Goddesses

Love Goddesses

Carole Buck
Paula Detmer Riggs
Rebecca Paisley

St. Martin's Paperbacks

NOTE: If you purchased this book without a cover you should be aware that this book is stolen property. It was reported as "unsold and destroyed" to the publisher, and neither the author nor the publisher has received any payment for this "stripped book."

LOVE GODDESSES

"Tickle My Fancy" copyright © 1996 by Rebecca Paisley.
"Myth and Magic: Helen of Troy, New York" copyright © 1996 by Paula Detmer Riggs.
"When Mona Lisa Smiles" copyright © 1996 by Carol Buckland.

All rights reserved. No part of this book may be used or reproduced in any manner whatsoever without written permission except in the case of brief quotations embodied in critical articles or reviews. For information address St. Martin's Press, 175 Fifth Avenue, New York, N.Y. 10010.

ISBN: 0-312-95716-5

Printed in the United States of America

St. Martin's Paperbacks edition / February 1996

10 9 8 7 6 5 4 3 2 1

Contents

Tickle My Fancy

Rebecca Paisley

One

"*H*ow much do y'think Annette would want for that stove sittin' out there in the front yard, Cleopatra?" Speaking without moving her mouth so she wouldn't crack her facial mask, Opal Clooney pulled back the pink chiffon curtains that hung above the shampoo sink and peered out of the window.

"Opal, you don't want Mama's old stove," Cleopatra replied while putting the last roller on Miss Iris's head. Rolling Iris Miniver's hair only took a little over two minutes. The old dear was almost bald, so each roller only held about twenty or thirty hairs apiece. "That stove's as useless as gossip that ain't worth repeatin'. The oven's out, only one burner works—"

"I didn't say I wanted it," Opal said. "I only offered to buy it to get it out of your front yard. It's the tackiest thing I've seen since Francine Collins wore that orange tube top to Mavis Silcox's weddin'."

"Did you know there's a family of werewolves livin' not five minutes from here, Cleopatra?" Miss Iris asked, pinching off a bit of chewing tobacco from the supply she kept in a black vinyl change purse. "Saw 'em with my own eyes yesterday. Oh, they try to act like humans, but they don't fool me for a minute. That's the hairiest family I've ever laid eyes on. I bet they all have hairy palms, and hair between their toes, too. And the howling! Goodness gracious, I've never heard such howling as what comes out of that house at night."

"Miss Iris, that's the Hunsucker family," Cleopatra said. "They have seven dogs."

Miss Iris snapped the vinyl change purse closed. "They're werewolves. The whole family, from the grandfather down to the baby. Have you seen that child? The day his mother brought him home from the hospital he had long enough hair to braid. Newborn humans do not have that kind of hair. Werewolves, all of them, and that is all I will say on the subject. Cleopatra, you and your mama'd best get out of this neighborhood, honey. In fact, I'm going to speak to Annette just as soon as you've finished my comb-out."

"You do that, Miss Iris, but wait 'till *The Price Is Right* is over, hear?" Cleopatra popped a black jelly bean into her mouth. "Sleepin' in a waterbed with long toenails'd be a sight safer than interruptin' Mama when she's watchin' that game show."

" 'Course, after *The Price is Right,* she'll turn the channel to *Bewitched,*" Opal reminded Cleopatra and Miss Iris. "Then her soaps'll start. I declare, sittin' in front of the TV all damn day . . . you know, I read somewhere that television rays can eat up your brain."

Cleopatra rolled her eyes. "Opal, that's the silliest thing I've ever—"

"You ever gonna buy her that satellite dish she's been wantin'?" Opal asked.

Opal's question almost reduced Cleopatra to tears. There was no one in the world she loved more than her mother. Times had been hard through the years, and Annette had worked herself nearly to a nub trying to give her daughter everything a young girl could want.

Cleopatra had been the only child in her class to own a brand new lunchbox every September rather than having to use an old one year after year. She also had a sterling silver ID bracelet that her mother had found and purchased at a pawn shop in a nearby town. It didn't matter that the name on the bracelet said LEWIS rather than CLEOPATRA. It was a beautiful bracelet, even if it *was* a man's.

And no other child had ever had a toothbrush with his or her name stuck on the handle in shiny gold letters. Annette special ordered that toothbrush and paid nearly ten dollars for it. Cleopatra had been so proud of it that she'd brushed her teeth four times a day at home and once a day at school so all the other kids could *ooh* and *ah* over the fancy handle.

Cleopatra had never had a cavity. Nor had she ever been able to pay back her mother's generosity. She tried. God only knew how hard she tried, but there was just never enough money for the things Annette wished she could have.

"Cleopatra?" Opal prompted.

"If I ever get enough money, Opal," Cleopatra finally answered, caressing the silver ID bracelet she still wore on her left wrist. "A satellite dish is just about all Mama talks about, and do you know that if she had one she could probably get shows from Japan?"

"Japan?" Opal frowned so hard that a piece of her facial mask popped off her forehead and settled on her eyelashes. She blinked it off. "Why the hell would Annette want to watch a show she couldn't even understand?"

"There's werewolves in Japan, too," Miss Iris commented, giving a grave nod. "The entire planet's crawlin' with the S.O.B.'s."

Cleopatra suppressed a smile and patted Miss Iris's shoulder. Werewolves. Miss Iris suspected nearly everyone in Snyder's Dock, Georgia, of being a werewolf. Because of her age, no one had known her long enough to understand why she was so obsessed with the mythical creatures, but everyone accepted her eccentricity without batting an eye. Not even the local movie house manager would consent to run werewolf movies in his theater for fear of upsetting the sweet old lady.

Dear Miss Iris. Many a day came when folks saw her walking down streets and peeking into windows in search of some sort of werewolf activity in progress. Edna Chester, a newcomer in town, had tried to get her arrested once, but quickly dropped the notion when Miss Iris pulled a handgun out of her pocketbook. Edna had moved out of Snyder's Dock soon after that, never knowing that Miss Iris's pistol was simply a semi-

sweet chocolate novelty that she'd won at a county fair.
Miss Iris claimed the weapon was loaded with solid silver bullets to pump into the heart of any werewolf she
might meet up with, but she only carried it in the winter, when it wouldn't melt. In the summer she kept it in
her freezer.

"I'm ready for the dryer now, honey," Miss Iris said,
struggling out of the beauty chair.

Cleopatra escorted Miss Iris to the hair dryer across
the room, sat the woman down, and handed her a small
plastic cup for when she felt the need to spit tobacco
juice. Then, for a moment, she patted Miss Iris's shoulder again, pondering the deep affection she felt for the
elderly lady.

And for Opal, too. For all her customers and everyone else in Synder's Dock. The tiny community wasn't
shown on any map she'd ever seen, but the people who
lived here were as close as any family could be. And
folks cared about each other. Tried to help each other,
because life in the little town wasn't easy.

If only Synder's Dock was bigger, more attractive to
businesses and industries. As it was, there was little opportunity for the residents here. No one earned much
money because well-paying jobs were non-existent.
Some people moved to larger towns, but the majority
chose to stay, living each day as best as he or she could.

"Cleopatra?" Miss Iris said. "Didn't you hear me? I
said you could turn the heat on now."

"Here comes Rhonda Faye," Opal announced, still
stationed at the window. "Her boys, Wylie Owen and
Howard Errol, taggin' along behind her and little
Vernon Newton in her arms. I don't know why in the
world she can't get somebody to keep them young'uns
o' hers when she comes in here for her wash and set.
And I'll tell you another thing. If she flips that tit o'
hers out in front of me one more time, I'll—"

"She's nursin' Vernon Newton, Opal," Cleopatra
said, lowering the hair dryer down over Miss Iris's head
and setting the heat control switch. "She can't very well
feed that child if she doesn't."

"Wonder if she'll nurse Vernon Newton as long as

she nursed Wylie Owen and Howard Errol?" Opal queried. "Rhonda Faye never should have had him in the first place, if you ask me. Can't barely take care of Wylie Owen and Howard Errol. It's that shiftless husband o' hers. How she puts up with his gamblin' is beyond me. He—well, good Lord. Here it is a sunny June day, and Rhonda Faye's wearin' that red blouse with the snowmen embroidered on the sleeves. I've never seen anything so tacky in all my—"

"Opal, you could clip a hedge with that tongue of yours," Cleopatra scolded, and smiled.

"Well, Rhonda Faye Dean!" Opal exclaimed as the young, harried housewife stepped into the beauty salon. "Lovely blouse. Just lovely. I've always liked you in red."

Rhonda Faye handed Vernon Newton to Wylie Owen, then reached inside her shirt to pull her bra strap back onto her shoulder. "I haven't had a lick of time to get to the laundry and this blouse was the only clean thing I could find this mornin'. Wearin' a Christmas shirt in June seems a bit—"

"Tacky?" Opal supplied. "Nonsense. It's a festive look, Rhonda Faye. And where's it written that snowmen can only be worn in December?"

"Wylie Owen?" Cleopatra addressed the redheaded boy. "Take Vernon Newton over to the loveseat and sit down while I tend to your mama's head. And Howard Errol, you go over there and rub Miss Iris's fingers the way she likes you to do."

Howard Errol shook his head. "Last time I rubbed her fingers, she missed her cup and spit brown slobber all over my arm."

"Howard Errol, you mind your elders or I'll get a switch after you," Rhonda Faye snapped. "Do what Miss Murphy says and go rub Miss Iris's arthritic fingers. And while you're doin' it, say some prayers that *you'll* have someone to rub *your* fingers when they're a-painin' you sixty-some years from now."

"Go on now, darlin'," Cleopatra said. "And getcha some jelly beans to suck on while you're rubbin' Miss Iris's fingers."

"All's you've got are black ones. I like red ones." Kicking at all the cut hair on the floor as he walked, Howard Errol crossed the room, took Miss Iris's hand, and began to rub her gnarled fingers.

"Rhonda Faye, give me a minute to get Opal's mask off and then I'll get to you," Cleopatra said. "There's some new makeup catalogs and magazines over there you can browse through while you're waitin'."

Rhonda Faye sat down on the sofa beside Wylie Owen and began to unbutton her blouse.

"She's gonna do it, Cleopatra," Opal whispered as she took a seat in the beauty chair. "She's fixin' to flip out that tit o' hers—"

"This is such a nice little sofa," Rhonda Faye said as she took little Vernon Newton from Wylie Owen and put the baby to her breast. "If it was mine, I'd have it right in my livin' room."

Cleopatra glanced at the piece of furniture. A sigh gathered in her chest. "I bought that loveseat five years ago, and half of it's still new."

"Well, it's no wonder you don't have a man," Opal said as she leaned back in the beauty chair. "Spendin' all day in this salon—"

"I've had *two* men in my life," Cleopatra argued.

"Billy Wicket and Clyde Motts were shallow as pie pans, both of them. Neither one of them cared a fig about anything but themselves, and you know it. You're lucky to be rid of them."

Lucky, Cleopatra repeated silently. *Unlucky* was more like it. Unlucky in love. At age thirty-one, she'd nearly resigned herself to life as a spinster.

Still, she was proud of her accomplishments. Her salon, Murphy's Make-over Miracles, was as much of a success as it could be in a town like Synder's Dock. Run out of the garage and decorated in various hues of pink and lavender, the place was as pretty as a polished pearl. She was especially proud of the neon sign that hung over the door outside. In lights of bright purple, it spelled out the name of her establishment. She so loved the way it looked that she kept the lights on even during the day.

"You're just too young to let yourself waste away," Opal continued, blinking when another stiff piece of facial mask fell on her eyelashes. "And you're the purtiest woman in Synder's Dock. What with that long black hair, that silky smooth skin, and those big brown eyes of yours . . . you could get any man y'wanted if y'could just find some to get. I know Murphy's Make-over Miracles means a lot to you, Cleopatra, but . . . culture's what y'need. A taste o' fine food, a look-see at fine places, and the company of a fine hunk. Closest thing we have 'round here that's culturelike is that marble statue of the naked man that Ima Puggins put in her marigold garden. Statues of naked men are what cultured people look at, you know, though Lord knows, Ima Puggins is about as refined as a cabbage."

"Opal, I can't just run off lookin' for the finer things of life. Someone's got to run the salon." With a warm, wet cloth, Cleopatra began to remove the hardened mask from Opal's face.

"I don't know why Annette can't get her behind back in here," Opal responded. "She could move the little TV out o' her bedroom and set it up in here so she wouldn't miss any of her shows."

"How many times do we have to go through this? Mama can't work the salon anymore. Her nerves got too frazzled after she almost put Loreen Mickler's eye out with that eyeliner pencil."

"Wouldn't have been any more'n Loreen deserved," Opal replied. "I've never known a woman who gawked at men the way she did."

"But she only liked the well-off ones," Cleopatra clarified. "Y'know, it's hard to imagine what she would have found attractive about men if she'd lived before money was invented."

"If that ain't the truth, God's a possum," Opal agreed.

After removing the last bit of mask from Opal's face, Cleopatra reached for a bright yellow mustard bottle and squirted its lime green contents into the palm of her hand. The silky cream was her grandmother's recipe. Cleopatra whipped up a new batch every Sunday after church services. Her customers' eyes lit up every time she picked up the bright yellow mustard bottle, a container she found perfect for the cream.

"Put a lot on me, Cleopatra," Opal said, closing her eyes and relaxing in preparation for the application of the wonderful cream. "Last time you were stingy with it."

"Well, I wish you'd look at the model in this magazine," Rhonda Faye blurted out from across the room. "She's so skinny she doesn't have enough on her to itch."

"Is it that Sonia What's-Her-Name?" Opal asked, sighing with pleasure as Cleopatra massaged the fragrant beauty cream into her cheeks.

"Sonia Brockman," Cleopatra said, slipping another black jelly bean into her mouth. "She's worldwide famous. Heard tell she makes millions with that face and body of hers."

Opal snorted. "If she ever swallowed an olive whole, she'd be rushed to the maternity hospital. I don't know why on earth those fashion companies think bein' so thin is beautiful."

"Says here that that big makeup company, Dresden, is havin' an exhibition in New York City," Rhonda Faye said. Quickly, she handed Vernon Newton to Wylie Owen, then walked over to the beauty chair, her left breast completely exposed. "Look here, Cleopatra. Beauty consultants from all over the nation are invited to attend the show."

Upon hearing that information, Opal sat straight up in the chair, grabbed the magazine out of Rhonda Faye's hands, and scanned the article. "Says a slew o' makeup artists'll be demonstratin' their art on models, usin' all Dresden products. You've gotta go, Cleopatra! Well, you *are* a makeup artist, don't forget. Remember when you made up Viola Swanson before her funeral? I declare, I've never seen such a lively-lookin' corpse. After you got through with her, she looked better dead than she ever did alive. Rhonda Faye, for God's sake, put your tit back in your shirt!"

Rhonda Faye complied. "Opal's right, Cleopatra.

There's no good reason in the world why you can't go to that show, set up your own little booth, and put all them other makeup artists to shame."

"And just imagine all the culture in New York City!" Opal exclaimed. "There's so much culture in that city that you could shovel it off the sidewalk. And what about the men? Some o' the best lookin' men in the country live in New York, Cleopatra, and they've all got Romeo blood in their veins."

"Just look at that one," Rhonda Faye said, pointing to a photograph in the magazine. "M. Anthony Mazzini. I bet he's Italian. His last name sounds like somethin' I ate at that Italian restaurant over in Pittsville last October. Says here Mazzini's one of Dresden's vice-presidents in charge o' new products. Looks rich, don't he? Sure is a good-lookin' devil."

Cleopatra stared at the color photo of the man named Mazzini. He had black wavy hair, and her experience told her that it was thick and soft. His skin was tanned, not from the sun, she knew, but from his genes. In the picture he stood beside a woman she recognized as Sonia Brockman. Sonia was tall.

Mazzini was taller.

He had dark eyes. They shone, but not really. They laughed, but not really. They held a put-on shine. A false happiness.

Cleopatra wondered how many other people realized that the slight smile on his handsome face was deceiving.

The man wore mystery the way other men wore cologne.

She swallowed her jelly bean whole. The soles of her feet warmed, a certain indication that her feelings were those of desire.

Lord have mercy, she was getting all hot and bothered by a picture of a man she'd never even met.

"Ain't he handsome, Cleopatra?" Rhonda Faye asked again.

"Yes," she whispered, intrigued by all that she'd perceived from the photograph and more than a little aroused by his looks and the enigma he presented, "he's very handsome."

"He ain't only handsome," Opal said, lifting the magazine closer to her eyes, "but get a load o' the bulge in his pants. Looks to me like Mazzini's weenie's so big that a mere picture of it would weigh five pounds."

"Opal!" Her lips trembling with mirth, Cleopatra struggled to keep laughter at bay. She failed miserably.

So did Rhonda Faye, and all the loud laughter finally reached Miss Iris's ears, who wanted to know what was so funny.

"Cleopatra's goin' to New York City," Opal informed the woman. "And I think we should all pitch in our loose change so she can—"

"There's werewolves in New York," Miss Iris claimed. "I wouldn't be surprised if that city was their headquarters."

"It's all decided," Opal said. "You're goin' to New York City, Cleopatra. I've got a hundred and thirty-some dollars I'll give you to pay for—"

"And I've got a little over sixty," Rhonda Faye added.

Miss Iris lifted her plastic cup toward her mouth, but spit on Howard Errol's arm instead. "I'll give you an even hundred if you'll promise to look for a book about how to recognize a werewolf when you see one. Mr. Weaver over there at Weaver's Market? Well, the only books he carries are those outer space stories and a few romances. You'd think he could order a few werewolf books, seein' as how I've been after him to get me some. And to think of all the money I've spent in his store! You know, now that I think on it some, Mr. Weaver might be a werewolf himself. He *is* a mite hairy. Maybe that's the reason why he won't order—"

"You'll need bus fare, Cleopatra," Opal interrupted, impatient with Miss Iris's rambling. "And once you get to the city, you'll need a place to stay. Says in the magazine that the show's bein' held in the Windsor. A hotel with a fancy name like that ain't gonna be cheap. The rooms are probably almost fifteen dollars a night."

Cleopatra gasped. "Fifteen dollars a night?"

"Yeah, and I think y'have to tip them hotel maids when they put those paper strips over the toilet seat. They put those paper strips there so's you'll know the toilet's been cleaned, y'know. Dumbest thing I've ever heard of. All y'have to do to know if a toilet's clean is look at it. Still, I reckon it's all a part of culture."

"You'll have to eat, too, Cleopatra," Rhonda Faye said.

Opal nodded. "But don't eat anything that has a name you've never heard of. They eat strange stuff up there in New York City. Stuff like slugs that you pick up with little metal slug holders, and they give those slugs a fancy French name so's folks'll think they're eatin' somethin' exotic. You can take the culture thing only so far, Cleopatra. There's a fine line between culture and downright nastiness, and slugs for dinner crosses that line."

Cleopatra took the magazine from Opal and looked at all the pictures of the models, the makeup artists, and heads of the Dresden cosmetic company. "It really would be a thrill to go," she murmured. "I *do* have over three hundred dollars in my Christmas Club account at the bank. And Fred Wigginton said he'd give me five hundred for the trailer. I kinda hate to part with that trailer, though, seein' as how Mama and I stay in it when she sees a roach and sets off those fog bombs in the house."

"Oh, sell the damn thing," Opal pressed. "You can come stay at my house on Annette's roach-killin' days."

"Who would run the salon while I was gone?"

"Annette," Opal replied. "Her frazzled nerves don't have a damn thing to do with hairstylin'. She can do hair while you're gone just to keep the salon open, and the makeup part can get up and runnin' again when you get back. Nobody's gonna die if you ain't here to put on makeup, Cleopatra."

"Well . . . " Cleopatra hedged.

"And just think what your trip would do for Synder's Dock," Opal went on. "If you were to go and make good up there in New York City, all o' Georgia would hear about it. Alabama might hear, too."

"Make good?" Cleopatra asked.

"Y'mean to tell me y'don't think y'could show them New York makeup artists a thing or two?" Opal rose from the beauty chair and turned Cleopatra toward the mirror. "Just look at how nice you put your own makeup on."

Cleopatra stared at her image in the mirror. A thick line of coal-black eyeliner swept gracefully over her eyelids, ending in small curlicues at the corners of her eyes. Three coats of ebony mascara thickened her lashes into the thin clumps she felt made them look longer. Dark pink blush—the same color as the apron she wore while working—painted her cheeks, a beautiful contrast to the pale foundation and powder she used to hide the smattering of freckles on the tip of her nose. And oh, how nicely the generous smudges of blue and purple shadows enhanced her eyes!

But she especially loved her lipstick. Sort of red, sort of brown, sort of orange, the color was of her own invention. She'd created it by mixing several old lipsticks together in a plastic yogurt container, and she called it Autumn's Passionate Kiss, a name she'd often thought of submitting to a makeup company.

"Dramatic, that's what your makeup is, Cleopatra," Opal said. "You can *see* it; that's what *I* like about it. Those makeup artists in New York don't use enough color. Hell, some o' them models don't look like they're even *wearin'* any makeup. Makeup's s'posed to be *seen*, for God's sake, or there ain't no use in even puttin' it on."

"You know," Rhonda Faye began, she, too, staring at Cleopatra's reflection in the mirror, "it wouldn't surprise me a bit if Dresden offered you money to teach its artists all the things you know about makeup, Cleopatra. If you went to that show, you might come home with enough money to buy Annette that satellite dish she's been wantin' for so long."

Rhonda Faye's comment echoing through her mind, Cleopatra needed only a few seconds to make her decision. "I'll go."

Opal and Rhonda Faye both hugged her. "It'll be so excitin', Cleopatra!" Rhonda Faye squealed.

"Swallowed up by all that culture," Opal said.

"Just be on the look out for them werewolves," Miss Iris warned. "They're hairier than humans."

New York, Cleopatra mused, looking down at the magazine again. "The Statue of Liberty," she whispered. "The Empire State Building."

"Broadway," Rhonda Faye added.

Opal peered down at the magazine Cleopatra held. "And don't forget Mazzini's weenie."

Two

"*Six* seventy-five?" Cleopatra stared at the cab driver and felt her right eyebrow begin to rise, a sure sign that she was about to lose her temper.

"The meter, it says six seventy-five," the New York cabby replied with a heavy accent.

"Yeah?" Her eyebrow now fully raised, Cleopatra leaned forward in the back seat. "Well, it can say six *thousand* seventy-five for all I care, you triflin', common-as-dishwater thief! You think I've never been in a taxi before? That ride from the bus station to this here Windsor hotel couldn't've been more'n a few blocks. And don't think for one minute—"

"Traffic."

"—that I didn't see you charge me a dollar fifty right up front!" Cleopatra continued smoothly. "A dollar fifty on the meter before you'd even taken the gear out of park. You're so crooked that if you swallowed a tenpenny nail, you'd spit up a corkscrew!"

"Lady, you pay the fare, or I call authorities."

Cleopatra longed to continue arguing with the man, but remembered that in only a few more hours the Dresden Cosmetics exhibition would be over. She'd planned on arriving to New York a whole day early so she wouldn't miss a minute of the show, but her departure from Snyder's Dock had been delayed.

Damn that old Claudine Wigginton, Fred's wife. It had taken nearly forever to talk the old biddy into letting Fred buy the trailer. Since the trip to New York wouldn't have been possible without the five hundred dollars Fred offered for the trailer, the whole venture had been on hold until Claudine finally relented.

Her eyebrow raised so high that her forehead ached, Cleopatra paid the cab driver, grabbed her bags, and stepped out onto the sidewalk. It wasn't until the cab driver drove off and she turned toward the hotel that she realized she'd stepped in a wad of sun-warmed chewing gum. The sticky yellow mess encased the spiked heel of her new black velvet shoes.

She closed her eyes. "Cleopatra," she whispered, "considerin' the kind of luck you've had lately, if you bought a cemetery folks'd stop dyin'."

Finding a more-or-less clean napkin in the trash can on the corner, she removed as much of the gum from her shoe as possible, then started toward the doors of the luxurious hotel.

Red carpet lay in front of the doors. Plush, red carpet on cement! She'd never seen the beat of it.

This was culture at its best. Opal would go into a tizzy if she could see it.

"May I help you with your bags?" a uniformed hotel employee asked.

Cleopatra shook her head. "Don't have time to mess with these bags right now. I need to know where the makeup show is. I'm a makeup artist, y'know, here from Snyder's Dock, Georgia, to demonstrate my talents to the Dresden makeup company."

"I see." The young man stared at her hair, makeup, and attire for a long moment, then glanced at the small green Naugahyde bag she held in one hand, the powder blue hanger bag she held in her other hand, and the plastic grocery store bag that swung from the crook of her elbow. The grocery store bag said WEAVER'S MARKET. "The Dresden Cosmetics exhibition is being held in the ballroom on the sixth floor."

Cleopatra dropped her purse as she started for the hotel doors.

The employee picked the blue canvas bag up for her.

"Just stick the strap in my mouth," Cleopatra instructed him. "I can't carry all this stuff without droppin' somethin'."

The employee obeyed, and lifted the purse toward her parted lips.

Her purse strap clamped firmly between her teeth, Cleopatra finally entered the hotel, stepped into the glass elevator, and did her best to act as though she'd ridden in hundreds of glass elevators before.

Her purse fell out of her mouth and she nearly lost her lunch as the elevator soared upward. "Good Lord," she murmured to the woman who stood beside her, "this elevator's so fast, I reckon its shadow needs fifteen minutes to catch up."

The woman turned away.

"I'm a makeup artist," Cleopatra said.

The elevator doors opened and the woman stepped out. After retrieving her purse, Cleopatra followed.

There was no mistaking where the exhibition was taking place. What seemed to be a million people were crowded into a large, elegant room done in white and gold. Long tables laden with various Dresden products, brochures, and flower arrangements filled the room, each of them manned by makeup artists, models, or representatives of Dresden Cosmetics.

Glittering. That was the only word that described the show. Everything Cleopatra saw twinkled, sparkled, and flashed. The very air she breathed seemed laden with radiance.

Excitement surged through her. The time had come, the opportunity to show off the skills she'd acquired through the years at Murphy's Make-over Miracles, and earn money from Dresden by sharing her talents with the company's cosmetic artists.

Annette's satellite dish was going to be the envy of everyone in Snyder's Dock.

Quickly, she found a place to store her hanger bag, pushing it behind a potted tree that looked to her like a cross between a magnolia and a stunted scrub oak.

Now for a table. Her green Naugahyde bag full of makeup supplies and her Weaver's Market grocery store bag filled with brushes, combs, hair picks, and pink sponge rollers dangling from her fingers, she made her way through the crowd of people, searching the lower level and the balcony level of the ballroom for a table she could use to set up her display.

Cosmetic artists, models, and Dresden spokesmen occupied every single table she saw. Undaunted, and determined to take advantage of what was probably the only shot she'd ever have to promote her craft, she hurried to create a makeshift table. Several empty cardboard boxes suited nicely, especially after she draped a few white linen napkins over them to cover the plastic packaging tape. For a final touch, she added to the top of her carton table a small silver cream pitcher she found on a waiter's serving tray. The gleaming vessel added just the right stroke of culture.

Opal would have been so proud.

Smiling at all the people who passed by, she arranged her supplies on the table. "Hey, ma'am?" she called to a well-dressed woman who was examining various Dresden products at the next table. "Come on over here, honey, and I'll show you how to hide those deep lines you've got around your lips."

Her eyes narrowing with irritation, the woman marched away.

"Well!" Cleopatra exclaimed to the makeup artist who sat at the table next to hers. "That lady was like a prune with legs, and all I tried to do was help her. There's just no understandin' some people, huh?"

Before the man could reply, another man arrived in front of her display. "What, may I ask," he said, "are you doing?" His eyes widening with each passing second, the man gawked at her attire.

She wore metallic pink leggings that might as well have been painted on and a short black summer sweater that stretched tightly across her full breasts. Two long strands of pink and white plastic beads hung down her chest, huge gold hoop earrings swayed from her earlobes, and a shiny silver ID bracelet sparkled around her wrist.

Her long hair was black, and she'd teased the top of

it in such a way that it stood up off the crown of her head at least a good six inches.

He was certain she was the gaudiest woman he had ever seen. Clearing his throat, he gave her a stern look. "I asked you what you're doing."

Cleopatra noticed his name tag and realized he was with Dresden Cosmetics. "Cleopatra Murphy," she introduced herself. "I've come all the way from Snyder's Dock, Georgia, to join y'all's makeup show. Proud to meetcha, Ted Wallace. Y'know, I knew another Mr. Wallace once. Otis Wallace was his name, and he's who sold my mama all the supplies she needed when she first opened up our salon in the garage years ago. Otis was—"

"Miss Murphy," Mr. Wallace cut her off, "I think you've misunderstood. The beauty consultants attending this exhibition are invited to look and learn, not participate." He looked down at her display and frowned at the colorful array of household containers she'd placed upon her cardboard table.

Two yellow mustard bottles sat beside a brown glass jar of coffee creamer and a small plastic tub that said WEAVER'S PORK BARBECUE—BEST IN ALL OF GEORGIA on the lid. A bottle of squeezable margarine, a vegetable shortening can, and a large bottle of garlic salt were lined up behind several yellow ice trays.

Each square in the ice trays was filled with colored powders.

Mr. Wallace looked back up at Cleopatra. "May I assist you in gathering up your things and disassembling your table?"

"Disassembling my . . . " Her voice faded away as she realized that the man was politely forbidding her to continue her demonstration. "No," she said softly.

"Very well. I trust you'll hurry then?"

"No," she said again, this time louder. "I came here to New York to earn money by teachin' y'all's makeup people all the things I know. I've got to get Mama that satellite dish, and this is the only way—"

"Miss Murphy," Mr. Wallace said, leaning over her

table, "if you do not get your things out of here this very minute, I'll call hotel security."

Desperate to make a favorable impression on the man, Cleopatra took the arm of the bare-faced model who had just arrived at the next table. "Sit down here, honey," she said, grabbing a chair for the young woman. "Now, ordinarily we'd start with some of Grammy's beautifyin' cream, but I ain't got the time for basics right now."

She pulled the lid off the vegetable shortening can. "This here's Dresden foundation," she explained to Mr. Wallace. "I use so much of it at Murphy's Make-over Miracles, that I started pourin' it into this can. It's much easier to get at in this can than it was from those little bottles y'all sell it in."

Mr. Wallace signaled to a nearby waiter. "Get security at once."

"I do eyes best," Cleopatra blurted, frantic to prove her talents before she was arrested. "Eunice Gish back home has the smallest eyes you ever saw in your life, but when I get done with her she looks like she's wearin' two blue saucers on her face."

Pushing back the model's head, she quickly smeared lavender eyeshadow across the girl's eyelids and smudged sky-blue shadow above the lavender. A thick pat of pastel pink shadow in the center of the model's lids and a dab of lemon yellow beneath her eyebrows served as highlighters. "I call this look April Sky on account of it reminds me of spring," Cleopatra explained, picking up a stick of dark purple eyeliner.

But a pair of strong hands prevented her from applying the eyeliner. "Come with me, miss," the hotel guard said while another guard collected her things and put them into her green bag.

Nearly every head in the room turned as the man escorted her toward the doors. Miserable with anger and humiliation, Cleopatra struggled with tears and her captor's hold on her.

And then she saw him.

M. Anthony Mazzini.

He stood in the lobby right outside the ballroom

doors, the cluster of beautiful models around him all vying for his attention. She didn't need to read his name tag to know who he was; she'd stared at his picture too many times to fail to recognize him.

Lord, he was even more handsome in real life than he'd been in the magazine photos. Dressed in a dark gray suit that shimmered slightly, a stark white shirt, and a beautiful black and white tie, he was the most cultured human being she'd ever set eyes on.

"Mazzini," she whispered. "Maz—"

She quieted; her mouth opened wide. Mr. Mazzini was one of Dresden's vice-presidents . . . if anyone could help her, he could!

"Mr. Mazzini, y'got to help me! I'm here all the way from Synder's Dock, Georgia, to show y'all how to put on makeup, but that there Ted Wallace varmint is havin' me thrown out!"

Ted Wallace glared at her. "Now, see here, Miss—"

"The next time y'wash your neck, wring it, Ted!" Cleopatra shouted at him.

"Get her out of here," Ted ordered the guard. "Quickly. I'm sorry, Mr. Mazzini," he said when the guard disappeared into the elevator with Cleopatra.

"Who was that, Ted?"

"She thought she could just breeze in right off the street, set up a table, and perform make-overs at our show. When she refused to abandon the notion, I was forced to have her removed. Brazen, that's what she was."

"I see." Anthony glanced at the elevator. He could no longer see the woman the guard had dragged away, but he sure remembered what she'd said.

The next time y'wash your neck, wring it, Ted!

Anthony almost smiled.

"Brazen and outrageous," Ted continued. "She even had an outrageous name."

"Oh?"

"Cleopatra. Can you believe that? Who would name their daughter Cleopatra?"

"Someone in Synder's Dock, Georgia, apparently."

With that, Anthony Mazzini entered the ballroom, the gathering of models following him inside.

Long years of practice made it easy for him to look happy.

"Psst! Hey you, mister," Cleopatra whispered from her hiding place behind a marble pillar in the Windsor lobby. "You work here, right?"

The young man struggled to get his burden out of the elevator before the doors shut, but the rolled-up carpet was difficult to maneuver. "Yes, ma'am," he panted.

Cleopatra scanned the lobby in search of the security guards who had escorted her out of the ballroom earlier, then stepped out from behind the pillar and helped the hotel employee get the carpet out of the elevator.

" 'Preciate it, ma'am," he said. "I'm a mite wilted today, what with havin' to work all through that makeup show that just ended. I'll tell you the truth, that show had me movin' faster'n a worm on a barbecue grill."

Cleopatra stared at him, his accent flowing through her mind like beautiful music. "You're from Georgia, huh?"

He stared, too. "Pittsville."

"Pittsville? Well, good Lord, it sure is a small world! I'm from Synder's Dock, for goodness sake, and my friend, Rhonda Faye Dean, ate Italian food over in Pittsville last October!"

"At Betty's Lasagna and Chicken 'N Dumplins Paradise?"

"That very restaurant!" Smiling broadly, Cleopatra took the man's hand and pumped it wildly. "It sure is good to see a face from back home. I'm Cleopatra Murphy, here for the makeup show."

"Lonnie Boatright, Miss Murphy."

"Call me Cleopatra, Lonnie. What are you doin' all the way up here in New York City?"

"Workin' here at the Windsor. I want to be a Broadway actor, but I ain't been picked for nothin' yet. I will, though. I surely will on account o' I'm as patient as a cat camped out under a birdbath. Did you enjoy the makeup show?"

"I wasn't there but twenty minutes before gettin' thrown out. Listen, Lonnie," Cleopatra said, looking all around the lobby again, "I need to see a Dresden man by the name of Mazzini. I saw him for a whip-stitch of a second durin' the show, but I got dragged out so sudden like that I didn't get a chance to talk to him. My mama's future happiness depends on me speakin' at him. Can you find out where he is?"

"Mazzini?" Lonnie looked down at the rolled-up carpet. "Matter of fact, this rug's from his room. Some makeup man got lipstick smashed all over it, and I'm s'posed to bring up another one."

"Mazzini's stayin' here?"

"He's in the penthouse havin' a meetin' with two men and a woman. But I can't get a visit with Mr. Mazzini for you, Cleopatra. I'd like to oblige you, seein' as how we're both from the same neck of the woods and all, but I'm not even allowed to talk to the guests unless they ask me somethin' that needs answerin'."

Cleopatra glanced down at the carpet. A slow grin spread over her face. "Y'ain't got to say a word when you get back up there, Lonnie."

"But—"

"Here's what you do."

When she took his arm and pulled him behind the marble pillar, Lonnie had no choice but to listen to her whispered instructions.

A half an hour later, he entered Mr. Mazzini's penthouse. Sweat beading his forehead, he laid a clean, rolled-up carpet on the floor of the living room, and left the suite so quickly that he fell out into the hall before managing to shut the door.

Anthony Mazzini was the first to notice the black velvet spike sticking out of the end of the rug.

It appeared to have yellow gum on it.

Three

*J*ust before Cleopatra began trying to squirm out from inside the rug, she felt someone lift the edge of the carpet and pull hard. Helpless, she rolled across the floor like a ball down a bowling ally. When she stopped, she was lying on her back under a window sill.

Eyes peered down at her. The darkest eyes she'd ever seen, blacker even than her jelly beans. "Mazzini." Not a wisp of breath escaped her while her lips formed his name. The soles of her feet warmed, even felt hot.

Until she saw his eyes grow darker. She recognized anger when she saw it, and knew that Mr. Mazzini was none too pleased by her unconventional arrival into his rooms. "Don't blame this on poor Lonnie," she blurted. "I made him do it. Held a pistol to his head." She sat up, dug into her blue canvas purse, and withdrew a gun.

Semi-sweet chocolate oozed over her palm and squeezed through her fingers. "Dang it. I told Miss Iris her gun wouldn't last in this heat, but she made me bring it anyway. Said I'd need it if I met up with any New York werewolves."

Anthony stepped away and looked at his companions, Ted Wallace, Sonia Brockman, and one of Dresden's best makeup artists, Hubert Fritz.

"It's her," Ted announced, rising from the striped satin sofa. "That Cleopatra—"

"Murphy," Anthony finished for him. He took Cleopatra's arm and assisted her off the floor, noticing she wore a man's ID bracelet that said LEWIS. "Miss Murphy—"

"Cleopatra." Lord, the man had a gorgeous voice. Deep, masterful, and it made her yearn to hear what he sounded like when he was murmuring. Speaking softly the way men were supposed to do when sweet-talking a woman.

"Not that any man's ever sweet-talked me," she whispered.

"Pardon me?" Anthony asked.

She glanced down, thinking about how good her hand felt in his. He had long, strong fingers, and his nails were clean. His wristwatch looked like pure gold, and his cologne smelled even more expensive.

The man had money—lots of it.

She raised her head. He had a little scar in the middle of his forehead, she noted, and small crinkles at the corners of his eyes.

They weren't laugh wrinkles. Whether they came from being out in the sun or from years of frowning, she didn't know.

But they weren't laugh wrinkles.

Money, apparently, didn't make him too happy.

There was someone else behind that handsome face of his. A different man from the one he presented now, and it kind of made her wonder if he was empty, as if there was a place inside him that was too deep, too hidden to find and fill.

It beckoned to the same sort of place inside her own body, a deep, hidden place no one had ever brought to life.

She had to restrain herself from slipping her arms around his waist and hugging him. Instead, she cupped his cheek in her hand.

He stepped away, unnerved by the warmth of her palm, the soft touch of her fingers.

The profound look in her eyes.

Who was this woman, and how was it possible that she affected him so strangely in such a short time?

"I'll call security, Mr. Mazzini," Ted Wallace said, reaching for the phone.

"No!" Instantly pulled from her contemplation, Cleopatra clasped Anthony's broad shoulders and dug her nails into thick swells of muscle. "Please, Mr. Mazzini. I emptied my savin's account, fought with that old biddy, Claudine Wigginton, rode on a Greyhound bus for what seemed like forever, got cheated by a foreign cab driver, stepped in gum, and then got flung out of the makeup show. I've just *got* to show you my skills before you have me pitched out into the bitter, cold, icy streets of New York again."

"It's summer." For some reason he couldn't fathom Anthony had to fight back a smile. Bewildered by his instant amusement, he removed Cleopatra's hands from his shoulders and rolled his eyes when he noticed two chocolate handprints on his gray coat.

"I'll have her out of here in just a few minutes, Mr. Mazzini." Phone in hand, Ted started dialing.

"It's now or never," Cleopatra muttered, reaching for the two bags she'd tucked into the carpet. "Honey," she said to the model who sat in a chair beside the sofa, "you sit still now, hear?"

Sonia Brockman gasped when she saw Cleopatra hurry toward her with a green Naugahyde satchel and a plastic grocery bag. "Anthony!"

Cleopatra stopped in front of the chair and stared. "Well, you're Sonia Brockman! Lord have mercy, I'd do anything to know what it feels like to be a world-famous model! Wait 'till I tell Opal, Rhonda Faye, and Mama that I slapped makeup all over Sonia Brockman!"

"Sl-slapped?" Sonia repeated.

"Now see here, young woman," Hubert Fritz admonished. "I am Hubert Fritz, the *only* person allowed to touch Sonia's face."

Cleopatra gawked at the man. Never in her life had she seen a hairier human being. The man even had hair on his neck!

She took a step backwards, Miss Iris's words of warning sounding through her mind. "Are you . . . uh . . . Are you afraid of silver bullets by any chance?"

Hubert stared at her. "Silver bullets?"

"Security is on the way up, Mr. Mazzini," Ted stated.

Realizing she had only a few precious minutes to demonstrate her skills, Cleopatra dismissed the werewolf makeup man from her thoughts and yanked open her green bag. Taking out a pink dish towel, she wiped the chocolate off her hands, then reached into her bag again.

She withdrew a yellow mustard bottle. After squeezing a bit of the lime green cream into the palm of her hand, she smoothed the homemade, sweetly-scented emollient over Sonia's cheeks, under her eyes, and over her forehead.

"Dear God!" Sonia shouted. "Anthony, *do* something!"

Anthony, Ted, and Hubert all advanced toward Sonia's chair.

"Y'all, this ain't nothin' but beautifyin' cream!" Cleopatra hollered. "It won't hurt her none!" Fast as her fingers could move, she continued to massage the cream into Sonia's skin.

"That is quite enough," Ted gritted out from between clenched teeth. He reached for Cleopatra's hands, having every intention of dragging her out into the hall.

"Wait," Anthony ordered. "Stop just a minute, Ted." Leaning over Sonia, he gaped at her skin. "Well, I'll be damned."

"What?" Ted asked.

"What is it, Mr. Mazzini?" Hubert queried. Puzzled, he, too, bent over Sonia and stared at her face. "My God," he whispered.

Sonia covered her cheeks with her hands. "What has this wild woman done to my face?" she wailed. "Tell me what she's done—"

"Sonia, calm down, for God's sake," Anthony snapped. Quickly, he reached for the mustard bottle in Cleopatra's hand and smelled its contents. "What is this cream of yours, Miss Murphy?"

Before Cleopatra could respond, Sonia grabbed a hand mirror from Hubert's makeup case and held it up to her face.

Her eyes widened. She smiled. "My skin," she murmured. "Why, it's—it's *glowing!* And I don't have a single line anywhere! I haven't looked this good since I was a teenager!" Lowering the mirror, she stared straight at Cleopatra. "What *is* that cream?"

Cleopatra retrieved the mustard bottle from Anthony. "I didn't come here to show y'all my cream. I'm here to demonstrate my makeup talents."

Anthony continued to stare at the mustard bottle. Excitement welled within him. No Dresden product he'd ever handled could do what Cleopatra Murphy's concoction had done. The lime green cream in the mustard bottle was nothing short of miraculous.

And as executive vice-president in charge of new products, Anthony knew he'd discovered a gold mine. Glancing at Ted, he saw the same exciting realization in his assistant's eyes. "Where did you get the cream, Miss Murphy?" he asked, looking back at her again.

Cleopatra dropped the mustard bottle back into her bag. "I made it. Mix up a new batch in the kitchen every Sunday after church."

"And did you invent the recipe yourself?"

"No. My grammy did. It's been in the family for years."

Anthony folded his arms across his chest. A family recipe. Most likely a secret formula the Murphy family guarded carefully.

Cleopatra would not reveal a family secret, he realized. No, he would have to think of other means with which to procure a list of the ingredients. "Miss Murphy—"

A loud knock at the door cut him short. "Get rid of them, Ted," he instructed. "Miss Murphy is welcome to stay at the Windsor as my guest for as long as she pleases."

Understanding that Anthony was going to charm the secret to the beauty cream straight out of Cleopatra's little mind, Ted smiled and crossed to the door.

"Champagne, Miss Murphy?" Anthony asked while Ted spoke to security. Without waiting for her answer, he poured her a flute of champagne and pressed the fragile glass into her hand.

"I'd like some champagne too, Anthony," Sonia said.

Hearing the whine in Sonia's voice, Anthony poured another glass of champagne and quickly set it down on the table next to Sonia's chair. "Is it to your taste, Miss Murphy?"

Cleopatra took a sip of the bubbling liquid. "It's all right, but what I really like is Boone's Farm Strawberry Wine. Comes in a bottle with a screw-off top, and I get it over at Weaver's Market. Mr. Weaver, he's all the time goin' on and on about how sinful it is to drink, but Opal Clooney and I caught him with a bottle of Wild Turkey one time at a Shriners' convention."

Anthony stared at her for a long moment. "We'll do everything we can to provide you with a bottle of Strawberry Farm."

"Boone's Farm."

"Yes, of course. Boone's Farm. Ted?"

Ted left the room, wondering where in the world he would find a strawberry wine he'd never even heard of. Still, if the wine could be found, he'd find it. Anything to help Anthony Mazzini procure the recipe for Cleopatra Murphy's miraculous cream.

"Please sit down, Miss Murphy." Anthony indicated a plush velvet chair.

"Cleopatra," she corrected him for the second time. "And can I call you Anthony?"

Anthony decided she could call him anything she desired as long as she gave him the recipe for her cream. "Of course. Now, I'd like to discuss a certain matter with you," he began, glancing at the bag in which she'd dropped the mustard bottle. "As executive vice-president in charge of new products at Dresden, I'm at liberty to—"

"You know, Miss Murphy," Hubert broke in, walking nearer to Cleopatra's chair, "you've got beautiful eyes. The problem, however," he said, clasping her chin and lifting her face toward the lamplight, "is that your makeup is overbearing. Would you allow me to experiment with—"

"I like my makeup." Smoothing her fingers across the swath of bright pink blush upon her cheekbone,

Cleopatra crossed her legs. "Now, what were y'sayin', Anthony?"

"What? Uh . . . " Anthony couldn't help but notice the lean curves of her long legs. She had nice breasts, too, full, firm, and nicely rounded.

A tiny waist, he mused, a tight, sexy bottom, and a cascade of luxurious coal-black hair.

Not even her tawdry attire and heavy cosmetics could disguise the beauty of her body.

Like Hubert, he caught himself wondering what her face looked like without the ton of makeup she wore. She did have nice eyes. Dark, reddish brown, like mahogany. No, like expensive whiskey, rather intoxicating, actually. And her cheekbones were the sort that other models had to create with contouring makeup. Her lips—

Instantly, he interrupted his own train of thought. Wondering what the hell had gotten into him, he reminded himself of the pressing business at hand. "Cleopatra," he said softly, then cleared his throat, "Dresden would be happy to purchase the list of ingredients—"

"Anthony, darling," Sonia interrupted, "I'd like some more champagne." Her eyes mere slashes across her face, she glared at the black-haired woman who had somehow captured Anthony's undivided attention.

Sonia clenched her fists. How long had *she* tried to win Anthony's attention? Three long years, that's how long, and this Cleopatra Murphy woman had needed but fifteen minutes! "Anthony?" she called softly.

"What?"

"Miss Murphy," Hubert broke in, "I do wish you would allow me to reapply your makeup in such a way as to bring forth your natural beauty. It couldn't hurt, and if you don't like what I do I promise to remove the makeup—"

"Well . . . " Cleopatra wavered. "Well, all right."

"Hubert, if you don't mind," Anthony reprimanded.

"Oh, I'm sorry, Mr. Mazzini," Hubert said. He reached for his cosmetics bags.

"What are you doing, Hubert?" Sonia asked. She

watched as he assembled his supplies on the table beside Cleopatra's chair. "You're *my* makeup man."

Hubert pretended not to hear the snap of irritation in the model's voice. Gut instinct told him what he would find beneath Cleopatra's thick layers of cosmetics, and nothing thrilled him more than discovering hidden beauty. "There now, Miss Murphy, we'll gently remove the makeup you have on," he mumbled, busy dabbing cosmetic remover on Cleopatra's eyes. "Easy, easy, does it."

"Hubert," Anthony growled, "I'm trying to talk to—"

"Yes, I know, Mr. Mazzini, and I promise I'll be finished in only a few moments."

Knowing that nothing short of death could stifle Hubert's eagerness to perform Cleopatra's make-over, Anthony quelled his frustration and took a seat on the sofa.

"Yeah, my grammy could make just about anything," Cleopatra said out of the blue. "Not only did she invent the beautifyin' cream, but she could cook like nobody's business, God rest her sweet soul. I mean to tell you, the woman could make a five-course meal out of a bone's smell. I used to sit in her kitchen and talk to her while she cooked. Times come now when I still talk to her. Makes me feel good."

Anthony frowned. Cleopatra Murphy was certainly sentimental, talking to a woman who'd been in her grave for God only knew how many years.

Anthony couldn't comprehend that kind of sentimentality. Maudlin, that's what it was. Maudlin.

"Oh, that feels good, Hubert," Cleopatra murmured, closing her eyes as the man continued removing her makeup. "You've got a nice touch, a way with fingers. And since I'm always the one puttin' makeup on other faces, it's kinda nice havin' someone else do the same to me. But Lord have mercy, if Miss Iris could see me now. Lyin' back gettin' makeup put on me by someone who's yet to prove he ain't a werewolf . . . Miss Iris'd swallow her wad of chewin' tobacco, that's what she'd do. Pinks tickle my fancy, Hubert. Pinks, blues, and purples."

Hubert worked quickly, his skills telling him exactly what shades to use, his expertise advising him precisely how to apply the colors, none of which were pink, blue, or purple.

Ten minutes later, astonishment slammed into Anthony like a bullet from a gun.

The girl who sat before him now looked nothing at all like the girl who'd entered the room rolled in a carpet.

Cleopatra Murphy was beautiful. Incredibly so.

"I knew it," Hubert stated, smiling broadly. "I knew that under all that heavy makeup was a million-dollar face! Tell me, Miss Murphy," he said, resting his chin on the steeple of his fingers, "how old are you?"

"Thirty-one."

"Thirty-one? But—but you don't look—how could you be—I—you look like a nineteen-year-old!" Hubert turned and caught Anthony's equally surprised gaze. "The cream," he mouthed. "The cream."

"So she's thirty-one," Sonia said, her irritation deepening to anger. "Hubert, come show me that new highlighting trick you were telling me about earlier."

Hubert nodded, but continued to examine Cleopatra's face. "What do you think, Mr. Mazzini?"

Anthony couldn't stop staring.

I knew that under all that heavy makeup was a million-dollar face!

Lord have mercy, I'd do anything to know what it feels like to be a world-famous model!

A million-dollar face, Anthony mused. A world-famous model.

Well, he had the power, didn't he? Had all the influence he needed, didn't he?

Yes.

He smiled.

Every woman could be bought. Two decades in the cosmetics business had taught him that.

And Anthony had no doubt that he'd just realized what Cleopatra's price tag was.

Four

"*M*ama, Opal, and Rhonda Faye are plumb swelled up with elation that I'm stayin' in New York to be a model," Cleopatra announced to Anthony, Hubert, and Ted while Hubert prepared her for her first day in front of the camera. Sitting in a swivel chair in front of a well-lit makeup mirror in the photo studio, she crossed her legs and tried to pull down her short skirt. "I've never heard such gleeful hollerin' in all my days than when I called 'em with the news. Mama's so excited that she promised to get back to puttin' on makeup like she used to do before almost gougin' out Loreen Mickler's eye. Much as I want to be a model and all, I was worried about Murphy's Make-over Miracles, but turns out everything's gonna be fine."

"Murphy's Make-over Miracles," Ted repeated slowly. "Who came up with that name?"

"Mama." Cleopatra smiled, pondering her little salon back home. "She set up shop right in our garage when I was just a young'un. Bought makeup supplies from a travelin' salesman by the name of Otis Wallace. I told you I knew another man named Wallace, Ted. Anyway, Otis Wallace? Well, Mama took a heart-burnin' to him on account of he reminded her of Larry Tate, that character on *Bewitched*. You know—Darren Stevens's boss? Mama always thought Larry Tate was some *kinda* handsome. 'Course, 'round about that time was right after Daddy left us, so Mama was pro'bly a mite lonesome for a man. When Otis Wallace came around, Mama'd just about drown herself in liquid lure and then she'd—"

"Liquid lure?" Ted asked.

"Perfume. Y'know, Anthony, that there cream of mine works on men, too," Cleopatra announced, watching as Anthony squirted a bit of the lime green cream out of the mustard bottle.

He rubbed the silky cream into the top of his hand, his curiosity over its formula intensifying.

"Mama bought just about ever'thing Otis Wallace had to sell," Cleopatra continued, opening her eyes wide so Hubert could apply a final touch of mascara. "He was pretty slick, Otis Wallace was, accordin' to Mama. She said he was such a good salesman that he could've sold clothes hangers at a nudist colony if he'd set his mind to it. So, she had all this makeup, see, and then she opened Murphy's Make-over Miracles."

"Be still," Hubert said, then plucked the black jelly bean out of Cleopatra's fingers. "These candies will make your mouth gray. And since I've already applied your lip color, you can't brush your teeth." He tossed the sweet onto the makeup counter, then adjusted Cleopatra's chair toward the mirror so she could better see the face that would soon be plastered on magazines across the country. "Well? What do you think?"

Cleopatra stared at her reflection. "I've seen more color on bleached bones! Good Lord, Hubert, you've been rubbin', blendin', smoothin', and pattin' makeup on me for near about an hour, and nothin' you used even shows up!"

Hubert cast a silent plea for help toward Anthony's direction. Try though he had, he still couldn't make Cleopatra believe that less makeup was more.

"Cleopatra," Anthony began, "we're going for a completely natural look. Just two days ago, when I first offered you a modeling job with Dresden, you agreed to abide by—"

"And one more thing!" Cleopatra slipped out of her chair and stood. "Just look at this skirt, Anthony! If this dang thing was any shorter, it'd be *collar!*"

Anthony couldn't suppress a quick burst of laughter.

Even as amusement rolled through him, his own mirth sounded strange to him.

It sounded odd to Ted and Hubert too, who both stared at him as if he'd suddenly sprouted two heads. "Mr. Mazzini?" Ted asked. "Are—are you all right?"

"Is he all right?" Cleopatra echoed, frowning. "All's he's doin' is laughin'."

As soon as the words left her lips, she realized the significance of what she'd said. Was it possible the man never laughed? "Anthony?" she asked softly.

Anthony regained control of himself immediately. He didn't care for the way Cleopatra was looking at him, as if she could see straight through him.

It was damned unsettling.

"The skirt is fine, Cleopatra," he stated firmly, pulling at one of his shirt cuffs. "So is the makeup. You have great legs and a gorgeous face."

She caught his gaze and held it fast. "Real—really?"

What was the matter with her? he wondered. Couldn't she see her own beauty every time she looked in a mirror?

Obviously not, and her complete lack of conceit astonished him.

And it pleased him, for some odd reason he couldn't understand.

"Really," he answered, floored by the warm, bright smile of delight she gave me. "But I'm afraid you'll have to take off that silver bracelet."

She fingered the ID bracelet. "But—"

"Who's Lewis, anyway?" Anthony asked. Perhaps she had a boyfriend waiting for her in Snyder's Dock, he mused.

"I don't know who Lewis is."

"Then why do you wear the bracelet?"

"Because Mama gave it to me."

When she looked at him as though his mind was totally void of logic, Anthony tried his level best to understand why anyone would wear a bracelet with a stranger's name on it. He failed.

"When a loved one gives you somethin', then whatever that somethin' is becomes a treasure," Cleopatra explained as she dropped the bracelet on to the table. "You sure and certain I have enough makeup on? I'm nervous, Anthony. If I bite my nails anymore, my stomach'll need a manicure."

His lips twitched. "You're perfect. Trust me, okay?"

She did. And so began her life as a model.

The days were long and tiring. Dresden's representatives allowed her only a bit of fruit for breakfast, a small salad for lunch, and not a single jelly bean, claiming that if she gained the least amount of weight she would lose the wonderful hollows beneath her cheekbones. And every morning at five o'clock, a muscle man named Chico made her daily exercise class so difficult that some nights came when she felt she could sleep on a barbed wire fence.

The camera lights made her perspire. As soon as the first sheen of moisture appeared on her face, Hubert hurried to repair her makeup. Other people were constantly fiddling with her hair, and others couldn't seem to leave her clothes or jewelry alone to save their lives.

But tired, hungry, and sore as she was, Cleopatra loved every exciting second of her new profession.

Especially when Dresden's publicity department initiated one of the most spectacular promotional campaigns the beauty industry had ever conceived.

The company took full advantage of the fact that she was named after one of the most beautiful women the world had ever known, a woman who had chosen death by snakebite. To strengthen the idea and capture the public's fascination, every photo of Cleopatra that appeared also featured a snake.

But the serpent was always hidden in the photos, prompting everyone who saw the pictures to search for the scaly creature. Once, a green reptile lay coiled in the mass of lush foliage where Cleopatra sat. Another time a small brown snake laid over the strap of her handbag, blending in with the leather so perfectly that it was fairly impossible to find. In another photo, a very thin black snake hung over her shoulder, looking so much like one of her ebony tresses that not even Anthony spotted the reptile without help from one of the photographers.

The promotional gimmick seized instant attention from the press. Grocery store tabloids printed her picture, reporting that the real Cleopatra had risen from the dead. She made the covers of *People* and *Us,* which also featured stories about her life in Georgia, the outlandish manner by which she'd come to Dresden's attention, and her resulting rise to fame.

She became the beauty industry's hottest find in decades, and every time she thought about her picture being displayed next to cash registers in nearly every grocery store in America—including Weaver's Market —a thrill spiraled through her.

Opal and Rhonda Faye wrote to inform her that the media had descended upon Snyder's Dock like a pack of starving wolves and that articles about her had appeared in newspapers all over Georgia. Annette had given most of the interviews.

But only after showing off the satellite dish her famous daughter had bought for her.

All of Synder's Dock was proud of Cleopatra. Grateful, too, since Cleopatra had sent a great deal of money to the little town. Opal made it her business to distribute the cash to anyone who needed it.

"I paid for Rhonda Faye's tube-tyin', Anthony," Cleopatra announced when she'd finished reading Opal's most recent letter.

Sitting across the table from her in one of New York's finest restaurants, Anthony lowered his dinner menu. "Her tube-tying?"

Cleopatra leaned back in her chair as the waiter placed a silver basket of warm bread on the table. "Rhonda Faye had her tubes tied last week. Opal says it's the best thing she's ever done, what with that gamblin' husband of hers. Opal claims the cravin' for gamblin' is inherited and the world sure doesn't need for Rhonda Faye to breed more gamblers. My modelin' money paid for Rhonda Faye's surgery. Next week they're havin' a tube-tyin' party for Rhonda Faye over at Miss Iris's house. Miss Iris's house ain't real big, but it's the only place in town where Miss Iris feels safe from werewolves. We had a hemorrhoid party for Benny Shrugg last year when he got his hemorrhoids taken care of. 'Course, Benny didn't really have a good time at his party on account of he still couldn't sit down good. But I reckon other folks had such a good time at that party that they decided to do one for Rhonda Faye."

"A hemorrhoid party." Bending his head, Anthony smiled at the napkin in his lap.

"Miss Iris is Snyder's Dock's oldest citizen. No one really knows just how old she is for sure, but folks are fond of sayin' she knew the Big Dipper when it was only a drinkin' cup. I sure do hate to miss Rhonda Faye's tube-tyin' party, Anthony."

His smile vanished; he swiftly lifted his head. "You aren't thinking of going home, are you?" he asked, alarmed by the very thought of her leaving New York before he'd gotten the recipe for her beauty cream.

Damnit, when would the time come for him to ask her for the ingredients? He knew she was enjoying her modeling career. And she loved her new home too, an apartment in the same building where he lived. True, he hadn't been able to spend as much time with her as he realized he needed to, what with his pressing work schedule and her long hours as well, but he tried to meet her for lunch whenever possible. He'd managed to take her out to dinner on several occasions, and he'd even found time to escort her to bookstores, where she'd purchased a multitude of books about werewolves for the little old lady named Miss Iris.

She was happy. Her vivacious smile assured him of that.

But he still didn't feel he could request the recipe from her. Not yet. It just seemed too soon.

"What's the matter, Anthony? You look as worried as a duck in the desert."

He struggled to present a more normal expression. "I asked if you were thinking about going home."

His worry over her returning to Georgia gave her a warm, all-over feeling that made her smile. Maybe An-

thony liked her. *Really* liked her. He was very nice to
her, always opening doors for her, pulling out her
chairs at tables, and carrying packages for her. He'd
even bought her a five-pound jar of black jelly beans.

No man she'd ever known had shown her such con-
sideration. And yet . . .

He was so stiff-acting. Like he dipped his character
into a bowl of starch every morning.

And there was still that vague unhappiness about
him. She couldn't shake the feeling that something important was missing in his life.

"Do you ever have any fun, Anthony?"

Her out-of-the-blue question took him aback mo-
mentarily. Hadn't they been discussing the tube-tying
party? "Fun? I—"

"Work's the most fun thing y'do, huh? Doesn't anything else tickle your fancy?"

"Tickle my fancy?"

"Yeah—you know. When you like somethin' a whole,
whole lot, that means your fancy's tickled."

"I enjoy my work. You like your modeling too, don't
you?"

"Oh, sure, but I don't eat, drink, and breathe it. I
only have two or three photo shoots a week, and when
I'm off I like to walk the streets and hunt down famous
people. I saw Sylvester Stallone last week, did I tell you
that? I wanted his autograph, but he ducked into a
buildin' so fast I didn't have time to ask him for it. So, I
got his limousine driver's autograph instead. Sent it on
to Mama, and she framed it after showin' it off to all of
Synder's Dock.

"And even when I was still workin' my salon back
home, I didn't let work keep me from havin' fun," she
added. " 'Course, workin' my parlor's fun on account of
my friends are there all day, but I do other stuff too. On
Saturday night I like to go bowlin' or play bingo with
Opal and Rhonda Faye. Sometimes Mama comes
along, too, but only if the Saturday night movie is a
rerun. And on Sundays I like to piddle. Y'don't do
much when you piddle, but sometimes not doin' anything is fun. And sometimes piddlin' leads to real fun.

Like the time I was piddlin' around the kitchen, just wipin' the counters, rearrangin' the refrigerator magnets, and cleanin' out the junk drawer. Guess what I found in that junk drawer?"

She answered her own query before the question had even registered in Anthony's mind.

"I found a scrap of wallpaper."

Anthony tried to understand if he was supposed to feel excited over her find. "A scrap of—"

"Wallpaper. Mama'd been goin' to repaper the kitchen and had had that sample tucked away for years. Well, right then and there I carried her over to the hardware store. We picked out some purty paper with big green cabbages and bunches of carrots on it, and we papered the kitchen. It was so much fun, and it all started with piddlin'. I reckon you don't ever piddle though, huh?"

Still unsure as to what piddling truly entailed, Anthony decided to address a subject he understood. "Do you do this Sunday piddling before or after you've made your weekly batch of beauty cream?"

"After."

"How long does it take to make the cream?"

"About an hour or so. Less if I have all the ingredients, but sometimes I have to slip over to Weaver's Market and buy stuff for it."

"What makes it green?"

Cleopatra smiled. "Food colorin'. That lime green's purty, huh? When I first started makin' it, I used red food colorin' and tried it out on Opal. Must've used too much red in it. Opal looked like a cranberry for three days before the colorin' finally wore off. I finally settled for green. Anyway, back to the question you asked me before I started ramblin' about piddlin'. No, I'm not goin' home for Rhonda Faye's tube-tyin' party. I can do more for Mama and my friends here than I can there in Snyder's Dock. The people there—well . . . "

Anthony heard worry in her soft voice. "What about the people there?"

Cleopatra took a deep breath then released a long, slow sigh. "Snyder's Dock's a small town with no opportunities. The people there struggle, Anthony. I always thought that if only some big businesses would move there, the folks'd have a better livelihood. But no businesses ever come, so my friends, neighbors . . . everyone gets by as best as they can. I've been sending as much money as I can to try to help, and Opal's been handin' it out to anyone who needs some.''

Anthony gave a nod of comprehension, but he didn't understand at all. She *gave* her modeling money away? Giving it to her mother was one thing, but to the entire town?

He could hardly believe such a thing. But he *did* believe it because he saw no evidence of dishonesty in Cleopatra's beautiful eyes. She really and truly was sending her money to the township of Synder's Dock, Georgia.

Perhaps such generosity was her way of paying back the people who watched out over her mother for her while she was gone, he reasoned. Or maybe she was paying back debts to the people who were receiving the money she was making now. It had to be one or the other or both, he knew, because no one would just pass out money.

"You'll be receiving a substantial increase in salary before much longer," he told her. "If all goes as planned, you'll be soon be featured on the covers of *Glamour* and—"

"Then I'll be able to do even more back home," Cleopatra said, laying Opal's letter aside. "Y'know? Not only did I pay for Rhonda Faye's tube-tyin', but Opal writes that I also bought a new pulpit for the church. A big mahogany one, Opal says. The old one was so rickety that once when Reverend Lubbins leaned over the top of it? Well, it fell right over, and Reverend Lubbins crashed into the floor and hit his head on the front pew. Had to get five stitches in his forehead. That scar he's got ills him somethin' awful, too. Etched across the wrinkles he's got on his forehead, together it all looks like a tic-tac-toe game. How'd you get that scar on *your* forehead?"

"What?" His mind reeling with the rambling tale

she'd just told him, a moment passed before Anthony could answer. "I . . ."

He reached up and drew a finger across the small scar.

He'd been nine, he remembered. Maybe ten, and he'd set up a wooden lemonade stand in front of his house in Rome, New York. He'd passed out all the lemonade to his friends for free.

His father hadn't agreed with the idea of giving away lemonade on such a hot day. His mother had expounded upon the fact that the sugar and lemons he'd used to make the lemonade had come out of her grocery money.

Anthony quietly had disassembled the stand. As he worked, a board with a nail sticking out of it had hit his forehead. The next time he manned the lemonade booth, he'd charged ten cents a glass, earning one dollar and ninety cents by late afternoon.

Now, every time Anthony saw the scar in the mirror, he was reminded of the lesson he'd learned that long-ago day. Everything came with a price; nothing was free.

Nothing.

"Anthony?" Cleopatra pressed.

"A board," he said, and took a sip of wine. "A board fell on me when I was a boy."

"What were you doin' when the board fell on you?"

"What does it matter?"

She shrugged. "It doesn't, I reckon. I just want to know. I like knowin' stuff about you. 'Course, I don't know much because you don't hardly ever talk about yourself."

Her interest in him encouraged him. Perhaps all the time and energy he'd spent making sure she was content in New York was finally paying off. He felt renewed hope that he would soon acquire the secret to her cream.

And he felt something else too, something uncomfortable, and for one brief moment he considered naming it guilt.

But he wasn't going to name it anything because if it

had a name then he'd be forced to acknowledge its existence.

He looked at his wine glass. Candlelight glinted off the fragile crystal, reminding him of the way Cleopatra's eyes twinkled when she smiled that drop-dead gorgeous smile of hers.

It was such a real smile. So unlike those of other women he knew.

He twirled the stem of his glass between his fingers, watching the burgundy liquid swirl, and summoning to mind things he thought might impress her. "Talk about myself, huh? Well, I was born in Rome, New York, but I've lived in New York City for twenty-some years, ever since landing a position with Dresden's marketing department. I remember debating as to whether I really wanted to work for a cosmetics company. The job seemed . . . well, the product is for women. But I accepted the job, and before long I realized it wasn't any different than marketing beer or selling cars. I'm executive vice-president in charge of new products right now, but I'm working toward being promoted to president. The position is—"

"Anthony?"

"Yes?"

"That's not the kinda stuff I was hopin' to learn about you."

He couldn't imagine what other "stuff" she wanted to know.

"What's your favorite color?"

Oh, that "stuff", he realized. "Blue."

"Men always say that. I think it has something to do with their masculinity. Like, it wouldn't be manly to fancy pink or yellow. Wonder who decided which colors were for women and which were for men?"

A stranger question had never been put to him. "I have a pink shirt."

"But would you ever put a pink sofa in your house?"

He smiled. "Touché."

"I have a pink loveseat in my salon. Do y'think I could send for it and put it in my apartment here in the city?"

Nodding, he made a mental note to arrange for the shipping of the loveseat. He'd make all the calls first thing in the morning.

A pink loveseat, he mused, watching happiness play across Cleopatra's face. He smiled again, thinking of the day he'd taken her furniture shopping so she could fill her new apartment with the things she liked.

She'd purchased a lavender and white striped sofa and two red easy chairs, one a deep, dark red, the other the color of a fire engine. A brass and smoked glass coffee table sat in front of her sofa. On the table she'd placed knickknacks such as coasters made of seashells, a yellow plastic ashtray which she'd filled with strawberry potpourri, and a stack of Archie comic books in case any of her guests wanted to read.

She'd also purchased a painting done on black velvet, the kind of painting that small time vendors sold on the side of the road in rural areas. The artwork depicted the face of Lucille Ball. "I watch *I Love Lucy* whenever I have time," she'd explained to him. "I especially like the one when Lucy sets her clay nose on fire in front of William Holden while she, Ricky, Fred, and Ethel are out in California for Ricky's Don Juan movie."

Her apartment was completely filled now with furniture, wall hangings, set-arounds, and throw rugs. Nothing in the place matched. . . .

And yet, everything matched Cleopatra. And when Anthony pondered that notion, his thoughts were not disparaging. On the contrary, he felt a happy sort of acceptance.

"I ain't never had no lovin' on my loveseat, though," Cleopatra said abruptly.

Pulled out of his reverie, Anthony sat up straighter in his chair. "You've never had a boyfriend?" He leaned forward to hear her answer.

Cleopatra stared at the gold rim around the edge of her bread plate, pondering the ill luck she'd had with the men in her life. "I've had two," she stated softly. "First one was Clyde Motts. He was so handsome. But Clyde? Lord, he was so lazy that he walked in his sleep so he could rest and get his exercise at the same time."

Anthony fairly choked while trying to keep laughter at bay.

"The second one," Cleopatra continued, "was Billy Wicket. I loved him somethin' fierce at first, but he turned out to be a hypochondriac. He was always so full of penicillin that every time he sneezed, he cured a dozen people."

Anthony could no longer suppress his amusement. His loud laughter caused heads to turn throughout the elegant restaurant.

The rich sound of his laughter made Cleopatra feel the way she always did when standing in the first rays of spring sunshine after a cold, hard winter. Warmth seeped through her and her heart seemed to smile.

Anthony needed to laugh, she realized. Laugh every single day.

"I'm sorry," Anthony said, still struggling to tame the quick and irrepressible mirth caused by her outlandish way of expressing herself, "for my outburst."

"Well, good Lord, I've never known anyone who apologized for bein' happy."

"For being happy? I'm not apologizing for being—" He broke off, suddenly unsure of what he was about to say. Was he apologizing for being happy? Or for laughing?

But weren't being happy and laughing one and the same?

"I don't think Sonia Brockman likes me, Anthony. The other day at that photo shoot we did at the airport? Well, I said hey to her and she walked right past me without even lookin' at me. Kinda hurt my feelin's on account of I've never done anything to her to make her hate me. You ever do this when you were a kid?" Leaning forward, Cleopatra drew her finger through the flame of the candle. "It used to fascinate me that I could put my finger through fire and not get burned. I reckon it still fascinates me, else I wouldn't still be doin' it."

Anthony watched her move her finger through the flame again, remembering when he'd done the same thing. God, he hadn't thought of the finger-through-the-flame trick in years.

Another memory came to him. He'd also liked to stick each of his fingers into the warm, melted wax that pooled beneath the candle flame. The wax would dry on the tips of his fingers, forming perfect little cups.

"What I really like to do," Cleopatra continued, "is stick the tips of my fingers into hot candle wax. When the wax dries—"

"You have ten hollow wax shells."

She smiled. He'd done it too, she realized. He'd stuck his fingers into hot wax just like she had. "So, what were you doin' when the board fell on you and cut your forehead?"

He'd forgotten she'd asked him that question. Strange. It was a rare occasion when he forgot anything. "Taking apart a lemonade stand."

"I like lemonade, but there's a secret to it, y'know. Most folks don't know that a smidgen of mint makes it taste better. All's you've got to do is stick your fingernail through a few mint leaves and drop 'em right in the lemonade."

She tasted a bit of the bread. "I don't reckon y'all have any cornbread around here, do you? I like mine fried. 'Course, it's not real good for you fried. Wonder why all the things that taste good are so bad for you? I made a lemonade stand once."

"Oh?" Anthony wondered if she'd been a better sales person than he. "How much money did you make?"

"Not nary a cent."

He leaned back and folded his arms across his chest, unable to suppress a smug smile.

"Didn't make a single cent," Cleopatra continued, popping another piece of bread into her mouth, "on account of I gave all the lemonade away for free."

Five

*S*he wanted to soak up culture.

He took her to see *Phantom of the Opera*.

She didn't like it. If *she'd* written the play, she'd have let the phantom win the girl in the end.

He escorted her to the ballet.

She couldn't understand a story that had no words. How was it possible to know what was going on just by watching some dancers leap and twirl around the stage?

He invited her to accompany him to the opera.

She fell asleep, and when she woke up she admitted that the only language she spoke was English. Therefore, she hadn't a clue as to what the Italian opera singers were singing about.

Anthony began to realize that culture and Cleopatra went together about as well as a pearl and a pebble.

"All right, Cleopatra," he said one evening when he'd come to her apartment to take her out again, "what do *you* want to do tonight?" While waiting for her to emerge from the bedroom and answer him, he took a seat on her lavender and white striped sofa, and slipped the small, wrapped gift he'd brought her into his inside coat pocket.

A swirl of fragrances assaulted his senses. There was the strawberry potpourri she kept on her coffee table, but he also detected a floral scent and something that smelled like apple pie.

"Did you bake apple pie?" he called.

Cleopatra limped out of the bedroom with one shoe

on. "Apple pie?" Standing on her left leg, she slipped her other shoe on her right foot. "Oh, that's cinnamon-apple lamp oil. I put a few drops on the lightbulbs around here. And the other smell you pro'bly smell is the gardenia-scented candle that's lit over there on the table by the window. I love smells, Anthony."

Strawberry, gardenia, and cinnamon-apple, he thought. If he'd been with any other woman, he'd consider the fragrance combination a peculiar one. But since he was with Cleopatra, the mixture of scents seemed perfectly ordinary.

"Y'want me to bake you an apple pie one day?" Cleopatra turned off the lamp in the living room, a standing fixture whose base was a miniature version of the Statue of Liberty. It was the statue's raised hand that held the lightbulb. "I make 'em real good, y'know, apple pies. The secret is usin' honest-to-goodness, high fat, heart attack–givin' lard in the pie crust."

Anthony remembered when his best friend's mother used to bake apple pies. Mrs. Birdsong was her name, and he'd loved her pies, her last name, and her son, Micah.

He wondered what happened to Micah and Mrs. Birdsong.

"I thought you said we were going to some important exhibition over at the art museum," Cleopatra said. "And now you're askin' where I want to go. I put on this fancy dress just for the special museum show."

Turning toward the full length mirror that decorated one of her walls, she smoothed her hand down the black lace dress. "Seems a little fancy just for starin' at paintin's and sculptures of naked men, but I—"

"Do you want to go to the art exhibition, Cleopatra?" Anthony rose from the sofa and walked toward her, closer, not stopping until he stood directly behind her, his chest touching her back, the top of his chin resting on the crown of her head. "We don't have to go if you'd rather not. After all, you weren't overly fond of the play, the ballet, or the opera, so it stands to reason that you might not care for the museum exhibition either."

His nearness stole her voice, her breath, and every thought she had but the one of him. Her gaze met his in the mirror.

He read every thought in her mind, felt every emotion flowing through her body. Tonight, he decided. Tonight would be the night.

He'd seen to her happiness with her modeling, her apartment, and her evening hours. Now he would see to her physical needs.

Her sensual desires.

And then he would broach the subject of her beauty cream.

He lifted his hands to her shoulders, slid them down the length of her slender arms, and gently grasped her wrists. "Well?" he murmured, savoring the soft, clean smell of her hair, "what do you want to do tonight?"

"My feet," she whispered. "The soles of my feet are gettin' hot."

Her feet, he repeated silently. He liked knowing he'd made her hot, but he could think of other parts of her anatomy where he would have preferred the heat to spread.

"One time?" Cleopatra said, still staring at his reflection in the mirror. "Well, one time I stuck a metal paper clip into the electrical socket in my bedroom. I saw sparks and got a shock that nearly turned me inside out. I never did it again, but I remember how fast that shock traveled into me."

He frowned. "What does that have to do with your feet?"

She sighed, and heard how shaky her sigh sounded. "That's what happened when you came up behind me and touched me the way you did."

"You got shocked?"

"No, my feet got hot. And they got hot just as fast as I got shocked that time I put the paper clip into the socket."

Anthony realized that somewhere in her twisted explanation there existed logic, but he'd be damned if he could discern what it was.

His confusion prompted him to return to a subject he

could understand. "What would you like to do tonight?"

She turned to face him. When her breasts slid across his hard, broad chest, her feet grew hotter. "Stay here."

He liked her answer. "You haven't eaten." Still standing close to her, he took off his coat. His fingers brushed her breasts, and he smiled inside when he heard her sharp intake of breath. "What about dinner?" Taking a step back, he casually untied his tie, pulled it out from beneath his collar, and draped it over his shoulder. "Do you want to have something delivered?"

She parted her lips to answer, but found speaking an impossible thing. Lord have mercy, all the man had done was take off his coat and tie, but the simple action made her feel as flimsy as a ribbon.

"Cleopatra?"

"Scram—scrambled eggs, toast, and orange sherbet?"

His gaze never leaving hers, he unbuttoned the first two buttons of his shirt. "I have rum raisin ice cream at my place."

His suggestion of a different dessert got her full attention. Rum raisin. How elegant. Cultured. Like the play, the ballet, the opera, and the exhibition at the art museum.

"You ever been fishin', Anthony?"

He doubted he'd ever become accustomed to her habit of changing the subject so quickly. "Yes. When I was sixteen my father took me deep-sea fishing in Mexico. I caught a swordfish. We had it mounted, and I hung it over my bed."

"What about minnows?"

"Mounted minnows?" The thought was the most ludicrous he'd ever entertained.

"Some minnows are see-through, and when you look at 'em you can see all their innards. I'll go make the eggs now." She left him standing by the mirror and headed toward the kitchen, singing "Flies in the Buttermilk, Shoo Fly Shoo" while she walked. "Oh, and Anthony?"

"Yes?"

"We're not at your place. We're at mine, and I have orange sherbet. So, guess what we're havin' for dessert?"

His answer was a grin and, an hour later, while he and Cleopatra lounged on the pink loveseat from Georgia and finished the last of the icy dessert, Anthony admitted to himself that orange sherbet *did* go better with scrambled eggs than rum raisin ice cream would have.

"Want anything else?" Cleopatra dropped her spoon into the empty sherbet container. "I have a smidgen of chicken-corn soup in the freezer that might tickle your fancy. It's my grammy's recipe."

"Oh?" Turning slightly, Anthony reached toward her face, trailed his finger across her cheek, down to her chin, and then over her lips. "It sounds as though you have many of your grandmother's recipes." He spoke the statement softly, all the while continuing to caress her lips. "Do you make them as often as you make the beauty cream?"

A long moment passed before she could reply. If she didn't know any better, she'd have sworn her feet were inside a blazing furnace. "Mama," she whispered, "does most of the cookin'. I don't close Murphy's Make-over Miracles till after seven or so on account of some of my customers don't get off work in time to get over there any earlier. Times come, though, when I'm still workin' after nine. When folks call wantin' to come, I just can't say no."

Anthony hoped she wouldn't be able to say no to *him* tonight, either. No to his sensual advances or no to his soon-to-come request for the secret to her cream.

"I have something for you, Cleopatra."

She watched him cross the room. The back of his shirt stretched tightly across his broad shoulders and the swells of muscle in his back. He had an easy gait, a sureness in each of his steps, and she liked thinking about his self-reliance.

He sure was different than Clyde Motts and Billy

Wicket, neither of whom possessed the skill or inclination to take care of himself.

Both of whom would have rathered *she* take care of them.

"Cleopatra?"

The sound of her name brought her back to the present, back to Anthony. "Is that what you have for me?" She glanced at the small, oblong box in his hand. Wrapped in pink paper, the present was topped with a perfect purple bow.

"You like pink and purple," Anthony said, sitting back down beside her and placing the box in her lap. "At least, those are the colors you always want Hubert to put on your eyes."

His thoughtfulness reinforced her comprehension of how special he was. How opposite he was from the other men she'd known in her life.

"Open it, Cleopatra."

She picked up the box. It lay heavily in her hand. "What's this present for?"

"No special reason." He looked away for a moment, uncomfortable with the lie he'd just told her and knowing he had to tell her a second one as well. "I just wanted to give you something, that's all."

Cleopatra removed the bow from the box. Carefully, so as not to tear the pretty pink paper, she unwrapped the gift, and then an emerald green velvet box lay in her hand. "Looks like a jewelry box," she murmured, longing to open it, but not allowing herself to do so yet. " 'Course, boxes can fool you. I once opened up a present from Mama? Well, imagine my all-over glee when I saw that the box had a picture of a fax machine on it. Not that I'd ever use a fax machine since I don't have anyone to fax, but just the idea of havin' somethin' as fancy as a fax machine is sorta thrillin', don't y'think? Turned out, though, that the fax machine box was only a fax machine box. Inside was a peach velour bathrobe from Sears. I'll have that bathrobe for years to come. Stuff from Sears lasts forever, y'know. One time I had a trainin' bra from Sears, and I mean to tell you, that thing lasted for three whole years. That's how long it took me to finally grow out of it. I was a slow developer. So slow that I used to wear enough cotton in my bras to open up a first-aid station."

"Cleopatra?" Anthony said, and chuckled.

"Yes?"

"Open the gift."

Slowly, so she could prolong the anticipation and also hear the delightful squeak of the box as its hinges separated, she opened the gift.

Inside, gleaming upon a puff of white satin, lay a gold bracelet. Cut out in intricate letters, the beautiful piece of jewelry spelled her name.

"Lewis doesn't suit you," Anthony told her. He lifted the bracelet from the box and clasped it around her right wrist. "I understand that the bracelet your mother gave you holds special meaning for you, but I hope you'll wear this one for me every now and again."

She held her hand up close to her face. Light leapt over the gold like a swirl of happy dancers, and she compared the pretty sight to the equally joyful feeling that skipped through her heart. "It's—it's one of the nicest things anyone's ever given me, Anthony. I promise to wear it everyday, and I can, y'know, just the way I can always wear the bracelet Mama gave me. It's sterling silver. This one's gold. Neither one'll turn my wrist green."

Her sweet and simple reasoning made him smile.

"Thank you, Anthony. Thank you so much." On impulse, she leaned toward him, and when he opened his arms she snuggled next to his chest, into his heat.

She found an unfamiliar security there, wrapped in his strength, his silence, and his kindness.

They sat quietly for many long moments, unmoving, the only sound in the room that of the traffic in the street below.

Then, in the space of a heartbeat, it happened.

So gently did Anthony kiss her that his touch was barely a touch at all. A whisper of a caress, that's what it was, Cleopatra decided. Made of air and tenderness.

She sighed, and when she did, so did he, and she felt

her breath mingle with his. There was no demand in his kiss, no unspoken request for anything more.

She'd never been kissed like this, so unhurriedly and without a hint of lust. That Anthony gave with such sensitivity, that his kiss imparted such unseeking sweetness deepened Cleopatra's affection for him.

She could love this man, she realized. Love him with all her heart, soul, and every other fiber that made her who she was.

"Soft," Anthony whispered, his lips moving upon hers. "So soft." Slowly, he inched his hand up her arm and across her shoulder. He tarried at her neck, his fingers and thumb stroking her skin.

She drew a deep breath, and he saw how her lush breasts pushed at the bodice of her lacy dress. She'd taken off her black stockings. He hadn't seen her remove them, but guessed she'd done so earlier while she was in the kitchen.

Her little black dress dipped low in the front, not so low as to be obscene, but low enough to heighten a man's appreciation of things unseen. What he could see of her breasts . . . white. Not stark white. Creamy. And smooth. Like her pale legs, one of which she'd tucked beneath the other.

She had such pretty feet, he thought. Small and delicate, and she'd painted her toenails pink, the kind of pink that made him think of the little pink stick-on notes his two secretaries used.

No, not the notepads, he amended.

Cleopatra's toenails were more the color of cotton candy and rainbows. He liked that comparison better, and wasn't so close-minded that he didn't realize that he'd never have thought of it before knowing her.

He drew his gaze back up to her breasts, to the lush cleavage hugged by all the fragile black lace. In only moments, he would hold her there and feel her softness in the palm of his hand. And when she whimpered at his touch, showed him she wanted more, he would satisfy her.

By midnight the secret to her beauty cream would be his.

He edged his hand downward.

But when she spoke, he stopped and looked into her eyes.

"Y'know, Anthony?"

He thought her voice one of the softest things he'd ever listened to, softer even than the faraway peal of distant church bells, those delicate chimes that he heard when he paid enough attention.

"Back home," Cleopatra continued, absently circling the tip of her finger around one of the buttons on his shirt, "at night . . . when the house is quiet, I hear night birds and tree branches. Crickets, and sometimes Vinny Orville's horse a-runnin' through the field behind where I live. Ole Vinny, he sure sets a store by that horse. Ain't much more'n swayback nag, but to hear Vinny tell it that critter's right up there with Man o' War. Here though, Anthony? Here in my apartment while I'm in bed, I hear cars and sirens and airplanes. It gets to me, and nights come when I'd pay money just to hear a cricket chirp or Vinny's horse run. Or even to hear Mama snorin' in the next bedroom. She snores so bad that I just know that one mornin' I'm gonna go in there and see that she's sucked the drapes off the walls.

"Now, though, Anthony, right now, I don't feel so homesick. That pinin', yearnin' feelin' . . . you lessen it, or somethin'. I like bein' with you, and y'want to know why? Truly why?"

"Tell me."

She shifted in his arms, lying her head on his shoulder. "On account of you don't want anything from me."

He stiffened.

"Remember when I told you about Clyde Motts and Billy Wicket? Both of 'em needed me for somethin'. Clyde because he was so dang lazy. Wanted me to work all day and cater to him all night. And Billy . . . sick as he always thought he was, all I ever really was to him was someone he could complain to. Didn't either one of 'em ever want me for nothin' but selfish reasons. Makes me feel real stupid to remember how long it took me to figure that out. Even stupider to think of how I didn't let it happen with just one man, but two."

Anthony didn't answer.

"Don't y'have anything to say, Anthony?"

He searched his mind for a proper reply, but guilt sat in his mind like a rock and not a single thought could get past it.

"Anthony?"

"Let's not talk about things that make you sad tonight, okay?"

Or things that made him admit he was the third son of a bitch who'd come into her life, he added silently.

"What do y'want to talk about then?"

"How about things that make you happy?"

"Eatin' raw cookie dough. And you?"

"Completing a difficult and time consuming business project." He thought about the beauty cream again. *That* business project certainly was proving to be difficult and time consuming.

"Our happy thoughts can't have anything to do with work, Anthony. They have to be simple stuff. You know —ordinary things that people do all the time."

He couldn't think of anything.

"How about shavin' without nickin' yourself?"

He smiled. "You're right. That does make me happy, especially when I'm in a rush to get to the office."

The office, Cleopatra mused. Always work and the office. "It's still your turn on account of I had to think of the first happy thing for you."

"All right." He deliberated for a moment, struggling to come up with a simple, happy notion. "Organizing my briefcase."

"Organizin' your briefcase?"

He sensed she was less than pleased with his simple, happy notion. "Your turn."

"Lightin' the fireplace with a week's worth o' junk mail."

"Discarding business cards I know I'll never need."

She realized that he was incapable of thinking of simple pleasures. "The smell of onion grass just after the lawn gets mowed. And the smell of ginger lilies. My grammy had ginger lilies in her yard, and when she died and we had to sell her house, Mama dug the lilies up

and transplanted 'em in our yard. When they bloom
their perfume nearly takes your breath away, and it always makes y'think of Grammy."

Anthony wondered what ginger lilies smelled like.

"Your turn, Anthony."

"Oh. Uh . . . watching the stock market report."

How much more boring could he get? "Gettin' free
samples of cereal and leg shavin' cream in the mail.
Your turn again."

What else made him happy? he struggled to think.
"Um . . ."

"How about when you're not quite awake but not all
the way asleep, either, and you tell yourself what y'want
to dream, and then you dream it?"

Her happy thought made him smile again. "That
doesn't really work, does it?"

"It does for me. Your turn."

"Kissing you."

"Eatin' sun-warmed cherry tomatoes right off the
vine, and—" Cleopatra lifted her head from his shoulder and looked into his eyes. "What did you say?"

His answer was another kiss, another long, leisurely
kiss that had her squirming in his arms, sighing into his
mouth. . . .

A kiss he ended before he succumbed to the fire her
ardent response poured through his loins.

Gently, he edged her back. For reasons that bewildered the hell out of him, he simply could not go
through with his plans to seduce her. Not tonight, a
night that had been filled with things like orange sherbet, minnow innards, the smell of apple pie, cookie
dough, and velour bathrobes from Sears.

Sex just didn't seem to go with tonight.

"It's late," he whispered.

"Yeah," she whispered back.

"I'll see you tomorrow?" He smoothed a lock of her
ebony hair away from her cheek.

"Y'don't have to work?"

He remembered he had two important meetings the
next day, one in the morning and another in the afternoon. "Ted can handle the office for one day."

His reply delighted her, but a sudden thought erased her smile. "I forgot. I *do* have to work. I have a shoot in Central Park in the morning. But if everything goes right, I should be done by one or two."

"Call me when you get home then."

"And we'll hunt for minnows and celebrities."

"Maybe we'll kill two birds with one stone and find Barbra Streisand fishing in the harbor."

He bid her goodnight then and left for his own apartment two floors up. Once in bed, he thought of all the things Cleopatra had told him during the course of the evening.

One thing especially piqued his curiosity.

A long while passed before he neared the brink of slumber, but when he reached it he told himself he wanted to dream about Cleopatra.

And he did.

Six

"She's a bitch, Kay," Sonia flared, standing beside another of Dresden's models and watching Cleopatra's photo shoot in Central Park. "That shoot she did last week for *Mademoiselle* was to have been mine. I wish that snake wrapped around her belt would bite her."

Smiling, Kay took a seat on a stone bench. "She's not a bitch, and you were only being *considered* for the cover of *Mademoiselle*. And as for the snake . . . Do you really think they'd have her pose with a venomous one?"

"I—"

"I'll admit I was jealous of Cleopatra, too. At first anyway, when Dresden made such a fuss over her, and Anthony Mazzini started paying so much attention to her. But after being with her during two shoots last month, I couldn't help but like her. When she told me that the roaches in Georgia were so big that people had to have hunting licenses to kill them, I thought I'd die laughing."

Sonia looked down at Kay, a model from the Philippines whose exotic beauty had made millions of dollars for Dresden. "What interest in Anthony do *you* have?"

Kay shook her head and laughed. "Do you really believe you're the only model whose secret fantasies involve Anthony Mazzini? A man like him with looks, power, and enough money to light his fireplace with? Not to mention that he'll be even more successful when Dresden promotes him to president. . . . What woman *wouldn't* lose her head over him? We talk about him all the time. Just yesterday, Wendy and Gabriella were wondering what it would be like to be in his bed."

Sonia had been wondering the same thing for three years. What did Anthony see in Cleopatra? He so refined, so educated; she so ill-mannered and ignorant. It just didn't make sense, the relationship Anthony had begun with the girl. Didn't add up.

There had to be *something* that Anthony wanted from Cleopatra. Something vitally important, or else Anthony never would have lowered himself to pay suit to the little heathen.

"Gotta go," Kay said, rising from the bench. "Cleopatra's done, and they're calling me."

As Kay left to begin her own shoot, Cleopatra entered the trailer where the models changed clothes.

Sonia followed her inside.

"Sonia," Cleopatra said, surprised by the woman's visit. "What—"

"Am I doing here?" After making sure no one else was in the trailer, Sonia shut the door. "I came to talk to you."

An uneasy feeling came over Cleopatra when she saw Sonia's expression. The woman's smile could have put another hole in the ozone layer. "What do y'want to talk about?"

Sonia walked away from the door, peered out of a small window, then faced Cleopatra again. "How does it feel to have achieved overnight success?"

"Overnight?" Cleopatra's wariness deepened. "Nothin's happened overnight, Sonia. I've had my picture taken lots of times, but I've still never been on the cover of any big women's magazines like you have."

"But you will. Soon, I hear. Sooner than any of the rest of us did when we first began."

"Are you—jealous?" Cleopatra asked incredulously. "Of—of *me?*"

Sonia forced a laugh. "Of you? Don't be ridiculous! Why would I be jealous of an illiterate—"

"*Illiterate?*" Cleopatra felt her right eyebrow rise.

"Lady, my daddy might've left my mama, but they were *married!*"

For a moment, Sonia only stared. "I said *illiterate,* not *illegit—*"

"You—"

"I asked you how instant success felt, Cleopatra. I mean, to a country girl from some tiny okra patch in the South, such glittering accomplishments must—"

"Snyder's Dock ain't no okra patch."

"Oh? A turnip patch then?"

One slow step at a time, Cleopatra approached Sonia, stopping only when she could see the pulse jump inside the woman's powdered neck. "Y'know? I used to stare at your picture for hours on end, wonderin' what it would be like to be you. Then, when I first met you the day of the Dresden makeup show, I'd never felt such excitement in all my life. When I signed up with Dresden to be a model, I hoped we could be friends and do stuff together. But now? Well, now, Sonia, I couldn't warm up to you if we were cremated together. *Mean's* what you are, and—"

"Of course, success *would* be easily attained for a model who was sleeping with one of Dresden's most important executives," Sonia interrupted smoothly. "A fact that has been thoroughly discussed among the company's other models, I can assure you."

"Wh-what?"

"I refer to Anthony Mazzini. It's common knowledge that the two of you have been—"

"I ain't sleepin' with Anthony! We ain't done nothin' but kiss!"

That Cleopatra had shared kisses with Anthony deepened Sonia's ire. "Oh, come now, Cleopatra. Do you really expect me to believe that? Your quick popularity is unheard of in this business. You are no more beautiful than any of the rest of us, so it stands to reason that your success has come about because of other reasons. I, on the other hand, am self-made."

So angry that she could barely take her next breath, Cleopatra pulled back her shoulders and confronted her adversary with the only weapon she had. "Self-made? Well, I reckon you ain't got nobody but yourself to blame for leavin' out the workin' parts."

Cleopatra's stinging wit rendered Sonia mute.

But Cleopatra was far from finished. "You got a beau, Sonia?"

"What? I . . ."

"I bet you could've married any man you pleased. Trouble is, you ain't ever pleased one, huh?"

Sonia gasped so quickly that she almost choked. "How dare you talk to *me* that way!"

"Why? On account of you're the worldwide-famous Sonia Brockman? Lord have mercy, lady, it's a damned good thing you don't have to pay taxes on what you think you're worth. I reckon I could try to knock some sense into you, but why should I try to put anything in your head when nature saw fit not to?"

"I don't have to stand here and take this from you!" Sonia clenched her fists so hard that three of her porcelain nails popped off. "I'm leaving!"

"Well, if y'can't think of a place to go, I can suggest one."

Sonia whirled toward the door.

When the spiteful woman was gone, Cleopatra calmly changed into her own clothes and left the trailer. A quick cab drive got her home in short order. Only when she was safely in her apartment did she give in to her true feelings.

She wept.

"Is something the matter, Mr. Mazzini?" Ted asked, sitting in a chair on the other side of Anthony's mahogany desk. "You seem preoccupied this afternoon."

Anthony drummed his fingers on the side of his coffee cup, glancing at the phone every few seconds. Why hadn't Cleopatra called yet? It was almost four, and she'd said the shoot in the park would be over by one or two. They were supposed to go minnow and celebrity hunting.

He missed her. Of course, missing her didn't mean he possessed any feelings for her. He didn't. Not at all because the last thing he needed in his life was a woman. He had his work, and it made him happy. A woman would get in the way of everything he'd worked so hard to attain, and she'd also need attention, which he would never have time to give her.

Still, he admitted that he missed Cleopatra. And it was perfectly all right to miss her because, after all, she was one of those fun kinds of people anyone would miss being around.

Yes, she was fun to be with, and that was the logical and acceptable reason why it was justifiable for him to miss her. That was that, and he'd dwell on the matter no longer.

"Mr. Mazzini?"

"What?" Anthony fought to remember what Ted had just asked him. "No. Nothing's wrong. How do the reports look?"

Ted looked down at the papers in his hands, summaries concerning the new cosmetics products that Anthony was considering investigating. "Great. Only . . ."

"Only what?"

Shifting in his chair, Ted pulled at the knot in his tie. "Well, there's still nothing in these reports about Miss Murphy's cream."

"You bring up the subject of the cream every week," Anthony snapped. "I'm getting tired of hearing it."

Ted laid the papers aside. "I have your best interests in mind," he said quietly. "You and I have been working together for going on five years now, and I'd like to see you reach that next rung on the corporate ladder."

Anthony picked up a pencil and bounced the eraser on the polished surface of his desk. Why *wouldn't* Ted Wallace want to see him become president? As Anthony's personal assistant, the man's own position would rise.

Everyone was out for something, he thought bitterly. Greed was a disease in the business world.

He'd been sickened by the malady himself.

Still rapping the pencil on the desk, he glanced at the phone again.

"You know, Mr. Mazzini, there's a rumor circulating

that Michael Varner is being considered for the position of president of new products. I thought you should know, sir."

Anthony rose from his chair, turned toward the huge window behind his desk, and ran his fingers through his hair. He'd heard the same rumor, only it wasn't a rumor. Michael Varner *was* a prime candidate for the coveted presidential position.

"Isn't Miss Murphy willing to sell the formula?" Ted pressed.

His impatience with Ted's interrogation rising, Anthony rammed his fingers through his hair again.

"If you could only acquire the secret to the cream," Ted added, "Michael Varner wouldn't stand a chance—"

"I know."

"There isn't much time—"

"I'll get the recipe."

"With a product like that, Dresden would be—"

"I said I'd get it, damnit!"

Finally understanding the depth of Anthony's frustration and anger, Ted rose from his chair and crossed to the door. "I'm sorry Mr. Mazzini. During all your time with Dresden, you've never failed with an important project, so I shouldn't have questioned you. You'll get the formula. I know you will."

With that, Ted exited and closed the office door. Outside in the reception area, he walked past two secretarial desks and headed for the elevator, which opened as soon as he reached it.

Sonia Brockman stepped out of the compartment, looking at the three fresh nails she'd just had applied. "Oh, hello, Ted. Is Anthony in?"

"Yes, but I wouldn't go in there if I were you."

She glanced at Anthony's door. "Why not?"

"It's that beauty cream. I know damned well he wants the formula, but for some reason I can't understand he hasn't gotten it from her."

"Her?"

"Cleopatra. Anyway, he's mad as hell right now, so consider yourself forewarned."

When Ted disappeared into the elevator, Sonia stared at Anthony's door so hard that her eyes began to sting.

So *that* was the reason Anthony was paying so much attention to Cleopatra. He didn't really care about the silly little hayseed at all!

He was using her to get the beauty cream formula.

Sonia smoothed one of her new nails across her bottom lip.

And smiled.

"Cleopatra, open the door." Anthony stood outside her apartment, talking into the peep hole. "I know you're in there because I heard you swear when I started knocking."

In the living room, Cleopatra gave a great sigh. Knowing her eyes looked like two cherries in a bowl of buttermilk after her long bout of crying, she'd hoped to keep Anthony from seeing her.

"Cleopatra."

He wasn't going to go away. "I . . . I'm not dressed."

"I've no objection to that."

His quip made her smile, and it sure felt good to smile again. "I'm tired."

"You can take a nap in my arms, and I won't care if you snore."

"I drool."

"In that case, you can nap on the sofa and I'll watch from across the room."

She giggled at that.

"Are you going to let me in, or do I have to stand here all night kissing the door? I'd rather kiss *you*, you know."

The soles of her feet warmed.

"I know your feet are warming," Anthony said.

She smiled again, pondering all the little things he knew about her. How desire made her feet hot. Her fondness for black jelly beans. Her penchant for piddling. Her preference for the California episodes of *I*

Love Lucy, and her fascination with minnows and the finger-through-the-flame trick.

Little things that Billy Wicket and Clyde Motts never took the time to discover, much less remember.

"Damnit, Cleopatra, open this door."

"Anthony—"

"If you don't let me in, I'll just get the superintendent to give me the key. He'll give it to me, you know, because I'll convince him that you're sick and in need of help."

"I'll tell him you're lyin'."

"And I'll tell him that you're only saying that because your illness has made you incoherent. He'll believe me because I've lived here longer than you have, and when you've known someone for a long time you trust him more than a person you've only known for a short while."

"No one can ever say you aren't persistent, Anthony," Cleopatra replied. She opened the door.

"You said you weren't dressed." He stepped inside and closed the door.

"I'm not." She looked down at her attire, an old blue and white polka-dotted house dress that she'd donned for the sheer comfort it gave her to wear it. "This is the rattiest thing I own, but I've had it for so long that I can't bear to throw it away. It's like old sheets, y'know? Buy new sheets and they're purty and fresh and all, but they aren't near as soft as old ones. Besides that, new sheets haven't ever been dreamed on like old ones, so it's not as easy to fall asleep on 'em." She wondered if he'd noticed she didn't have anything on under the ratty dress.

Studying her simple shift, he realized immediately that she didn't have a stitch on beneath it.

The thought aroused the hell out of him. "Why didn't you answer any of my calls? I called you at least eight times."

"Ten."

"You've been crying," he said, suddenly noticing her red, puffy eyes.

Avoiding his gaze, Cleopatra walked into her bed-room and entered the closet.

Anthony followed her into the bedroom. "Cleo—"

"I been slicin' onions, Anthony. What should I wear?" She stared at her hanging clothes, sighed, and shook her head. "It's almost seven. Too late to hunt minnows, and I don't feel like lookin' for celebrities. Maybe we could just stay home and do a jigsaw puzzle and make butterscotch puddin'."

"Onions don't make swollen eyes."

"Well, if I look that bad—"

"I didn't say you looked bad." Anthony walked into her closet and took her in his arms. "The truth, please. You've been crying, and I want to know why."

Her feet warmed again and her mind whirled with lies. "I miss Mama."

He didn't like seeing her so sad, and sought a way to make her smile for him. "Fly her up here. Opal, Miss Iris, and Rhonda Faye could come, too. Your mother would probably love Broadway, watching actors in real life rather than on the television set. Miss Iris could scour the streets in search of werewolves, Rhonda Faye could take her boys to Schwartz toy store, and we could treat Opal to escargot so she'd realize that so-called slugs are really a delicious fare."

Funny, he thought. Cleopatra talked about her mother and friends so often that he felt he knew them. "Well?"

"Anthony?"

He pressed his lips to her forehead, inhaling the sweet scent of her hair. "Yes?"

"I lied to you."

He grew very still. Her admission of fibbing merely illuminated her pristine honesty.

Honesty. The very thought of the word forced him to focus on the fact that he'd built his relationship with Cleopatra on a foundation of deception. He'd never dealt with guilt before meeting her. Now he fought his conscience constantly, and so far he'd won every battle.

He wondered how long he'd keep winning.

You know, Mr. Mazzini, there's a rumor circulating that

Michael Varner is being considered for the position of president of new products.

Ted's words sliced through his thoughts.

The position.

Damnit, for years he'd poured his heart and soul into his work. Had expended every drop of energy and ideas he possessed to reach presidential status with Dresden. His goal was so close now. Almost tangible, as if he could reach out his hand and hold it in his palm.

And he was going to allow a bit of remorse and this woman from Georgia to keep him from achieving the most important accomplishment of his life?

He drew away from her, determined to see his original plans through to the end, intent on ignoring any personal emotion that weakened his purpose.

"What did you lie to me about, Cleopatra?"

"Mama."

"You mean you *don't* miss her?"

"Yeah, I miss her, but—well, that's not the reason I was cryin'." She walked out of the closet and sat down in the middle of her bed. Her legs crossed Indian-style, she rested her elbows on her knees and cupped her cheeks in her palms. "I had a run-in with Sonia Brockman today at the shoot. Lost my temper when I should've ignored her. I said some purty awful things to her. 'Course, the things she said to me weren't compliments either. I can't believe I was ever so fascinated with her. Now I know she ain't worth the spit it takes to wet a postage stamp."

"She made you cry?" Anthony left her closet and moved toward the bed.

"Would y'hand me my cream, please? It's over there on the dresser, settin' on top of the vegetable shortenin' can."

Glancing at the dresser, Anthony saw an array of household containers. Besides the vegetable shortening can, there was a brown coffee creamer jar, a squeezable margarine bottle, two yellow ice trays filled with colored powders, a garlic salt bottle, and a small plastic tub that said WEAVER'S PORK BARBECUE—BEST IN ALL OF GEORGIA on the lid.

He retrieved the mustard bottle and ran his thumbs over the smooth plastic. Inside, in the form of lime green cream, was his presidential position with Dresden. When he acquired the formula to the emollient, he mused, he'd have the color changed. An iridescent hue, the color of pearls.

His sense of purpose heightened.

"Anthony?"

He returned to the bed and handed the bottle to Cleopatra. "Sonia's jealous of you, Cleopatra." He watched as she squirted a dollop of the silky cream into her hand and massaged it into the skin on her elbows, knees, and heels. "You've become a popular model in a short amount of time, and she feels threatened—"

"I've accomplished what I have on my own, haven't I?"

The soft, timid squeak he heard in her voice alerted him to her vulnerability, but he didn't know how to connect her question to her argument with Sonia. "Of course you did it on your own." Well, she might have made it on her own, he told himself. He'd helped her, yes, but if he hadn't, she still might have found success by herself.

She was, after all, an incredibly gorgeous woman.

But even so, he admitted silently, beauty was not everything in the cosmetics industry. Luck played a major part as well.

And he'd made sure she'd gotten lucky.

He picked up the mustard bottle. "This cream . . ." he began. "Ever since the day you used it on Sonia, I've been curious to know what the ingredients—"

"I haven't slept with you, Anthony."

He snapped up his head and stared at her. "What?"

"It's not like sex had anything to do with anything."

"What?"

"Sonia Brockman ain't nothin' but a snob. It'd do her good to go to a plastic surgeon and have her nose lowered, and I don't know why I'm wastin' time worryin' about what she said. It's dumb to fret over stuff that isn't even true." Cleopatra leaned back into a mound of pillows, wiggling her bare toes. "Did you say y'wanted to kiss me?"

"What?"

"Is 'what' all y'can say? Goodness sake, Anthony, you're actin' more empty-headed than Gertie Rawson back home. Y'know what Gertie did one time? Broke a mirror just so's she could be sure she'd live another seven years. Ever heard of anything so silly in all your days? Now, about that kiss . . ."

Desire almost sent Anthony to his knees when she turned to her side and patted the mattress. His gaze riveted to hers, he stretched out beside her.

They gasped in unison when her breasts flattened against his chest and their hips met, his cradling hers.

"Anthony, my feet—"

"I know, Cleopatra, I know." Her *feet* were hot, while he felt as though his entire *body* was swallowed by flames.

"We're gonna make love, aren't we?" Cleopatra murmured, her lips moving upon the chiseled crest of his cheekbone.

Her question . . . the breathy sound of her voice . . . the way she molded her body to his . . .

God, she drove him mad.

"Anthony?"

"The thought had occurred to me."

Nothing, he mused. She wore nothing beneath her dotted dress but skin. And warmth. And the barest hint of her perfume.

He dropped the mustard bottle, absently noticing that the bright yellow container rolled to the other side of the bed. "Cleopatra, I want to see the nothing you're wearing under your dress."

She didn't object when he grasped the hem of her shift. Indeed, she eased his task by sitting up and holding her arms up so he could tug the dress off.

And then she lay naked before him. His all-consuming gaze—as he stared at the length of her body—didn't make her shy. Didn't make her nervous.

Because the desire that smoldered in his dark eyes convinced her he liked what he saw.

"Anthony, get them clothes of yours off. I'm hotter'n a French-kissed fox in a forest fire."

He'd only unfastened two buttons on his shirt before she sat up to help him. In only moments, he was as bare as she, and the sense of urgency between them deepened when skin met skin, softness met hardness.

Femininity met masculinity. . . .

Seven

*H*is breathing harsh, uneven, and a husky groan rumbling in his chest, Anthony slid his hand between her thighs, his fingers immediately moistened by her sensual essence. "God, you're hot," he whispered.

"You ain't so disinterested yourself." She arched her body into his, glorying in the feel of his thick, hard staff as it slid over her belly. "Hurry. Please, hurry."

Her ardor strengthened his own, but he held his blistering need in check. Hurry? He resolved to make love to Cleopatra slowly, bringing her to fulfillment only after a long, delicious session of foreplay.

Those ends in mind, he lowered his head to her breast, suckling her pebbled nipple, drawing the bit of pouting flesh in and out of his mouth even while his fingers performed the same motions within the slick petals of her sex.

But Cleopatra would have none of the leisurely attentions he offered. She didn't need them, had no patience for them. "Anthony—"

"I'm only trying to—"

"I know, but—"

"I want to make it good for—"

"I understand that, Anthony, but I can't wait—"

"God, Cleopatra, me either." With one fluid motion, he straddled her, his knees beside her hips, his every muscle tense with anticipation as he prepared to intimately join his body with hers.

And then he noticed Cleopatra's huge, laughing

smile and the fact that her total attention was centered upon his groin.

He felt an instant urge to cover himself with his hands. "What's so funny?" he asked, his voice edged with wariness, discomfiture, and a hint of ire.

Cleopatra couldn't answer. All she could do was stare and remember words she'd forgotten until this moment: *Looks to me like Mazzini's weenie's so big that a mere picture of it would weigh five pounds.*

"Cleopatra?" He saw laughter come into her eyes, and then felt himself begin to wilt. "I asked you what was so funny!"

"Nothin'," she replied, still smiling. "I was just thinkin' about how right-on-the-mark somethin' was that somebody said to me once."

That she could concentrate on such trivial things during the heat of passion made Anthony frown. But his scowl disappeared immediately when Cleopatra gently clasped his arousal and began to move her hand up and down.

Her soft fingers and sensual activity filled his loins with flowing pleasure within seconds, and he knew that if he did not soon bury himself inside her, their love-making would be over before it had even begun. "Stop," he demanded huskily, and in the next moment he drew back his hips and entered her, driving her toward the head of the bed with the sheer force and momentum of his penetration.

Cleopatra cried out as irrepressible bliss skimmed through her. The enormous strength of Anthony's body and need engulfing her, she caught his pace quickly, circling her hips in such a way so as to rotate her tightness around his rigid length. Her hands clutching at the hard, contracting muscles of his buttocks, she pushed and pulled at him, her actions a silent plea for release from the exquisite torment.

In answer, Anthony tunneled his hands beneath her thighs and lifted her legs so that they were wrapped around his back. The position affording him even better access to her luscious depths, he plunged into her more quickly, deeply, and the helpless moans that escaped her parted lips brought him to vivid awareness that she'd almost reached the peak of ecstasy.

"Anthony."

His name seemed torn from her throat, part whisper, part groan . . . a feral sound that hurled him toward the same point of desire where she continued to hover and strain.

He felt the first shuddering spasms of her release, barely-there pulses that gradually strengthened and quickened. The deep contractions hugged him rhythmically, so sweetly that he could barely resist surrendering to his own mounting pleasure.

"Not yet," Cleopatra panted into his ear. "Stay with me, Anthony. Stay . . ."

From somewhere within the recesses of his mind came the realization that she was experiencing a second bout with pleasure. His shoulders and back beaded with perspiration and his teeth clenched tightly, he fought to subdue his furious desire and continued to foster Cleopatra's bliss, pumping into her smoothly, swiftly, and to the measured beat she'd set.

"Oh, Anthony."

When she climaxed again, his own release exploded from him, attacking every part of his body with a pleasure that he'd never experienced with any woman but Cleopatra. His arms curled around her, he embraced her with every shred of every emotion surging through him.

"Dear God," he whispered.

She made no reply. She couldn't. She clung to him. She shouted with soundless words so full of ecstasy that her eyes glistened with tears of joy.

She came completely apart in his arms.

And at that moment, while her sensual pleasure mixed and melded with his, she knew she'd fallen in love with Anthony Mazzini.

"I've just come up with another happy thought." Holding Cleopatra close after their lovemaking—her long ebony hair spilling across his shoulders and chest—Anthony caressed her cheek with his thumb and planted several tiny kisses upon her temple.

"Is it a happier one than cleanin' out your briefcase and organizin' your business cards?" She snuggled even nearer to him, cupping the hard mass of muscle beneath his nipple and lying her leg over his hips. "Tell me what it is, Anthony."

"Making love with you."

His answer thrilled her to no end, and a long while passed before she could reply. "You know," she began softly, tilting her head so she could look into his eyes, "I've never had two . . . I—well, what I mean to say is that this is the first time I've had a double dose . . . of . . ."

He knew what she was trying to tell him, and her shyness enchanted him. She'd certainly shown no inhibitions during their lovemaking. "Next time we'll go for three."

The very notion warmed Cleopatra's feet again. "Thank you, M. Anthony Mazzini. For tonight. For yesterday, for the day before that, for last week. Thank you for not throwin' me out of your room the day of the makeup show so long ago. If you had, tonight never would've happened."

His guilt returned. Damnit, he hated the way it struck at the most untimely moments!

"Anthony?" Cleopatra lifted her upper torso, using his chest for support. "What name does your initial *M* stand for?"

He smoothed her hair away from her face, forcing himself to ignore his guilt and concentrate on the way the mixture of moonlight and city lights played upon Cleopatra's pale skin. "Mark."

She gasped softly, her eyes widening. "Mark Anthony?"

"Yes."

"Well, Lord have mercy, I'm Cleopatra! Don't that just beat all?"

It *was* rather amazing, he thought. And how strange that he'd never caught the significance of their names.

"I'm named after Elizabeth Taylor's role in the

movie, *Cleopatra,*" Cleopatra continued merrily. "Thirty-some years ago, Mama saw that movie in the theater, and I mean to tell you, her apron was a-ridin' high. She was pregnant as pregnant could be with me, and went into labor right there in the theater. That's where I was born—in the movie house, on account of Mama waited a tad too long to go to the hospital. 'Course, fascinated with the movie as she was, it stands to reason that she didn't even feel her labor pains. But she *did* feel the fancy to name me after some ancient Egyptian queen who committed suicide with a snake. What about you? How'd you get your name?"

The happy sound of her chatter relaxing him, Anthony smiled a lazy smile. "Every first born male in my family has had the same name."

"I once knew a girl named Delilah," Cleopatra went on, and then took a second to press a tender kiss to Anthony's chin. "Now, she didn't marry a man named Samson, but she came pretty close. Her husband's name was Sam, and y'know what? He had long hair just like the real Samson, and he was a body builder so his muscles were real big. He cut off his hair one day. Didn't lose his strength, but his ears sure did stick out. Delilah told him that if he didn't grow his hair back she'd leave him. He let her leave on account of he couldn't cotton to livin' with a wife who didn't want him just because his ears stuck out. I haven't thought about those two in years."

"I've recently thought of two people I haven't seen or heard from in years, either," Anthony said. "Mrs. Birdsong and Micah. Mrs. Birdsong used to make apple pies for me, and Micah was my best friend. He and I used to take Taekwondo classes together. That's the martial art from Korea. I remember Micah and I made a vow that when we grew up we were going to be just like our instructor. Master Pinaroc was his name, and we were sure there was no one in the world who could ever beat him in a fight. The man was amazing."

Cleopatra realized that Anthony was sharing a part of his life that not even *he* thought of very often. The fact that he was reliving little-boy memories with her caused her heart to swell with happiness. "Mama likes martial arts, too. She watches *Power Rangers* every afternoon, and she's seen every Chuck Norris movie ever made. I never took Taekwondo classes. I took ballet lessons once, but I wasn't very good. Fell right off the stage durin' my first recital and wouldn't ever do ballet again. Are you hungry?"

"You fell off the stage?"

"Right smack on the record player. It broke, the recital was called off, and my ballet teacher, Mrs. Muckleson, set to wailin' so loud that she busted a tendon in her throat and had to wear a neck brace for almost two months. Are you hungry?"

"Some."

Cleopatra got out of bed and left the room. Shortly, she returned with a tray. "I emptied the fridge and pantry. Tonight's hodgepodge food night. Hope that tickles your fancy."

Anthony stared at the meal: a small plate of smoked cocktail sausages, a bag of cheese puffs, several chocolate cupcakes, a half-empty carton of blueberry yogurt, a little bowl of carrot sticks swimming in ranch dressing, a jar of black jelly beans, and a big glass of tomato juice with a lemon wedge floating in it.

"Your fancy ain't tickled," Cleopatra said.

"No." He lifted his gaze to hers. "Can't we have a can of sardines with soda crackers and ketchup, too? And maybe some caramel popcorn, dill pickles, and banana popsicles?"

She couldn't believe he was serious. But he was. She could tell by the expression in his eyes. Only recently had she begun to notice this playful, roguish side to him, and it made her love him all the more. "I'm fresh out of sardines, caramel popcorn, and dill pickles. I have some popsicles, but they're cherry."

"I like banana." He stuck his bottom lip out.

His feigned childishness compelled her to hug him. When he hugged her back—a strong, real embrace that sent joy skimming through her—she wondered if her unlucky streak with love had finally come to an end.

Maybe, she thought, just maybe she'd finally found a

man who wanted her for all the right reasons. Anthony
didn't need her for anything, after all. Didn't want her
for his own selfish gains, but desired to be with her
because . . .

Just because.

She hugged him one last time, then pulled back and
gently pinched his cheek. "Let's eat."

Smiling and naked, they proceeded to devour the
odd supper, feeding each other and then fighting over
who would get the last bite of blueberry yogurt.

Anthony finally spooned it into Cleopatra's mouth,
but only because he'd gotten more of the sausages than
she had.

"This is the nicest time I've had with you so far,
Mark Anthony Mazzini," Cleopatra announced, stifling
a yawn. She moved the empty tray to the bedside table,
then curled up next to Anthony and thought of all the
things they'd chatted about during the course of the
evening. "Wonder what ever happened to old Delilah,
Sam, Mrs. Birdsong, Micah, and Master Pinaroc?"

She yawned again and closed her eyes. The sound of
Anthony's heart stroked her ear. She listened to the
soft beat, thoughts of him lulling her into tranquillity,
thoughts of him making her smile inside.

Thoughts of Anthony . . . "I love you, Anthony."

Her whispered declaration hit his ears like a sudden
crash of thunder, but he had no time to reply. In only
moments, her deep, steady breathing told Anthony that
she'd fallen asleep.

He lay still for a very long while, deliberating upon
her admission of love. Part of him wanted to wake her
and tell her that he didn't deserve her affection.

But another part of him wanted to hold her love in
his hand, stare at it, and caress it, much the way one
would handle an exceedingly rare and precious jewel.

She wasn't the first woman who had told him she
loved him.

But he knew deep in his soul that she was the only
woman who really meant it.

An unfamiliar warmth, a feeling of tenderness he'd
never experienced before tonight filling his mind and

heart, he moved to draw the covers over Cleopatra and himself. As he pulled at the sheets, he spied the yellow mustard bottle on the other side of the bed.

He stared at it for so long and with such intensity that his vision blurred.

The beauty cream.

Cleopatra.

I love you, Anthony.

He threw the mustard bottle across the room and gathered Cleopatra more securely into his arms.

And he thought about how right it felt to have her there.

Eight

$\mathscr{S}$itting at his desk in his office, Anthony hung up the telephone receiver, leaned back in his chair, and smiled just as Ted entered the office.

"I see you're in a better mood today, Mr. Mazzini."

Still smiling, Anthony nodded. "Micah really did it, Ted."

"Micah, sir?"

"He turned out just like Master Pinaroc. I didn't, but he did. I just got off the phone with him. He's a fourth-degree black belt now and works as head instructor at one of Master Pinaroc's six Taekwondo academies. I spoke to Master Pinaroc, too, and he remembered me. Reminded me of the time he made me do one hundred push-ups for questioning his teaching methods. I'd forgotten that. But as I recall now, I couldn't move my arms or shoulders for days after those hundred push-ups.

"And Mrs. Birdsong," he continued, his grin widening, "still makes apple pies. I asked her if she used honest-to-goodness, high-fat, heart attack–giving lard in the pie crust. She laughed and said yes. That's why her pies were so good, you know."

"Lard? Uh . . . yes."

"Micah, Mrs. Birdsong, and Master Pinaroc. They're all well and happy."

Ted shuffled his feet on the thick, midnight blue carpet, bewildered by Anthony's strange conversation. "I'm glad to hear it, sir. Now, about these reports—"

"Wasn't there anyone in your life you've now lost track of? Someone you ought to get back in touch with?"

"What? I—"

"Take the day off, Ted. I'm doing the same."

"The day off?" Ted frowned. "But it's not even ten o'clock. You have a meeting with—"

"I'm not certain we'll find any minnows, but then, we really won't have time to look for any," Anthony rambled on. "Celebrities, however, are an entirely different matter. Dresden has supplied cosmetics for several of Tom Hanks's movies, you know that, don't you, Ted?"

"Well, yes—"

"Tom Hanks is here in the city." Continuing to grin, Anthony pulled at his shirt cuffs. "I found a few strings to pull, yanked the hell out of them, and managed to arrange lunch with Mr. Hanks today at one o'clock. I don't imagine minnow innards could compare, do you?"

Ted made no reply. He simply stared at Anthony, wondering if the man had been drinking.

"Have a nice day, Ted."

Whistling the melody of "Flies in the Buttermilk, Shoo Fly Shoo," Anthony left the office and stopped to speak to one of his secretaries. "Call Miss Murphy and tell her I'm picking her up in an hour. And tell her to wear something nice."

"Right away, sir." The woman picked up the phone.

"On second thought, tell her I'll be there in two hours." He'd go find Cleopatra a bouquet of ginger lilies first, he decided. "What are ginger lilies?"

The woman shrugged her shoulders. "I've never heard of them, but I'm sure any good florist would be able to help you."

"Right." Anthony turned and headed for the elevator.

Cleopatra was in for the biggest surprise of her life, he thought as the elevator doors opened and he stepped inside. Soon, all of Snyder's Dock, Georgia, would know that she'd had lunch with the famous Tom

Hanks. Annette would probably shout the news from the rooftops.

Completely unable to stop smiling, Anthony pushed the elevator button for the lobby of Dresden's office building and recalled his morning with Cleopatra. She'd awakened him at five thirty with coffee and a kiss. He'd let the coffee get cold, but God, had their lovemaking been hot.

Lovemaking in the morning, lunch with Tom Hanks in the afternoon, and more lovemaking at night.

Anthony hoped that this day would be the best day Cleopatra had ever had.

The sound of the doorbell made Cleopatra glance at the clock on her dresser. It was only ten thirty, and she hadn't expected Anthony until noon. At least, that was the time his secretary had said he'd arrive.

He was early, and she was glad. Dressed in her blue and white polka-dotted shift and with her wet hair wrapped up in a towel, she left her bedroom and went to answer the door. "Anthony—"

"I'm afraid not," Sonia said, standing in the hall but for a moment before brushing past Cleopatra and entering the apartment.

Cleopatra glanced at Sonia's outfit. Dressed in a beautifully shaped cutaway jacket and slim-fitting skirt made of honey-colored linen, Sonia Brockman looked every inch the famous and successful model she was.

Painfully aware of her own shabby attire, Cleopatra closed the door and unwrapped the towel from her head. "What do you want, Sonia?" she asked, running her fingers through her long, damp hair.

Before answering, Sonia took a moment to scrutinize the apartment. The words gaudy and vulgar came to mind.

The place certainly reflected its owner's character. "I've come as a friend, Cleopatra," she announced, reaching up to move a shimmering blond curl off her shoulder. "You haven't been in the business long, but one thing you should know is that Dresden's models look after each other. Stick together, if you will. And that's why I'm here. To tell you about a bit of hearsay that I happen to know is the truth."

"Well, ain't you just the top man on the quote-'em pole. Look, Sonia, I don't have time to stand here listenin' to you sling slander ever' which way. I—"

"It's about you—and Anthony. Dresden's grapevine is extraordinary. Everyone knows." Sonia almost laughed when she saw the expression on Cleopatra's face, an absolutely hilarious blend of uncontrollable curiosity, growing alarm, and not a little dread.

Now that she had Cleopatra's undivided attention, Sonia turned and sauntered into the living room, where she saw a man's tie draped over the back of a hideous pink loveseat.

She smiled, and almost laughed, but didn't. Didn't because the time for laughter would be when Cleopatra's feet once again were planted in that stupid okra patch in Georgia.

Whirling on the heel of her shoe, she faced Cleopatra again. "Anthony's using you."

The statement hit Cleopatra like a brutal punch in the belly. She didn't believe what she was hearing. Couldn't.

Wouldn't.

But the look in Sonia's gleaming eyes made her wonder.

"He's been wining and dining you for the past months because he wants something from you, Cleopatra. I knew it from the start, you know. Anthony Mazzini . . . rich, handsome, and powerful man that he is . . . why would he want *you?* It didn't make sense. From the very beginning, it just didn't make sense."

Sonia picked up the tie she knew belonged to Anthony, and slowly pulled the silky strip between her fingers. "Anthony is refined. He's accustomed to elegance. I mean no disrespect when I say this, but what have you to give him? What do you know about culture? About upper class lifestyle? Do you even know what to order when dining at a posh restaurant? When reading the menu, do you look for cornbread, catfish, and collard greens?"

Twisting her towel in her hands, Cleopatra remembered when she'd asked Anthony if they served fried cornbread at the restaurant where they'd been dining.

He hadn't answered.

Had he been disgusted?

"He wants something from you, Cleopatra," Sonia continued, "and he wants it badly."

Cleopatra clutched her towel so hard that her hand began to shake.

"He's one of the vice-presidents in charge of new products at Dresden," Sonia purred, thoroughly enjoying the panic creasing Cleopatra's flawless complexion. "As such, his job is to find and investigate fresh ideas for the company. Such finds mean promotions, prestige . . . even more success in his career. He's stumbled upon such a find, and do you know what it is?"

When Cleopatra didn't answer, Sonia had to suppress laughter again. "Why, it's the secret to your homemade beauty cream, my dear. You saw his reaction to the cream that day you applied it to my face, didn't you? Surely he's mentioned the cream again since then."

Coldness came over Cleopatra then, a chill that caused her skin to ripple into goose flesh.

Do you do this Sunday piddling before or after you've made your weekly batch of beauty cream?

She remembered. Remembered Anthony asking her that question once.

She remembered. . . .

How long does it take to make the cream? What makes it green? It sounds as though you have many of your grandmother's recipes. Do you make them as often as you make the cream?

This cream . . . ever since the first day you used it on Sonia, I've been curious to know what the ingredients—

"Ingredients—" Cleopatra repeated. Lifting her hand to her neck, she clutched her throat, then felt her knees begin to shake. "Ingredients."

"As much as I hate being the bearer of such ill tidings, I thought it best that you know the truth, Cleopatra."

Somehow, with a will she never realized she possessed, Cleopatra pushed back her shoulders. When she spoke, it was with a calm, self-assured voice that surprised even her. "I think it best that you know the truth, too, Sonia. I already gave Anthony the beauty cream recipe. I gave it to him last night."

She turned and opened the door. "Now, if y'don't mind, I'm busy gettin' ready for my day with him. He'll be here to pick me up right around noon."

Sonia didn't move. She simply gawked. "Noon?"

"Noon."

"You gave him the recipe?"

"Last night. Now please leave."

Her smug mood shifting to fury, Sonia marched out of the apartment.

Softly, Cleopatra shut the door. Her eyes closed, she pressed her forehead against the wall.

Anthony. Her Anthony.

It had happened again. A third time. He wasn't any different than Billy Wicket or Clyde Motts. They'd used her, wanted her for their own selfish reasons.

And so had Anthony.

Her pain was too deep for tears.

Her actions becoming mechanical—as if someone had put a key in her back and wound her up—she returned to her bedroom, dressed, and packed. That accomplished in short order, she then picked up the phone and made a flight reservation for the next plane to Atlanta.

As she hung up the phone, the gleam of her gold ID bracelet caught her eye. Her fingers trembling, she removed the jewelry and carried it to a small writing table in the living room. There, she sat down, scribbled a note, and placed both the bracelet and the letter in an envelope.

She left the envelope on the floor right in front of the door.

Ten minutes later she sat in a cab that headed for the airport, her luggage in the seat beside her. There was nothing inside her bags but the belongings she'd brought from Georgia.

She wanted no reminders of her time in New York City.

She didn't need any.

The hurt in her heart was reminder enough.

"Open it," Anthony demanded of the building superintendent. "Something's wrong."

"Mr. Mazzini—"

"Look, I know her! I was to pick her up at noon, and she's not here. She didn't call or leave me any sort of message. It's just not like her!"

The undeniable alarm in Mr. Mazzini's voice and eyes convinced the man that something was, indeed, wrong in Miss Murphy's apartment. Without another word of argument, he slipped a key into her door and opened it.

Anthony rushed inside. "Cleopatra?"

She didn't answer.

Deep foreboding rising within him, he raced into her bedroom. Many clothes still hung in her closet and he felt a small measure of relief.

Until he noticed that all her makeup containers were gone. The brown coffee creamer jar. The plastic tub that said WEAVER'S PORK BARBECUE—BEST IN ALL OF GEORGIA on the lid, the squeezable margarine bottle, the vegetable shortening can, large bottle of garlic salt, the yellow ice trays filled with colored powders.

And the mustard bottle.

Anthony knew then that Cleopatra was gone.

"Mr. Mazzini?" The superintendent walked into the bedroom. "I found this on the floor in front of the door."

Anthony took the envelope.

"Mr. Mazzini, if Miss Murphy's really gone, the manager will have to be advised, you know. She has a lease, and if she's broken it—"

"I'll take care of it—of everything."

Satisfied, the superintendent left the apartment.

Only when Anthony heard the door close would he

allow himself to look at the envelope. On the front, Cleopatra had written, ALL'S Y'HAD TO DO WAS ASK.

Bewildered by what she'd meant by the words, Anthony opened the envelope. The bracelet he'd given to her fell out, landing on his shoe then slipping to the floor. He picked it up and sat down on the bed.

On *her* bed, where he'd made love to her only hours earlier.

He dropped the bracelet into a pocket in his coat. It lay heavily in the pocket.

But not as heavily as his heart lay in his chest.

There was a note in the envelope. A good-bye letter, he was certain. He didn't want to read it because he didn't want to believe she was really and truly gone.

Why had she left?

He pulled the paper out of the envelope, already knowing that he would read her parting words.

But words of farewell were not what he saw when he glanced down at the paper in his hands. Other words met his gaze:

GRAMMY'S BEAUTY CREAM RECIPE

A list of ingredients and a block of directions followed, but Anthony could concentrate on nothing but the words on the front of the envelope.

All's y'had to do was ask.

She knew. Somehow she'd discovered that everything he'd done for and with her had been in an effort to acquire the secret to her cream. How she'd found out didn't matter.

Nothing mattered but that she was gone. She'd left thinking the worst about him.

And the worst was true.

Well, damnit, so what? "So what?" he yelled, his voice reverberating throughout the bedroom.

He didn't need her. She kept him from work. She wasted his precious time by causing him to do things like fight over blueberry yogurt, call people he hadn't seen in years, and scour New York City in search of a stupid bunch of ginger lilies.

He had what he wanted now. Right in his hand was

the secret formula that would make him executive president in charge of new products.

Please, Mr. Mazzini. I've just got to show you my skills before you have me pitched out into the bitter, cold, icy streets of New York again.

Memories of her slid through his mind like water through a sieve.

Just look at this skirt, Anthony! If this dang thing was any shorter, it'd be collar!

I'm hotter'n a French-kissed fox in a forest fire.

I love you, Anthony.

Anthony's tears smeared the ink on the note in his hands, running all the letters together and making the recipe impossible to read. He didn't care.

Because he didn't want the damned formula anymore.

He wanted Cleopatra.

Nine

A bottle of permanent solution in her hands, Cleopatra glanced at the clock that hung above the door of her salon. Two thirty. Usually by two thirty, at least three or four women, sometimes five, were in the beauty parlor waiting for their turn in the chair.

Now there was only Opal. Even Rhonda Faye was gone. She and almost every other citizen of Snyder's Dock were taking employment training classes in the armory, which was the only place in town large enough to hold so many people. The instructional program had begun several weeks ago and still had four weeks left to go.

"Good Lord, Cleopatra!" Opal exclaimed, closing her eyes as a cold, foul-smelling dribble of permanent solution trickled off her forehead. "You're pourin' that stinkin' mess all over my face!"

Cleopatra set the bottle of powerful hair curling chemicals on the counter behind the chair. "Sorry, Opal. I wasn't payin' attention."

"You ain't been right since y'got home from New York four months ago." Opal wiped her face with the bright pink cloth drape clasped around her shoulders. "Been goin' about business like a damn robot. Last month y'put red lipstick on my eyebrows, and just the other day, y'sprayed my hair with bug spray instead o' hairspray. Call the man, for God's sake, and—"

"No." Cleopatra turned toward the counter and pretended to be busy, straightening various bottles, swiping at invisible dust, and then turning the sink faucet on and off. "And I've told you time and time again, Opal, that I don't want to—"

"Talk about him. All right, all right. But if y'ask me, talkin' about Anthony Mazzini is exactly what you need to do. It's been four months!"

"He hasn't called me either." Hearing the tremble in her voice, Cleopatra cleared her throat and took a deep breath. "Which means he didn't care one iota that I left. Why should he have cared? He only wanted the recipe for the beauty—"

"Yeah? Well, I ain't seen no new beauty cream out by Dresden. All's I've seen so far is your picture there on the fronts of *Glamour* and *Mademoiselle.*" She pointed to the two magazines lying upon a nearby table. "If Anthony was so all fired up to market that cream o' yours, then why—"

"Things like that take time."

"He—"

"Opal, please."

"Oh, all right." Opal huffed, settled back into the chair, and tried to think of a different subject to discuss. Lord knew Cleopatra sure couldn't think of anything to talk about anymore. The woman's heart had been heavier than a bucket of hog livers since her return from New York, and she showed no sign of coming out of her depression any time soon.

Men, Opal thought. There were millions of them in the world, but it was just Cleopatra's luck to have gotten involved with three rotten ones. "I miss Rhonda Faye hangin' around here," she finally said. "I even miss them boys o' hers. It just ain't the same here in Snyder's Dock anymore, what with everyone takin' them trainin' classes for that big factory."

Fiddling with one of the plastic rollers on Opal's head, Cleopatra pondered the huge factory being built right outside town. The news that a brand new cosmetics company had decided to manufacture makeup and other beauty supplies only a few miles away from Snyder's Dock had created a blast of excitement that hadn't yet let up. Word had it that the factory would be up and running in only a few more months, and the majority of Snyder's Dock's population had been hired to work there. For weeks, the residents had been learning the skills their new occupations would require them to have, everyone thrilled to no end to have the good paying jobs that had once been non-existent in Snyder's Dock.

The town would never be an obscure, sleepy little community again.

"'Course, Miss Iris won't take none o' them trainin' classes," Opal added. "Says that factory ain't bein' built by no cosmetics maker. Swears it's the new werewolf den of the world, and she won't even go near that side o' town no more. I thought Annette said that your apartment manager in New York sent your pink loveseat back to you. When are you gonna put it back in here? That space over there's awfully empty lookin' without it."

Cleopatra glanced at the spot where the loveseat had once stood, but could only "see" how the little sofa had looked in her New York apartment.

Memories stung her heart. The first time Anthony had ever kissed her had been on that loveseat. The night they'd had scrambled eggs and sherbet for dinner.

Her eyes filled with tears she refused to shed. Viciously, she wiped them away with a corner of Opal's drape.

But one escaped and rolled down her cheek.

"Don't cry no more, honey," Opal cooed, rubbing Cleopatra's arm. "Ain't no man in the world worth four month's o' constant sobbin'. Things'll get better. You'll see. Just wait till that factory opens up. Lot's o' folks'll be movin' here to get 'em a job, y'know, and half of 'em'll be men. One of 'em just might be the one—"

"Cleopatra!" Annette called from inside the house. "Cleopatra!"

Once again, Cleopatra looked at the clock. "Lord have mercy, somethin' must be wrong. Mama's soaps are on, and she never makes a peep before they're over."

Holding up her gloved hands the way a surgeon does

before beginning an operation, she crossed to the door that opened into the house and twisted the doorknob by clasping and turning it with her elbows.

Inside the kitchen, she met Annette, whose makeup-smeared eyes shone with something that Cleopatra thought could have been either excitement or fear. "Mama, what in the world—"

"There's a man here!" Annette whispered, and pointed toward the living room.

"A man got in here? Did y'leave the front door open again? Dear God, does he have a gun? Did he hurt you, Mama? We've got to call the police, for heaven's sake!"

"Wait!" Annette stopped Cleopatra from reaching for the harvest gold phone that hung on the wall by the refrigerator. "He ain't no criminal, darlin'. He's with that new cosmetics company that's buildin' the factory, and he wants to know if you'd be interested in workin' for him. Must've heard about you bein' a top New York model. Pro'bly wants the glory your name and face'll give to the company, seein' as how you're plastered all over *Glamour* and *Mamselle.*"

"*Mademoiselle.*"

"French. I only speak English. Oh, Cleopatra, he's such a nice-lookin' man. Must be rich, too. Drove up to the house in a car that's nearly a mile long. Has his own driver, too, who got out and opened the door for him. Could be Mr. Right, just the man to make y'forget that Mazzini monster y'met in New York. Go on in there and talk to—"

"No."

"But—"

"Mama, I don't want anything else to do with any makeup companies." Quickly, Cleopatra turned her back to her mother, faced the window, and stared at the satellite dish in the back yard. Memories of Anthony assaulted her like a handful of sharp stones. "Now, if y'don't mind, I left poor Opal in the chair with permanent solution all over her head, and I—"

"You go talk to that man right now in this day and time, young lady," Annette demanded in her best voice of authority. "I've already told him you'd join him and bring him a swig of iced tea. Carry him in some o' that tomato soup cake I made yesterday, too."

"Mama—"

"Well, at least go tell him y'don't want to work for his company. It's the polite thing to do, ain't it? I didn't raise you to be rude, darlin'."

Cleopatra realized her mother wasn't going to give in. She sighed with irritation, then left the kitchen and walked into the living room.

What she saw there nearly shocked her senseless.

There, on Annette's avocado green sofa, holding a pillow with Elvis Presley's face embroidered on it, sat Anthony.

She held her breath while staring at him. He was a bit leaner than she remembered, but every bit as handsome.

Every bit as devastatingly sexy.

"Anthony." She spoke his name without making a sound, elation filling every part of her.

And then, in the next moment, grief killed all her happiness. This man had used her for his own gain, she reminded herself. Had led her along as if she were naught but a helpless little puppy.

She was just before giving him a piece of her mind when she heard the shuffle of footsteps behind her and realized her mother had entered the room. "Go on back into the kitchen, Mama, and take Opal with you."

Sensing that Cleopatra would stand for no arguing, Annette and Opal returned to the kitchen, both of them staring at Anthony.

"Cleopatra," he said.

His voice made the emptiness inside her even emptier. But she wouldn't cry in front of him. Instead, she looked him directly in the eye and gave him what she hoped was a good, hard glare. "What's the matter, Anthony? The beauty cream recipe wasn't enough, and now you've come to see if I have anymore cosmetics secrets you can trick out of me for Dresden? I guess y'got that promotion you wanted, huh? You're president in charge of new products now."

"No." Anthony tossed the Elvis pillow aside and rose

from the sofa. "I resigned from Dresden four months ago."

Cleopatra frowned. "Resigned?"

He walked toward her.

She backed away.

He continued toward her.

Her back met the wall.

"Cleopatra—"

"Stop," she demanded when he reached for her shoulders. Tears clouded her vision despite her efforts to stem them. "You shouldn't have come here, Anthony. Please go now."

"Not until you hear what I have to say." He dropped his arms back to his sides, wanting nothing more in the world to hold her, but knowing that he couldn't touch her in the slightest way until he explained himself. "I'm here in Snyder's Dock because I'm the one who's building the factory outside of town. The new cosmetics company belongs to me."

His news astonished her, but she feigned a nonchalant demeanor. "Oh? Well, you ought to make a zillion dollars manufacturin' and sellin' my cream."

The hurt in her beautiful eyes cut into him like a knife. "I don't have the recipe for your cream, Cleopatra. I never even looked at the list of ingredients—"

"Liar." She fairly spat the word.

He didn't blame her for not believing him, but he wasn't going to give up until she accepted the truth. "I swear I don't have it."

She searched his eyes for evidence that he wasn't lying.

"Cleopatra, I swear on minnows and banana popsicles. On finger-through-the-flame tricks, lemonade stands, and ginger lilies. I never even read the recipe."

There it was, she saw. The light of truth. It shone from his eyes like diamonds on black velvet. "Anthony—"

"After you left, I realized it wasn't the cream I wanted." Slowly, he reached for her shoulders again, relieved when she allowed him to touch her.

God, it felt so good to hold her again. "It was you I

wanted, Cleopatra. It still is. I don't give a damn about the cream. I don't give a damn about anything but you."

When he drew her close to him, next to his chest, Cleopatra didn't resist. She couldn't. Her mind swam with incredulity, even as her heart swelled with joy, and she could do nothing but let him have his way.

"After you left," Anthony whispered, his lips moving upon her earlobe, "I left my job and, using every shred of experience I acquired at Dresden and almost every penny I had to my name, I planned and started my own company."

"Your own company," Cleopatra repeated on a sigh.

"And I built it here in Snyder's Dock on purpose. Because of something you once told me. It was the only way I could think of to prove how much you mean to me."

At that, Cleopatra moved slightly away from him so she could see his face. "Somethin' I said?"

She thought. And thought.

And thought some more, but couldn't remember having said anything to him that would have prompted him to build his factory near Snyder's Dock.

"Once," he said, "when we were at a restaurant, you told me that Snyder's Dock was a small town with no opportunities. You said the people here struggled, and you added that if some big businesses would move here, the citizens would have a better livelihood."

He bent to kiss her cheek. "When you left New York, I remembered everything you ever said to me. And when I recalled your worry over all your friends here, I knew what I'd do to try to win you back. It was the only thing I could think of that you said you wanted—for your town and its people to prosper. To the best of my ability, I've tried to make that wish come true for you, Cleopatra."

She stared into his eyes so deeply that she felt she could see his very thoughts. To think that he'd resigned from his job at Dresden . . . had spent months and all the money he had in an effort to win her back. . . .

"I love you, Cleopatra."

Tears ran freely down her cheeks, but this time she didn't try to stop them, for they were tears born of the deepest joy she'd ever known in her life. "Anthony," she squeaked.

His arms around her waist, he picked her up off the floor and swung her around and around and around. It wasn't until he set her back down again when he realized she'd smeared something that smelled God-awful terrible all over his suit.

"Oh, Anthony," she whispered. "I was givin' Opal a permanent, and I forgot that this smelly stuff was all over my gloves."

He looked at his shoulders, seeing two glossy handprints. The sight striking his sense of humor, he began to laugh. "The day I met you, you smeared chocolate all over my coat. And now, today, the day I've got you back again, you smear—"

"I'll buy you another coat."

He grinned at her. "I don't want another coat. I only want you. Marry me."

"Yes."

He kissed her, softly at first, but then with a passion that soon had them both trembling.

"My feet," Cleopatra murmured.

He laughed again, realizing then that he would laugh every day of his life with her. "I can't describe how much I missed you. The day you left, my whole world ended."

"But you've got another now. Your own company, Anthony! Just imagine!"

He smoothed his finger down the graceful slope of her neck. "I named the company after you."

"Cleopatra?" she asked.

"You'll be right up there with Mary Kay, Elizabeth Arden, and Estee Lauder. On every cosmetics package that leaves my factory, there will be a picture of your beautiful face. I want the whole country, the whole damn world to know I'm in love with you."

Overwhelmed by all that he'd done for her, Cleopatra hugged him again, smearing even more permanent solution on his coat.

"And as for Murphy's Make-over Miracles," Anthony said, "you—"

"I have to give it up? Anthony, I can't—"

With a finger on her lips, he hushed her. "I wasn't going to ask you to give it up. I know how much the salon means to you. But my corporate offices are in New York, and I—"

"You have to be there. Well, I'll be there with you, Anthony. Then, when you're here, seein' to the factory, I'll run my salon. Half the time in New York, and the other half here. How does that tickle your fancy?"

He pulled her close again, so close that his heartbeat melded with hers. "From the moment I first saw you . . . now . . . tomorrow . . . *you* tickle my fancy, Cleopatra, and you always will."

Myth and Magic:
Helen of Troy,
New York

Paula Detmer Riggs

SEATTLE, WASHINGTON. (AP)—In a recent ribbon-cutting ceremony, Helen Delorio, 33, originally from Troy, New York, and now head of the wildly successful Fantasy Vacations division of Seattle-based Greek Isles Cruise Lines, officially opened the latest fantasy island retreat, this one designed to represent the ancient island of Troy where her namesake once was held captive by her devoted suitor, Paris. Assisting Ms. Delorio at the ceremony was Greek Isles chairman, Constantine Paristeri. Also in attendance was eleven-year-old Nicholas Paristeri, Delorio's son by a previous marriage, and Constantine Paristeri's nephew. Troy will be available for rental beginning July 1.

At the end of the ceremony, Mr. Paristeri surprised the guests with an announcement of his impending marriage to Ms. Delorio. The big day is scheduled for June 14 of this year and is to be held at Paristeri's waterfront home on Bainbridge Island.

One

A storm was coming, a big one from the looks of the black thunderheads piling up over Puget Sound. In a matter of minutes, the twilight sky Helen Delorio had been admiring through the wraparound windows of her fifth floor corner office had turned dark and dangerous.

"I hate storms," she said with a sigh to her friend and colleague, Celia Franks. "They make me feel . . . well, helpless." And she hated them because eight years ago nearly to the day her ex-husband had walked away from her in a violent storm very much like this one.

It had taken her a long time to stop missing the father of her only child. Alexandros Paristeri lived in Greece now, in the tiny fishing village his parents had left five decades earlier, and, in four days, she was going to marry his older brother, Constantine. It had been Con's idea to hold the ceremony on the anniversary of the very date her divorce from Alex had become final. A final end to a lingering nightmare, he'd said with his version of the legendary Paristeri grin, the same one her son, Nicky, invariably used on her when he was trying to wheedle her into changing her mind about something or other.

"You hate storms because they excite you too much," Celia declared as she came to stand next to her. "Heaven forbid you should actually give in to that wild side you worked so hard to squelch."

"Uh oh, you've been editing your husband's book again, haven't you?"

"Nope. I don't need Grant's knowledge of human behavior to know how different you've become from the scared baker's daughter I met in the lobby of this same building umpteen years ago."

"Thirteen," Helen corrected automatically, then scowled at Celia's knowing look. "So I'm compulsive about a few minor things."

"Like your entire life?" One year Helen's senior, the thirty-four-year-old Celia was as dark as Helen was fair, and, at a generous five feet ten, a good head taller. A native of Southern California, she had a ready grin, a year-round tan, and a yen for adventure Helen envied. They'd met when they'd each answered an ad for part-time work in the Greek Isles marketing department. Helen had gotten the job and, in the process of a long wait for the interview in the lobby of this very building, a roommate.

A theater major, Celia had a passion for creating illusion and a flair for set design. Seven years ago, when Helen had gotten the go-ahead to test market Fantasy Vacations, Celia had been the first one she'd recruited for her team.

Replicating ancient Troy on a company-owned island in the San Juan chain to the north of Seattle had been the latest product of their collaboration.

In a little over a month, after almost three months of offering travel agents the opportunity to preview the destination resort for their clients, Troy would be available for rental to the general public.

Helen had asked Celia to a pre-launch meeting with marketing in order to fill them in on the special, last-minute features she'd incorporated into the final package—like the terra-cotta bathtub patterned after one found near the Acropolis, and a fresco on the wall near the swimming pool that was an exact reproduction of one discovered on Crete.

The meeting had ended at half past six, almost an hour ago. She and Celia had remained in the office, going over specs for the next vacation site already in the planning stages. And then they'd shared a glass of wine, decompressing after long months of hard work, the way they'd done in college after a long study session.

" 'A trip back in time,' " Celia quoted softly from the TV ad that would begin in two days.

"Believe me, we didn't have *anything* like this in New York when I was growing up," Instead, she'd lived above her father's bakery in a working class neighborhood. By the age of five when she'd entered kindergarten, she'd become accustomed to strangers laughing at her name. *Helen of Troy, New York? You've got to be kidding.*

"Good thing you grew up tough, kiddo."

Helen shot her friend a long-suffering look. "I wish."

"Hey, didn't you read the article on the ribbon cutting? That reporter, I can't remember her name, but you remember her, the one who showed up wearing Army boots and tweed? Anyway, she was so impressed she called you Seattle's premier lady executive."

"I told her Troy was a team effort, and it was."

"Yeah, but an article about teamwork is boring."

"Boring or not, it's true."

Helen finished her wine, and with one last apprehensive look at the menacing clouds, carried her empty glass to her desk and sat down.

After pausing by the three-dimensional model of Troy to straighten one of the miniature fir trees near the Greco-Roman villa, Celia, too, returned to her chair.

"Hot damn, Celia, we really pulled it off," Helen said with a tired grin. The wine had made her mellow and slightly less inhibited.

"You had doubts?" Celia settled back and crossed her legs.

"Only every step of the way."

Celia chuckled. "Not me. Not with Wonder Woman in charge." Helen took a swat at her, and Celia ducked.

"I still say we should have waited for the horse to be finished before we accepted reservations from the public."

"It wasn't made available to the public. Mary Ruth at Northwest Travel specifically requested the early date for an important client, and since we get a hefty share of our business from Northwest, I couldn't see turning them down. Besides, except for the staff we intend to have available next month, Troy is ready for occupancy, and Mary Ruth made it very clear to her client that he would have to supply all the amenities."

Celia finished her wine and set her glass near Helen's on the gilded desk. "Shoot, I was all set to volunteer as the first 'Helen' to be kidnapped, with my dear husband as 'Paris,' of course. Or you and Constantine could have hidden away there for your honeymoon."

Helen has a quick image of her austere fiancé slinging her over his shoulder in a sham kidnapping and nearly burst out laughing. Constantine treasured his dignity far too much to resort to such primitive methods of wooing a woman. No, he'd planned his campaign as precisely as the launching of another Greek Isles liner, but of course, without the public hoopla.

It had taken a year of dinner dates and Sunday brunches before his brotherly kisses had edged toward passionate, and even then, he'd been a gentleman, never pushing her too fast or too far. Maybe his kisses didn't make her heart go wild, but they aroused a nice warm feeling of security, and his courtly attention was dependable and, well, solid, like the Greek Isles liners themselves. After four years of saying no, she'd finally agreed to marry him.

"I still can't believe I scheduled my wedding to coincide with our busiest season," she said, flipping through her desk calendar. Tomorrow she had a final fitting on her wedding gown in the morning, a meeting of her Fantasy staff in the afternoon, and then at six she was scheduled to pick Nicky up at SeaTac. It had taken her some heavy-duty juggling, but she'd cleared her Friday calendar of everything except the wedding rehearsal at four and the dinner afterward. Whatever Nicky wanted to do during the day they would do. She'd missed him terribly in the six weeks since he'd gone away to military school, and the time they would have together before the wedding was precious.

"Actually, I seem to remember that it was the groom

who set the date for this nuptial bash," Celia commented wryly. "And chose his place on Bainbridge as the site. And picked out your dress, and—"

"Enough! I get the message." Helen selected a jelly bean from the heavy crystal jar on her desk and popped it into her mouth. She preferred the yellow ones, just as she preferred yellow daisies to imported orchids and sunshine to gray skies. "Contrary to the current feminist thinking," she said as she savored the tart taste of lemon on her tongue, "I happen to like decisive men."

Celia snorted. "Decisive, my Aunt Fanny. Constantine Paristeri is the most controlling man I've ever met, and believe me, toots, I've met my share."

"You just don't understand the mind set of a Greek male, especially Con," Helen countered while digging into the jar for another jelly bean. "He's very reliable and solid and, well, protective."

"That's one way of putting it," Celia drawled before leaning forward to draw the jelly beans closer. After a moment of deliberation, she shrugged and settled for a random handful. "And speaking of solid and protective, has Con decided to let you work after you get back from your honeymoon cruise?"

"Of course. I wouldn't have agreed to marry him otherwise: Con knows how I value my financial independence. That's one reason we waited so long to set the date. I wanted to have a college fund set aside for Nicky and get my house paid off first."

"God, ain't it great to get carried away by passion?"

Pointedly ignoring Celia's customary sarcasm, Helen smiled into the eyes of her son beaming back at her from his latest school photo sitting in a place of honor on the desk. "Naturally, I'll cut back my hours when I have another baby." They would like to have two children of their own, perhaps three. She was hoping for at least one little girl.

Celia narrowed her eyes. "You're not pregnant now, are you?"

Helen felt her face growing warm. "Not this time," she said, remembering her first wedding. The day before she was to walk down the aisle of St. Mark's Cathedral to marry Alex, the two-masted schooner he'd taken out on a whale-watching expedition had crashed into the rocks near Deception Bay during a sudden squall. Though he'd gotten everyone safely aboard lifeboats before the pounding surf had splintered the vessel, a mother and her daughter had drowned when their lifeboat had sunk.

Alex had been convicted of criminal negligence in not making sure the lifeboats were safe before setting sail and sentenced to two years in prison. Helen had been five months pregnant when he'd finally gotten permission to marry her in the prison chapel. Their honeymoon had consisted of a single kiss and three hours of stilted conversation in the visitors' lounge.

After she'd left the prison that gray morning, she'd sobbed for three solid days. Coming to check on her, Con had found her huddled in her bed, miserable and sick. He'd seen her through her pregnancy and kept her spirits high so that she would be able to smile during the one visit a month Alex grudgingly accepted.

"Actually, Con and I haven't slept together yet," she admitted with only the barest trace of embarrassment in her tone.

"You're joking!"

"No, and don't look at me like I just grew another head. Con has very strong feelings that a bride and groom should wait to consummate the marriage until *after* the wedding." She hesitated, then added sadly, "Con still holds it against Alex for getting me pregnant."

"Are you sure he wasn't just jealous of Alex? I mean, Con did ask you out first."

"Yes, but he was also a perfect gentleman when I turned him down, and he seemed genuinely sad when Alex and I divorced. Not to mention the fact he waited for six more years before asking me out again."

"Which just might have been because you were walking around like a zombie for nearly that long."

"I was not!"

"Uh-huh." Celia shifted her attention to the candy jar, this time taking several seconds to make her selection. "So, how's Nicky handling this wedding brouhaha?" she asked when she'd chewed and swallowed a lime-flavored bean.

"Not too well," Helen admitted with an unexpected catch in her voice. "He claims he wants to live with Alex after the wedding."

Celia lifted her sun-bleached eyebrows. "Have you discussed this with Alex?"

"Alex prefers to communicate with me by letter—when he communicates at all."

"You sound bitter."

"Do I?" Helen feigned indifference, but her throat was suddenly constricted.

"You *are* over him, aren't you?" Celia smoothed an imaginary wrinkle from her skirt before slanting Helen a telling look.

"I'd be a fool not to be, now, wouldn't I?" Helen turned to gaze through the tinted window at the neat row of Greek Isles ships berthed at the company pier below.

She'd answered an ad for a part-time job as a shipping clerk, and had been hurrying to make her appointment with Greek Isles personnel department. Too busy gaping to notice where she was going, she'd stumbled over a short metal post shaped like a fat mushroom and nearly had fallen flat. Only a bit of fancy footwork had saved her.

"Sorry, miss, someone must have put that ballard in the wrong place," a rusty, masculine voice had called from the deck of one of the smaller boats. She'd been mortified to have been seen flailing about by the most gorgeous male she'd ever seen in all of her nineteen years.

Her stomach did somersaults as he'd vaulted over the rail and onto the pier with the agility and grace of a well-trained athlete. She'd guessed his age at early twenties, his ancestry as Mediterranean, though the eyes smiling at her from beneath straight black brows were slate blue and steely rather than a soft Latin brown. His hair was black and curly, tumbling to his shoulders, and he had strong features and an interesting mouth.

He'd been scrubbing the deck and the well-worn jeans sheathing his strong sailor's legs were damp to the knees. Though the air still carried a touch of winter frost, he had discarded his shirt, revealing a brawny chest the color of oiled teak. For a frozen moment Helen merely stared, all that was female in her responding to the sight of his wide shoulders, muscular arms, and tapering torso. He was at least six-three and lean, a virile, sexy advertisement for sea air and exercise.

"Hi, I'm Alex," he'd said, extending a large, work-callused hand.

"I'm . . . Helen," she'd blurted out as she'd let her hand be enfolded in his. "And I'm desperate for a job so I'd appreciate it if you didn't let on to the personnel director just how much of a klutz I really am."

His grin flashed in a dazzling smile saved from perfection by a chipped tooth. "I promise, she'll never hear it from me."

"She?"

"Yeah, a fire-breathing dragon named Martina Drood."

"You're joking," she'd accused, biting off a nervous giggle.

"Scout's honor," he intoned solemnly as he laid the same large hand that had swallowed hers over his heart. "Marty's got to be in her seventies now, but when she was my age she cleaned fish for my dad on this very pier. He was from the old country where loyalty mattered, so when he struck it big during the Second World War, he passed on his good fortune."

"Your dad?" she remembered asking with a sinking heart. "You mean, *you* own Greek Isles?"

"I have a few shares, yeah. But my brother's the one who sits in the fancy office and issues orders. Me, I collect my pay like the rest of the skippers." He nodded toward a banner advertising the line's whale-watching excursions. "Mostly I chase migrating orcas for the enjoyment of the tourists."

"Sounds like fun—at least for the humans. I'm not sure about the whales."

He'd laughed then, a rich, deep sound that warmed her from the inside, and his grin had slashed wider. It was then she'd noticed a dash of cynicism in the blue-gray eyes smiling down at her. "From the looks I've gotten from some of those big guys, I suspect they'd like nothing better than to dunk us all in the drink."

"Why do I think you wouldn't blame them if they did?"

Something warm and appealing had flashed in his eyes then, attracting her to him. "I hope you get that job, sunshine." He lifted a hand to smooth a tendril of hair from her cheek, his raspy fingers lingering a beat too long before he removed his hand.

"Thank you," she remembered saying with a bemused huskiness. "However, I'd probably have a better chance if I knew where I could find your dragon lady, so if you could just point me in the right direction, I'd appreciate it."

He'd done that and more, Helen thought as she stared at the fluttering Greek Isles pennants flying from the forest of masts. Much, much more.

"You're thinking about Alex, aren't you?"

At the sound of Celia's gentle question, Helen swiftly put aside the past for the present, although the part of her heart that Alex had stolen that misty morning would always linger somewhere on that old dock.

"What makes you say a thing like that?" she bluffed, sitting just a bit straighter.

"The sad look in your eyes, for one thing, and the wistful look around your mouth for another."

"Delorio women are never wistful," Helen informed her haughtily. "We're much too practical for that."

Celia cocked her head and looked unconvinced. "At the risk of ruining a friendship that means a lot to me, I'd like to point out it's not too late to call off the wedding."

Helen let a smile play over her lips as she shook her head. "The orchids are already on the way from Brazil, and, at last report, the wedding consultant Con hired is busily cornering the market on phlox and gardenias. Just think of the waste if we called it off now—not to mention what that would do to Greek Isles stock. Why, the entire economy of greater Seattle might simply collapse."

Celia sighed. "Why does this sound more like a merger than a marriage?"

"Because, contrary to the persona you present to the world, you, my dear Celia, are a true romantic. You think all couples should be wildly in love when they say 'I do.' "

"You were once."

Helen felt a pain in the vicinity of her heart. "That part of my life is ancient history."

"True, but making ancient history come alive is what you do best, isn't it?"

Helen opened her mouth, then closed it when she couldn't think of a clever rebuttal. She was about to suggest they call it a night when a rusty male voice said softly, "She's got you there, sunshine."

Two

"*A*lex?" Her voice was little more than a rush of sound.

"Hello, sunshine." He was standing with one hand in the back pocket of his jeans, the other braced against the doorjamb. He had a half smile on his tanned face, and a look in his distinctive blue eyes that Helen couldn't decipher.

"Speak of the devil," Celia murmured before offering him a huge smile.

"And he appears?" Alex finished, his grin slanting wider.

"Something like that," Celia admitted before treating him to a coquettish head-to-toe inspection. "You look darn good for an old guy, Alex. What's your secret?"

If he was annoyed at being characterized as "old" at thirty-seven he gave no sign that Helen could see.

"No secret, just clean living," he said, sauntering closer. Helen felt her heart lurch at the sight of his familiar rolling walk, the indication of a man more at home on the pitching deck of a ship than anywhere else. According to Nicky, Alex was working as a hand on a Greek trawler, which was just about the hardest work there was, especially when the sea was winter wild, and the water pouring over the decks was only a few degrees above freezing. Only the strongest of men survived for more than a decade under such circumstances. Though it hadn't been quite that long for Alex, his eyes had the tired look of a man squinting into the sun for hours on end, and his thick black hair was liberally salted with silver where it curled back over his ears. As he paused to inspect the model, she noticed a small gold hoop affixed to his left ear lobe. Glancing up, he caught her staring and cocked one thick eyebrow. "Did I cut myself shaving, or are you refreshing your memory?"

Helen drew a quick breath before framing her answer with a polite smile. "I'm not likely to forget the father of my only child."

"Perhaps not," he said, hardening his tone. "But you did forget to consult him when you shunted *your only child* off to that fancy Virginia prison."

Helen flinched at the bitterness in his tone. "You make it sound like I exiled him to the wilds of Siberia instead of enrolling him in one of the best schools in the country."

"*Best* meaning what?"

"Best meaning scholastic excellence and character building," she said through a suddenly tense jaw. "And I didn't consult you because I knew you'd act exactly as you're acting now."

Alex took a moment to complete his study of Troy before shifting his lazy gaze her way again. "Oh yeah? How's that?" he drawled, looking relaxed, even bored, but Helen wasn't fooled. Unlike Constantine, who tended to get red in the face and raise his voice when angry, Alex simply went deadly still, while his eyes grew darker and darker until they were as dark and as potentially violent as the storm clouds outside.

She reached for the gold fountain pen Constantine had given her when he'd promoted her to vice-president in charge of the Fantasy division. "In point of fact, you're being utterly unreasonable, bull-headed, and . . . pugnacious," she said, curling her fingers tighter to keep them from shaking.

"Pugnacious?" He shook his head as he ambled closer. When he reached the desk, he angled his hip on one corner and rested a hand on one hard thigh.

"Yes, pugnacious," she repeated for emphasis. "As in, always ready to pick a fight."

He considered that, then rejected it with a look. "Not true. In fact, these days I watch more often than I wade in."

"Much as I'd love to stay and watch the fireworks, I know an exit cue when I hear one," Celia said with a grin as she gracefully got to her feet. "Grant keeps saying I've been working so many hours lately, he's hard-pressed to recognize me when he turns over in bed."

"Grant's the psychology professor Nicky said you married a few years back?"

"The very same. I'm crazy about his mind, and he loves my chimichangas."

Alex laughed. "What man wouldn't?"

"You sweet man. No wonder I've missed you." Celia leaned forward to kiss his cheek. "Will I see you at the wedding Saturday?"

Alex glanced Helen's way before offering Celia a shrug. "I haven't been invited."

"Since when has that ever stopped you, Alexandros Paristeri? As I recall, you pretty much did what you wanted, polite conventions be hanged."

His big hand flattened over his heart. It was his left, the one that had worn Helen's ring so very briefly. She refused to care.

"Trust me, Celia, I'm a changed man."

"In that case, I'm officially inviting you to attend as the guest of the matron of honor—me."

"In that case, I'm officially accepting."

Helen ground her teeth and cursed Celia's macabre sense of melodrama. "Please don't feel you have to be polite, Alex," she said, shooting Celia a killing look.

"Saturday, two o'clock sharp," Celia sailed on blithely. "Your brother is a stickler for promptness."

"Yeah, I remember."

Careful to keep from catching Helen's eye, Celia slung her purse over her shoulder before picking up her briefcase.

"Drive carefully," Helen urged as she exchanged hugs with Celia. "A storm's coming."

"Something tells me it's already here," Celia murmured before making her exit.

"So you're finally getting the wedding you always wanted," Alex said when the sound of Celia's footsteps had faded.

Helen's gaze came his way again, her soft pale lips compressed, her eyes a clear, cool emerald. Gone was the honeyed mane he'd loved to spread over his chest after they'd made love, replaced by a sophisticated knot hugging the nape of her slender white neck. His wild daisy had become an elegant lady.

"Actually, it was Con's idea to have a formal ceremony," she told him with a smile that felt almost natural. "Since this is his first marriage, I didn't have the heart to protest."

His jaw pulled taut, but the surface of his gray-blue eyes remained unruffled. "Where's this dog-and-pony show taking place?"

"The *ceremony* is to be held on the lawn of Con's place on Bainbridge Island."

He narrowed his gaze. "On the lawn? Not the beach?"

"Hardly. Not with three-hundred guests expecting a sit-down dinner and vintage wine." Even as she managed a laugh, Helen's heart ached a little for that starry-eyed twenty-year-old who'd longed for a wedding on the beach, with daisies in her hair and the soothing swish of the waves against the sand as the only music. Though Constantine hadn't actually laughed at her ideas, he'd quietly and firmly insisted upon hiring a tony wedding consultant who'd summarily vetoed Helen's choices of flowers, locale, and a small guest list.

"Nick tells me he's giving you away." he said, settling his big body into the chair Celia had just vacated. "Nice touch."

"Since my father died a few years back, I don't have any other close male relatives."

"What about me?" he asked, his mouth taking a stab at a teasing grin. "Don't I count?"

Yes, you count, she wanted to shout. I wish you

didn't. "Now that would cause a stir, wouldn't it? One Paristeri handing over his former wife to another."

"Might be interesting to give it a try, just to watch the reactions of the guests." He flashed her another grin, more genuine this time, stirring something dangerous inside her. The initial shock of seeing him again was fading, and a disturbing awareness of her ex-husband as an extremely handsome, sexy man was rapidly taking its place. Every time he smiled, she remembered the warmth of that hard mouth seducing hers. And every time he moved, she was acutely aware of the long, lean stretch of his muscular body. His shirt was open at the throat, revealing the dark chest hairs curling over the V above the third button. After they'd made love, she had delighted in rubbing her kiss-swollen lips over that downy mark of masculinity.

Because she was longing to touch him again, she made herself speak coldly. "Is that why you came all this way, Alex? To cause trouble at my wedding?"

"No, sunshine, I came because Nicky sent me an SOS. Seems he's not crazy about the idea of my big brother becoming his stepfather. Or about the way Con has taken over his life."

Leaning forward, he picked up the silver frame holding Nicky's picture and studied it intently before returning it to its place of honor. "No wonder Con wanted to get rid of the kid. He looks more like me every year."

Helen drew a quick breath that did little to calm her suddenly jittery nerves. "It wasn't like that at all, Alex, believe me, it wasn't. I admit I hated the very idea of military school, but when Nicky was expelled for fighting, I realized that Con was right. Nicky needs more discipline and structure than most kids."

"Why, so that he can end up as stuffy and unforgiving as Saint Constantine?"

"That's not fair and you know it."

Alex saw the fast shimmer of anger in her beautiful eyes and felt a stir. The image of the serene lady executive in her glass-walled office had been intriguing for a fast five seconds, and then he'd started missing the awkward, adorable girl he'd met on a dirty pier about a thousand years ago. The sky had been overcast, but she'd made her own sunshine. He remembered smiling for the pure pleasure of watching her face light up and her eyes grow wider and wider. The breeze had teased her hair into a soft golden cloud around that perfect face, and he'd had a yen to bury his face in the silky thickness.

That image had sustained him through the hellish years he'd spent locked for the better part of every day in a prison cell. No matter how hard he'd worked or how tired he'd been at the end of the day these last eight years, that image was the one he'd invariably taken with him into sleep. He knew now he'd always figured to come back and fight for her. Fool that he'd been, it hadn't occurred to him he might be too late.

"Look, we got way off course here," he said in clipped tones. "Nick wants to spend the whole summer with me this year instead of the usual four weeks in August, so that's why I'm here—to take him back with me."

Helen fought the impulse to refuse outright—even though she had the legal right to do just that.

"His counselor thinks it would be best if he stayed at school for the summer term in order to make up a math class he flunked, and I didn't seen any reason to object since classes end the last of July. He'll still have August with you."

Alex felt his frustration rising. Give him a design problem to solve and he would plod through to a solution. But that was logic and deduction and imagination. Putting his thoughts and feelings into words was the nearest thing to impossible for him. It always had been.

"He's more man than boy now," he told her. "He needs to test himself. To figure out his own course, not sweat blood on some parade ground all summer."

"Yes, but within limits, which is what Mount Vernon Military Institute provides."

"You try living by somebody else's rules twenty-four hours a day and see how you like it."

Restless, he got to his feet and walked to the west-facing window. The rain had started, beating hard against the windows. It was a sound he used to love once. Now it only made him feel more alone.

"Does my brother give you the sex I couldn't?" He didn't turn to receive her answer. He'd faced hell itself and survived, but he had no faith he could survive a look of pity in her eyes.

"Alex, please don't do this."

The soft plea sliced into his soul, leaving him bloody. He turned slowly, steeling himself to meet her gaze. "Are you in love with him?"

She returned his gaze with only a slight flicker of feathery lashes. "I care about him very much."

"Does he know you like to have your tummy rubbed when you're having your period? Or that you like to swim nude and make love on the beach when the tide is coming in?"

"What Con knows or doesn't know is none of your business. Besides, why should you care one way or the other? By the end of our marriage, you couldn't even stand to sleep in the same bed with me."

Alex raked a hand through his hair, then realized what he was doing and returned his hand to his side. "Because I couldn't touch you without wanting to make love to you," he grated, acid spilling into his belly. Each time he'd tried and failed, he'd died a little inside until, finally, there hadn't been anything left but shame.

"A lot of men who've been in prison have sexual problems when they get out. The chaplain even warned me that might happen."

She drew a breath and made herself go on. "We could have worked it out, Alex. But you didn't care enough to try. I think that's what hurt the most." She drew another shaky breath. "And in the end, that's why I divorced you. Because your pride mattered more to you than Nicky or I did."

"Damn it, Helen. I tried."

"I loved you, Alex. It didn't matter to me whether you made love to me with your hands or your mouth or—"

"I was there, remember?" His voice was cold, almost

disinterested, but Helen saw a jagged pain come into his eyes before his thick, black lashes wiped away all expression.

"I shouldn't have said that," she apologized softly before rolling back her chair and getting to her feet. "I'm sorry."

Alex felt something twist inside him. "For what it's worth, I am, too. For a lot of things."

She accepted that calmly, though her heart was thudding. "We both want the best for Nicky," she said, moving toward him. "Maybe if you went to Mount Vernon and spent a few days, you'd realize it's not such an awful place."

"Or you could call off your wedding, and come with Nick and me to Pyrgos. You'd like Greece."

"Maybe, if you'd ask me a year ago, or two, I might have said yes."

"I never should have left." He caressed her cheek with his thumb, sending shivers running over her skin, and then he was sliding his hand to the nape of her neck.

Don't, she tried to order, only to find the word dammed behind the tightness in her throat. Lifting her hands, she braced them against his chest, intending to push him away. Through the soft cotton she felt the heat of his skin, the contraction of hard muscle, the twitch of power rigidly controlled. She saw his face looming larger, the flaring cheekbones, the bold eyebrows, the sweep of blunt eyelashes. Heat kindling in stormy eyes an instant before his mouth found hers.

His lips pressed softly, teasing the tension in her own into submission. He stepped closer, bringing them thigh to thigh. Her breasts brushed his chest, sending ripples of warm excitement over her skin. Inside, she felt herself softening.

His lips moved, tasting, nibbling. His breath mingled with hers, warm and moist, flavored with coffee. "Relax, sunshine," he whispered against her lips. "Let it happen."

Even as she told herself to resist, she was sliding her hands over the hard slope of chest and shoulder. His arms came around her, one big hand flattening against her spine to urge her closer.

One kiss tumbled into another and another, each one more hungry more insistent. Her senses spun, her mind fogged. He tasted like Alex, he felt like Alex. Suddenly everything was right. Glorious.

He lifted his head, sucked in air. His expression was tortured, his eyes hungry. Her mind was reeling, and she shook her head to clear it, but the fog seemed to swirl thicker. She started to speak, only to have his mouth come down on hers again. His lips were hot, eager, tempting her to an eagerness of her own.

His arms tugged her closer, his body crushing hard against hers, thigh against thigh. The bulge of his arousal pressed her belly, sending fire through her veins. Her body took control, and she let it, glorying in the silky feeling of desire. She arched closer, feeling the hard stab of rigid flesh. *Yes,* her mind shouted.. This was what she was made for, what she craved. To be filled with him, to be loved.

She moaned, and felt him jerk. He drew back, his eyes shiny, his breathing harsh. "Look at me, Helen. Who am I?"

Blinking, she tried to level her frantic breathing. "What?" she managed to get out.

"I'm the guy you divorced, remember? The guy you said you don't love anymore."

Helen started to sway, then caught herself. She tried to move away, only to feel the muscles in his arms turn to steel. "I . . . know who you are. What I don't know is why you started this in the first place."

His eyes took on a tortured gleam and his jaw bunched. "Damnit, I started it because I still want you," he grated, his voice low and thick. "Even when I found out you were going to marry my brother, I still wanted you. And you want me."

Don't think now, she told herself. Just get him out of here as fast as you can. "It was an interesting experiment, I grant you, but the party's over, and I have things to do. I'm sure you do too, so let's call it a night."

Interesting? Alex thought, staring at her flushed face.

Infuriating was more like it. Like the feeling he'd gotten when he'd had too much to drink and knew he'd pay dearly the next morning.

"You're right, Helen. We both have things to do." Still watching her eyes, he let her go and took a step backward. The room tilted like a ship's deck in a blow, and his body felt heavy. Awkward.

A gentleman would apologize. He'd be damned if *he* would, but he would back off while he still could. "I'll be there on Saturday to watch you walk down the aisle —and to pick up my son for the summer."

Before she could answer, he made himself walk away. Again.

Three

*S*mitty's had a new sign hanging outside and a sturdy new door, but, inside, the waterfront bar and grill was the same seedy dive Alex remembered. Like waterfront bars everywhere, the place smelled like fried onions, stale cigarette smoke and fish. The atmosphere was smoky and hot, and the music was country-western and loud. Behind the scarred bar, the bartender had hard eyes and a knack of knowing which drinks he could safely water and which had better be served full strength and brimming.

The dinner crowd, such as it was, had come and gone, making room for the hard-core boozers who'd arrived within minutes of each other and bellied up to the bar with an eagerness Alex had once shared. Before he'd taken to staring into the amber contents of the glass in front of him, he'd noted a few familiar faces. He'd noted, too, enough gape-jawed looks to know he'd been recognized.

Once, he would have gotten a kick out of baiting the biggest and brawniest of the lot into a one-on-one, just to let everyone know he was still the same tough son of a bitch who'd never walked away from a fight in his life. Yeah, he'd been a piece of work, all right. A real hell-raiser. The family devil.

Constantine had been the family saint, his mother's shining example, to be constantly taken out and polished like the silver urn she'd prized so highly. Alex was the fuck-up, the kid she'd proudly sent off to school in ironed blue jeans and starched white shirt, only to have him straggle home a few hours later with the shirt half-torn off and a beaut of a shiner already blossoming.

He was pretty sure he never consciously decided to cultivate a reputation as a troublemaker. Once he'd had the name, he hadn't bothered to shake free. Just the opposite. So he was a devil, was he? Well, hell, let's show 'em what a really bad one he was.

Oh yeah, the bad boy of the Paristeri family had done a damn good job of thumbing his nose at life, he thought as he threw the remainder of his drink down his throat in one gulp. He'd been fifteen and drunk when they buried his mother. Ten years later, when his father had been laid next to her, he'd been saved from disgracing himself at the funeral only because he'd been in prison at the time.

Craving numbness, he signaled the waitress for a re-fill, then contemplated the empty glass as though he'd find his forgiveness at the bottom. Instead, he was treated to a crystal clear vision of the wounded look in Helen's eyes right before he'd walked out on her.

"You new in town?" the waitress asked as she traded him a full shot glass for the one he'd just emptied.

"Been gone a while."

"Want some company? I get off at ten."

"Another time, maybe," he said, summoning what he hoped was a decent enough smile.

The gleam in her eye faded, leaving her face a little sad. "Yeah, another time," she echoed before walking away.

Alone again, he flexed his tired shoulders and thought about heading back to the *ESPIARE*. He'd been at sea two weeks, just him and the boat he'd built damn near with his own hands. When the sea was calm, he'd managed to drop anchor for a few fast hours of sleep before setting off again. Coming up the coast after a brief provisioning stop in San Diego, he'd fought rough seas all the way, and he was dead tired.

Old Dad blew it, son, he thought as he brought the glass to his mouth. Conscious of the raw burning in his gut, he sipped this time, then winced as the whiskey hit bottom.

He'd promised Nick he'd talk to her. Try to make her see reason. Instead, he'd gotten all tangled up in feelings he'd thought he'd left behind. But damn, she'd been sweet.

"Mind if I join you?"

Caught up in his own thoughts, it took Alex a beat to realize he was no longer alone. Glancing up, he found himself looking into the cold blue eyes of his brother. Emotion stirred somewhere in the black pit where he'd stuffed his feelings. An emotion, he realized, he didn't care to identify.

"Since when have you needed my permission to do anything?" he drawled, lifting his glass in a mocking salute before draining it dry. Though it was late in the day, his brother looked freshly shaved, and the collar of his natty striped shirt was laundry crisp. Alex didn't need to see Con's shoes to know they'd been recently shined to a high gloss.

"Still as civil as ever, I see," Constantine said as he slid into the seat opposite.

"You got that right, brother." Straightening, he summoned the waitress.

This time her hips seemed oiled as she approached, an ingratiating smile on her freshly glossed mouth. Alex figured they didn't get too many corporate types in Smitty's this time of night, and what the hell, a girl had to make a living anyway she could.

"What can I bring you, sir?" Her question, like her fluttering gaze, was directed at Constantine.

"I'll have what he's having," Con ordered with a polite smile. "And bring him another, my tab."

"Two double Jack Daniels," she said, her voice lowered to a purr. Alex thought about warning her off, then decided that Con could do a better job with one of those icy looks of his.

"Anything else?" she prodded when it became obvious Con wasn't going to rise to the bait.

Con flicked her another smile. "No, but thanks for asking."

"Any time," she murmured before reluctantly turning away.

Alex sat back, one hand fisted on his thigh, the other flat on the scarred tabletop. Since Con was paying for the drinks, he'd be polite and let his brother get in the first shot. He didn't have long to wait.

"What the hell do you think you're playing at, Alex?" Constantine challenged in a low tone one notch below explosive.

Alex settled back, one hand hooked around his drink. "I take it Helen called you," he stated, his tone deliberately bored.

Con's heavy brows pulled together over the bridge of his nose, which unlike his own, had never been hammered by someone's fist. "No, she did not call me. I found out you were back when security called, strictly as a courtesy, to tell me they'd okayed my brother to visit the fifth floor. Said you showed him your passport to prove your identity."

Alex let his mouth relax into a lazy grin. "Impressive set-up you've got there, brother. Made me feel real safe knowing that no two-bit terrorist was going to blow up your building while I was in it."

"You son of a bitch, don't you take anything seriously?"

"You'd be surprised."

Constantine shook his head. "Nothing about you surprises me anymore, Alex." He started to say more, only to fall silent when the waitress approached.

"Here you go, gents," she murmured, bending just a bit lower than necessary as she transferred the glasses from tray to table. Alex watched Con's gaze flicker to the generous breasts straining against the tight white blouse and tried not to think about his brother making love to his ex-wife. He didn't succeed. Worse, the image of Helen's slender arms around Con had him biting down hard.

"Here's to brotherly love," Con said when the waitress was out of earshot. "And if you hurt Helen again, I'll kill you."

"If I hurt Helen again, I'll load the gun," Alex said

before downing the double shot in one long, burning swallow.

Constantine was watching him warily as he returned the glass to the table with a soft thud. "Am I supposed to believe you've actually developed a conscience?" he asked when Alex met his gaze.

"I stopped caring what you thought about me a long time ago." Still holding Con's eyes, he leaned forward slightly, his expression still tightly controlled. "What I do care about these days is my son."

"An admirable sentiment," Con muttered before tasting his drink.

"He doesn't belong in some lousy military school."

"That's your opinion."

"Not opinion, fact." They locked gazes, dark blue shot with steel against blue ice. "Nick is out of there. Got it? As of now."

"Not your call, little brother. Not anymore."

"I'm making it my call."

"Sure you are. Hell, it's easy playing good guy twice a year. Making the boy big promises you know you won't have to keep." Con's mouth snaked up on one side. "You're a great role model for the boy, Alex. A real sterling example of a man."

Alex knew he was being baited. Con had a knack for pushing his buttons. Not this time, brother, he thought as he sat back. "This isn't about me, Con. It's about a half-grown kid who's being punished because he's too much like his father."

Con snorted, but his eyes had changed. "If you mean he's already too far down a dangerous road, you're right." He leaned forward, looked right and left as though checking for eavesdroppers. "This is a small town, in spite of the population explosion. Being in business here, having a name that's easily recognized, is both a curse and a blessing. It's been rough on Nick, growing up with the stigma of being the son of a . . ."

"Jailbird?" Alex supplied when Constantine paused.

Con flashed him a grin more derisive than amused. "A man with your sordid reputation."

Alex didn't bother to dispute fact. "No problem. He can finish his growing up in Pyrgos."

"Yeah, right. And in six months, maybe less, he'd be back here, totally out of control and more confused than ever."

Alex moved his shoulders in an effort to ease a sudden tightness. "Again, a matter of opinion."

"A matter of experience. You're a quitter, Alex. Oh, a charming one, I'll give you that, but you're unreliable. I'll grant you have good intentions, but when crunch time comes, you fold."

Because he wanted to smash a fist into his brother's face, Alex made himself go perfectly still. "Go on, get it all out if it makes you feel better."

"You want chapter and verse, fine. You graduated high school only through the generosity of your teachers. God only knows how you wangled your way into the university, but instead of buckling down and taking advantage of your good luck, you flunked out after one semester."

Con paused for breath, his face taking on the dull red of rising temper. "For a while, after you met Helen, I really thought you'd pull it together, maybe go back to college. Even when I found out you'd made her pregnant, she'd seemed so happy, I . . . " He stopped, cleared his throat. "Jesus, Alex, why couldn't you have checked that damn lifeboat before you put to sea in marginal weather?"

Alex's insides knotted. Only through extreme force of will did he keep his breathing even and his expression controlled. "Christ, don't you think I've asked myself that same question? The point is, I screwed up. I assumed the boat had been fixed."

"Too bad the jury didn't believe you." Con smirked as he spoke.

"With a little help from my brother—"

"I couldn't lie. The repair order wasn't in the files."

"Lucky for you and Greek Isles, right?"

Con's eyes sparked with anger. "What the hell are you implying? That I took it?"

Something hard and painful knotted more tightly in

Alex's chest. "I thought about it a lot in prison, about how you had a key to every office, access to every computer file. I can't prove that you took that repair order. I just know that you did."

Con gave a harsh laugh. "You're out of your frigging mind."

Alex lifted his tumbler in a mock toast. "What I am is Nick's dad. Whatever he needs me to do, I'll do."

"Then disappear. He doesn't need his ex-con father hanging around and stirring up gossip to further humiliate him."

"Nice shot," Alex said softly. "Only it won't work on me these days, Con. I'm not running from the truth anymore. I can't pretend the shipwreck didn't happen or that people didn't die. I don't lie to myself by pretending I haven't hurt the people I love. But I paid my dues. Served my time. I still have the next half of my life to live, and, by God, I mean to make it up to my family—whether you like it or not."

"Too little too late. Helen's going to be my wife, and Nicky's going to be my son. I intend to do everything I can to erase you from their minds—and their future."

"You can try, big brother," Alex drawled, his voice whisper quiet.

"That's the difference between us, Alex. I finish what I start." Con took his wallet from the inside pocket of his suit coat and extracted a hundred-dollar bill. "That should cover the tab, with enough left over to pay for a night in a cheap hotel," he said before he finished his drink and slid from the booth.

Alex had lived in the vicious world of prison long enough to know exactly how easy it was to kill. A flick of the wrist, a flash of steel, and a man could be left bleeding out his life on a dirty floor. Life was cheap. Death was easy. Hanging in, doing the decent thing, finding a reason to stay alive one more day—those were tough.

Leaning back, he smiled up at his brother, while beneath the table his fist was murdering tight. "I'll see you Saturday, bro. Two o'clock."

It was a cheap shot, but Alex felt a stab of satisfaction nevertheless when Constantine's face reddened. "Stay away from her, Alex."

"Sorry, no can do. We have unfinished business, remember? And like you said, it's time I saw something through to the end."

Con's face twisted. "Tell you what, Alexandros. When I see that state-of-the-art yacht you were always talking about designing, then I'll start to worry."

Alex sat perfectly still, accepting the look of scorn Con threw his way. All of a sudden, he felt sick.

Four

It rained in the early hours of Saturday morning, but by two in the afternoon Bainbridge Island was bathed in sunshine. To the rear of the stone and cedar house, the lawn sweeping down to Puget Sound had been pampered into a carpet of kelly green plush, and the air was perfumed by the scent of a thousand gardenias flown in from California. Overhead, the sky was a dazzling blue canopy under which the guests, over three hundred at last count, were assembling leisurely.

While the men in their perfectly tailored summer suits compared stock tips and interest rates, women in butterfly finery greeted each other with kisses in the air and murmured insincere compliments before ambling to the ribbon-bedecked chairs.

Traditionally divided as though inside a church, half the seats were on the groom's side, half on the bride's. The two sections flanked a white carpet runner, the length of which a very nervous Helen soon would walk to join her future husband in front of the rose arbor to exchange vows. To the left a small blue and white striped tent sheltered the tuxedoed twelve-piece orchestra that was well into the prenuptial selections.

Hidden from view behind the caterer's screen of gardenias and ivy, Helen clutched her bridal bouquet with hands that trembled violently every time she thought about the promises she was about to utter and told herself to relax. Twenty-six minutes before the ceremony and counting was no time for second thoughts.

"Lord, smell those gardenias," Celia exclaimed after drawing in an exuberant breath. "Talk about a conspicuous display."

"Be nice, Celia," Helen pleaded through suddenly numb lips. "The last few days have been stressful enough without your shooting poison darts at my future husband."

"You're right. I'm being a bitch." Celia lifted her bridesmaid bouquet to her nose and sniffed before glancing up at the puffy clouds. "Anyway, it sure turned out to be a gorgeous day. I wish Grant hadn't had to teach a master's class, the workaholic rat."

Helen smiled her condolences, then searched for her son's dark head in the crowd. She saw friends, co-workers, the society columnist for the paper, the catering staff all standing at attention in front of the huge striped tent, but no Nicky.

"Alex isn't here yet," Celia said pointedly as she swept her gaze over the throng.

"I was looking for Nicky. I told him to stay close so I could signal to him when it was time." Any second now she expected to hear the orchestra break into "The Wedding March."

"He'll be here, and looking very grown-up in that gorgeous tuxedo."

Helen felt her face soften. "He does look handsome, doesn't he?"

"Yep, almost as handsome as his dad."

Helen scowled. "I was thinking of Con, actually."

Standing at uneasy attention, Helen resisted the urge to poke at the garland of gardenias digging into her scalp. After enduring five endless hours of pampering from the bridal consultant's silently efficient staff, Helen was finally manicured, coiffed, made up, and buttoned into a bead-encrusted silk gown so tight she was afraid to breathe.

Sensing movement, she turned stiffly to see Nicky heading toward them. For an instant she was sorry Alex wouldn't see his son looking so grown-up and responsible.

"Mom, are you sure you want to do this?" Nicky

asked when he and Celia had exchanged greetings and mutual compliments. Seeing the troubled look in his eyes, she forced a reassuring smile.

"I'm sure. And I'm especially happy because you're here to walk down the aisle with me."

"I just hope I don't mess up," he muttered, checking his watch.

"Don't worry, you're going to do just fine."

"Uh, yeah." He bit his lip, then glanced toward the sparkling waters of the Sound where a dozen or so luxury yachts swung at anchor. Following his gaze, she spied another vessel nosing into the slip by the pier. A good forty feet in length, with a hull the color of midnight and a gleaming superstructure, it was easily the most beautiful vessel she'd ever seen. And fast, she decided. Definitely fast. With a skilled captain at the helm, a ship such as that could easily outrun the fastest ship in the Greek Isles line.

A smile curved her lips as she pictured herself standing at the rail, with the wind teasing her hair away from her face and the sun caressing her skin. In less than an hour, she could be on the Pacific, with Seattle's distinctive skyline astern and . . .

"Hang tight, Mom, I'll be right back."

Before she could draw breath to stop him, Nick had taken off running toward the house. "Hurry back," she called after him, but Nicky seemed not to hear her.

"Poor Nick," Celia murmured when he disappeared into the throng. "I've never seen him so shook."

"At least he's no longer acting like a pill about the wedding."

"Reconciled, is he?"

"I hope." Helen sighed and fussed with the gown's satin and lace train, which she'd unfastened and unfurled only a few minutes ago. The thing was at least ten feet long, and ridiculously impractical for a garden wedding.

"Here, let me help you," Celia said, stepping back. Just then a gust of wind came in off the sound and caught Helen's veil, drawing the exquisite Alencon lace across her face. Through the blur, she saw the minister and Constantine move to stand at center front before the arbor. An instant later, the orchestra began to play the prelude to "The Wedding March."

"Oh Lord, Celia, where's Nicky?"

"I don't know, but he'd better rustle his buns, or I'll be the one giving you away." Celia went on tiptoe and craned her neck. "Wait, I think I see him over by the house. I'll be right back."

"Celia, don't leave me!" Helen called, but Celia was already dashing toward the house.

"Damn and double damn," she muttered, taking a tighter grip on her bouquet.

A sudden lull came in the music, and Helen knew by the suspended chord that "The Wedding March" was about to begin. Frantically, she searched for a glimpse of Nicky or Celia. Someone—anyone—to walk with her down the aisle. But she saw only the stranglers hastening to their seats.

Vaguely aware of an odd hissing sound, Helen straightened her shoulders and made ready to move. Just as she put her foot forward, the hissing noise became more a sharp sputter. Then, *splat!* Something ice cold and wet slapped her in the face, plastering her veil to her skin. She gasped at the shock of it.

Someone screamed, "Oh, my God, the sprinklers!"

Then there was pandemonium. Chairs tipped over. People, ducking to avoid the Rainbird spray, began running in all directions. Struggling to peel the veil from her face so she could see where she was going, Helen tried to find shelter, but every direction she turned, she encountered bodies—and water. Fixing her gaze on the house, she tried to make her way toward it, elbowing aside bodies as she went. Then one of her spike heels sank into the soft earth, making her lurch. She grabbed helplessly at the back of a man's suit jacket in a vain attempt to keep from falling.

At the last possible second, an iron hard arm caught her about the waist. Glancing down through her veil, Helen glimpsed a man's white sleeve rolled tight against a wide, burnished forearm. Twisting, she saw the scowling face of her ex-husband.

"For heaven's sake, Alex, what are you doing?"

"At the moment, trying to stay dry."

Leaning into her, he supported her weight with the muscular length of his body while he hauled in her bridal train, much as a cowboy might his lasso.

"But what—"

Before she could finish what she was saying, Alex vised his arm tightly around her. The next second, Helen found herself being lifted and tossed rather unceremoniously over his sturdy shoulder. Bouncing her about to reposition her weight, he caught her behind the knees with one arm and began shoving his way through the swarming bodies with his other.

His well-padded shoulder impacted with her midriff again, shoving all her breath from her lungs and sending the spray of rare orchids flying out of her hand. Gasping for air, Helen made a wild grab for his belt in an attempt to lever herself upward.

The beautiful setting had turned to chaos, a dizzying kaleidoscope of color and noise.

"Al—ex," she tried to shout, only to feel her teeth knock together. At the same time, she saw the weathered boards of the dock coming toward her face. Flinching and blinking, she threw up an arm to protect her face, realizing only at the last second that he wasn't dropping her, but turning. Glancing around wildly, she saw the dark hull of a ship and a ladder. Terrified, Helen bicycled her feet furiously.

"Goddamnit, Helen," Alex grated. "Be still before you get us both killed!"

"Hurry, before he sees us!" she thought she heard Nicky call.

"Nicky? What's . . . going on?"

"Don't worry, Mom. Everything's cool."

"Nicholas Paristeri, you run get help, right now!"

Completely ignoring her, the boy looked straight at his father. With a victorious whoop and a thumbs-up, he cried, "Dad, that was ominous! I can't believe it. They're swarming around up there like ants on an anthill. It's the funniest thing I've ever seen, all of them either looking for the sprinkler controls or running for cover! Uncle Constantine doesn't even know Mom's gone yet!"

"He will, soon enough," Alex said tersely, swinging her in a wide arc that made her dizzy. "Untie the bow lie, son, then climb aboard and get ready to let go the stern line when I give you the signal."

"Nicky, listen to me!" she managed to get out between gasps. "Your father's gone crazy. Go tell Uncle Constantine. Hurry!"

"Forget it, sunshine. Big brother's too busy trying to save his dignity to bother about a minor thing like a missing bride."

"You bastard, I'm going to have you thrown in jail for this," she shouted, her words ending in a rush of air as Alex shifted her for better purchase, then climbed aboard.

Five

"Nick, cast off!" Alex shouted without stopping.

Arching upward, Helen caught blurred glimpses of a gleaming teak deck, a neat coil of rope, and her suitcases standing in neat row next to another flight of stairs.

"I am—going to—kill—you," she managed to grind out between jarring steps as he climbed.

"Later. First we're hauling ass out of here."

Inside the bridge, he plunked her down on a tall admiral's chair. She had an impression of gleaming stainless steel surrounding an impressive array of radar and communication equipment. Her heart sped up when she saw the microphone attached to a complicated-looking console.

"Let me go, you idiot," she shouted, scooting forward.

Grinning, Alex grabbed handful of sodden veil and stuffed it into her mouth. Sputtering, she struggled to spit out the gag.

"Take it easy, sunshine. You're going to do yourself some damage." Gathering her train in one hand, he gave the chair a spin with the other, and wound her up tight in the gauzy stuff like a mummy.

"You make a very neat package, sunshine," he said with a devil's grin. "As soon as we get clear of the island, I'll cut you loose, so be a good girl and sit still, or you'll end up taking a nasty tumble."

Curses muffled by the gag, she glared at him. He'd

pay for this, she fumed. Oh, yes, in spades. No black-haired son of Satan was going to ruin her wedding and get away with it. As soon as she got loose, she'd . . . she'd . . . think of something, all right.

"Damned if you're not gorgeous when you're flashing daggers at a man." He sounded annoyed, as though she'd offended him.

She called him a name through the mouthful of veil, then realized she was shivering. The air temperature was a good ten degrees lower over the water, and the wind had picked up, becoming even more chilly as it skimmed moisture from the water's cold surface. Her heavy gown was wet through and through, three layers of clammy fabric clinging to her skin.

Alex frowned, flexed his shoulders, and disappeared through a door to the rear of the bridge. Craning her neck, she tried to peer over the wing of the bridge. The crowd on shore was a blur of shifting color beneath the big striped tents. She was still trying to spot Constantine among the throng when Alex returned with a heavy foul-weather jacket in his hands.

"Twenty minutes tops, and you can take a nice warm shower. If you're nice to me, I might be persuaded to join you."

Laughing at her attempt to flay him alive with a look, he dropped the coat over her shoulders, draped it carefully in front to keep the wind off the bodice of her gown, then leaned forward to kiss the tip of her nose before removing the gag. She tried to bite his fingers, but he was too quick.

While she fumed, he stepped to the wheel, flipped a half dozen switches overhead, and the gently purring engines became a deep-throated rumble.

Nicky was shouting something below, his voice whipped away by the wind. On the shore, a man in a white tuxedo was running toward the pier.

"Constantine, help!" she shouted, knowing that he couldn't hear her. At the same time, she heard feet pounding the steps to the bridge.

Nicky came in panting, his cheeks red and his eyes shining like Christmas morning. "All set, Dad!" he said between gasping breaths. "I think Uncle Con's figured out what happened."

"No *think* about it, son." Alex flicked a gaze toward the shore, then snagged a pair of aviator glasses hanging on one of the switches and put them on.

"See to it your mom doesn't end up on her fanny," he ordered the boy before checking fore and aft. Seconds later, the boat surged forward, throwing her back against the seat.

She slipped sideways and banged her shoulder against the chair's arm. She barked out a word that had Nicky staring wide-eyed. "Help me up," she ordered, blaming Alex for her lapse of ladylike decorum.

Looking slightly dazed, Nicky pushed her upright, his face seamed with worry. "Mom, you're not really mad, are you?"

Teeth clenched, she stared at him in disbelief. "I can't believe you're asking me that question, Nicholas Paristeri."

"But Dad and me thought it was kinda romantic, you know?"

"You and your dad have a lot to learn about women, young man." She kicked one foot sending her satin pump flying across the bridge to land with a thud against the white bulkhead. "And if one of you two scoundrels doesn't get me out of this shroud *right now,* I am going to make every waking moment the three of us are forced to spend together a miserable, nonstop nightmare!"

Nicky shot a baleful glance at his father, who nodded. "It should be safe enough."

"Maybe we'd better wait. She might jump overboard."

"If she does, she'll sink like a rock in that dress."

Nicky stepped behind her, looking like a criminal being marched to his doom. "Lean forward so I can get rid of the jacket."

"Don't you dare snap at me, young man. If you're inconvenienced, it's your own fault."

"Sorry," he mumbled contritely.

Somewhat mollified, Helen leaned forward enough

for him to slip the heavy jacket free. She felt oddly lost without it—and without the scent of soap and wind that had clung to it. Alex's scent.

She heard the jacket hit the floor, then felt a tug on the material binding her. "Stuff feels slimy," Nicky complained, tugging harder. After several more hard jerks, she felt the material loosen. Instead of spinning her around, he held on to the end of the train and walked around her twice before letting the end of the train fall to the deck. What had once looked regal now reminded her of a painter's drop cloth, all splotched and ragged.

Poor Con, she thought. Spending all that money for nothing.

"Uh, guess it's ruined, huh?" Nicky said, following the direction of her gaze.

"Totally—thanks to you and your cohort."

"It was just a plain, old white dress. You've got lots of others."

"A plain, white *Dior* dress," she corrected, thinking about Con's face when he found out he'd spent ten thousand dollars for nothing.

Looking competent and relaxed and much too pleased with himself, Alex grinned at her. "Women set a lot of store in weddings, son. I never knew exactly why."

"Probably so they can put on all that gunky makeup and high heels and pretend to like it."

Alex threw his son one of those smug male looks she'd always hated. "You have to admit your mom looked pretty as a picture in one of those glossy ladies' magazines."

"Thanks very much, Mr. Fashion Expert." She put enough venom in her voice to bring down a horse. Alex merely grinned and kept his gaze on the water ahead while she fumed.

Puget Sound was crowded with Saturday sailors, making swift passage tricky, if not downright dangerous. Keeping the engines throttled back to what she suspected was far below maximum power, Alex handled the wheel with one hand, the other resting on his hip, fingers splayed casually. A klaxon sounded in the distance, and a small engine whined somewhere to the rear. Bainbridge was already a blur of green behind them. Ahead was the Kitsap peninsula and the Strait of Juan de Fuca leading to the Pacific and open water.

Standing at his father's elbow, one leg cocked forward at the same angle as Alex's, Nicky studied one of the radar screens, his expression rapt. "Mom wanted to elope this time," he said without looking up. "Only Uncle Con said he'd waited too long for her to sneak off to some justice of the peace."

"Sounds like Uncle Con all right."

"He said something else, too, only I didn't understand what he meant." He directed a quick glance toward his father who lifted one black eyebrow.

"Nothing good, if I know my brother."

Nicky giggled like a little boy, then caught himself and sobered. "He was talking to this bridal lady, the one he'd hired to make Mom all fancy. He said he wanted to make this wedding perfect, not . . . uh . . . sordid like her wedding to you."

Alex turned to glance at her over Nicky's head. Though dark lenses hid the expression in his eyes, she felt his gaze, penetrating and yet oddly vulnerable. "Maybe it wasn't perfect, but it was the best we could manage at the time," he said gruffly.

"It wasn't so bad," she found herself telling Nicky solemnly. "Your dad was there, and a chaplain. That's all that mattered."

"You should have had flowers." Alex's voice was rough, his mouth hard at the corners. "Those yellow daisies you were always so crazy about."

"I didn't miss them." But she had, desperately— along with the music and the candles and—

"Liar," Alex said with only a hint of humor in his husky voice.

Helen realized she was smiling at him with the same wildly beating pulse she'd had the first time she'd laid eyes on him. Nostalgia did strange things.

"I don't regret our marriage," she said with an unexpected catch in her voice. "Only the way it ended."

His gaze burned into hers, dark and full of remorse. And something more, something powerful and dangerous. "You called it right the other night," he grated, his voice rough. "When things piled up, I ran." Abruptly, he directed his attention to the sea, his spine ramrod straight, a muscle ticking hard in his jaw.

"Dad, which one of these screens is the weather satellite?" Nick asked a few tense minutes later.

"Not now, son," Alex said, flicking him a glance. "Let me get clear of this traffic first."

"Can I help?" Nicky sounded hopeful, yet tentative, as though he expected a brush-off. Helen bit the inside of her cheek and tried to signal Alex with a glance. Hero worship was a heavy load to lay on anyone, especially a man who saw his son only two months out of the year.

Taking his gaze away from the water ahead for only an instant, Alex reached out a hand and ruffled Nicky's hair. The thick waves so like his father's had been shorn to a military closeness by the school's barber.

"Still remember how to read a chart and plot a course?" Alex asked as he returned his attention to the sea.

Nicky nodded. He beamed, Helen thought, a sudden lump in her throat. "I've been practicing with the chart of the Med you gave me."

"Puget Sound isn't as big, but it's just as tricky in spots. Best check out the course I laid out, see what you make of it. Once we're clear of the worst of the crowd, I want you to take the helm while I get your mom settled in her cabin."

"Yes, sir!" Nicky's chest expanded a good inch, and the glance he shot Helen was dancing with excitement.

Alex grinned. "Lose the military talk around old dad, okay?"

"Okay!" Nicky circled behind his father and hunkered down over the plotting table tucked efficiently into a sheltered corner away from the wind. A chart was spread on the surface, held down by a heavy ceramic coffee mug and a thick paperback book with a torn cover. Helen's jaw dropped open when she read the title. It was *The Iliad,* by Homer.

Six

Alex throttled back the engine to a nice easy three knots, checked the heading, then stepped aside and let Nicky take the wheel.

"Questions?" he asked when Nicky glanced up.

"Keep her on this heading, watch out for trouble, and holler for you if I need you," Nick repeated with a grin just shy of cocky.

"You have the con," Alex said, flipping him a little salute that he returned with a lot more expertise. But then, the poor kid had had six weeks of practice, he thought, as he turned his attention to the wilted bride in the chair.

"All set?"

She scowled at him, her eyes snapping. The twenty minutes he'd promised her had stretched to thirty, and though he'd caught her looking pained more than once, she hadn't complained.

"Don't you dare—" The fierce order ended with a squeak as he circled that tempting waist with his hands and lifted her out of the chair.

He put her down, waiting until she found her balance before removing his hands. His fingers were wet from the sopping material, and guilt knotted in his belly. His shirt had dried quickly in the wind, but the damp denim of his jeans was damned uncomfortable. She had to be downright miserable.

"Okay, now?" he asked when she glanced up, her fingers still clutching his arm.

"Fine." She turned, took two limping steps toward the door, then stopped, an odd look coming over her face. "It feels like I'm towing the damn boat behind me," she muttered, glaring down at the sorry-looking pool of satin at her feet.

"No wonder. There's enough material in that thing to make a good-sized sail."

"It unhooks in the back." she said, twisting, her hand groping at her waist. While her attention was focused on the back of her gown, his was drawn by the clear outline of her nipples against the wet material. Nipples that had hardened when her awkward movement had stretched the material taut over her breasts. Nipples that looked as tempting as the sweetest candy.

Biting off a groan, he jerked his gaze to her hands, then frowned at the lack of progress, and pushed them away. With one sharp tug, he tore the train free and kicked it aside.

"Now look what you did," she exclaimed, glaring at him again. "My dress is ruined for sure now."

"So sue me," he said, scooping her into his arms.

"Put me down," she ordered, her voice one notch below seething. "I can walk."

Alex felt the softness of her breasts settle against him, and his libido gave him a jab. He tried not to think about the last time he'd had a yen to make love to her. "If it's all the same to you, I'd just as soon not take half a day getting from here to the cabin."

"Oh, shut up," she muttered, clutching at his neck to keep from falling. He settled her more firmly, shot Nick a glance to make sure the kid was watching the channel instead of his parents, and left the bridge.

By the time reached below decks, he was sweating, as much from the fire kindling in his loins as from exertion. But he'd be damned if he'd let her know he was hurting.

"Damn dress weighs a ton," he muttered as he propped one knee by the door to the cabin and held her there while he twisted the knob.

She drew back far enough to see his eyes. Her own were still simmering. "Must be tough to get old."

Alex swung the door inward, then let his gaze linger on the soft, pink mouth pursed so silkily only a few inches from his. He'd never tasted a mouth as sweet, or wanted another taste so desperately. But the hem of her dress was still dripping water onto the deck and she'd started shivering again.

Gritting his teeth against the hunger spiking hot below his belt, he carried her inside and set her down near the door to the head. "Bathroom's through there, even has a tub if you want to soak out the chill."

Tucking his hands into his back pockets, he glanced around, trying to see the cabin through her eyes. When his gaze skimmed the bed, he felt a rush of heat. He'd had a lot of lonely years to think about making love to his sunshine girl again. Years and years of wanting, of sleepless nights and empty days.

Now that she was close enough to touch, he was to-the-bone scared. In his dreams, she always said yes. In his dreams he surged into her, hard and strong. He knew better than most just how fragile dreams could be.

"Uh, look, you're cold," he said, his pulse rattling in his throat. "While you jump in the shower, I'll bring your bags down, then check on Nick."

Hands pressed together at her waist like a child in prayer, she gave the room a fast once-over, then nodded. "I think I will take a bath."

"Good idea." He'd forgotten how tiny she was when she climbed down from those skinny-heeled stilts she wore because she thought they made her legs look sleeker. And how utterly desirable, even now, with her hair falling down from the fancy knot and a ruined bunch of flowers drooping over her forehead.

Helen saw his eyes change and knew he was thinking about kissing her again. Her pulse skittered erratically, then settled into a gallop. In the warm, secret places somewhere inside her, she felt a sweet stirring, like the first hint of a smile.

The Delorio temper he'd stirred to boiling was now simmering, with only a few bubbles rising to the surface now and then. She suspected the anger would return once she'd had a chance to rest.

"I'm furious with you, you know," she said, framing her words with a scowl that felt strangely soft on her lips.

His eyes crinkled into deep lines at the corners, but his mouth remained resolute. "Yeah, I figured you would be."

"By tomorrow it'll be all over Seattle that Constantine Paristeri's bride was kidnapped. Slung over her ex-husband's shoulder like a sack of wheat."

His mouth relaxed slightly. "If I know Con, he's already got his PR lackey spinning out damage control."

"Tell me the truth, Alex. Is that why you pulled this stunt, to embarrass your brother?"

His eyes hardened to blued steel. "I gave you my reasons."

"Because you don't think I should marry Con?"

"I won't repeat all the reasons why that's a mistake. You already know what they are."

"I know I won't break my promise to Con. He's been so unfailingly kind and patient—"

"Bullshit! He's been trying to take you away from me since the first moment he laid eyes on you. Even hinted he'd be willing to pay big-time bucks if I'd agree to disappear for a couple of years."

"That's not true!"

His eyes flashed, and for an instant tension sizzled between them. "I've made my share of mistakes, done things that I'll never shake free of, but I don't lie."

She drew a shaky breath, regretting now that she'd started this. "I know that," she said softly and with feeling that surprised her as much as it seemed to surprise him.

"Give me a chance to prove I've changed, sunshine. Pretend I really am Paris and you're the real Helen of Troy."

Helen blinked, but the drawn look around his eyes was still there. Worse, he was looking at her with so much longing it actually hurt to meet his gaze. The carefree boy she'd met on a misty dock one winter morning had become a man with sadness in his eyes and a scar on his soul.

The urge to caress that dark, world-weary face was nearly overpowering, but she made herself stand very still. "You . . . you're the man who paid triple rate to rent Troy before the official opening?"

"Mary Ruth Costas and I went to high school together. She was only too happy to do an old friend a favor—and earn herself a decent piece of change in the bargain."

"That reservation was made a month ago."

"Something like that. Our son put a lot into that letter he sent me. And no, I didn't come halfway around the world just to spring him from military school, though I can't deny that was part of it."

He captured her hand in his and closed hard fingers around hers. His skin was callused yet wonderfully warm against hers, and she experienced a rush of longing. She'd always loved his hands.

"Nicky was just a baby when I left. We never had a chance to be a family," he said in a husky voice. "I don't know if we can make it work after all this time, but . . ." He broke off, his storm-dark eyes searching hers. She saw currents in the dark depths, the dangerous kind that drew you down fast. "Damn, I'm saying this all wrong."

Helen had to lick her suddenly dry lips before she could make them form words. Even then, her tongue felt thick. "Saying what?" she managed to articulate in a dismayingly husky tone. "That you're sorry for leaving me to raise our son alone? That you're sorry you broke my heart? What exactly are you trying to say, Alex?"

Alex battled back a smothering sense of panic. He was damn near forty years old and yet, all Helen had to do was touch him and he turned into a kid with his first crush. For eight years he'd struggled day and night to convince himself she was better off without him. That Nicky, too, was better off without the anchor of his father's past hanging around his neck.

In Pyrgos he was respected for his ability to work as long and as hard as any other man in the village. He was known as a man who kept his word and the kind of sailor you wanted to have at the wheel in a storm.

"For what it's worth, I'm asking you for a second chance," he said in a voice that came out too fast and too angry. "I'm not rich like my brother, but I can promise you and Nicky will never have to go without." Once the *ESPIARE* was sold, he added to himself.

Helen was too stunned to do more than stare for several endless moments before she managed to summon enough reason to speak.

"I . . . are you asking me to . . . to . . ." Floundering, she pulled her hand from his and used to it gesture helplessly. "To reconcile?" she managed finally.

He ran a hand through his curly hair, leaving furrows in the soft thickness. His expression was solemn and edging toward self-conscious, but his jaw was hard. Determined. "I know that's asking a lot, but, yeah. At least to give it a shot."

Helen drew a careful breath and an even more careful look into his eyes. She saw determination and intelligence and a quiet steadiness that hadn't been there the day he'd left her standing in the rain on the courthouse steps, her divorce decree still clutched in her hand.

"Alex—"

"No, don't give me your answer yet. Give it some thought first."

She drew a careful breath. "I realize that we've always had a certain . . . chemistry between us, but—"

"Chemistry, hell. What we have is spontaneous combustion."

"Physically, yes, but—"

"Damn straight it's physical. I felt it in your office the other night. So did you, although I'm not sure you have the guts to admit it yet."

"You took me by surprise. I was feeling nostalgic."

The pain was there, deep and dark. No matter what tack he took, she took the opposite, staying just out of reach. Like the shimmer of light on the sea at dawn.

Fighting down the need to beg, he cocked his head and regarded her coolly. Sun streaming through the skylight caught fire in her hair and touched her clear skin with gold. Her makeup was smudged, her lips pale without artificial gloss and beguilingly soft.

He'd learned self-discipline in prison and patience in the long years he'd spent without her. What he hadn't learned was a way to resist the invitation of that tempting little mouth.

"Nostalgia, huh?" he mused aloud, his voice lowering a full octave of its own accord. "Interesting concept." He cupped her chin, felt it jerk, and tightened his grip just enough to gentle her without bruising that creamy skin.

Keeping his eyes open, his gaze on her, he brought his mouth to hers. Though he schooled himself to go slowly, the taste of her was intoxicating, making his heat swim and his heart race. Softly, so softly, he increased the pressure until her lips parted with an involuntary sigh.

Her skin smelled of flowers, her hair of sunshine. Instead of the waxy white flowers now drooping forlornly, he saw her with daisies in her hair and in her hands. Daisies and sunshine and the sea—they were Helen. Only Helen.

Her lashes fluttered, then dipped, another breath whispered from her mouth to his. Beneath his fingertips, her pulse throbbed faster, harder, and her skin warmed to the sudden rush of blood.

The same heat was surging in his veins, throbbing in his head, pooling in his groin. The urge to bend her backward onto the wide bed was strong, the fear that he would suddenly prove inadequate stronger.

Easing back, he waited until her lashes fluttered open and her eyes lost their dreamy sheen, waited until the roaring in his head eased off and his blood cooled.

"You'd better get out of those wet things before you catch cold," he said when he felt in control of his voice again.

Helen slowly uncurled her fists and took a few testing breaths. "Don't . . ." She paused to clear a sudden thickness from her throat. "Don't you dare give me orders."

"Okay, so don't change. Suits me either way." His mouth tightened slightly as he looked deeply into her eyes. "If you refuse to give me another chance, that's my loss. But for God's sake, don't turn a deaf ear to your son. He's crying out for help, and if you won't listen, who the hell will?"

With that, he stepped out into the companionway and closed the door.

Seven

True to his word, Alex had brought her bags to the cabin while she'd been soaking away the chill. Wrapped in one of the soft bath sheets she'd found in the bathroom, she lifted the smaller of the two bags to the bed and snapped it open.

A soft groan escaped her lips as she stared at the neatly folded clothing. Everything inside had been purchased expressly for her honeymoon, every item, from the skin out, skimpier and more seductive in design than the garments she usually wore. Now, instead of going on a honeymoon with her new husband, she was heading to Troy as Alex's captive. To live out a fantasy, one that she herself had created.

A reluctant smile tugged at her lips as she imagined the picture they must have made slogging through the sprinkler spray. If it had been Constantine sweeping her away, she would have found it utterly irresistible—and utterly out of character.

Slowly she sank to the bed, her fingers pressing the lips Alex had kissed into tingling fullness. She'd fallen in love with a rogue and a charmer. A man who'd had tears in his eyes when he'd slipped the plain gold band on her finger.

Though he hadn't allowed his lawyer to tell the jury, he'd sold his shares in Greek Isles and set up a trust fund for the two children the drowned woman had left behind. He'd forgotten to check the lifeboat only because one of the passengers that morning had become

separated from her five-year-old daughter, and he'd
scoured the ship until he'd found the child raiding the
refrigerator in the galley. Already behind schedule,
he'd set sail immediately.

It had been Constantine who had drummed promptness into all the skippers. Greek Isles ships left on time
and they arrived on time. All part of the service.

Not once had Alex blamed anyone but himself, not
even when the head of ship maintenance had sworn
under oath he'd never seen a repair request bearing
Alex's signature.

Helen remembered begging Constantine to force the
man tell the truth, only to have Alex's big brother very
calmly, very regretfully tell her that he was convinced
there had never been such a chit.

Con was wrong. In her heart she knew that Alex
hadn't lied. People in maintenance had—callously, deliberately branding him a reckless murderer. She could
still hear the scorn in the judge's voice when he'd pro-
nounced the maximum sentence. Alex had flinched,
then squared his shoulders and allowed the marshal to
shackle those big powerful wrists. She could still see the
look in those smoky blue eyes when the marshal had
taken him away that awful day. Buried in the shock and
guilt had been a grief so terrible she never wanted feel
its like again.

He'd changed in prison, aged overnight. Even after
his release, he'd still been locked up. Caged by his own
conscience. When she'd tried to reach him through the
invisible bars he'd put around himself, he'd pushed her
away. Coldly, silently, the way he'd gone through the
days.

Without his skipper's license which had been revoked
while he'd been in prison, the only jobs he could find
were menial. Humiliating. Still, he'd tried. Just as he'd
tried to make love to his wife—and failed.

Time after time.

Until one night he'd smashed his fist against the
headboard of their bed and broke two knuckles. From
that moment until their divorce six months later he
didn't touch her once.

In a way, she'd died inside.

No other man had ever been able to bring her to life again. Not even Constantine, though she'd told herself a million times all that would change once they married. She knew now that she'd only been deluding herself.

Perhaps she no longer loved Alex Paristeri, but she wanted him. Desperately. She was also terrified to trust her heart to him again.

Frustrated and on edge, she tugged a bra and panties from the bag's side pocket. Fashioned of French silk the color of champagne, both were decidedly skimpy. Certainly nothing like the unadorned nylon she preferred.

Why didn't I at least pack one of my old faithfuls? she asked herself peevishly, even as she ran caressing fingers over the smooth, shimmering silk.

Suddenly she was thinking of Alex and the soft brush his mouth over his. His lips had been smooth as sun-warmed satin, and far too seductive. A nun would have trouble hanging on to her vows when Alex was in a kissing mood. Important things like dignity and decorum and Puritan values were far too easy to forget when that clever, greedy mouth was teasing hers.

And then what? she thought. Watch the heat smoldering in his eyes turn to anguish when his erection wilted. Feel the shudders of self-hatred shaking his big body again? Die a little because she couldn't love him enough or hold him tightly enough to make the pain go away.

But maybe, he'd changed. Maybe he'd found a measure of peace in Greece, maybe even learned to forgive himself.

Maybe they could make it work this time.

As she fitted the silky bra over her breasts, she realized how badly she was shaking. It took three tries to catch the hooks over the eyes.

After throwing on a pair of slacks and a silk blouse, Helen stepped to the mirror above the cabin's built-in dresser to check her reflection.

"Dear God," she muttered, lifting a hand to the once-elegantly smooth upsweep that had taken the

haughty stylist two hours to create. Instead of the calm
and collected executive she'd worked so hard to become, the woman staring back at her looked more like
an eighteenth-century wench who'd just been tumbled
in the hayloft. Or slung over the shoulder of the only
man she'd ever loved.

Alex waited until the spew of threats spilling from the
radio's stereo speakers broke off, then keyed the mike.
"Don't worry, brother, I'll take good care of your fian-
cée for you." He signed off without giving Constantine
a chance to reply. Hell, he had every right to stick it to
the supercilious bastard, in spades, he thought as he
brought the ship closer to land. He should be celebrat-
ing. Instead, he felt sick inside, and more than a little
sad.

They were well north of Seattle now, far enough so
that he'd decided to risk anchoring in a little cove he
knew where the fishing was usually good. Good enough
for Nicky to wet a line while his parents shared a drink,
and maybe a little conversation.

He hoped.

Shifting to put the wind at his back, he checked his
watch, then the sky and figured they would drop anchor
off "Troy" around sundown. If all went well, they'd
have their first meal ashore. He'd included a dozen bottles of Helen's favorite Washington Chablis in the pro-
vision order he'd given to the Fantasy people.

A lifetime ago they'd bought it by the jug and drunk
it over ice on hot summer days. They'd made love to
each other on a beach very much like the one to star-
board.

Yeah, and it would be just his luck she's switched to
something red and expensive. Something Constantine
preferred.

Feeling more tired than he wanted to admit, Alex
watched the Stars and Stripes fluttering from the stan-
dard on the stern.

A lump lodged in his throat as he watched his son's
rapt expression. The boy had seawater in his veins and
a need for adventure in his soul. No wonder he was

going crazy in that landlocked loony bin they called a school.

Well, the kid was done with that.

Alex had given his word and nothing short of death would make him break it. Not this time.

Nicky interrupted his search for seals long enough to cast a worried look over his shoulder. "It's already been an hour, Dad. Maybe you should go check on her."

Alex hid his own worry behind a teasing grin. "Ladies need a lot longer than we do to get themselves organized, so you might as well get used to waiting." He widened his grin, man-to-man. "Course it's almost always worth the wait."

"Yeah, sure, only Mom's always ready way before it's time to leave for work or whatever. She says it's not polite to be late."

"She's right about that." Alex wondered if he would ever make her understand why he was eight years late in coming after her. Or if she would even care.

It almost had destroyed him to leave her once. He had no confidence he could survive losing her again. Since he'd finally learned to like himself enough to fight for what he wanted, he intended to wage all-out war on the lady.

His sweet, adorable, sexy lady.

As though he'd summoned her from the depths of his small store of treasured memories, she suddenly appeared on the bridge. She had changed into white slacks and a shirt the color of fog over a morning sea. Her feet were bare, offering a glimpse of bright pink toenails, and a tantalizing hint of the girl who'd poleaxed him with a smile. Alone in his narrow bed in Pyrgos, that time had seemed a thousand years ago. Now, with the sun warming his face and surrounding her with golden light, it seemed like yesterday.

Suddenly shaken at the thought of all he was risking with this stunt, he drew in a lungful of brine-flavored sea air and courage. It cost him to move slowly toward her when every part of him prodded him to sprint to her side.

As soon as Nicky caught sight of her, he abandoned

his watch by the rail. "Hey Dad, Mom's here," he called, twisting to give Alex an encouraging look.

It hurt Alex to see how eager the boy was to get his mother and father together again. And it humbled him to realize just how lucky he was to have a son as generous with his love and forgiveness as Nick.

Conscious that Helen was eyeing him warily, he made himself relax. "Looks like she put all that extra time to good use, doesn't it, son?" he said as he ambled toward the awning shading the port side cabin.

Nick looked puzzled for an instant before his eyes cleared. "Yeah. Like you said, it just takes ladies longer, but it's worth the wait."

Helen caught the look that passed between father and son and her heart turned over. She'd never seen Nicky more excited, or more eager to please. He was like awkward puppy, desperate to be accepted, and yet, there was a sparkle to him that had been missing for months.

If for nothing else, she should be grateful to her ex-husband. Should be, but couldn't be. Not when her emotions were in a tangled knot and her usually reliable common sense seemed hopelessly scrambled. For the first time in years, she didn't know her own mind—or her heart. She felt adrift without a compass, helplessly at the mercy of a powerful current.

Damn and blast the man, she thought as she brushed the short spiky wisps of hair away from Nicky's broad forehead. He shied from her touch, then seemed to catch himself and went rigid. From the instant he'd popped into the world, red-faced and squalling for his dinner, he'd always been a cuddly boy. Her snuggle bunny.

No matter how absorbed he'd been in a puzzle or how energetically he'd been tearing around their small house, pretending to be Batman one minute, a Ninja turtle the next, he'd invariably gravitated to her side for a quick hug or a flurry of teasing kisses before racing off again. It seemed he needed affection as much as he needed healthy food and fresh air in order to thrive—and laughter. Lots of laughter to hoard against the time when the pain came, as it invariably would. He was just like his father, she realized suddenly and with a clarity of insight that stunned her.

Beneath the sexy, off-center smile and maddening male arrogance was a lonely little boy who only wanted to be loved. And the casual brush of callused hands over her cheek or her arm or the sensitive spot behind her ear was more than a sexual signal. Much, much more, she thought as she tipped her face upward and meshed her gaze with his.

Eyes narrowed against the sun, he offered her a slow, teasing grin that had shivery ripples running her spine. Yet, beneath the laughter in his eyes there was a wariness she'd never noticed before. No, hadn't understood, she corrected with the insight of experience and distance.

The hell-raising rebel who'd fought against restraint of any kind was really a facade, a shield behind which he hid his softer feelings, feelings she suspected now ran deeper and stronger than anyone knew. That was it, wasn't it, she thought. What she'd once called pure cussedness was really a defense against letting himself want too much.

But then, she had her own defenses—against the pain of being left behind, against the anguish of loving a man who fought that love at every turn.

"So, you decided to join the good guys," he teased, reaching out to smooth her collar into place.

Though she longed to fold her hand around that sinewy wrist and hold him close, she did as he expected and batted his hand aside.

"No-good scoundrels, you mean," she declared, flicking Nicky a pointed look that had his face turning red. "A genetic trait obviously passed along through the male line."

Nicky drew his black eyebrows together over the bridge of his sunburned nose and darted a questioning look at his father. "Uh, that's good, right, Dad?"

"Damn straight it is, especially when it comes to impressing the ladies. Particularly the ones who pretend to mind when you steal a kiss."

Before Helen could duck, Alex lowered his head and pressed a hard, possessive kiss on her lips. She felt heat, loneliness, a whisper of danger. And a dark and insidious longing to fold herself into those powerful arms and shelter there forever.

Drawing back, he offered Nick an infuriating look of smug male triumph. "See what I—"

She plowed her fist into Alex's hard stomach and felt a savage satisfaction as the air whooshed from his lungs. "Son of a bitch," he muttered, narrowing his eyes and rubbing his belly. Beside his father, Nicky was biting his lip, his eyes dancing with laughter, his face even redder now.

Alex took a couple of testing breaths, then straightened slowly. His gaze was wary, his mouth twitching. "Okay, maybe I owed you that one."

Apparently losing his battle with hilarity, Nicky burst out laughing, earning himself a dark scowl from his father. "She's got you there, Dad."

"Shut up," Alex muttered, but there was more amusement than sting in his tone. Meeting his gaze, she lifted her head a little higher and refused to acknowledge the pain in her knuckles.

"Now that we've established the rules, how about offering the kidnappee a drink?"

Eight

 *N*icky offered to make the drinks. "Mai-tais," he said, beaming her a grin. "Your favorite—okay?"

"Lovely," she murmured, unwilling to see the eager glow in his eyes disappear.

"You and Dad make yourselves comfortable," he ordered, glancing toward the deck chairs under the awning. "Get to know each other again, or . . . whatever. I'll be right back."

"Yes, sir," Helen teased, though her heart had raced at the thought of the "whatever."

Nick turned to leave, then abruptly spun around. "And Dad, maybe you'd better keep up your guard this time. Mom can be real tough when she's mad."

Alex pressed his hand to the spot that still stung on his belly and grinned his thanks to his son. Nicky lifted a thumb, then took off toward the galley.

"You know, we usually have our fantasy guests sign releases, absolving Greek Isles of any liability," she said when they were alone and seated a few feet from one another in the cool shade.

"Signed it this morning."

"Aha, but I didn't."

"Actually, you did. Nick told you it was a release form allowing him to try out for the soccer team."

"But that's fraud. Or something equally illegal."

"Not if you don't press charges."

"Don't count on that, buster."

He lifted her hand from the arm of the chair and

balanced it on his wide palm. Her skin was shades
lighter than his, her hand smooth where his was rough.
"I thought all women liked to be swept off their feet."
He glanced down at her toes and grinned. "And such
pretty little feet."

She wiggled her toes at him, feeling lighthearted in
spite of her churning emotions. "Not that I care, you
understand, but why are we anchored?"

"The crew needed a breather."

Leaning back, he pressed her hand to his thigh,
stretched out his legs, and regarded her through drowsy
eyes. Sheathed in jeans worn white at the stress points,
his long, lithe muscles looked powerful, even at rest.
He'd crushed the femur of the left in a motorcycle accident in his teens, leaving him with a slight limp that was
only noticeable in rainy weather, or when he was very
tired.

"Did you have trouble getting time off for a visit?"
she asked, imagining those long legs planted wide on
the slippery deck of a trawler in a fierce Mediterranean
gale.

"Not enough to matter."

"Nicky said you're first mate now?"

His mouth slanted. "Yeah, I get all the cushy jobs,
like scrubbing the fish scales off the deck after the grunt
labor has gone home to a hot meal and a bottle of
retsina."

"Have you ever thought about owning a boat of your
own? Maybe one like this one someday?"

"What makes you think this isn't mine?"

"The price tag, for one. I figure upper six figures."

"Quote I heard was closer to seven." Between the
thick blunt lashes his eyes had a sleepy look she didn't
trust. Like most everything he did, Alex had no middle
ground. When he was tired, he slept, rarely moving, his
mind shut down and recharging. When he'd had
enough sleep, he came awake in an instant, fully aware
and ready to move.

Restless suddenly, she pulled her hand free, shifted
against the soft cushion, and looked around for Nicky.
A seagull landed on the stern, took a moment to preen

his wing feathers, then took flight again, soaring upward with a freedom she envied. It would be lovely to wake up to a day that wasn't packed with appointments or meetings. By the time she'd given a few minutes here, a few there, there was usually precious few left to squander on personal pleasure.

A smile flitted through her mind as she thought about two solid weeks on Troy. If only she'd packed books, she thought, or the half-finished sweater she'd started to knit for Nicky two summer ago. She hadn't, however, because she'd expected to be in Acapulco. With another man entirely.

A man she didn't miss nearly as much as she should, she realized with a pang of guilt.

"Painful thoughts?" Alex asked, drawing her startled gaze.

"Actually I was thinking about time."

He arched an eyebrow, giving him a diabolical look she found utterly adorable. "Any conclusions?"

"Yes. There's never enough."

"Depends on who's controlling your life. Me, I've got all the time I need. Too much, sometimes."

Before Helen could reply, Nicky returned with their drinks, which were perched precariously on a silver tray. With a mother's instinct, she took one look at the wobbling glasses and leaped up to him, reaching automatically for the edge of the tray and one of the drinks.

"Not that one," Nicky said sharply. Then, softening his tone with a grin, he added, "I just made yours special. More bananas and pineapple on the stick."

"Mmm, a man after my heart." Helen took the drink he turned toward her and treated herself to a cautious sip, and smacked her lips at the drink's sweet bite. "Very good, Nicky! I'm impressed."

He watched her take another sip. "Do you really like it?"

"Oh, yes, it's wonderful." Helen resumed her seat, holding her drink carefully to keep it from spilling. "Although I have to admit I'm wondering where and when you learned to mix drinks." She directed a pointed gaze toward Alex who shook his head. "Don't look at me, Mom. I take my drinks neat."

Remembering too many nights when he'd come home drunk and brooding had her lips tightening. Determined not to ruin Nicky's triumph, she returned her gaze to his face. "So what's your secret, honey? Inquiring minds want to know."

Though he beamed her a blazing smile, he looked a tad uneasy. "Uncle Costas taught me how to make maitais. Not from scratch or anything. He uses a mix."

Costas Paristeri, Nicky's great-uncle, had come to the states last summer for a prolonged visit. While she and Constantine had gone on their engagement cruise, he'd offered to stay with Nicky at the house on Bainbridge Island.

"Well, your uncle Costas uses a very good mix," Helen observed. "I'd like to get the name of it, in fact. A person would swear an expert mixed it."

"There's plenty left," Nicky offered quickly. "I made lots, just in case."

"Just in case what?" Alex asked as he bit down on a chunk of pineapple.

"I just thought you guys might be in the mood for a party. Us being together like a real family and all." Nicky shifted his gaze from one to the other before fixing his attention on his glass. "Dumb idea, I guess."

Helen took a deep breath. "Honey, your dad and I don't hate each other. We never did. We just couldn't live together."

"Maybe if you tried harder to get along, like you're always telling me."

"That's enough, son. You're embarrassing your mother." Alex spoke softly, his tone mild. He rarely raised his voice. He didn't have to. Not when he could lay a person open with a glance, or shiver your spine with a whisper.

"Sorry, Mom," Nicky muttered, looking anything but.

"That's okay," she returned, forcing a smile.

Her good spirits muted, Helen settled back in the cane-backed chair and tried to relax. For Nicky's sake.

More thirsty than she realized, she found herself sipping frequently until her glass was empty. Fast as a thought, Nicky replaced her empty glass with another that was all but brimming.

"You did make these light, I hope," she murmured, taking another testing sip.

"Sure thing. I mean, you never drink much, except fancy wine."

"I like wine, fancy or otherwise," she agreed before treating herself to another swallow. "But this—" She tapped her glass with a glossy nail. "This is ambrosia."

"Oh no, Mom, it's a mai-tai. Remember?"

She giggled and thought that Nicky really was becoming a thoughtful young man. Mount Vernon was working wonders, and Alex wanted to yank him off to Greece. Which, of course, she simply would not allow, no way. Having her baby gone for a month at a time at Christmas and in summer was torture enough, she reminded herself as she savored another swallow. Alex just didn't understand. Or did he?

Blinking, she tried to imagine what it was like for him, seeing Nicky so seldom, having to maintain a long-distance relationship the best way he could. With letters and cards, a weekly phone call that had to cost him a good chunk of his paycheck.

She leaned her elbow on the arm of the chair and studied the two exasperating males who'd turned her day—and her nicely ordered future—upside down.

Handsome devils, both of them, she mused, running her tongue over the sugary taste of mai-tai clinging to her lips. Though Nicky's face still carried the softness of youth, the promise of his father's lean angular looks was more than clear. Around the mouth, mostly, where the dimple that winked so boyishly now would someday have females of all ages preening whenever it flashed their way.

His eyebrows, too, had the same fierce slant, the chin the same stubborn jut. Nicky had her nose, dotted with freckles instead of sun-burnished. Alex's nose was crooked, where it had taken a fist once too often; and his face carried an entire collection of scars, mostly lit-

tle ones that added seasoning to a face that would have
been much too pretty without them. A warrior's face on
the man, an intriguing promise on the son.

"Hey, look, Mom's glass is empty," Nicky said suddenly, springing to his feet. "I'll get the pitcher."

Sweet boy, she thought. Trying so hard to make them
into a family. Which maybe wasn't such a terrible idea.

"Helen?"

She loved Alex's voice, especially when he was
amused. Like velvet whispering over razored steel.
"Hmm?"

"Are you okay? You seem a little . . . distracted."

She considered that with the solemn attention it deserved. Only suddenly, she was nineteen and falling
hopelessly in love.

"It was the eyes," she mused. "You have beautiful
eyes, especially when you smile. I think I missed your
smile most of all. For a long time, till I made myself
stop." She saw his mouth firm, and felt a deep sorrow
run through her.

"We could have worked it out, you know. . . . It
wasn't your drinking that drove us apart, or even the
impotence. We could have gotten through all that if
you'd just swallowed that blasted Greek pride of yours
and gotten professional help. But you didn't care
enough to try. I think that's what hurt the most." She
drew a shaky breath, set aside her empty glass and went
out onto the side deck to stand at the rail.

The water lapped against the midnight hull in a
rhythm all its own, and the air was salt-scented and
moist. The sun, which had still been hanging in the
sky not long before, had suddenly sunk onto the lip of
the horizon, its radiance casting dappled silver across
the water, making it look as though every ripple was the
setting for a magnificent diamond.

Feeling unaccountably light-headed, Helen tried to
focus on the individual sparkles. They swam together in
a shimmering blur. As impossible as it was, she felt a
little tipsy. Scotch that. She felt a whole lot tipsy.

She jumped with a start when she felt the heat from

Alex's body warming her skin. "Do you have to sneak up on people like that?"

Lord, but he was the softest walking man. Like a big, cautious cat, wary of getting too close. A panther, she thought, reaching up a hand to touch his hair.

He trapped her hand with his, his fingers linking in a warm bracelet around her wrist. "Honey, I've been standing here next to you for over five minutes."

Watching her while she watched the sunset? "You have?"

Did Constantine ever watch her so quietly? she mused. Or was he always too busy telling her what to do?

"Sunshine?" Alex leaned down to look more deeply into her eyes. He smelled good, like the sea, and the gold ring in his ear gave his hard face a hint of mystery.

"I like the earring." She moved closer to him.

"It's my wedding ring," he murmured. "I had it converted a few years back."

Helen's heart caught. "Why?"

"At first, to remind myself of all I'd tossed away. And then . . ." He stopped and shrugged.

"Then what?" she prompted, knowing that she had just crossed a very dangerous line, yet unable to stop herself.

His eyes darkened, turned potent. Drew her in. "I needed to feel close to you."

She swayed toward him, only to have his big hands grasp her shoulders to steady her. "Steady, there, sailor," he teased, but his eyes were nearly as dark as the highest slice of twilight sky.

A feeling she didn't want to analyze ran through her, causing her to stiffen. His grip gentled, then his hands fell away.

"Where's Nicky?" she demanded, glancing over his shoulder.

"He went to get us refills on our drinks."

Hers, actually. He'd barely touched his own. The drink he'd downed at Smitty's had broken an eight-year abstinence. His stomach hadn't totally recovered from the shock.

Uncomfortable with his nearness and the memories, she glanced around. "I wish he'd hurry. Not that I need another drink. Just the opposite." She laughed suddenly, then wondered what had prompted the giggle. "I feel sort of woozy."

She moved to prop an elbow on the rail and missed her mark by a good inch. Alex grabbed her by her other arm to steady her.

"Sunshine, are you drunk by any chance?"

"No, I'm Helen of Troy. And you're the man who stole me away." She ran her tongue over her lips and realized they'd grown numb. "Oops, I think I'm losing my face."

He curled his large hands over her shoulders. "Son of a bitch." Glancing toward the galley, he called, "Nick! Get your butt on deck, now!"

It seemed to Helen that Nicky popped up from between the deck boards, gone one moment, there the next. He looked anxiously at his father.

"Is it working?"

"Is what working?" Alex demanded, making no attempt to gentle his tone. He knew that look. The kid was up to something.

"The Jamaican rum. Uncle Costas says its so strong that it can tote double and kick up behind. I thought it might make Mom relax and start feeling romantic."

Alex stifled a curse, and contented himself with a long, hard look that had Nick's grin fading. "Mistake, Nick. Big mistake."

Dimly Helen realized that Alex had an iron-hard arm clasped around her waist and that her breasts were flattened against his ribs. She leaned back to get some distance between their upper torsos, becoming aware an instant too late that her spine seemed to have lost all its starch.

"Alex?" she said softly.

"Hang on, sunshine," he murmured before returning his attention to their mutual offspring. "Exactly how much did you put in the damn drink?"

Nicky shrugged. "I dunno. I just poured and kept

tasting to make sure it wasn't strong enough for her to notice."

"Alex?" Helen tried again, with more urgency this time.

"What?" he asked with a sharp edge to his voice.

Helen tried to focus on his swimming face. "I think . . . any minute now . . . I'm going to be sick."

Nine

*A*lex woke gasping for air. For an instant he was still in the prison shower room, his hands tied behind him, his face smashed into the slimy concrete floor. He'd fought hard, but there were three of them. Seasoned cons, lifers, with nothing to lose.

He'd taken a knee to the groin and gone down. They raped him, then. One after another, and then kicked in his ribs when they'd finished. Bastards would never do that to another green con again, he thought, running a shaky hand through his sweat-wet hair.

He hadn't had a nightmare this bad in years. Not since he'd started construction of the ship on which he now sailed. The final design had evolved from the sketches he'd done in prison to keep himself sane. It had taken him seven years to scare up enough backing to lay the keel. He'd done much of the work himself, his body growing as hard as the steel he'd welded day after day, and sometimes long into the night. He'd lived like a monk, his needs few, an aching loneliness his constant companion. Night after night he dreamed of the woman he'd left, yet loved more than life itself.

Fighting down the need to bolt, he left the narrow bunk in the captain's sea cabin and walked through the dimly lit companionway to the ladder leading to the deck. Topside, the night sky had a clarity that soothed his jittery nerves, and he spent a long moment reciting the names of the stars until his heart rate settled into a more even rhythm and the last of the terror had leeched from his mind. Breathing deeply, he turned his gaze toward the darker shape fifty yards to the east.

Helen's Troy.

And his last shot at winning her back.

They'd arrived at the tiny island around nine and anchored where the sea bottom started its sharp slope upward. With only Nick to help him, he'd decided to wait until daylight to tie up to the short pier.

The charts showed shallow water rimming most of the land mass, with only a narrow channel gouged into the sea floor where the pier had been constructed. Given the state-of-the-art navigation on the bridge, he could, if pressed, thread an even smaller needle. And only if he were alone, with no one else's safety at stake. Never again would he take foolish risks with anyone else's life.

Curling his hands around the railing, he dropped his head and asked forgiveness from a God he scarcely knew nor truly trusted. Still, the habits of youth were hard to break, if not particularly comforting.

No, making amends to the dead was beyond him. It wasn't all that easy with the living. In fact, it was turning out to be damn painful. But then he deserved more than his share of suffering for the stupid mistakes he'd made.

Sometimes, in one of the black moods that came less frequently now, he suspected that what happened to him in prison was a fitting punishment for his sins.

With memory came a wave of discouragement so deep he felt swamped with it. Saturated. What if he hadn't wrestled the demons inside him into silence after all? What if he wasn't able to get past the fear of failing her again that clawed at him night and day?

"Stow the self-pity, Paristeri," he muttered, watching the phosphorescent curl of a wave angling toward shore. He'd set his course. Now it was up to him to go the distance.

Lifting his hot face to the cooling breeze, he let his mind linger on the image of her tucked into the big bed below decks, her face flushed from the lingering affects of the rum.

Poor baby, he thought, scrubbing his hands down his now-stubbled checks. By morning she would have a hell of a headache and, if she got lucky, little memory of the hour she'd spent hanging over the rail while he'd rubbed her back and ran through a mental series of fitting punishments for their ornery son.

By the time her stomach had emptied, the rum was already in her bloodstream, enough, by his rough estimation, to take down a stevedore. Sick with worry at the gray tinge to her skin, he'd come damn close to returning to port and hustling her to the nearest hospital. But once she'd stopped retching, some of the color had returned to her cheeks and her pulse had been strong, if a bit too fast.

Damn that kid and his bright ideas, he thought, scowling into the thick darkness. Once he'd gotten Helen bedded down and reassured himself that she wasn't in any danger, he'd blistered Nicky's ears, but good.

Letting his shoulders droop, he thought about the things he'd done at Nick's age. Half-assed, stupid things. Pranks that could have turned deadly. Shit, he'd been a poor excuse for a human being. No wonder he'd ended up on the outside looking in like a pitiful character in a damn story by Dickens.

Suddenly bone tired, he turned toward the cabin, only to give a start at the sight of his son standing stiffly a few feet away. The boy's features were shadowed in the dim glow of the mast light, his eyes huge.

"Trouble sleeping, son?" he asked when Nicky tried for a smile—and failed miserably.

"I guess," came the dispirited reply.

"A guilty conscience is a bitch, isn't it?"

Nick lifted one bony shoulder in a half-hearted shrug that stabbed Alex's heart. "I didn't meant to make Mom sick," he muttered in a sullen voice. "But I guess you don't believe that."

"Why wouldn't I?"

Nick slid his gaze from his, looking first at the inky surface of the sea and then at the scuffed sneakers he'd put on to replace the sodden black dress shoes.

"That first day at my new school, Uncle Con told the commandant I was a liar," he said in a voice dulled by hurt. "I think he meant for me to hear him say it, too."

Alex had learned the hard way that the man who lost his temper first lost his edge—and the fight. Consequently, he'd devoted considerable time and energy to controlling the sudden rages that seemed to come boiling up from some dark, angry place inside. It had been a lot of years since he'd felt fury so searing he had to take more than a split-second or two to master the urge to kill his brother.

Even as he felt his blood pressure leveling and the heat fading from a sudden pit in his belly, he'd allowed himself a fast image of his brother's face after he'd finished with him. Then, banishing the image, he dropped his around his son's slumping shoulders and managed a decent imitation of a smile.

"I don't know about you, son, but I'm getting damn cold out here. How about we raid the galley for some of that hot chocolate I saw in one of the baskets."

Alex finished the last of the chocolate he'd allowed to sit untouched and cooling while he'd worked to put Nick at ease. For the first fifteen minutes or so he'd done most of the talking, pulling a topic out of the air and tossing it into the pot. Finally, just when he was about to come right out and ask Nick what the hell he got excited about, he'd mentioned an old Samurai sword he'd seen once in a shop window.

That had done it.

Nick had been talking nonstop since then. About the difference between a sword and a cutlass, about the secrets of tempering steel, anything and everything, bouncing from one topic to another, his eyes shining and his restless feet thudding against the door of the counter where he had perched during a particular intense and surprisingly technical discussion of broadswords.

"There's this shop near the school that had one for sale. The guy said if I'd put down a hundred dollars, he'd hold it for me until I could save the rest."

"Sounds like a good plan."

"I had almost enough, too. Twelve hundred dollars."

Gut tightening, Alex tightened his fingers around the heavy mug. "Had?" he asked quietly.

Nicky's mouth drooped into a sullen line, and the light faded from his eyes. "Uncle Con made me use it to replace a stupid stained glass window in his stupid house on the island."

"Yeah? Why was that?"

The boy suddenly developed a fascination with the tips of his sneakers. "He was trying to teach me how to putt, but the dumb ball kept going every place but the hole."

Alex thought about the time when he'd gotten hooked on Little League and Con had tried to teach him to hit a curve ball. They'd ended up screaming obscenities at one another. A year later, Alex had taught himself to hit the curve, and Con no longer came to his Little League games.

He shifted, uncomfortable with the feeling the recollection aroused. "Made you mad, did it?" he asked mildly.

Nicky nodded. "Uncle Con kept going on and on about not paying attention and keeping my eye on the ball, and how I would never amount to anything unless I learned to take orders, and the next thing I know, I hauled off and whacked the damn ball with the putter. I didn't mean for it to break the window. It just . . . did."

Alex pushed his chair onto the two back legs and folded his arms over his chest. "I assume that's when Uncle Con went ballistic."

"Completely." One corner of Nick's mouth quirked. "I never saw anyone get so red in the face."

"Sounds like my brother hasn't changed much over the years."

Nick rummaged in the basket next to him for a candy bar. "Did he get mad like that when you a kid?"

"Constantly."

"Yeah?" Nicky tore off the candy wrapper and treated himself to a huge bite.

Seeing the rapture on the boy's face reminded him that he'd skipped dinner in order to watch over Helen. "Toss me one of those, will you Nick?"

"Sure," the boy muttered through a mouthful of caramel.

A man who savored his pleasures, Alex took his time peeling back the wrapping, then bit into the chocolate and chewed. He liked the taste of chocolate. Craved it, actually, which was why he rarely allowed himself more than a bite or two.

"Dad, are you sure Mom's okay?" Nicky asked before licking chocolate from his fingers.

"Yes, Nick, I'm sure."

"She's probably gonna be royally pissed at me, though? Right?"

"Wouldn't you be?"

"Yeah, I guess, only . . ." The boy paused. Swallowed hard. "Will she hate me forever, do you think?"

"Son, on your worst day, you couldn't do anything to make your mother stop loving you. If you never believe another thing I tell you, believe that."

Nicky chewed on his lip, considering. "How come she stopped loving *you?*"

Alex grabbed extra oxygen. "I blew it, son. Big time. I had this vicious hate going on in my belly, and nothing else seemed to matter. Not your mom, not you. Nothing."

"On account of you killing those people when your ship wrecked?"

Careful to keep his gaze steady on his son's, he nodded. "That was part of it, yeah. A big part. But there were other things, too, things I don't intend to tell you or anyone else." Except Helen, he added silently—provided he managed to work up the courage.

"Do you still love her?"

Funny, in all the times they'd spent together, Nicky had never before asked him that question. "I guess I must," he said, glancing toward the island that had cost him the best part of his bank balance to rent for fourteen short days. A lifetime.

Shifting his gaze to his son's somber eyes, he forced a

grin. "Hell yes, I love her," he grated as he got to his feet.

"So you're going to fight for her, just like we talked about?" Nicky prodded with the unabashed eagerness of a kid half his age.

"Damn straight, I am," he said with more bravado than hope of winning.

A light blazed in Nicky's eyes for an instant, then winked out. "What if it's too late? What if she decides to marry Uncle Con after all?"

Over my lifeless carcass, Alex though, clamping down hard on the same fear. "Then I guess you and I had better figure out a way to live with it."

Ten

*H*elen opened her eyes, winced at the flash of searing pain lancing her eyeballs, and closed them again. But not before she'd had a glimpse of deep-set blue eyes in a bronzed face hovering somewhere above her.

Like a disembodied wraith, she thought, frowning. Even that slight movement of her facial muscles hurt and she let out a low moan.

"How do you feel?" Though Alex had very kindly pitched his voice low, scarcely above a whisper, she winced at the sound.

"Like I've died and gone straight to hell," she managed to grind out.

"Any particular section?"

"Mm, the place where they send the mothers of almost-teenage sons." Opening one eye, she glared at him. "I'll never forgive you for this."

His mouth quirked. "How about if I bring you a Bloody Mary?"

The thought of pouring more alcohol into her queasy stomach made her gag. "I'd rather you just shoot me and toss my body overboard," she murmured before turning to bury her face in the pillow.

She thought she heard him laugh softly—right before he brushed his mouth over her hot forehead. "Go back to sleep, sunshine. You'll feel better when you wake up again."

She was just drifting toward oblivion when she felt a

wonderful coolness settle on her forehead. Eyelashes fluttering, she sighed in relief—and thought she heard Alex murmur her name in a voice so full of longing she knew she was dreaming.

When she woke again, the haze of early morning had been replaced by bright sunshine filtering through the portholes. The cabin was blissfully still, with only a distant drumming noise coming from somewhere beyond the four walls. Inhaling slowly so as not to jar her still-aching head, she closed her eyes the better to savor the salty scent and fresh air.

Cautiously she took stock. She was lying under a single white sheet, wearing only her bra and panties. The monstrous headache was gone, as was the horrible roiling feeling in her stomach. Still her mouth was painfully dry, and she felt kitten weak. Maybe five on a scale of ten, she decided glumly. Definitely not top-notch.

As soon as she could summon sufficient strength to rise from the huge bed, she intended to have a straightforward talk with her son, the little idiot. Imagine, trying to get his mother looped in order to help his father fast-talk her into bed.

As if she would be that foolish. That gullible. That . . . tempted.

Forgetting why she'd ended up in bed in the first place, she started to get up, only to freeze as a knife sliced through her skull. She moaned, and neon squiggles darted across her field of vision. At the same time the odd drumming noise she'd noticed earlier ended abruptly.

Must be the engines stopping, she thought, and wondered if Alex was on the bridge. Two seconds later the door to the bathroom opened and Alex, dressed only in white shorts, the boxy kind he'd once hated but wore because she considered them sexy. The thin cotton stretched taut against his hard buttocks, stark white against the dark skin of his heavy thighs.

When he saw her watching, he smiled and veered toward the bed. "Good morning, sunshine." He smoothed back her hair and brushed a kiss across her forehead before sitting down on the edge of the mattress. He smelled of clean male flesh and soap. His hair was damp and pushed back from his face, the ends curling against his corded neck.

His chest was rock hard, sinewy muscle layered on sinewy muscle. The inky triangle of chest bisecting his corded midsection, arrowing down to the elastic band of his shorts had been towel dried to soft, clinging curls, his two nipples hard, white pebbles in the thatch. He was so beautifully formed she could count each individual rib. His stomach was flat, taut as a drum. She couldn't see his navel very well. It was hidden inside a sexy swirl of hair.

"Still think you're in hell, sunshine?" His tone was gentle, with only a whisper of amusement shading the husky baritone.

"I must be, since you're here too." Though her fingers itched to pull the sheet over her head, she refused to let him see her discomfort, discomfort that increased when he reached for her hand and entwined their fingers snugly. His hand was hard, calluses over calluses, as familiar once as her own.

"Ah, sunshine, you wound me deeply."

"Good!"

His laugh filled the room, a deep rich sound that rumbled from that wide, deep chest like a precious gift. "Don't tell me you're still holding a little thing like kidnapping against me?"

"I certainly am, plus destruction of property and mayhem. Definitely mayhem." She tried not to think of three hundred sodden party guests stampeding for cover, thousand-dollar hats drooping and custom-tailored suits shrinking, but the image refused to fade. "As we speak, Con's lawyer is no doubt dealing with three hundred claims for damaged wedding finery."

He flashed her a grin that was as much ingenuous delight as determined male. "I'd pay major money to anyone who'd caught it on tape."

Helen bit her lip, but the laughter bubbling inside finally erupted. "It's not funny," she declared when she caught her breath.

Something changed in his eyes, like a door opening a crack. "I'd almost forgotten how adorable you are when you laugh." Though he was grinning, his voice had taken on a haunted quality that moved her deeply.

"Forget it, Paristeri, I'm immune to your flattery," she teased, though her throat was suddenly tight.

"Adorable and irresistible and just a bit hungover, I suspect."

"Don't remind me, please."

"Head still hurting?" His thumb moved slowly, seductively over the back of her hand, sending sensual signals spiraling through her brain.

"A little." Was that her voice coming out so breathless, as though she actually wanted to encourage him?

"Want some aspirin?" He lifted their entwined hands to his mouth and kissed her wrist. Powerless to stop the shivers running through her, she frowned.

"Not on an empty stomach." Her voice hitched.

His mouth slanted, easing long deep grooves into both lean cheeks. "A kiss to make it better?" Before she could shake her head, he was leaning closer, his gaze hot on her lips. Instead of covering her mouth with his, however, he lowered his head to her breasts and rubbed his cheek back and forth over the nipples.

Though the sheet covered her, she felt her flesh respond as though his mouth was sliding over bare flesh, growing hot where the hardening nipples tugged her breasts taut. She felt her skin grow damp where his breath filtered through the sheet. A soft moan escaped her lips, and, with an answering groan, he opened his mouth and touched each nipple with his tongue.

She drew breath through her parted lips and dug her head deeper into the pillow. She should stop him, and she would have, but the delicious tingling spreading through her felt so good after so many years of wanting.

"I . . . Nicky?"

"Busy." He buried his face between her softly giving breasts, his breath hot and moist. Shivering, she burrowed her fingers into his hair. Cool to the touch, it curled around her finger, dark as night. Through half lowered lids she saw the flash of gold in his ear. The ring she'd given him.

Instantly, it all came back, the bleak look in his eyes whenever he looked at her, the long scary nights he'd spent thrashing through some terrible nightmare, his harsh refusal when she tried to comfort him. And always, the rage in his eyes when he tried to make love to her and failed.

"Please, Alex," she heard herself pleading in desperation. "Please stop."

He stiffened, then eased backward and lifted his head. His face was taut, his thick black brows drawn over eyes as dark as charcoal with only a hint of blue. "Too soon?"

She drew a breath. Shook her head.

"Worried about Con?" His eyes turned guarded.

"I should be, but . . . somehow, I'm not." Perhaps the guilt she should feel would come later. If it did, she would deal with it.

"Tell me you don't love him," he grated, his voice rough and a whisper short of pleading.

"I don't think I ever really did." For an instant, the rogue's mask he wore to cover a lifetime of hurt slipped, showing the vulnerable man inside.

"Thank God," he muttered as he pried her hand free of the sheet and pressed it palm down against his chest, holding it there. "Feel the power you have over me, sunshine." His heart was slamming hard against his ribs, sending shock waves bouncing off his skin. Her throat went dry, and, in spite of the residual affects of too much mai-tai, she felt her body coming alive in secret sensitive places only he had mapped.

"I'm . . . afraid to love you again."

Pain flooded his eyes as he brought her hand to his mouth and kissed her wrist. "It will be better this time," he murmured, his voice thick.

"It hurt so much when you would start to kiss me and then . . . turn away. I could never make you understand that it was okay. I was willing to wait for you to work through the pain."

"I was an idiot. Selfish." He separated her fingers

and kissed the tips one by one, his breath moist and tickling, his lips ardent. "God, you're beautiful," he murmured, his gaze hot on hers. "All of you. I nearly went out of my mind when I put you to bed."

Bemused, besotted, she glanced toward the neat pile of clothes on a nearby chair. Shirt, slacks. "I could have slept in my clothes."

His face changed, reddened. "You, uh . . . when you were hanging over the rail, the wind—"

"Spare me," she pleaded hoarsely, closing her eyes.

"Don't be embarrassed, honey. You cleaned me up plenty of times in the past. I was happy to return the favor—even if I did have to take a cold shower afterward."

"Shut up," she murmured, but somehow her hands were busy stroking his hair, and she was looking up into the eyes of the man she loved, had never stopped loving.

"Make love to me, Alex. Please."

Even as a smile lit his eyes, his face grew tortured. "I'll do my best, but . . . " He hauled air into his granite chest, then mustered a smile. "I don't know if . . ."

"If it doesn't work this time, we'll just keep . . . working at it until we get it right," she said, brushing his hard cheek with the back of one hand.

"Ah, sunshine, I love you. God help me, so much." His mouth came down on hers, searing her with his need. Heat spread like wildfire until her body was trembling.

Drawing back, he eased the cover to her waist. Her nipples were yearning hard beneath champagne silk, and her breasts felt swollen and aching.

"Touch me, Alex," she pleaded, arching upward. "I . . . hurt."

"So do I," he whispered, bending low to swirl his tongue around one breast, then the other. She moaned, her hands clutching the sheet.

"Ah, sunshine, let me . . . damn bra."

She sighed a giggle as she rolled to the side. His hands seemed to tremble as they freed the hook and gently, caressing eased the straps from her shoulders and down her arms. He caressed her with his eyes, his face lined with emotion. She held her breath, waiting.

"I thought I remembered," he whispered before laving one pink nipple with his tongue. "So beautiful." He nipped swollen flesh with his teeth, sending a flare of pleasure sizzling deep. "And I've never stopped wanting you. Not ever."

Enthralled, she moaned his name, tension building. His hand moved the sheet lower, and she felt the cool whisper of sea air over bare skin. She ached with love for him. She burned.

She felt his hands on her thighs, stroking, caressing, parting her legs to brush over the thin silk barrier between them. Her breathing stopped, then changed rhythm, becoming rapid, straining.

"Easy, love," he whispered, but when he stood to slip free of his shorts, his movements were jerky, impatient.

Released from the underwear's constraint, his flesh stood rigid, swollen with blood. Throbbing.

For her.

With one hand he swept the sheet back, then gently eased himself down next to her. Between kisses, he freed her from her panties, then replaced their cool texture with the hot moisture of his breath as he slipped his tongue into that downy nest and tasted.

Shivering, helpless, she raked her fingers over his hard shoulders, desperate to take all of him inside, yet knowing he had to set his own rhythm, find his own way through the morass of past failures.

"Honey, I can't . . ."

"It's okay," she managed to whisper in an agony of disappointment.

". . . wait much longer," he went on before sliding upward, his chest skimming her breasts, his arousal pressing against her soft mound. He braced his arms, hovered over her, his eyes smoldering, hungry.

The erotic message made her weak, and she whimpered, half-plea, half-pleasure. "Now, Alex, now. Please, oh please."

She spread her legs wider, reached for him as he thrust slowly into her, filling her to her core, hot and hard. She heard him cry out, felt him begin to move, and then she was moving with him, her hand clutching, his mouth ravishing. His plunging thrusts became frenzied, his flesh harder. Hotter.

Mindless, moaning, she railed against the delicious tension, building, building. Tipping over the edge, she cried his name, heard his answering cry. She shuddered at the explosive release, felt him shudder. Needing to see him, she opened her eyes, saw him watching her. There were tears in his eyes.

Eleven

*A*lex lay on his back, one hand tucked under his head, the other curled around his lover's waist. Lying unabashedly naked, she curled against him like a sleepy cat basking in the sun, one sleek leg crooked over his thighs, one arm lazily hooked around his neck.

He had never been so happy—or so scared. Now that he knew his body wouldn't fail him—or her—he knew he would want to make love to her again and again. In this bed, on deck under the stars, on a beach somewhere. In his solitary bed in the shabby little apartment above Minerva's Bistro.

She'd made love with him, yes, but she hadn't said she would go with him to Greece. Sooner or later, he had to know. At the moment, however, he only wanted to savor the feeling of her warm soft flesh against his.

He'd never fully understood just how entwined his heart and his body were before. Now, with Helen in his arms, he knew he would never be able to separate the two again. Knowing he might lose her even now terrified him more than the worst of his nightmare.

"Mmm, you smell good," Helen murmured, nuzzling his neck with her nose. "Soapy, with just a hint of manly sweat."

Alex angled his head to look into her face. Her cheeks were pink, her eyes clear and just a little sleepy. Smiling, he mentally added sex to his long list of hang-over cures, though he doubted he would ever take another drink. Why should he, when just holding Helen close made him drunker than any booze ever could?

"You smell like woman," he murmured, kissing her nose. "And sex."

Her eyes clouded, and he felt his guard drop in place. "Is that what we just did? Have sex?"

Alex felt his heart thud. "Is that what it felt like to you? Straight sex, no strings, no commitment?" Though he let a lazy smile play over his lips, his mouth went dry.

Helen watched his eyes narrow at the corners. Not much, but enough to know he had drawn inside again to protect that vulnerable heart few others had ever seen. Her own swelled with feeling. Wanting him to know how marvelous she thought he was, in body and soul, she lifted her head and brushing a long, lingering kiss over that hard, proud mouth. "We've never had straight sex," she murmured, her lips close to his. "Not from the first moment you touched me."

"And with Con?" He knew he was out of line, a jealous ass with no business asking that question. He'd had to ask it anyway.

"Con and I never slept together." Her gaze stayed level on his, as enticing as the sea.

"I'm . . . glad," he said, his tone hoarse.

"So am I," she murmured, returning her head to his chest. Her hair sifted over him like a silken mantle, alive with the color of the sun. Lifting a hand, he played with the soft strands, his body stirring again.

"Marry me again?" he asked, his tone light, his gut tight.

"I want to, but . . ."

He stilled his angle, shifted to see her face. "But what?"

"I have responsibilities to consider. To the company and Con. I know now I was crazy to even think of marrying a man I knew I didn't love, but—"

"Trust me, Helen. Con will survive."

Helen heard the harsh note in his voice and sighed. "I know he will. And I know Fantasy would survive without me."

"But you love what you do, is that it?"

Helen drew a relieved breath. "Oh Alex, I do! We started with so little, just a crazy idea I came up with when I was reading Nicky a story one night, and a staff of three, all green as grass." Remembering had her sitting up on her knees, her hands splaying over his soft chest hair.

"So do the same thing in Pyrgos." She heard the confident tone in his voice and marveled at his belief in her.

"It would take start-up capital," she mused, taking a quick mental inventory.

He traced the veins in her hand with a raspy fingertip. "How much?"

"More than I have, even if I sell my house." His body was beautiful, she realized, skimming her gaze over the roped muscles lying relaxed and yet firm under the bronzed skin.

"Could be I might be able to raise the rest, once *ESPIARE* is sold." He rubbed his palm against her nipple and she inhaled in pleasure.

"ESPIARE?" she managed to inquire fairly rationally.

"Mmm." He gestured with his free hand toward the cabin.

Swiveling slowly, she studied her surroundings, her throat growing tighter and tighter. The wood was dark and rich and rubbed to a delicate glow. The thick blue carpet under her feet had a luxuriant feel, and the brass accents on the built-in dressers and closets gleamed. Above the bed was the window to the stars she'd always envisioned. This room, at least, was just as she'd described her dream ship to Alex years ago.

Feeling disoriented all of a sudden, she glanced down to see him watching her intently, his head cocked to one side, his fathomless blue eyes focused on her face, an absorbed half smile playing over his mouth, just as he'd watched as she sat on a blanket spread over sand and described the ship she wanted him to build for them someday.

Instead of laughing as she'd feared, or, worse, dismissing her dream with a disinterested shrug, he'd fired

question after question at her. Did she want her ship to
be big enough to live in? So big it needed a crew, or
sleek enough for one man to master her? She remembered thinking long and hard about that, then deciding
her ship must be both.

*We'll need a crew for the times when we feel lazy and
decadent, or perhaps when the children are small,* she'd
said, her smile curving at the thought of a half dozen
dark-haired replicas of Alex swarming over the decks.
*And when we feel romantic, we can take her out alone,
just the two of us.*

Alex had kissed her then, and whispered to her of the
wildly romantic ways he intended to pleasure her on
that same ship.

This ship. Her ship.

A ship he'd named *ESPIARE*. To atone, if she remembered her Italian verbs correctly.

"Oh, Alex, she's exquisite," she murmured, bringing
her gaze back to hers. "How can you bear to sell her?"

Alex felt his breath whoosh out and realized he'd
stopped breathing. "I have to sell her so I can build
another. Bigger, but not much, with twin screws this
time, and . . . oh, shit, don't cry, baby." Reaching up
with a hand that suddenly felt too big and too rough, he
wiped the tears from her cheeks. When he finished, she
was still biting her lip and looking at him with huge
eyes. He couldn't get a fix on the emotion swimming
there, and that made him edgy.

"Look, the deal is only pending, not cut in stone. If
you don't want me to sell her, I'll find another way to
raise the money." Though he smiled to reassure her, his
gut was churning at the thought of starting over from
scratch—endless hours of sweating in foul weather
clothes, pulling in nets until his back was so sore he'd
had trouble standing straight for hours after they'd off-
loaded at the pier.

"Sunshine, talk to me. What's wrong?"

"Wrong?" She blinked, then shook her head. "Oh
no, everything's right, Alex. Wonderfully, beautifully
right. I'm so proud of you." Before he could sort
through the emotions tearing through him, she was on

top of him, raining kisses on his face, his neck, his shoulder. "You might look like a tough guy—"

"Hey, watch it, lady. I'm more than just a pretty face."

"—but you have the soul of a poet."

"The hell I do." Somehow he managed to keep his tone light, but when her mouth settled on his again, gentle as butterfly wings, and yet so potent he had to suck in, he felt his eyes sting.

Linking his arms around her waist, he crushed her to him and felt the violent fluttering of her heart beneath her breasts. "Kiss me again," he begged when she drew back. "I'm starved for you."

Her eyes sparkled, grew dark. Her lips curved in a saucy courtesan's smile, and he ground his teeth. He'd never wanted another woman so badly, or with such consuming emotion. Or wanted so fiercely to shake her for daring to taunt him.

"Nicky will be wondering where we are," she murmured, touching one corner of his mouth with her finger. He tried to capture it with his mouth only to have her whisk it back. "We really should get ourselves on deck."

Alex narrowed his gaze. "You're enjoying this," he accused, his frustration level soaring.

"Yes, aren't you?" She shifted position, deliberately, he suspected as he bit off a groan and eased his hold.

Slipping free, her gaze eased to one side, her gaze absorbed as she ran her fingernails through the hair on his chest, raked his nipples, swirled her fingers lower. He felt a spike of need, and fought to hang onto his reason.

Helen heard his swift intake of breath and felt his hand grip hers. "Careful," he warned in a hoarse voice. "You're dealing with a guy who's been celibate for eight years."

Stunned, she jerked her gaze to his face and saw the truth in his eyes. She saw it all then—the vulnerability he'd hidden beneath the swagger, the need to be cherished for who he was inside, not the things he had or did, the loneliness hidden by a devil's grin.

Arching closer, she brought her mouth to his, and

she felt him tremble. "I love the taste of your mouth," she whispered, her lips close to his. "And I love that cute little dimple that only shows up when you relax." She touched her finger to the spot just above his mouth and he groaned.

"Sunshine, I'm just hanging on by a thread here."

"Maybe you should let go."

She turned her head and pressed hot kisses against his throat. He tried to hold himself still, but her hands were touching him everywhere, arousing sharp spasms of pleasure where her fingers trailed until he felt his control splinter.

She slid lower, searing his skin, sending shock waves to every part of him. She was climbing over him, her long sleek legs tangled with his, her breasts rubbing his chest. Need roared through him with sharp edges, leaving him raw.

He rasped out her name, fisted his hand in her hair. She moaned, moved. Her lips were silky, sliding over his skin. He drew in air, expelling it in a hoarse cry of surprise as she touched her tongue to his rigid, swollen flesh.

She felt him shudder, heard the ragged rasp of his breathing. Needing to see him, she raised her head, only to gasp at the savage need seething in his eyes.

Her own breathing faltered even as her heart raced. He groaned her name, reached for her with those strong, callused hands. And then they were thrashing together, hands touching in a frenzy of need and exploration, mouths welded. He was in control now, his hard thighs vising hers, his tongue plunging. She bucked, arched, bringing heat to heat. His flesh was hot, she was moist.

He was blind, nearly senseless, driven now by needs he'd ignored, had to ignore. Her body was warm, eager, her flesh scented by the musky smell of passion, her arms urging him closer.

Arching his head back until the tendons of his neck strained, he eased slowly into her, feeling her body sheath his, inch by inch. He gritted his teeth, began to move. She moved with him, faster, faster until they were wild with the pleasure of flesh rubbing flesh.

Through the thunder in his head he heard her cry his name, felt her convulse around him. Need clawed at him, gouging, scourging. And then he came in a rush of hot pulsing release, draining him of reason. Of doubt. Of pain.

Alex woke with a start, and for an instant, thought he was still dreaming. He'd slept in this bed only once, his first night in Seattle. It had been too big, too soft. Too lonely. After that, he'd bunked in the sea cabin, But now, with Helen curled against him and the sun streaming through the tinted skylight, he never wanted to leave it again.

He turned his head and planted a kiss against the tangle of golden curls covering her forehead. She stirred, frowned, ran her tongue along her lower lip. And then smiled, a secret dreamy smile that wrapped his head in velvet and brought a lump to his throat.

Drowsy lashes fluttered, lifted. "I had a lovely dream," she murmured. "You were making love to me."

"I had the same dream, my love." He nudged her chin higher and brushed his mouth over hers. "The best ever."

Her lips curved, sought his for a long, lingering kiss that, to his utter amazement had his body stirring again. "It's almost noon," he whispered between kisses.

"Mmm."

"Time to get up, my wild temptress."

Her eyes opened wider. "There's no such thing as time here," she murmured, with only a tiny catch in her voice. "We're on Troy, remember?"

"Not yet, but soon." He started to ease away from her, only to have her clutch his arm.

"Don't leave," she murmured, her voice sultry.

"One of us has to."

"Don't you want to make love to me again?" She skimmed teasing fingers over his belly.

"You know I do." His voice was shading toward frustration.

"Then why don't you?"

He swallowed hard and tried to think about tide tables and wind-shifts, anything but slipping inside her again. "For one thing our son has been alone all morning, and for another, I want to get docked and the supplies off-loaded as quickly as possible so I can lock you in the master bedroom for two weeks."

He found her mouth and treated himself to a belated good-morning kiss before rolling to the edge of the bed. He heard her yawn, then gasp.

"What?" he demanded, swiveling to face her.

"Your back," she murmured in dismay. "You're bleeding." Scooting closer, she raised a hand to touch his shoulder. "Did I do that?"

He captured her hand and kissed it. "My lady Helen has sharp little claws," he teased.

Her eyes clouded. "You should have said something."

"Sunshine, you could have sliced me open with a knife and I wouldn't have cared." That won him a grin and took most of the worry from her eyes. But not all.

"Alex, we have to talk. About where we go from here." She drew a deep breath, and he found himself watching her breasts move as her chest rose and fell. The nipples were still swollen and rosy, and her breasts seemed fuller. A faint pink tinge still covered her throat, fading into the swell of her breasts.

When he was young and stupid, he'd considered her breasts dainty and sweet and on the small side. Enough to whet a man's appetite for more. Now, he knew better. Everything about her was perfect—her breasts, her small waist, her curvy hips that swayed with a subtle sensuality when she walked on those spiky high heels.

Feeling his loins grow heavy, he took a deep breath and managed a smile. "Love, until you get some clothes on, talking is going to be awfully low on my list of priorities."

Helen saw his eyes heating and managed a tiny, "Oh," before scrambling for the sheet. Drawing it close, she scooted backward until she felt the pillow behind her.

Alex watched her with brooding eyes, then shook his head. "Me and my big mouth," he muttered, his expression so dejectedly frustrated and male she had to laugh.

He shot her a baleful look, then heaved a noisy sigh and bent forward to retrieve his shorts. He slipped them over his long legs, hitched them higher, then stood to slide them over his hips. His back muscles rippled beguilingly with every movement, and when he stood, his buttocks tightened, drawing the white cotton taut.

Helen didn't realize she'd sighed until he turned to look at her and cocked one eyebrow questioningly. "Nicky," she blurted. "He's so eager for us to get back together."

His grin flashed, uninhibited by his customary control. "His father's son, through and through."

She grinned, but her eyes remained somber. "I want . . . I *need* to go slowly this time, Alex. When we were kids, it didn't matter what we did, but this time around we have our son to consider. And, well, to protect."

"Protect from what? The fact that his parents are going to get married again? Or that they're just sleeping together?"

"Alex, please. You know what I mean. Nothing's settled. We've slept together, yes, and I've already admitted I want to be with you, but—"

"But what?"

"Don't look at me like that. I can't help it if I have to do things slowly now. Step by step." She drew a hasty breath, desperate to erase the wounded look from his eyes. "It's only been five days since you came barreling back into my life. Kissing me. Abducting me, in my *wedding* gown. My head is still whirling."

He shifted, ran a hand through his tousled hair. "Okay, I'll grant you I've had a lot longer to think about my feelings."

Feelings he had skimmed over only lightly while they'd been making love. Feelings she needed time to anchor into some kind of foundation for a marriage. "Then you'll be patient?"

He sighed. Heavily. "You can have two weeks, but before we leave this island, I want to have a course mapped out, straight to the altar."

She felt a flare of panic, a jolt of anger. "Don't give me orders, captain. I'm not part of your crew."

His eyes grew still, hardened to blued steel. "No, you're the woman I love, damnit. The woman I've been dreaming about for eight years."

She blinked. "Well, you don't have to sound so angry about it."

His eyebrows bunched. "What the hell should I sound like? Grateful that you deigned to let me share your bed? Thankful for any crumbs you can give the pathetic bastard who came crawling back damn near on his knees because he couldn't stand to spend one more day without you?" His voice was silky, his lips curled into a mocking line.

She drew a shaky breath, regretting now that she'd started this. Alex was not a man to be pushed too hard.

"That's not fair," she murmured, edging the sheet to her chin. Her head was beginning to ache again, and her stomach felt wobbly. "And by the way, thank you for ruining a perfectly wonderful afterglow."

"Ah, hell!" He turned quickly and stalked to the built-in closet, opening the door with a savage jerk. His movements were rigidly controlled, his wide back stiff as he jerked a shirt from its hanger and shrugged into it without bothering with the buttons. Another jerk and he had a pair of khaki shorts in his hands. He pulled them on with a ripple of muscle and a grunt of impatience, zipped the fly, and snapped the waistband closed. He seemed driven, frustrated, and very possibly violent, a stranger with a hard jaw and prodigious strength.

He returned to the cabin, swept a hard gaze her way, then grabbed his watch from the dresser and checked the dial. "I'll be on the bridge."

"Aye, aye, captain," she shot back.

Emotion, dark and violent, flickered in his eyes, but when he spoke, his voice was soft. "Don't push me, Helen. *Just don't push me.*" To her shock, he slammed the door when he left.

Twelve

$\mathcal{F}$ifteen minutes later, somewhat revived by a shower and the three aspirins she'd discovered waiting for her on the bathroom sink, she arrived on deck to find it glistening from a recent hosing.

The sun was shining, and the sea reflected the deep blue of a cloudless sky. To port, the island the Indians had christened the hiccup of the gods and now renamed Troy lay basking in the sun like a lazy sea turtle. Splashes of exotic color marked the path from the dock to the villa sparkling white against velvety foliage.

Though built of modern materials with modern equipment, the brand-new mini-resort replicated the legendary city-state in perfect detail, from the Greco-Roman-style villa to the high walls of stucco surrounding the sun-kissed grounds. Because of the building codes and safety regulations, they had had to provide modern plumbing, an overhead sprinkling system and electricity, all of which Celia and her staff of architects had tried to make as unobtrusive as possible. A true get-away paradise, there were no phones, no television, no VCRs. And no computer hookups.

Helen sighed, her smile going soft at the edges. Her father would have loved this Troy. A lover of the classics, he'd deliberately settled his family in New York's version of the ancient city and then had made certain Helen had understood the honor he'd bestowed upon her by naming her for the legendary beauty. Now, here she was, swept away to the very island she herself had

helped create—and by a man her father would have
liked very much. A man who worked hard and played
hard, and made her feel as beautiful as her namesake.

"Yo, Mom!" Nicky's voice had come from behind
and above. Turning slowly in deference to her still-aching head, she saw him on the bridge leaning from an
open window on the port side. He was bare chested,
and already his skin seemed to have taken on a darker
shade of tan.

"Nicky, be careful, you might fall."

He glanced down, then shrugged with a typical male
disregard for danger. "Guess what? Dad's gonna let me
take her into the pier." Though the brim of his
Seahawks cap shaded his face, she was able to see the
slash of his grin—Alex's grin.

"Sounds great, sweetheart," she called around the
lump in her throat.

"Come watch, okay?"

"Okay, but don't start without me," she called before
heading to the outside ladder leading to bridge.

Alex nodded as she entered, his gaze hidden behind
aviator sunglasses. He'd buttoned his shirt and tucked
the tails neatly into the shorts molding his buttocks. He
didn't seem angry, merely removed from her emotion-
ally.

"Permission to come aboard, sir?" she inquired for
Nicky's benefit and was rewarded with the lopsided grin
she adored.

"Permission granted," Nicky shot back, straightening
his spine and squaring his shoulders. "Right, Dad?" he
asked, glancing over his shoulder.

Alex smiled then, for his son, and for an instant he
seemed a different man. Younger, she realized. More
like the mischievous, fun-loving man who'd stolen her
heart. "You have the con. That gives you the right to
make the decisions and issue the orders."

Nicky bobbed his head, preening with pride. "Yeah, I
almost forgot."

Helen had never seen her son so full of himself. And
so . . . happy. After what seemed like months of his

morose rebellion, the change was startling—and wonderfully sweet.

"So, what do you think?" Nicky demanded impatiently from his place behind the wheel. "Is this one radical ship or what?"

Helen made a show of glancing around. When her gaze lighted on Alex, she felt her pulse jerk. "Oh, indeed, at the very least," she declared playfully, returning to gaze to Nicky.

"She's really, really safe."

"That's reassuring."

"And, see, with all this automatic stuff, one man can run her. Like Dad did coming here from Greece. Right, Dad."

"Right, son."

Nicky seemed to grow taller. "Dad says there's this rich sheik who wants to buy her."

"That's . . . wonderful. And he'll be getting a fantastic boat."

"Vessel," Alex corrected with an odd jerk to his voice. "Or yacht, if you prefer. The word *boat* is usually used for vessels small enough to be transported on larger ones."

He'd told her for the first time between wildly arousing kisses, the kind that ignited a flame that curled deep inside. "I . . . vessel, right," she said softly. "Do forgive me."

"Anything, sunshine."

She blinked. "I'll . . . keep that in mind."

Though she couldn't see his eyes, she felt his gaze as strongly as though he'd touched her.

"Dad says I'm old enough to have a boat of my very own," Nicky boasted, seemingly oblivious to the sudden tension crackling in the small space. "We decided on a sailboat, 'cause that's the best way to learn. Dad says he taught you how to sail once, like just a few miles from here."

A wave of heat that had nothing to do with the weather assailed her, heating her skin to fever temperature. After that lesson they'd spread their blanket on the sand and made love for hours.

"I wasn't very good at it," she murmured, her voice stiff. She hadn't intended to look at Alex, but suddenly she was. And, though the dark glasses hid his eyes, she knew that he was looking at her.

"How about it, Dad?" Nicky prodded when the silence lengthened. "I bet Mom was great, right?"

"Amazing," he said, his voice suddenly thick. "Once she got the hang of it."

"I tried," she murmured, her pulse leaping and her senses scrambling.

His mouth softened, curved. "You were perfect, sunshine. I was a lousy teacher."

"No, I was too scared to pay attention."

"But sweet."

From the corner of her eye she saw Nick glance from one to the other, then grin. "See, I knew you two would like each other again once you spent some time together." His voice was so full of hope it brought tears to her eyes.

Helen drew a deep breath. "I . . . uh, thought I smelled coffee when I was climbing up here," she murmured, blinking hard.

"In the sea cabin," Alex muttered, indicating a door in the rear wall of the bridge.

"Excuse me," she managed to mutter before all but running toward the door.

Safely inside, she leaned against the door and struggled to keep the tears flooding her eyes from falling. I can handle this, she told herself fiercely. Later, when the lingering effects of the hangover were gone and she had time to think clearly. Conscious of the two males waiting beyond the frail barrier provided by two inches of teak, she straightened and glanced around for the coffeepot.

Unlike the rest of the luxurious vessel, this small cabin with its own shower stall and toilet tucked into one corner was strictly Spartan in furnishings and design. There was room for a bunk with drawers built in below, a desk and chair nearly close enough to touch from her place by the door and a miniature galley with a sink, a tiny refrigerator, and a one-burner hot plate.

The coffeemaker was tucked into a corner of the stainless counter. The pot was half full.

She found a mug in the tidy cupboard beneath the counter and poured herself a cup. Recalling Alex's preference for coffee thick enough to chew, she took a testing sip, and then was glad for the instinctive caution. The brew was not only strong enough to strip paint, but also hot as sin.

Holding the cup carefully at arm's length she was reaching for the door handle when she stopped dead, her gaze frozen on a small picture frame sitting on the desk next to a portable CD player and earphones. The photo of Nicky was the same one she kept on her desk in the Greek Isles tower. The other one was of her, taken on board Alex's yawl, the one on which he'd taught her the rudiments of sailing. While Nicky's school photo was bright and new, the color in the snapshot had faded almost to a blur.

"Oh Alex," she whispered, torn by the thought of his keeping that picture for so many long years. The tears she'd willed away returned and this time refused to be damned. Using her free hand she scrubbed the tears from her cheeks, only to find them wet again a moment later.

She was searching for a box of tissues when a sharp rap sounded on the door. Before she could call out, the door opened and Alex slipped inside. One look at the concern on his face, and the stream of tears turned into a flood.

"Go away," she muttered, turning her back to him.

"I tried that once. It didn't work."

Please don't do this to me, she pleaded silently, squeezing her eyes closed. She heard him move, felt the mug being plucked from her fingers, and then she was being enfolded against a wide, hard chest smelling of soap and sunshine.

All of a sudden it was all too much—the agony of indecision over sending Nicky to military school, the stress of the wedding, Alex's startling proposal. Making love to the man she'd tried so hard to forget.

Clutching his shirt with both hands, she closed her

eyes, buried her face against his sheltering chest and cried. "Damn you," she murmured softly between sobs.

"It's okay, love," he murmured, dropping his check to the top of her silky hair. "If you want to go slow, we'll go slow. It'll cost me, but we'll do it your way this time."

He ran a gentle hand through her loosened hair, letting the soft strands shimmer through his fingers like silken sunshine. The scent of flowers teased his nostrils.

"I hate crying," she muttered, hiccuping. "I really, really hate it."

She drew back, her lashes spiky with tears. "Give me your hanky," she ordered, then realized it was Constantine who always carried a fine linen handkerchief.

"Will this do?" he said, jerking open one of the desk drawers and retrieving a tissue.

"Yes, thanks." She wiped the tears already wetting her cheek and tried to sniff back the rest.

He shot her an impatient look, plucked another tissue from the box and held it to her nose. "Blow," he ordered as though she were a recalcitrant toddler.

Too tired to argue, she blew, then snatched the tissue from his hand, wadded it into a sodden ball and threw it into the trash basket.

"I'm a mess," she muttered, bringing her gaze to his. He'd taken off the dark glasses, and his eyes looked tired.

"You're beautiful and I was a jerk." His grin slanted. "Forgive me?"

Helen felt her heart do a slow tumble. "If you'll forgive me."

His eyes warmed. "For what? Wanting to protect my son?"

"Alex—"

"It's okay, sunshine. Once I calmed down, I realized you were right. We'll take it slow and easy this time, and when the time is right, we'll talk to Nick. Okay?"

She smiled. "Okay."

He curved his big hands over her shoulders and squeezed gently. "Now that that's settled, how about we get Helen to Troy?"

Thirteen

"Mom, are you and Dad still mad at each other?"

Helen glanced up from the crossword puzzle she was doing and shaded her eyes against the sun as she glanced toward her son. "Of course not, honey. Why do you ask?"

His back to her, Nicky reeled in the line he'd just casted into the surf. "Ever since we got to this place you're never in the same place. If you're in the pool, Dad's running on the beach. And then when me and him are fishing and you show up, all of sudden he decides he wants to go swimming."

Helen shifted her gaze to the deep water beyond the breakers. Alex had always been a tireless swimmer, slicing through the water with the grace of an otter, his strong arms arcing out of the water in long, sure strokes. Watching, she felt her blood heating. Reluctantly, she returned her gaze to their son.

"Honey, we're not avoiding each other, honestly. It's just that we both want to spend time alone with you."

Nicky stuck his pole in the sand and came to sprawl next to her on the sand. His skin was nearly as dark as Alex's now, and he seemed to have gained a few pounds. She herself was having trouble buttoning several pairs of shorts that had been loose on her when she'd bought them. Not that she was surprised, she realized, glancing down at the expanse of skin above the skimpy bottom to her bikini. Whenever she was out of sorts, she ate. And she was most definitely out of sorts.

It had been three days since she and Alex had made love. Three days of furtive kisses when Nicky wasn't nearby, three days of sleeping in separate bedrooms because their son was a light sleeper, three days of pent-up sexual heat. Frustrated almost beyond bearing, she was beginning to wish she'd let Alex tell Nicky about the change in their relationship after all.

"Mom?"

"Hmm?"

Nicky grabbed a handful of sand and let it drizzle through his fingers. "Uh, you wouldn't be mad or anything if I wanted to hang out alone sometimes, would you?"

Helen studied his profile before answering cautiously, "Hang out how?"

"Nothing major, honest. Just kicking back on Dad's boat, maybe cranking some tunes on his CD player." Nicky scooped up more sand and added it to the tiny pile, then angled her a glance. "If Dad doesn't mind."

"I'm sure he won't." She glanced toward the sea and saw that Alex was now walking toward them through the breakers. Her breath caught at the magnificent picture he made with the sun burnishing his massive chest. "Perhaps you'd better ask his permission, though, before you go aboard."

Seeing his father approaching, Nicky scrambled to his feet and called out a greeting. Alex raised a hand and used it to sluice seawater from his chest. He was wearing a pair of paint-speckled jeans hacked off midthigh and riding low on lean hips.

He was so primally male, so earthy and strong and handsome. No doubt about it, she was wildly in love with him again. Every day they spent together she felt more certain she wanted to be with him forever.

"You two look thoroughly lazy," he said, stopping a few feet away to slick the water from one arm, then the other.

"And you look thoroughly wet." Her breath came out too fast and a little shaky.

His mouth quirked. "Water's nice and cold."

"Maybe I should try it." She threw him a towel and watched while he made a quick, careless pass over his hair, leaving it tousled and clinging to his neck. Her mouth went dry at the thought of running her fingers through that thick, damp silk during the throes of passion.

He flicked her a rueful grin, then spread the damp towel on the sand next to her beach chair and sat down. Viewed from above, his heavily muscled shoulders appeared a mile wide.

"Catch anything," Alex asked Nicky while shooting a quick look at the bucket next to the pole.

"Nah. Wasn't really trying that hard, though." Nicky flopped down next to his dad, unconsciously assuming the same pose—one leg crooked, one arm resting on his knee.

"I think Nicky's feeling a little smothered by too much parental attention," Helen said with a smile.

Lifting his eyebrows, he swung a gaze at the boy next to him. "Too much quality time, son?"

Eyes looking at the ground, Nicky shrugged, looking suddenly six again and achingly vulnerable. "I like being with you guys, honest, but I kinda thought, if it was okay with you, I'd like to hang out on *ESPIARE* tonight, maybe listen to some tunes on your CDs."

Alex shot a fast glance at the yacht tied like an impatient greyhound next to the pier. A man and his ship, Helen thought, watching his face soften. Though she'd never completely understood the masculine obsession with engines and speed, it was a passion she'd tolerated in her son. To Alex, however, the *ESPIARE* was a dream come true, a tangible result of long hours spent learning about marine architecture and shipbuilding. A validation of a sort, proof that he wasn't the loser his brother and just about everyone else thought he was.

Her heart swelled as he offered his son a cocky grin. "Sounds like a plan. Just make sure you leave her exactly the way you found her, which means no candy wrappers on the deck. And no fooling with the radio."

"Okay, but I get to sleep aboard, right?"

"No way, sport. Nobody sleeps aboard when I'm not there."

"But, Dad, nothing can happen while she's tied up."

Helen sensed a sudden tension in Alex an instant before she saw it reflected on his face. "Wrong," he declared with staccato harshness. "On the sea there are no guarantees. None!"

Nicky's expression turned sullen. "You just don't trust me is all."

Alex drew an impatient breath and she could almost feel the effort he was expending to level the uncharacteristic burst of emotion. "It's not a matter of trust, Nick. It's a matter of experience."

"Yeah, yeah, that's what Uncle Constantine always says." Looking disgusted, Nicky scrambled to his feet and took off running toward the villa, disappearing seconds later behind the surrounding wall.

"Ah, hell!" Alex raked both hands through his hair, holding his head with fingers spread in the dark silk as he gazed up at the sky for a long moment before dropping his hands and shaking his head. "I'm no good at this father business."

"You're wonderful at the father business, Alex." She laid a hand on his shoulder and felt him jerk. "You're just lacking day-to-day experience."

He scowled, his gaze fixed on a point above the horizon. "I don't know how to make up for all those lost years when I wasn't around," he gritted through a tight jaw. "I'm trying, but—"

"You're doing fine," she murmured, her heart aching. "Just fine." Instinctively, she slipped from the chair and settled down next to him. Silently, he took her hand and pressed it tightly between hard palms.

"Nicky knows you love him, Alex. Didn't you drop everything and sail halfway across the world because he needed you?"

A muscle worked in his jaw. "Maybe that's not enough," he said gruffly.

She drew a breath. "I saw how raw you were when you got out of prison. And how . . . angry you were inside. If you had stayed with us, Nicky would have come to see it, too. And it would have frightened him, just as it frightened me."

He stiffened, then slowly meshed his gaze with hers. "I hated the way I was then, Helen. I just couldn't seem to get past the garbage in my head."

"I know, my love." She caressed his ravaged faced with her gaze. Suffering had etched permanent lines beside his mouth and across his brow. Lines that seemed like battle scars won in a terrible struggle.

"In prison, something happened." The words seemed jerked from him, one by one. "I . . . was sodomized."

Helen went still. I should have known, she thought. I should have sensed it. Instead, she'd been too caught up in her own pain, her own misery. Fighting back tears, she reached for him and felt him stiffen a split-second before he allowed her to draw him close. She felt his anguish, his shame, and wished she could absorb it into her body, freeing him from its burden.

"I'm so sorry, my darling," she murmured, cradling his head against her breast. "So very sorry."

He allowed her to hold him for another moment, then broke free. "I felt dirty inside. Ashamed." He dropped his gaze. "I was afraid to touch you, afraid that filth would rub off on you."

"Oh Alex," she whispered, her lips trembling. "It must have been terrible for you when I . . ." She broke off, her face icy.

"When you tried to seduce me," he finished with a sad note twisted into his deep voice.

Too wrought up to speak, she simply nodded.

"It was hell," he said succinctly, and yet with what she imagined was momentous understatement.

"No wonder you left."

His smile was sad and a little forlorn. "I left because I loved you too much to stay."

The tears she'd tried to stem spilled from her eyes and ran down her cheeks in hot rivulets. Because she had no words, she laid her free hand gently against his lean cheek and brought her lips gently to his.

His mouth remained passive, unresponsive. Just

when she thought her heart would break, he groaned against her mouth, his arms going around her fiercely.

"God, I need you," he grated.

"Alex—"

"No more talk. Not now." Closing his eyes, he ground his mouth against hers with a savage hunger. Eagerly, she arched toward him, needing to feel his warmth and strength. He dragged her across his lap, his arms hugging with prodigious strength, yet with so much tenderness her heart melted.

"Love you," he murmured between long, draining kisses. "So much."

She answered in kind, her mouth as eagerly hungry, her body responding, aching to be filled. He stroked her back until she was breathless, slipped the fingers of one hand between her flesh and the thin fabric of her bikini bottom. His breathing was fevered, his body taut. She felt the swell of his arousal against her thighs, the heat of his desire in his kiss.

Eagerly, avidly, she threaded her fingers into his hair, twisting so that she could rub her tingling breasts against his chest. She heard him groan, a long keening sound that seemed to come from his soul, and then he dragged his mouth from hers.

"Don't move," he said, his breathing a harsh rasping in his throat.

"Is . . . are you all right?"

"No," he grated, offering her a lopsided grin strained at the edges. "I won't be all right until I can make love to you properly."

Helen felt her face warm. "I know what you mean." She pressed her face against his throat and sighed. "Don't take this wrong, but I wish you'd given our son permission to sleep aboard."

She heard him chuckle. "So do I, sunshine. But I can't change the rules, not even for a chance to tumble my ex-wife in privacy."

"I know," she murmured, reluctantly lifting her head. "Maybe we could slip him a Mickey at dinner."

His grin slanted, the tension she'd sensed in him earlier lingering in the corners. "It would serve him right at that."

"Perhaps, but I can't be too angry with him, considering the way my stint as a lousy drunk ended."

"You have a point, my love," he murmured, his eyes smoldering as he wrapped her in another hug before setting her to one side. Bemused, she watched him get to his feet and gaze toward the sea. Her cheeks flamed when she realized he was still very aroused.

"C'mon, sunshine," he said, extending her a hand. "Let's douse this party in seawater before it gets out of control."

"Good idea," she murmured as she let him pull her to her feet. Looping an arm around her shoulder, he led her toward the waves lapping the beach. Her heart full, she slipped an arm around his trim waist and walked with him into the surf.

"Oh, that is cold," she cried when the water washed against her calves.

"Yeah, isn't it?" he said with a crooked smile that suddenly turned tender. "God, I love you," he grated. "I can't imagine a future without you."

"I feel the same way," she replied quietly. "I do love you dearly."

His grin faded, replaced by a look so tender she nearly gasped aloud. "Does that mean you'll marry me?"

Helen had to take a deep breath before she could answer. "Yes, I'll marry you my darling. Just as soon as we get back to the real world."

Fourteen

$\mathscr{H}$elen's room was bathed in moonlight, the perfect addition to a midnight rendezvous, Alex thought as he slipped inside and quietly closed the door.

"Is Nicky asleep?" She was sitting up in bed, waiting for him, her sleek legs bare. His mouth went dry, and suddenly, he was as nervous as a kid on his first date.

"The way he wakes up at the slightest sound, I was afraid to open his door to check," he told her in a low tone as he crossed the room.

"He seemed happy enough at dinner," Helen murmured as she scooted sideways to give him room.

"Think so?" He shucked his shorts before sliding in next to her.

"Didn't you?"

He captured her hand and pressed his mouth to the palm. "No, I think he was humoring us," he whispered before working his way up her arm, trailing kisses as he went.

She shivered and threaded eager fingers into his hair. "He . . . seemed fine when we were playing poker," she murmured, her voice breathy.

Alex transferred his attention to her throat, breathing in the scent of wild roses. "He lost every hand," he told her before pressing a kiss in the warm hollow below one ear.

"Maybe, ahh . . . maybe he had a bad night."

"Not possible. Nick can run a bluff almost as well as I can." She was wearing silk, he realized, easing one thin

strap from her shoulder. Something skimpy. He pressed
a kiss to the swell of her breast and she moaned.

"So, you . . . ah . . . I love to feel your mouth on
my skin."

"Such soft skin." He opened his mouth over her nipple and sucked. Her breath sighed from her lips, and
with another soft moan, she scissored her legs open.

His body had been hard for hours. Now it pulsed, so
engorged he hurt. "Beautiful Helen of Troy," he murmured, easing her free of the other strap. "Your hair is
silver in the moonlight."

"Yours is as black as midnight," she whispered in an
achingly soft voice that seemed to fill all the lonely
places inside him. "My brave, impetuous Paris. My
bold, strong warrior."

"I feel strong when I'm with you." Alex felt emotion
stir in the deepest, most fiercely protected part of his
soul. Trapped for so many years, it struggled to get free.
Drawing back, he framed her face in his hands. "Helen,
I—"

Hearing an all-too familiar rumbling sound, he
stopped suddenly and cocked his head. "Son of a
bitch!" he grated, scrambling to his feet.

"Alex, what is it?" Helen's eyes were huge in the
silvered light.

"ESPIARE! Someone's started the goddamned engine." He thrust one leg, then the other into his shorts
and jerked them to his waist. "Check Nick's room," he
ordered as he crossed the room in three long strides.
"I'll check the boat."

"I . . . d-didn't mean to . . . wreck her," Nicky cried
through chattering teeth when Helen returned to the
steamy bathroom with another thick towel. "Honest!"

"Of course you didn't," she murmured, wrapping his
trembling shoulders in an additional layer of warmth.
He was sitting on a stool, a cup of hot tea gripped in
both hands. She'd already forced him to down two
mugs, extra-sweet, just as Alex had ordered.

"I'd studied the chart just l-like Dad taught me. I
knew the channel, Mom. I swear I did."

Helen smoothed his salt-stiff hair before dropping a kiss on his forehead, the way she'd done so often when he'd been a toddler coming to her to heal some small hurt. "I believe you, sweetheart," she murmured. "And so will Dad."

"No, he won't. He'll hate me. Just like Uncle Constantine hates me for fucking up his life."

"Nicky, don't." Helen drew a shaky breath and glanced toward the door.

By the time she'd found Nicky missing and hurried to the pier, the *ESPIARE* was wedged on a reef and listing badly. She'd shouted for Alex, but he'd been halfway to the boat, swimming hard.

It had seemed an eternity before he'd returned in the dingy with Nicky wrapped in the blanket she'd last seen on the bunk in the sea cabin. She'd taken one look at the blood-soaked bandage on his forehead and would have panicked if it hadn't been for calm texture of Alex's voice quietly issuing orders.

She'd run ahead to run a hot bath while Alex had carried Nick into the house. It was a surface cut, he'd told her, quickly skimming the boy's clothes from him. When the hull had scraped bottom, Nicky had been thrown backward, hitting his head on a bulkhead.

With a minimum of talk, his jaw tight, his hands gentle, he'd gotten Nicky into the tub, made sure the boy was conscious and alert, albeit shaken, then returned to the *ESPIARE* to call the Coast Guard. From the little he'd said, she gathered Nicky had ripped a deep gash in the vessel's hull, trying to take her to sea.

Oh, Alex, she thought, wrapping her arms around her sobbing son. Please don't destroy our son. Please.

Two hours later, when she returned from Nicky's bedroom, Alex had finished the tea she'd made him when he'd returned and was sprawled on the couch, his eyes closed, and his face gray with exhaustion. On the table in front of the couch lay the *ESPIARE*'S log book, by marine tradition removed only when a ship was no longer seaworthy.

She hesitated, then knelt in front of him and laid her

head on his chest. Beneath the shirt he'd pulled on
after the hot shower he'd taken to stop the ravages of
hypothermia, his heart thudded a slow and even beat,
like the rhythm of a funeral drum.

"Is he asleep?" he asked in a tired voice.

"Yes, finally." She felt his fingers in her hair and
smiled. "He hasn't cried like that since he split open his
head falling from a playground swing."

"It'll be a while before he forgets."

"You made it easier, telling him about the insurance," she said, lifting her head. Something in his expression had her frowning uneasily. "She *is* fully
insured, isn't she? You weren't just telling Nick that so
he wouldn't feel so guilty?"

"She's insured," His voice was hollow and terribly
quiet.

"Fully?" she prodded.

"Fully." He smiled then, and the dread that had been
gripping her heart eased off. "Trust me, sunshine, I
wouldn't have taken her to sea if she hadn't been. Not
even to carry Helen away to her Troy."

"I'm sorry you lost her," she murmured, running her
hands over his hard chest. "She was one of a kind, but
you'll build another. Just like you said."

"Yes, I'll build another." He sat up slowly, then
reached for her. "No more talk," he grated before
crushing his mouth to hers. Minutes later, they drew
apart, needing oxygen. Alex's hard features were
flushed and he was breathing hard.

"Now that Nicky's safe and sound, how about you
and me holing up in your bedroom for a while?" he
said when he'd caught his breath.

Helen managed a saucy grin, but her heart was racing, and her body tingling. "Hmm, you do look like you
could use a good night's sleep," she teased, only to have
him growl a warning.

"Or not," she squeaked as he scooped her into his
arms and stalked toward her room.

Later, when she was drowsy with afterglow and about
to drift into sleep, he told her that he wouldn't be going
with her to Seattle when the Coast Guard arrived in the

morning. He had to stay with the ship until the salvage crew arrived.

"Come when you can," she murmured, turning her head to kiss his neck. "Nicky and I will be waiting."

For an instant, before sleep claimed her, she thought she saw his eyes darken with the same agony she'd seen in the courtroom right before they'd locked him away.

Alex slung his oilskin over one tired shoulder and slowly climbed the rickety stairs leading to his second-floor flat. At the landing he paused to look out over the Aegean. The sea had been rough all day, requiring extra energy to haul in the catch. The wind was even stronger now, whipping the sea into froth where it pounded the shore line.

Overhead, storm clouds were massing, and the air was electric with a promise of the violence to come. In the distance lightning split the overcast sky, zigzagging a majestic path downward until it sizzled out in the sea. A split-second later thunder cracked and then rolled. Pyrgos was in for a bad blow, and already his neighbors were closing shutters and hauling in the precious pots of flowers.

Narrowing his gaze against the wind's bite, he scanned the horizon, checking the density of the clouds. This time of year the roads leading from the village tended to flood during bad storms, cutting off all traffic. Nick was due to fly into Athens in three days. Alex intended to be there to meet him, one way or another.

A shutter banged below, drawing his gaze. His own were already shut, battened down this morning when he'd seen the color of the sky. There'd be no fishing tomorrow which was just as well. Since his return to Greece six weeks ago he'd been working nonstop, trying to drive the memory of Helen's good-bye tears from his mind.

Squaring his tired shoulders, he pushed open the door, then froze. Nick's familiar duffel was there on the worn entry tile, along with a pile of suitcases and garment bags. He smelled something cooking, something with garlic and tomatoes. His heart stopped, then tripped into double time.

"Nick?"

Helen stepped into the shabby living room from the kitchen, a wooden spoon in her hand and a smile on her face. She was dressed in jeans and a T-shirt that clung enticingly to her breasts. Stunned, he lost his grip on the oilskin and it slid to the floor at his feet.

"Our son is downstairs, eating his way through an entire baklava," she said, her voice low and sexy. "I like your friend, Minerva, by the way. She's extremely kind and very . . . voluptuous."

"She's married to a friend." He took a step forward, then stopped. Maybe she'd just come to deliver Nicky. "What the hell are you doing here?"

"Making lasagna. I had to borrow most of the ingredients from Minerva. Your larder is pitiful."

"The hell with my larder!"

"Tsk, tsk. Minerva said you'd been in a foul mood since you've been back."

He stood ramrod stiff as she moved toward him. He wanted to touch her but kept his hands fisted at his sides. If he touched her, he wouldn't be able to let her go again.

"I gave you a month to come back for me," she said when he remained silent. "You didn't, so I came to you."

Infuriated, scared, he ground his teeth. "Damnit, Helen! I'm broke. Busted. After I paid back the bank there wasn't enough left from the insurance settlement to pay for a bottle of good whiskey."

Thunder cracked close aboard, rattling the shuttered windows. Instead of flinching, she smiled. "So you settled for rotgut?"

"Something like that."

"I know a great hangover cure," she murmured, her fingers toying with the middle button of his shirt. He stepped back, only to have her move close again.

"Stop it, Helen!" He could smell her scent wafting through the more pungent aromas, a light and airy hint of flowers. His senses clouded, and the need for her sharpened.

"Do you know how many hours there are in six weeks?" she murmured, slipping the button free.

"No." Alex's voice came out strangled.

"One thousand and eight." Her gaze welded on his, she slid her hand into the opening she'd made and touched him. His stomach muscles jerked, and his eyes burned with an emotion Helen wanted to think was love. Still, it *had* been six weeks with only a card from him, and a stilted phone call telling her about the settlement. He hadn't mentioned marriage, nor would he, she knew, until he had something to offer her. "I spent every one of those hours wishing I was in your arms."

"Helen, I'm warning you!" His blood was thudding in his head. The need was becoming acute.

"You have a lot to make up for, Alexandros Paristeri." She licked tomato sauce from the spoon, then tossed it onto the nearest chair. He swallowed hard, tried to speak, had to swallow again.

"Believe me, I know."

His gaze faltered, and her heart tumbled. He'd looked so terribly tired when he walked in, his rough cotton shirt stained with the sweat of a day's cruelly hard labor, his thick black hair tied in a sexy ponytail at the nape of his neck.

His eyes had blazed with hunger when they'd first sought hers, and she'd started to relax. His damnable pride had taken over, however, and those beautiful blue eyes had frosted over.

"I thought we'd have dinner first—Minerva has offered to entertain Nicky for us—and then I intend to sweep you away into the bedroom and make up for lost time." She lifted a hand and touched his cheek, and he flinched. His hand came up to grab hers, holding her with hard, punishing fingers that soon gentled. She took heart when he didn't release her.

"Look around, Helen. See the way I live."

She glanced around dutifully, then offered him an angelic smile. "It's disgustingly neat, like every ship you've ever skippered, but I'll try not to be too untidy."

Alex closed his eyes and prayed for strength. When he opened them again, there were tears standing in hers. "Don't you dare cry," he grated. "I can't stand it when you cry."

She sniffed, a smile hovering over her soft mouth. "Alex, I'm trying to tell you I don't care if you don't have two pennies to rub together or two drachmas or whatever. I love you. I want to be with you. I want to go to sleep in your arms, and wake up to your kiss. I want you with me, holding my hand when I have this baby I'm carrying."

Unsure of his knees, he let go of her wrist and clutched her shoulders. "Say that again," he demanded hoarsely.

"A little girl this time. I'm sure of it."

He dragged air into his lungs and tried to think. But logic seemed to have deserted him because all he could hear was her voice telling him he was going to be a father again. "I think I need to sit down," he said, feeling dazed.

Helen watched the color drain from his face with alarm. "Alex?" She clutched his forearms, felt him sway.

"A baby?" he whispered, his eyes dark and stormy. "You're having a *baby?*"

She nodded. "In the middle of March." When he simply stared, she began to tremble. "Alex? Don't you want this child?"

"God, yes!" he managed to get out before he wrapped his arms around her. A shudder ran through him, and he groaned her name. His hands trembled over her, stroking her back, the sides of her breasts, then sweeping lower to her hips. His fingers tightened, pulling her closer as though he wanted to absorb her into his big, warm body.

"I love you," she whispered, arching up to find his mouth with hers. A shudder ran through him, and he kissed her back, desperate for the taste of her.

"I adore you, need you, treasure you," he whispered, trying to gentle his kisses.

"Marry me," she begged, her lips as heated, her need as great.

He jerked back, breathing hard, his eyes tormented. "It'll be years before I have the capital to lay the keel for another boat."

"Of course, you're not broke. You have my dowry."

Alex stared at her, convinced that one of them had finally snapped. He figured it had to be him, because she was looking too damn serene. "What dowry?" he demanded, giving her a hard shake that only served to widen that angelic smile.

"If you'll stop behaving like a typical Greek male and let me go, I'll show you."

Reluctantly, Alex dropped his hands, but kept his gaze trained on her, just in case. To his utter amazement, she dipped a hand into the curved neck of her shirt to retrieve what looked like a folded envelope. "I kept it in my bra all the way here," she said, holding it out to him.

Cursing, he ripped open the seal and extracted a check drawn on his brother's personal account. A check for five hundred thousand dollars.

"Don't you *dare* tear that up," Helen cried, plucking it from his hand an instant before he was going to do just that. "And before you act on the notion I see in your eyes, I suggest you read the note Con included."

"The hell I will!"

"Fine! I'll do it." She jerked the envelope from his hand and took out a folded piece of pale blue Greek Isles stationery. Her voice was impatient as she read, "Consider this partial payment of the debt Greek Isles owes you." Frowning, she lifted her gaze to his. "Constantine said you would understand."

Alex closed his eyes and drew a long breath. "Yeah, I understand," he said, looking down at her. His gaze was fierce, his expression taut. "I can't take it."

"Okay, I will." She folded the check and slipped it back into her bra. "I have money of my own, too. From selling my house, and various perks from Greek Isles." She went on tiptoe and linked her arms around his strong neck. "But I'll need that for Helen of Troy Fantasies." She kissed him lightly, exulting when he parted his hard lips under hers. "That's what I'm calling my new business, in case you hadn't guessed."

Alex finally found his voice and used it. "I think I'm in big trouble here."

Helen waggled her eyebrows. "I certainly hope so."

He laughed, a rich rolling laugh that came from his soul. "God, I love you, woman!" With a smooth movement of his powerful shoulders, he lifted her from her feet and swung her around.

They were both laughing and dizzy when he set her down again. "About your plans for the evening?"

Her smile was dreamy and just a bit teary. "Mmm?"

"Forget the dinner." He scooped her into his arms and strode with long, confident strides to the tiny bedroom. "I love you, my Helen," he murmured as he laid her reverently on the bed. "Welcome home."

When
Mona Lisa
Smiles

Carole Buck

Prologue

$\mathscr{O}$nce upon a time there was a seemingly ordinary girl from Brooklyn, New York, named Mona Lisa Lefkowitz who went to Paris as a participant in her college's junior year abroad program. All but one of the members of her large and loving—but inclined to be critical—family agreed that the trip was a foolish idea.

The lone dissenter was her widowed, maternal grandmother, Sylvie Seinfeld. Sylvie was French by birth but had emigrated to the United States shortly before the start of World War II. According to family lore, she'd left her native land with a broken heart, the victim of a star-crossed romance.

"French?" a number of Mona Lisa's relatives muttered dubiously during a farewell party given in her honor on the eve of her departure for the City of Lights. "What kind of job can a person get in today's economy with a degree in French? A degree in Japanese, maybe. Or Spanish. But *French?*"

"Better she should stay home and major in something practical," her father's youngest sister's husband, a plumbing supply mogul, opined with great assurance. "Like business administration. Or computer programming."

"Better yet, she should find herself a nice boy and settle down," her mother's only brother's wife chimed in helpfully. "Like her older sisters."

Such a blessing that would be, nearly everybody

within earshot concurred but no one actually said aloud. Mona Lisa, turning out like Donna and Brenda.

Wonderful girls, both of them, the unspoken litany went.

The happily-wed wives of doctors who treated them like queens.

The adoring mothers of baby sons delivered just three days apart.

Fashion plates, who were back to wearing their usual size-6s less than two months after giving birth!

Progeny to be proud of, Donna and Brenda were. Whereas Mona Lisa . . .

More than a few pairs of eyes shifted from Martin and Renee Lefkowitz's chic, slim-figured older daughters to their bohemian, abundantly fleshed, youngest child. Heads shook. Tongues clucked.

She was back at the buffet table, observers noted with disapproval. Eating. Apparently enjoying herself, which was nice. But still. *Eating.* And with her hips!

She was wearing black again, too. Head to toe. Twenty years old and she dressed like she was expecting to be summoned to a funeral at any second.

Black was supposed to be slenderizing, of course. Plus it never really went out of style, no matter how frequently the leaders of the rag trade tried to brainwash consumers otherwise. Even so, anyone with a shred of fashion sense knew that a girl as washed-out as Mona Lisa needed a little color to brighten her complexion.

Not that a person could see much of it. Her complexion, that is. The way she wore her hair—just *look* at those split ends!—hid most of her face.

Which was a pity, several of the more perceptive guests paused to reflect. Because it was an attractive face, all things considered. Not attractive in the symmetrically pretty (and surgically perfected) way her sisters' were, to be sure. In truth, Mona Lisa's features were rather mismatched and she pigheadedly refused to get them fixed. Still, her dark eyes sparkled with a spirited intelligence that was hard to look away from if a person took the trouble to notice it. And there was something undeniably appealing about the way the corners of her generous mouth curved slowly upward at special moments. . . ".

"Maybe she'll fall in love in France," someone suggested, sighing.

"With a foreigner?" someone else responded distastefully. "God forbid."

"Perhaps with herself," Sylvie Seinfeld said in her musically-accented English, temporarily shutting everybody up. "I doubt God would make a prohibition against that."

Mona Lisa flew off to Paris the next day, acutely aware of her status as the least satisfactory member of the extended Lefkowitz family yet secure in her maternal grandmother's unswerving support.

During the eight months that followed, this seemingly ordinary girl from Brooklyn, New York, spent a lot of time in the Louvre studying the works of Peter Paul Rubens, Pierre Auguste Renoir, and Edgar Degas. She was also persuaded to pose for an aging, alcoholic, and apparently alone-in-the-world painter wearing nothing but a smile. . . .

But more about that later.

One

To say that Mona Lisa Lefkowitz's first impression of Adam David Hirsch had been a positive one would be to understate the case. Within a few minutes of making his acquaintance, she'd decided that this sandy-haired, hazel-eyed hunk probably was the most desirable man she'd ever met.

She'd subsequently decided that there was no—zip, zilch, zero—chance of them becoming romantically involved. Even if Adam had indicated a sexual interest in her (a scenario which she'd ranked as marginally less likely than pigs sprouting wings), she wasn't about to succumb to a man whose gilt-edged, Ivy-League credentials would win him an instant welcome by her family.

The reason for this was simple. Mona Lisa Lefkowitz wholeheartedly believed that someday, some way, she'd manage to earn the unconditional approval of her parents and her practically-perfect older sisters, Donna and Brenda. Precisely how she would accomplish this, she didn't know. But dating her way into her relatives' good graces was definitely *not* on the agenda.

Nearly three years of platonic friendship with Adam had done nothing to undermine her favorable initial assessment of him. Quite the contrary, the passage of time had cemented her preliminary opinion about what a special guy he was into absolute certainty.

And then, shortly after four in the afternoon on the second Thursday in May, Adam David Hirsch blew this absolute certainty to smithereens with an unexpected invitation to a supposedly sold-out concert at Carnegie Hall.

"You want me to . . . *what?*" Mona Lisa stammered, telling herself that there was no way the man—the good buddy—on the other end of the telephone line could have said what she thought he'd just said.

"To go out with me. Tomorrow night."

Oh, God. He *had* said what she thought he'd said.

Mona Lisa took a deep breath and glanced toward the flimsy door of her cluttered office to make sure that it was completely closed. Discipline at the Square Pegs Job Placement Agency—a business specializing in finding "unique" (read, *odd*) people for "unusual" (read, *really odd*) positions which she'd started two years ago —was iffy under the best of circumstances. She had difficulty maintaining the correct degree of managerial distance from her small but loyal staff. Because of this, she didn't want any of them to get the idea that she, their putative boss and superior, was having personal problems.

She knew from past experience what the result of such a perception would be. First, all work in the agency would stop. Shortly thereafter, her employees would present themselves to her *en masse* and demand to know what the matter was. Once she'd fessed up (and she always did), about half the staff would insist on explaining in excruciating detail how her troubles were nothing compared with theirs. The ones who weren't in the mood to play "My Life's More Dysfunctional Than Yours" would undoubtedly try to hug her.

Or offer to cleanse her aura.

Or worse.

"Go out?" she repeated, clinging tenaciously to the concept that the words she'd just uttered were open to a lot of interpretation. To "go out" with someone wasn't necessarily the same as—

"I'm asking you for a date, Mona Lisa," Adam specified.

He made it sound like such a reasonable request, she thought, gnawing at her full lower lip with the faintly

serrated edge of her orthodontically-aligned upper
front teeth. But it wasn't. Reasonable requests didn't
threaten to turn a person's life inside out and upside
down! Nor did reasonable requests force a person to
start questioning the validity of the assumptions on
which her most cherished relationship was based!

As a chronic magnet for the needy, the nerdy, and
the nebbishy, Mona Lisa Lefkowitz had long-since
come to the conclusion that *any* man who wanted to
date her had to be flawed in some fundamental and
probably irreparable way. It wasn't that she thought she
deserved to be stuck with members of the opposite sex
who, had they been items of clothing, would have been
labelled IRREGULAR or MARKED DOWN FOR CLEARANCE.
Things had simply turned out that way. And she . . .
well, she had pretty much gotten used to them.

At least, she'd thought she had.

Then again, she'd thought she knew Adam David
Hirsch, too. And the Adam David Hirsch she'd thought
she knew wouldn't want to date her.

Which meant . . .

What?

That the Adam David Hirsch she was talking with
wasn't the Adam David Hirsch she'd thought she knew.

Well, yes. Duh. Obviously.

So who was he?

More to the point—

"Why, Adam?" she asked bluntly.

"Why what?"

"Why do you suddenly want to go out with me?"

There was a fractional pause. Then, very softly, "Why
not?"

The counter-query sent a strange shiver skittering up
her spine. Mona Lisa shifted in her swivel chair, unnerved by the sensation. She glanced at the door to her
office again.

"Don't you know it's rude to answer a question with
a question?" she demanded crankily.

"Really?" Adam riposted without missing a beat.
"Who told you that?"

She had to laugh. A husky chuckle came through the

line, making her relax a little more. But the respite was very brief. All too soon, their shared humor tailed into an uneasy silence.

"It's not so suddenly," her platonic pal of nearly three years finally remarked.

She blinked, confused. "Huh?"

"My wanting you to go out with me." The words came slowly, almost reluctantly, as though their speaker wasn't quite sure he should be saying them. "I've been thinking about asking you for a date for a long time."

"It's been a tough sell, huh?" Mona Lisa retorted, batting an errant lock of brown hair off her face. Her retreat into self-deprecation was instinctive. It had become her psychological maneuver of choice over the years. Forget the clichéd counsel about he who laughs last, laughing best. Experience had taught her that she who laughed at herself before others got a chance to generally ended up feeling less humiliated when she became the butt of jokes.

"Only where you're concerned, it seems."

Mona Lisa stiffened, hearing an unfamiliar edge in Adam's cultured, resonant voice. He sounded defensive. Almost . . . *hurt.*

This shook her in a way she couldn't adequately explain. It wasn't that she thought the man on the other end of the line was impervious to emotional wounding. Heaven knew, she'd seen how deeply he'd suffered because of the break-up of his marriage. He'd taken a sucker punch to the psyche and it had come close to shattering him.

He hadn't whined about it, though. While Adam was a generous man, he wasn't given to sharing his pain. Nor was he given to blaming his ex-wife, Felice, for everything that had gone wrong.

"I screwed up, too," he steadfastly maintained, although he refused to volunteer how and Mona Lisa shied from pressing the matter.

She also tended to apportion the blame for the divorce rather differently than her friend did. She knew that Felice had walked out on Adam, dumping him for some twice-married bartender named Bruno Izbecki.

She also knew that this dumping had occurred *after* Adam had taken Felice on a two-week cruise around the Greek Islands to celebrate their seventh anniversary. Why wait 'til then? she'd fumed to herself on more than one occasion. Had Felice needed fourteen days of luxurious fun in the sun to discover how unfulfilling her marriage really was?

Mona Lisa had never met the former Mrs. Adam David Hirsch and she had no particular desire to do so. In her mind, the woman was either a hopeless flake (a bartender named *Bruno Izbecki?*) or an unmitigated bitch. Possibly an unpleasant combination of both.

"Adam—" she began.

"Look," he said simultaneously, "if you don't want to go out with me—"

"But I do!" The words erupted out of her, uncensored, unstoppable. Mona Lisa felt herself flush from breast to brow. Dear Lord. What had she just said?

The truth, she realized with a shock. The wave of hot blood drained out of her face, leaving her a tad woozy. Heaven help her, she'd just spoken the truth.

"I see." Adam's tone was neutral. Guarded. "So, what's the problem?"

It was a good question, Mona Lisa acknowledged, struggling to get a grip on herself. An *excellent* question, in point of fact. Too bad she didn't have anything close to an excellent answer.

"Well, uh—uh—" she floundered.

"Are you trying to say you've got other plans?"

Until this conversation, Mona Lisa Lefkowitz's relationship with Adam David Hirsch had been remarkably free of male-female games. Or so she'd believed until a few moments ago. It had been the kind of relationship in which she would have had no qualms about telling him that she planned to spend tomorrow night as she spent a lot of Fridays—in her jammies, scarfing down fat-free popcorn (slightly more tasty than Styrofoam pellets) and channel-surfing in hopes of catching a glimpse of the diet soft drink commercial that featured the shirtless construction worker with the killer abs.

Whether he'd intended to or not, Adam had changed

the rules when he'd asked her out. Friend-to-friend honesty was no longer a viable option. He was an extremely eligible thirty-four-year-old man. She was a thirty-one-year-old unmarried woman who'd been reduced to getting her thrills by slow-forwarding through *The Last of the Mohicans* to determine what, if anything, Daniel Day-Lewis was wearing underneath his loincloth.

In other words, she was going to have to lie. Flat out. Big time.

Only she couldn't. Not to Adam. Not . . . directly.

"Tomorrow *is* Friday," Mona Lisa stated after a few seconds, hoping her inflection made it clear that no woman as sought-after as she (hah!) could possibly be unbooked for the week's prime dating night at this late juncture. She tried to infuse the words with a touch of regret, too. Not a lot. Just enough to suggest that if he'd had the foresight to extend his invitation earlier—say, maybe a month ago—she would have been seriously tempted to accept.

There was a brief silence, then a sigh. "I understand. I know I should have called sooner. But as I said, I just lucked into these tickets—"

"And after running down the long list of women you know, you figured I was the most likely to be dateless tomorrow night?"

Mona Lisa's reversion to the self-mocking mode was automatic. But it was complicated by a perverse resentment of Adam's willingness to accept her "Sorry, I'm busy" excuse without even a *pro forma* challenge. What kind of man took an implied "no" for an answer?

Obviously, the kind of man who didn't *really* want to go out with her, she told herself.

"Wha—?" There was series of peculiar sounds—including a *thunk* and a muffled curse—from the other end of the line. Finally, forcefully, *"No!* God. Of course not."

"Then you must have figured I'd be the most willing to cancel my plans." Mona Lisa knew her insecurity was showing and that it wasn't pretty. But she couldn't seem to help herself. There had to be a catch to this invitation. And if it wasn't an underlying indifference to whether she accepted it or not . . .

"Hardly." The response was trenchant, carrying an unusual hint of temper. Adam almost never got angry. "I know you, remember? You don't bail out on people you've made promises to. When you say you're going to do something, you do it. If I'd been thinking along the lines of women who'd be most likely to cancel previous plans to accommodate me—well, at the risk of sounding like an arrogant *schmuck,* I can name at least three who'd break off their *engagements* if I asked them for a date!"

Mona Lisa slumped down in her chair, assailed by a very contradictory mix of emotions. She didn't doubt for a moment that Adam's last assertion was true. He was unattached. He was attractive. He was straight. And if scoring three-for-three on the dating-and-mating gauge of eligibility wasn't enough, he was also gainfully employed as an investment banker *and* the only son of a socially prominent family.

Which brought her back to her initial question.

Why?

Why her?

Why now?

And why the heck hadn't she seen this coming?

Maybe because she'd been too intent on shutting her eyes to her own feelings? she thought, a quicksilver rush of awareness coursing through her.

Or maybe . . . maybe because the possibility that she, Mona Lisa the Misfit Lefkowitz, could attract the attentions of a Mr. Oh-So-Right he might have stepped out of a dream scared her clear down to her unpedicured toenails?

"Did something happen to you in L.A.?" she asked abruptly. She knew Adam was just back from a three-week business trip to the West Coast. He'd phoned her five—no, six—times while he'd been away. He'd also sent her several postcards. Tacky, touristy-type things, with silly messages written on the back in his distinctively neat script. She'd taped them to the door of her refrigerator.

"Did something happen to me?" Adam echoed, plainly puzzled by this sudden change of topic. "Like what?"

Mona Lisa fiddled with the same lock of hair she'd batted away earlier. Although she'd traded the wild, non-coiffure she'd sported through her teens and early twenties for a sleek, shoulder-length bob about four years ago, she could still hear her mother *kvetching* that she needed a trim. And a hot oil conditioning treatment. And why didn't she try highlighting her hair, the way her older sisters Brenda and Donna did?

"Like, I don't know," she said. "Like . . . maybe you had an out-of-body experience and decided to alter your life?"

"Which subsequently caused me to ask you out on a date?"

"Could be."

"Sorry. No out-of-body experiences. No earthquakes or aftershocks, either. But as far as life-altering decisions go . . ."

A pause.

"Yes?"

Another pause. Then, very simply:

"I missed you while I was away, Mona Lisa. A lot."

She lowered her hand from her hair. Her fingers were trembling. She stilled them through sheer force of will then drew herself up very straight in her chair. After a third pause she said, "That's *not* a decision, Adam."

"True," he immediately conceded. There was a note in his voice she couldn't quite get a fix on. It made her uneasy. "Call it a . . . realization."

"Slow-dawning or sudden?" She tried to put a teasing spin on the question.

"Excuse me?"

"This realization. That you, uh, missed me. Did it creep up on you or did it hit you—*blam*—right between the eyes?"

"Somewhere in between, actually."

He obviously wasn't going to be distracted by her efforts to fend off the implications of his admission with jokes. This made Mona Lisa even more wary than she already was. She knew that Adam had a stubborn streak beneath his calm, consensus-seeking exterior. Inclined toward a more overt form of obstinacy herself, she'd remained oblivious to its existence for many months after their initial meeting. But she'd gradually discovered that for all his soft-spoken politesse, her friend was no pushover.

"Adam—"

"It's hard to explain," he forged on determinedly. "At first I thought I was suffering from the usual native-New-Yorker-goes-to-La-La-Land culture shock. But then . . . well, I found myself wondering how you'd react to the people I was meeting, to the situations I was getting involved in. I kept asking myself what you'd say. What you'd do. Talking on the phone with you every few days wasn't enough. I wanted you to *be* there with me. To . . . share . . . things."

Mona Lisa remained silent, thinking about the postcards she'd stuck up on her refrigerator door. She also thought about the way she'd waited around her apartment during the past three weeks hoping Adam would phone. She'd vehemently denied doing any such thing, of course, when he'd twitted her about always picking up on the first ring when he called. But denying didn't change the fact that she had.

"I missed you, too," she finally confessed, her voice small. Her heart was beating much more rapidly than normal. Her breath was coming in and out in shallow spurts.

"You don't have to say that, Mona Lisa."

"Yes, I do." She felt . . . strange. Rather like she imagined she might feel if she were ever insane enough to go skydiving. Imbued with a weirdly exhilerating sense of release on the one hand. Terrified that she'd just committed herself to a fatal plunge on the other.

"Why?"

"Why what?" She tried for the refuge of flippancy and almost managed it. "Why did I miss you? Or why do I have to say I did?"

"Either one." Adam cleared his throat. "Both, if you'd like."

"I don't know why I missed you, exactly," she answered after a moment or two. "As for why I have to say I did . . . well, because it's the truth."

There was a soft exhalation from the other end of the line. Mona Lisa was shaken by the realization that Adam had been holding his breath—literally, *holding his breath*—in anticipation of her response. She shifted her position again.

"So, what's the truth about tomorrow night?" her erstwhile escort asked after a long silence. "Aside from the fact that it's Friday."

"And . . . that I've already admitted I want to go out with you."

"Yes." Adam cleared his throat a second time. "I remember that bit."

Time to pull the ripcord and hope her chute was properly packed, she decided, swallowing hard.

"How about . . . seven forty-five, in front of Carnegie Hall?" Mona Lisa proposed.

"How about six thirty, at the Russian Tea Room?" her would-be escort countered.

"D-dinner, too?"

"Unless you'd prefer to sit in the bar and get tanked on vodka."

"I'll pay," she asserted quickly. It was acceptance, she conceded, but on her terms.

"No."

Okay. On to Plan B. She was willing to be flexible. "Dutch treat, then."

"Absolutely not."

"But, Adam—"

"*I* asked you out, Mona Lisa. *I'll* pick up the tab."

"Don't you think that's a little . . . old-fashioned?" She honestly couldn't remember the last time a man had paid her way. Her feelings about this state of affairs were decidedly ambivalent. She relished the idea of asserting her financial independence (fragile though it was), of course. But there were times—like when her credit cards were maxed out, her checking-account balance was down to pennies and the guy she was out with smugly announced that he had no macho hang-ups about splitting the bill for his steak and her salad right down the middle—when she wondered whether certain elements of the feminist credo weren't actually the products of a misogynistic plot.

"Not at all," Adam replied, his voice smooth and sure. "When you do the inviting, you can foot the bill."

Mona Lisa bristled instinctively. " *'When'?*"

"Sorry." He didn't really sound it. "*If* and when you do the inviting, you can foot the bill."

"We haven't even had our first date and you're expecting an encore at my expense?" She told herself that she should be seething at his presumption. Instead she felt herself starting to smile in anticipation of tomorrow evening and beyond.

"Let's just say . . . I'm hoping for the best."

TWO

" ' *Let's just say . . . I'm hoping for the best,* ' "
Adam David Hirsch mimicked himself with savage precision as he hung up the telephone. He yanked on the knot of his discreetly patterned silk tie with unsteady fingers, glancing around his spacious, well-appointed office. "God, Hirsch. You can be such a *jerk* sometimes!"

Well, yes. Undoubtedly. But jerk or not, he'd finally summoned up the courage to ask Mona Lisa Lefkowitz to go out with him and gotten the answer he'd wanted.

Tomorrow night was going to be a *date* date, he emphasized to himself as he bent to retrieve the stack of documents he'd knocked off his desk earlier. Not one of their usual buddy-buddy get-togethers. Which wasn't to say that there was anything wrong with those. Lord, no. When he reviewed the last few years, the hours that glowed the brightest in his memory were the ones he'd spent with Mona Lisa.

Funny thing, though. He knew he'd be hardpressed to explain to someone precisely *why* those hours stayed with him. Because all he'd ever done with Mona Lisa was hang out. Just . . . hang out. Oh, occasionally they'd take in a movie or check out a museum exhibition or art show. But more often than not they ended up sitting someplace—his East Side duplex, her lower West Side one-bedroom, a coffee bar, whatever—yakking about this or that.

Or, rather, *arguing* about this or that, he corrected

with a fleeting chuckle. Because the truth of the matter was, he and his date-to-be disagreed about almost everything. Including which one of the Three Stooges was the funniest.

Maybe that was one key to the appeal she had for him. That her mindset was very different from his—to say nothing of that of about ninety-nine and nine-tenths of the women he knew.

It was difficult for Adam to nail down exactly when he'd finally faced up to the fact that what he felt for Mona Lisa was more than friendship. It had taken him a long time to sort out his emotions. Part of the problem—if *problem* was the right word—was that she wasn't his type in any way, shape or form. He'd always had a thing for slender, self-contained blondes like his WASPy ex-wife, Felice. Mona Lisa Lefkowitz was about as far from a proper, preppie princess as a woman could get.

Nonetheless, he'd experienced a crazy itch-twitch of attraction the first time he'd encountered her. Hormones he hadn't known he'd possessed had kicked into action, advocating the joys of procreation.

It had happened on the Saturday afternoon of the week his divorce had become final. He'd been walking in Central Park. He'd heard someone shout "Stop! Thief!" then caught sight of a rat-faced teenager being chased by a buxom young woman with brown hair.

Rallying to what had later struck him as an inexplicable—certainly an atypical—impulse, he'd taken off after the kid. Forty, maybe fifty yards later, he'd blindsided him with a flying tackle and brought him down, shredding the left leg of his favorite pair of khakis in the process. A moment later, the pursuing brunette had arrived, apparently tripped as she'd tried to check her forward momentum and landed on top of him.

It had been a weird sensation, lying sandwiched between a skinny, obscenity-spewing juvenile delinquent and a voluptuous, panting-for-breath female. The sensible part of his brain had been warning that the youth struggling beneath him might pose a threat. Another

part—a part controlled by ascendant, atavistic urges—
had been relishing the press of warm, womanly curves
against his tautly muscled back and thighs.

Then a pair of police officers had shown up and
sorted out the bodies . . . in a manner of speaking.
That's when he'd gotten his first good look at Mona
Lisa Lefkowitz—at her clever, chocolate-colored eyes;
her wide, winsome mouth; and yes, at her ripe, Belle
Epoque–style figure. It was also when he'd discovered
that the young felon he'd captured had been carrying a
switchblade.

The damage the knife could have done to him, he
hadn't paused to consider. But the image of the blade
slicing into lush, creamy-skinned flesh had triggered a
explosion of emotion deep within him. He'd shifted his
gaze from the switchblade to the dark-haired woman,
his mind filling with a mixture of fury and fear.

"Are you . . . *nuts?*" he'd demanded hoarsely,
blood thundering in his ears. Had she been within
touching distance, he would have grabbed her by her
T-shirted shoulders and shaken her until her teeth rattled.

The brunette had obviously seen the knife, too, and
she'd gone a little pale. But a split second after he'd
hurled his angry challenge to her mental stability, her
dimpled chin had notched up and a defiant sparkle had
entered her wide, long-lashed eyes.

"No, I'm not," she'd countered, her throaty voice
laced with a hint of the "Noo Yawk" accent often lam-
pooned in TV sitcoms. "Are you?"

"I—" He'd opened and shut his mouth several times.
His previous impulse toward chastisement had trans-
muted abruptly into something else. He'd found himself wanting to kiss her. Right then. Right there. It had
taken all his considerable self-discipline not to act on
the urge.

He'd thought for a split second that she'd sensed
what he was thinking. The glint in her dark eyes had
softened and a tinge of color had entered her cheeks.
But then she'd stiffened her spine and lifted her chin
another fraction of an inch.

"I'm the one whose purse got snatched," she'd pointed out, her inflection indicating that *she'd* at least had good cause to give chase to a weapon-toting criminal.

"You're also the one who yelled for help," he'd snapped, still fighting to keep a lid on his unruly feelings.

"You two know each other?" one of the blue-uniformed cops had inquired with a phlegmatic, seen-it-all air.

"No!" they'd denied simultaneously, glaring at the officer.

But they'd gotten very well acquainted during several tedious hours of filling out forms and giving statements at the nearest police station. By the time they'd finished performing their civic duty, it had seemed the most natural thing in the world for him to suggest that they get a burger or something before going their separate ways. Mona Lisa had concurred with the proposal on the condition that she pay for his meal as well as hers. She'd also insisted on giving him a check to compensate for his ruined pants.

He hadn't really intended to see her again. But after a week or so of having thoughts of her insinuating themselves into his brain at the most inconvenient times, he'd heeded the prodding of his subconscious and dialed the telephone number she'd given him. She'd sounded startled but pleased to hear from him and they'd ended up chatting for nearly thirty minutes.

They'd gone to a baseball game the following weekend. The outing had been her idea. Mona Lisa was a diehard fan of the Mets. He, personally, preferred the Yankees.

And so they'd begun hanging out. No strings attached. Nothing serious. Strictly *ad hoc.* Because the circumstances of his marital break-up had left him fearful of trusting his responses to anything or anyone, he'd decided that it was best to write off his lust-at-first-sight reaction to her as a form of temporary insanity. By the time he'd gotten himself back on the emotional track and realized that his attraction to Mona Lisa wasn't a flash-in-the-pan aberration, he'd found himself curiously reluctant to disturb to platonic pattern of the relationship they'd established.

This reluctance had been reinforced by his conviction that the object of his unexpected desire was content with the status quo. It wasn't that Mona Lisa treated him like eunuch or anything. She simply didn't seem interested in him *that way*.

He'd accepted this apparent indifference with relative equanimity in the beginning. Different strokes for different folks, he'd told himself philosophically. Better to suffer a little frustration than to spoil a friendship with a one-of-a-kind woman by coming on to her.

Unfortunately, the little frustration had burgeoned into something much bigger and Adam had found himself increasingly aggravated by his "friend's" attitude. He wasn't oblivious to the fact that he was considered quite a catch in Manhattan's highly competitive matrimonial sweepstakes. And while he didn't take his status in this regard very seriously, he couldn't help but wonder why the hell Mona Lisa Lefkowitz of Brooklyn was immune to his assets when so many other women weren't!

Which inevitably made him recall the reasons Felice had given for walking out on him. To sum it up in a nutshell, she'd informed him that he was a bore in bed and a slave to convention every place else. Maybe, he'd told himself grimly, Mona Lisa wasn't interested in him *that way* because she'd somehow discerned that he did not have what it would take to satisfy her in the sack.

This wasn't to imply that she presented herself as some sort of mistress of the mattress. Quite the opposite. Mona Lisa was prone to sexual self-deprecation, putting herself down with quips she tossed off with the unthinking aplomb of a professional comedienne. How seriously she intended these comments to be taken by others—indeed, how seriously she took them herself—was something he was still trying to puzzle out.

No matter. He knew, in his gut and his groin, that she was a very passionate woman. She was too full of life, too uninhibitedly responsive to the world around her, to be anything but. Whereas he : . .

Adam sighed heavily, raking a hand back through his neatly groomed hair. Whereas he was . . . what? he demanded of himself. *What?*

He didn't know. Not now. Not for certain. And if truth be told, he wasn't sure he'd *ever* known.

Yet he'd sailed through the first thirty years of his life without stopping to wonder about it. His identity had seemed self-evident. Almost preordained. He'd understood what was expected of him—by his family, his personal acquaintances, and his professional associates—and he'd conducted himself accordingly. He'd followed the rules, met the required standards. He'd done just about everything he was supposed to do and had done it damned well.

Then one day at breakfast his blue-eyed, blond-haired wife—a woman whose elegantly featured face had still carried the burnished glow of two weeks of lolling beneath the Mediterranean sun on an anniversary cruise—had heaved a bran muffin at his head and shrieked that he was a failure as a husband and a human being.

"Living with you is like living with an android!" she'd cried. "You're so goddamned programmed for perfection! Well, I'm sick of it, Adam! Sick of it, do you hear? I'm sick of playing Barbie to your Ken! I need a *real* man! A man who—who—who *sweats* once in a while!"

Felice had said a lot of other things, including the comment about his inadequacy between the sheets, before she'd gotten around to the bottom line.

"I'm in love with somebody else," she'd declared, enunciating each syllable very, very clearly. "His name is Bruno. You don't know him. But he's asked me to marry him and I've told him yes, so I want a divorce."

Adam had been too stunned to speak coherently until that point. Finally marshalling his thoughts into some kind of order, he'd opened his mouth to offer a response. But his wife of seven years had preempted him, uttering words that had scorched him to the very core of his soul.

"You had no idea, did you, Adam?" she'd asked bitterly. "I've been having an affair for nearly a year and you haven't had a clue. And if I hadn't said anything this morning, you would have gone on thinking everything was just fine. Wouldn't you? *Wouldn't you?*"

"Yes, Felice," he'd confessed after a long, long pause. His voice had sounded hollow to him, as though it had travelled across a great, empty space to reach his ears. "I probably would have."

More than probably. Almost without a doubt. Because he'd genuinely believed that she was happy in their marriage.

Then again, he'd genuinely believed the same thing about himself.

Felice had stalked out carrying two suitcases shortly after he'd made his admission. He'd stumbled around their immaculately furnished apartment for a time before he'd ended up in the master bathroom, staring into the light-rimmed mirror over the double sink. He'd been strangely surprised to see a reflection staring back at him. Somehow, he'd expected to see . . . nothing.

Because nothing was what he'd felt like.

That feeling of nothingness—of numbed out non-existence—had eventually given way to anguish and anger. Once he'd finally battled his way through those emotions, he'd begun to rebuild himself.

Exactly who he was going to be when he finally finished the job was still a question mark. It was an unsettling situation in many ways, but it carried a potent kick for someone who'd once taken conformity as his creed.

Becoming friends with Mona Lisa had been a part of the rebuilding process. She was one of the most challenging people he'd ever met. Although tolerant of most human foibles, she had no patience for hypocrisy or complacence. On more than a few occasions, she'd caused him to rethink assumptions he'd accepted without question for most of his life.

Her importance to him had become acutely clear during his trip to Los Angeles. Three weeks away from Mona Lisa had intensified his physical longing for her to the point where the time-honored methods of deal-

ing with sexual frustration simply didn't cut it anymore.
The separation had also driven home how much he'd
come to rely on her free-spirited point of view. He
needed her. She complemented him in some ways, com-
pleted him in others.

He'd returned to New York determined to act on his
newly focused feelings as soon as possible. Fate had
apparently been conspiring in his favor. Within ten
minutes of his arriving back in his office, a colleague
had stopped by with a story about a last-minute change
of plans and offered to sell him a pair of the most coveted concert tickets in town at cost. He'd been on the
phone to Mona Lisa within ninety seconds of making
the deal.

And almost blown it.

The man he'd been for most of his life would have
and never understood why. But the one he was trying to
become had managed to pull things out with a little
help from his friend, Mona Lisa Lefkowitz.

As for what was going to happen tomorrow
night . . .

Adam David Hirsch grinned crookedly. He'd just
have to hope for the best.

And sweat.

Three

"*There* is a problem with your meal, madame?"

Mona Lisa looked from her half-eaten chicken Kiev to the balding, brightly-garbed Russian Tea Room waiter who was hovering solicitously at her elbow.

"No." She shook her head, her dark hair swaying against her cheeks. "Not at all. It's delicious. Really. I guess . . . well, I'm just not as hungry as I thought."

"I should clear, then?"

She hurriedly set down the fork she'd been using to poke at her entree, wincing inwardly as it clinked noisily against the fine china dinner plate. "Yes. Thanks. That would be fine."

"And you, sir?" The server turned toward Adam.

"I'm finished as well," he answered. "Thank you."

"You would like to see our dessert menu, perhaps?"

Mona Lisa's stomach roiled. "Well, actually—"

"Why not?" her escort responded easily. "It never hurts to look."

There was an awkward silence as the waiter cleared their plates, decrumbed their table and finally presented each of them with a calligraphed listing of desserts and after-dinner liqueurs. It was not the first awkward silence of the evening by any means. But as uncomfortable as it was, Mona Lisa almost preferred it to the painfully polite conversation that she and Adam had been attempting to carry on since they'd been seated about forty minutes ago.

"I will come back," the server promised gravely.

"Wasn't that Douglas MacArthur's line in the Philippines?" Adam murmured as the man pivoted on his heel and moved away to attend to other diners.

"More like Arnold Schwarzenegger's in *The Terminator*," she countered. Her palms felt damp. Slipping her hands beneath the table, she wiped them against the crisply starched napkin that was draped across her lap.

"Ah." One corner of her companion's fine-cut, flexible mouth kicked up. "Of course."

The wry movement of Adam's lips had a strangely disruptive effect on Mona Lisa's respiration system. "Have you . . . ever seen it?" she asked lamely, trying to smooth her ruffled breathing pattern.

"The Terminator?"

"Uh-huh."

Adam shrugged. "Just bits and pieces, on TV."

"Oh."

Silence. Again.

And another scintillating topic of discussion bites the dust, Mona Lisa thought dismally. She glanced around the crowded restaurant, wondering whether she could get away with another trip to the ladies room. She decided probably not. Although she was nowhere near matching her personal record of seven visits to the loo during the course of a single date, Adam had looked a tad suspicious the last time she'd excused herself. She felt self-conscious enough without worrying about his speculating that she had an incontinence problem.

"You have, I take it," he commented after a moment or two.

"What?" Her eyes met his again. She swallowed. He seemed so calm. So sure of himself. But then again, he almost always did. It was one of the many things that she admired about him. "Seen *The Terminator*, you mean?"

"Yes."

"A couple of times."

"Really."

"I liked it better than *T2*."

"T2?" Sandy-brown brows lifted inquiringly.

"The sequel. To . . . *The Terminator*."

"Oh. Sure." Adam nodded as though he was genuinely interested. "Right."

"Not that *T2* was bad," Mona Lisa stressed, feeling herself sinking deeper and deeper into a morass of verbal inanity but not knowing how to escape it. "It was actually very good. And the special effects were impressive. But—uh—uh—"

"You preferred the original."

She grabbed onto this interpolation with the fervor of a drowning woman grabbing a lifeline. *"Exactly."*

Their waiter returned. Mona Lisa asked for tea. Adam requested a brandy.

"No dessert?" he queried after their server had moved away once again.

"Not tonight." She crossed her legs, conscious of the pull of the skirt of her black silk dress against her pantyhosed thighs. While she was still a long way from being sylphlike, she'd slimmed down from blimpette proportions during her year in France and had managed to keep the upper hand in her ongoing battle against the bulge ever since. *Zaftig*—slang, from the Yiddish word for juicy—was the adjective she'd heard several of her relatives apply to her solidly size-12 figure in recent years.

Lord knew, it was a lot better than flat-out being called fat.

Adam studied her for several seconds then quietly asked, "Are you all right?"

"I'm fine," she said immediately.

"Are you sure?"

"Do I look sick to you?"

"You look terrific to me." The response was quick and unequivocal. "Only you seem . . . I don't know, exactly. You're not quite yourself."

"Because I didn't order dessert?"

Adam frowned slightly. "You haven't eaten very much of anything this evening."

"As opposed to my usual practice of stuffing my face with everything in sight." Somewhere in the back of her mind Mona Lisa realized that she hadn't sounded this defensive since the last time she'd joined her older sis-

ters and their husbands for dinner at her parents'
house. It wasn't the way she wanted to sound this evening. But she couldn't seem to dam up the treacherous
flow of words.

"I didn't say that."

"You were thinking it."

"No, Mona Lisa," her companion contradicted distinctly, the small muscles along the angular line of his
jaw quilting with obvious annoyance. "I wasn't."

Their waiter bustled back to their table at this point,
delivering a snifter of brandy and a tall glass of tea,
sweetened with a spoonful of preserves.

"There is something else I can be getting for you?"
he asked politely.

"I'll take the check when you have a moment,
please," Adam answered, matching his manner.

"Of course, sir." The server nodded. "Right away."

His departure was followed by yet another awkward
silence. Mona Lisa stirred her tea, her mood growing
bleaker with each passing second. God, she thought.
This was turning into a disaster. Why couldn't they have
left well enough alone? They'd had a wonderful friendship going! And now . . .

"I'm sorry," she said tautly.

Her escort seemed taken aback by the apology. "For
what?"

"You name it." She grimaced. "I'm also . . . feeling
a little nervous."

"Ah." Adam paused, a rueful look settling over his
face. "Well, you're not alone."

"Oh, sure," she muttered, giving the preserve-coated
spoon a final swirl through her tea and setting it aside.
Her fingers were slick and not quite steady. "I really see
you sweating."

Quick as a jungle cat, Adam reached across the table
and trapped her right hand with his left. The contact
was like the closing of an electrical circuit. It sent a
thrill of pleasure arrowing up her arm.

"Maybe you should look a little closer, Mona Lisa,"
he suggested softly.

She did, searching her friend's lean-featured face intently for several long moments. What she discovered there made her heart perform a single, swooning somersault. Although he might be better equipped to hide it, there was no doubt that Adam was feeling as vulnerable at this moment as she.

"Oh," she finally managed to whisper.

The waiter materialized yet again, placing the bill—discreetly hidden in a small folder—next to Adam. "Whenever you're ready, sir," he murmured.

"Thank you," Adam responded with automatic courtesy, not breaking eye contact with her.

The waiter moved away.

Mona Lisa moistened her lips. Her heart had recovered from its precipitous tumble and was pumping at double speed.

Still holding her gaze, Adam lifted his brandy snifter and took a slow sip of the potent liqueur it contained. After setting the glass down, he slowly . . . very, very slowly . . . released her hand, stroking from wrist to fingertips as he did. By the time he finally let go, every fiber of her body was tingling.

"So," he said, his voice as caressing as his touch had been. "What are *you* nervous about?"

The slight but unmistakable emphasis on the pronoun caused her breath to hitch in her throat.

"At the m-moment?" she responded shakily after a second or two. "Just about everything." She gestured, trying to convey the scope of her present uncertainty. Then, with less than her usual glibness she went on, saying, "It takes some getting used to, you know? Us going out like this. I mean, I know we've spent a lot of time together. But tonight . . . it's *different,* Adam, *You're* different. And I'm having a little trouble adjusting to that. Because I, uh, I never really thought of you as a—a—"

"As a potential date?"

Mona Lisa Lefkowitz uncrossed her legs and shifted in her seat. During the past twenty-four hours, she'd faced up to the idea that she'd spent nearly three years denying the true nature of her feelings about Adam David Hirsch. But that didn't mean she was ready to

admit the truth of those feelings to him—or to anyone
else.

"W-well—"

"Or a potential lover?"

"Adam!" His name broke from her lips on a gasp.

"Sorry." He sat back in his chair, plainly distancing
himself from the question he'd just asked.

Mona Lisa stared, more than a little stunned. Lov-
ers? she thought. They'd never even kissed! The closest
they'd come to physical intimacy was her accidentally
tumbling down on top of him in Central Park the afternoon they'd met!

"We're *friends,*" she finally said, knowing she was
sidestepping the real issue but desperately wary of doing anything else.

"And friends don't . . ." There was no need for him
to finish the sentence.

"Not in my experience." The response came out
more sharply than she intended, barbed by unhappy
memories. She inhaled on a shuddery breath, then
asked in what she hoped was a more temperate tone,
"What about yours? Were you and your wife . . .
friends?"

Adam considered this question for what seemed like
a very long time, his lids partially lowered. Eventually
he sighed and said, "I don't know what we were to each
other. People called us the perfect couple, right up until
the day Felice walked out on me. And I suppose . . .
well, I suppose I probably would have agreed with
them. *If* I'd stopped to think about it. Which I never
did."

Mona Lisa remained silent for several seconds. The
insulation from self-doubt Adam's comments suggested
had been his was something she'd spent a lot of years
wishing she could experience. But hearing him allude to
its impact in the way he just had made her think that
that kind of confidence might exact a cost she hadn't
considered—and wouldn't necessarily want to pay.

"Are you saying you took your marriage for
granted?" she questioned.

"More like my whole life." Adam looked at her with

disconcerting directness. "It's a habit I've spent a big chunk of the past three years trying to break."

The expression in his steady hazel eyes emboldened Mona Lisa in a way she couldn't explain. She took a deep breath, then let the inevitable question spill out. "Did you ever think of *me* as a potential lover?"

Although he hesitated for a moment, his gaze didn't waver. When he spoke, it was the verbal equivalent of a gauntlet being flung down. "Truth?"

She nodded once, accepting the challenge to her nerve.

"Yes."

That was all. Just . . . *yes.* An unequivocal affirmation that he *had* thought of her being in his bed, in his arms.

Mona Lisa's memory flashed back to Adam's confession that he'd thought about asking her out for a long time before he'd actually done so. "Is this a . . . recent . . . development?"

"The first time the idea occurred to me, I didn't even know your name."

She blinked several times, the implications of this assertion detonating within her like an explosive charge. In the park? she thought. *Adam had wanted her when they'd met in Central Park, nearly three years ago?*

"R-really?" He voice was about a half-octave above normal.

"You didn't know?"

Mona Lisa frowned at his tone. There had been a brief flash of *something* in his eyes at one point during that initial encounter, she recalled with a quiver. But she'd been so caught up in trying to cope with her own tumultuous responses that she hadn't honestly tried to puzzle out what it might mean. And since Adam had never made a sexual move on her . . .

"I knew you had a pretty strong reaction to me," she finally conceded, picking her words with care. "But I thought it was mostly . . . negative. I mean, you accused me of being crazy! And you looked at me as though—uh—"

"I wanted to shake you until your teeth rattled?"

She pulled a face, still remembering. "Or worse."

"Well, I did." Although the statement was unin-
flected, a sudden flush of color on the ridge of Adam's
chiseled cheekbones attested to the fact that it was not
easily given. "Want to shake you until your teeth rattled, that is. For a few seconds, anyway. Then"—his
voice dropped without warning into a deep, velvet-lined
register—"I realized that what I *really* wanted was to
kiss you."

"So why didn't—" Mona Lisa broke off abruptly, appalled by what she'd almost asked. It was one thing to
have a big mouth. It was something else entirely to go
shoving both her feet into it. She gestured, trying to
wave the inquiry away. "No. Never mind. I don't want
to know."

"Too bad," came the totally unexpected reply. "Because I would."

She gaped. "You must have *some* idea, Adam!"

"The closest I can come to an explanation is that I
don't do things like that." He paused, his eyes flicking
down to her lips for an instant then bouncing back up.
Mona Lisa grew very, very warm. Her blood fizzed in
her veins as though she'd been infused with champagne. "Or, at least . . . I didn't used to."

The concert at Carnegie Hall was a brilliant, once-in-a-
lifetime musical experience. Or so Mona Lisa read in
The New York Times late the next day. She had to take
the newspaper's word for it because her memory of the
event was rather vague. She'd sat through the performance lost in a fog of anxious, erotic speculation.

She knew what Adam David Hirsch didn't *used* to do
in terms of acting on his sexual impulses because he'd
told her and she'd believed him, her line of thinking
had gone. What she didn't know—and, apparently, neither did he—was what his present inclinations were.

But she had a few astoundingly explicit ideas about
what she'd *like* them to be . . .

She was aroused in a way she'd never experienced by
the time they departed Carnegie Hall, shortly before
eleven. Her pulse was pounding, her breathing was

shallow. She could feel her nipples pouting against the fabric of her bra. The crotch of her pantyhose was damp; the petaled flesh it pressed against, throbbing.

Walking a few blocks west to find a taxi did nothing to cool her imagination-fueled ardor. When Adam cupped her elbow to assist her into the cab he'd hailed, she honestly thought her knees might give way beneath her.

They made the trip downtown to her apartment in silence. But it wasn't awkward like the silences during dinner. It seemed intensely, excitingly expectant.

She glanced sideward at Adam several times during the ride. The first two times she did, she found he was looking at her and quickly averted her eyes. The third time, their gazes caught and clung. After a few heady seconds, her companion reached across the seat and took her left hand with his right. Their fingers laced of their own accord.

While it was not the slum which her mother sometimes suggested it to be, the neighborhood in which Mona Lisa lived was not one of the city's best. *Evolving,* was the real estate industry's current term of choice for the area. In other words, the yuppies had made a few gentrifying inroads but not yet conquered with their designer coffee shops and gourmet boutiques while the hooker-and-wino population had diminished a bit but by no means disappeared. As a result, the rents were— by Big Apple standards, at least—reasonable.

One of the aforementioned winos saluted Mona Lisa with a wave of a brown-bagged bottle as she and Adam got out of their taxi in front of the four-story stone walk-up which she called home.

"Hey, Myrna Louisa," the drunk drawled as he ambled by, listing to one side like the Tower of Pisa.

"Hi, Boyd," she responded automatically, reeling from the fact that her escort had just handed the cabbie some money and told him to keep the meter running because he'd be back in a minute or two. Dear God, she thought. Had she misread his intentions *that* badly?

"An acquaintance of yours?" Adam asked in a curious undertone as they crossed the sidewalk to her building's entrance.

"Boyd?" Mona Lisa fumbled through her purse and retrieved her keys with trembling fingers. "I see him around the neighborhood."

"And give him money?"

"No. He'd just spend it on booze." She stuck the key into the security lock and turned it with more force than was strictly necessary. "I make him sandwiches once in a while."

"More often than that, I'll bet."

"I don't keep track," she snapped, yanking the door open. She didn't know what game Adam was playing at, but she'd had more than enough of it. If he'd acted this way with Felice—coming on hot only to cool off once he'd gotten a response—she could understand why their marriage had gone bust! "Well, good night, Adam. Thank you very much for dinner and the concert."

"Hey, wait!" he exclaimed as she pivoted away. Catching her by the left upper arm, he forced her to turn back and face him. "Mona Lisa, please—"

She cocked her chin, nailing him with a look. *What?*

No answer. *Nada.* Nothing. The man—her friend of nearly three years, the first-time date she'd actually been contemplating making love with—just stood there, staring at her as though he was wondering who she was.

"You've got a cab at the curb with the meter running," she finally reminded him, blinking against the sudden, stinging pressure of angry, unshed tears.

"Forget the taxi."

"You told the driver you'd be back in a minute or two."

Adam's hazel eyes flashed emerald green. His grip on her flesh tightened. "I did that so you wouldn't feel obligated to ask me in, damnit!"

Mona Lisa's breath jammed somewhere between her lungs and her lips. Now *she* was the one who was staring. "So I w-wouldn't feel . . . ?" she echoed faintly.

The bruising hold on her arm eased. The vulnerability she'd seen during dinner returned to Adam's attractive face. "I also wanted to have a quick getaway handy if I made a hash out of our first kiss," he explained, his voice turning husky.

Oh, Mona Lisa Lefkowitz thought, a tremor of uniquely feminine reaction running through her. For the second time in less than twenty minutes, she wondered whether she might collapse in a heap at her companion's expensively shod feet. Oh . . . my.

"Why—" she paused, swallowing convulsively "—why would you possibly think you might do that?"

There was provocation in the question, and she knew it. There was permission as well.

"Why?" Adam repeated rhetorically as he released her arm and lifted his hand to cradle the left side of her face. "Because I've waited so long. . . ." He cupped the right side as well, his touch exquisitely gentle. "And wanted it so much. . . . " His fingers stroked her tenderly. "Call it a kind of stage fright."

She tilted her chin up in a movement that had nothing to do with defiance. Her lashes fluttered down. Her pulse was pounding so hard it was a wonder it didn't rupture a vein.

The passage of time seemed to slow . . . then stop. The world went utterly still.

And then, finally, Adam David Hirsch lowered his head and kissed Mona Lisa Lefkowitz full on the mouth.

Surging up on tiptoe, raising her arms to encircle his neck, Mona Lisa Lefkowitz kissed Adam David Hirsch back.

The caress went from sweet to sizzling in the space of a few frantic heartbeats. She pressed close, then closer still, mating their bodies from knee to chest as she opened her lips in an act that was as greedy as it was giving.

Breaths blended.

Tongues enticed and entwined.

"Adam," she whimpered, clutching the crisp hair at the back of his head.

"Mona Lisa," he groaned, his hands gliding down her body, mapping its lush curves and hollows.

The kiss became deeper. More demanding.

Mona Lisa shifted her hips in ancient, instinctive invitation. She felt the hard proof of Adam's desire grow even harder. She canted her head to one side, allowing him even greater access to her mouth. His tongue stroked over hers in sinuous exploration.

Yes, she thought, intoxicated by the taste of him. Yes . . . please.

A squawking honk from the taxi's horn—plus a paucity of oxygen—eventually broke them apart. They stood in shaken silence for several seconds, gazes locked, lungs laboring.

"Would you . . . like . . . to come upstairs?" Mona Lisa asked at last.

"More than anything in world," Adam replied.

She glanced toward the curb. "Well, then—"

There was another impatient *blat* from the cab's horn.

"Don't—" her lover-to-be caught her to him and brushed a hot, hungry kiss against her trembling mouth "—go away."

A giddy laugh bubbled up Mona Lisa's throat. "I wouldn't dream of it."

He returned to her within thirty seconds. As he took her back into his arms she asked, only half jokingly, "You don't think we're rushing into this, do you?"

Adam's even teeth showed white as his mouth relaxed into a remarkably roguish grin. "After nearly three years?"

Four

$\mathcal{F}$riendship—even the platonic kind—engenders a special kind of ease between people. Still, Mona Lisa experienced a few visceral flashes of uncertainty as she and Adam moved toward the consummation she knew she was wishing for with all her heart.

The first serious one occurred shortly after they arrived inside her apartment. They hadn't made it to her bedroom yet. Which had been fortunate, she reflected later. Had they gotten within tumbling distance of her queen-sized mattress without one of them broaching the issue of protection, she had the distinct feeling that they would have been beyond the point of stopping to do the right, responsible thing. Their sexual chemistry had been that volatile.

"Adam—" she pleaded breathlessly, trying to ease back from him just a little. It was difficult to bring herself to do so. Her body was clamoring to get as close to his as possible with the both of them standing up and fully clothed.

"Yes?" he murmured, kissing his way up her throat then nibbling at her earlobe. The delicate rake of his teeth sent a quicksilver sluice of anticipation cascading through her.

"Please." She twisted, acutely conscious of the rampant length of his manhood throbbing against her thigh. *"Stop."*

Adam stiffened a split second later and pulled away from her. His features were rigid, the lightly tanned skin of his face pulled taut over the strong bones that supported it. His breathing was unsteady, the wild jump of his pulse clearly visible at his temples.

"What's the matter?" he demanded.

"Nothing," she assured him hastily, shaken by his expression and the primal energy radiating from him. "At least, there doesn't need to be."

"I don't—" he inhaled sharply "—understand."

Mona Lisa swallowed, firmly reminding herself that they were intelligent adults, not hormone-crazed teens with illusions of immortality.

"I hope you won't take this the wrong way, Adam," she said after a moment, placing a hand on his still-shirted chest. She could feel the warmth of his firmly-muscled flesh through the fabric. "But I've got a package of condoms in the other room and I want you to use them."

His hazel eyes widened with something that looked a lot like shock. Whatever he'd expected her to say, it plainly wasn't this. Then, astonishingly, he started to laugh. There was an edge to the sound. *"All* of them?"

"Wha—? No!" She shook her head, confused. "Of course not!"

"Thank heavens." He pulled her to him again and feathered his lips across hers. "Because as willing as my flesh is at this moment, it gets weak after a couple of . . . of . . . mmm . . ."

Mona Lisa succumbed to the seductive lure of his kiss with a throaty moan. The hot, male taste of him flooded her mouth. His scent—natural musk with a hint of citrus-spice cologne—tantalized her nostrils.

Eventually, some vestige of common sense struggled to assert itself against the surging tide of intoxicating sensations. It was an epic effort, but common sense gained the advantage for a few significant seconds.

"Adam," she insisted, squirming in his embrace. It occurred to her, rather belatedly, that wriggling around might not be the most effective method of deflecting his attention to the matter they very desperately needed to resolve. "I'm serious."

This time, he didn't pull back. "About my using a condom, you mean?"

"Y-yes."

"No problem, sweetheart." Adam nuzzled against her ear, his voice reduced to a gritty whisper. "I brought my own."

Any offense Mona Lisa might have felt at the implications of the second half of this assertion was washed away by the intense thrill of delight she felt at his unexpected use of the endearment. *Sweetheart!* she thought tremulously. He'd called her *sweetheart!*

A few moments later, Adam swept her up into his arms and carried her into her bedroom. Although she knew herself to be no dainty burden, Mona Lisa felt as light as a feather during that brief journey.

But hard on the heels of this blissful, buoyant sensation came another pang of uncertainty. Sharper and more insidious than the one before, it was triggered by Adam's passionate avowal that he intended to know all of her before the evening was done. Every . . . single . . . inch.

The awareness that there were a lot of inches for him to learn assailed her with bitter force. She was stricken by a host of painfully familiar insecurities.

What if he decided her breasts were saggy? she wondered anxiously as he began undoing the front of her black silk dress with methodical fingers. Or her hips too wide? Or her tush too big and the birthmark on its left cheek just plain ugly?

Oh, God.

What if he thought she was fat?

Perhaps he did. Perhaps Adam David Hirsch registered each and every one of her deviations from society's norms for physical perfection. But if he did, Mona Lisa Lefkowitz never sensed it. Quite the contrary. He celebrated the abundance of her body with word and touch, encouraging her to flaunt what she had rather than apologize for it. While her inhibitions did not fall away quite as quickly as her clothing, she shed them soon enough.

He bared all, too, with her help, then attended to the

necessary precautions. Her heart missed a beat as she registered the size of her about-to-be-lover's masculinity. He was extremely well-endowed and intensely aroused.

She wanted him. All of him. Every . . . single . . . inch.

And then they were on her bed, in each other's arms.

Adam palmed her full breasts, circling their plush-velvet peaks with his thumbs. "So beautiful," he breathed almost reverently, lowering his head to take one budding nipple between his lips.

Mona Lisa shuddered at the moist, suctioning pressure and felt an exultant pulse of response deep within her womb. She clutched at his upper arms, made dizzy by the potency of what she was experiencing.

"You taste so good," Adam muttered as he ravished her mouth a few minutes later. "The more I get, the more I want."

"Don't worry." She stroked him intimately, relishing the sleek feel of his skin and the cording of conditioned muscle and connective sinew beneath. "There's plenty of me."

Mona Lisa made the statement proudly. Provocatively. Without a trace of self-mockery. For the first time in the decade-plus since she'd posed in the buff in a Parisian garret, she felt her voluptuous shape was an unalloyed gift and she was eager to share it.

Adam slid a hand downward across her stomach to the dark triangle of hair at the junction of her legs. His fingers coaxed skillfully against the creamy, quivering skin of her inner thighs. She opened to him, arching on a gasp as he gently probed the feminine secrets hidden beneath the tight cluster of mink-brown curls.

Mona Lisa moaned as he found the nerve-rich nubbin sheltered by the folds of her flesh. He teased it with an exquisitely calibrated touch, urging her closer and closer to the edge. She writhed against him, her nails biting into his shoulders.

"*Yes,*" he growled, deep in his throat. "Oh, *yes.*"

Finally, when she was half out of her mind with desire, he guided himself to the entrance of her body. He shifted up and over, then joined them with a single powerful stroke.

She caught her breath, the feeling of being filled to capacity almost shattering her. Fiery ribbons of pleasure unfurled from her core, twining outward until even the tips of her fingers and toes seemed to burn.

"Adam," she cried out. "Adam."

"Right . . . here," he promised, the gruffness of his voice betraying a desperate struggle for control.

Mona Lisa wrapped her arms around him and lifted her hips to deepen their joining.

He moved. She moved with him.

Again.

And again.

Release, when it came, was ecstatically mutual. Mona Lisa Lefkowitz and Adam David Hirsch surrendered themselves to the splendid maelstrom of sensation they'd created—and to the best within each other.

"Are you . . . okay?" Adam asked a long time later, combing his fingers slowly through Mona Lisa's perspiration dampened hair. They were lying together, legs tangled, in the rumpled wreckage of her bed. The rucked up sheets were redolent of lovemaking.

His partner gave a low, luscious-sounding laugh that skittered through his nervous system, disrupting his barely-settled respiration and heart rate.

"As compared to what?" She turned her head and languidly kissed the side of his neck. Her warm breath fanned across his skin in a teasing caress. The soft weight of one of her breasts pressed against his chest.

Adam closed his eyes for a moment, a very elemental kind of self-doubt gnawing viciously at his gut. The sumptuous woman he was holding in his arms had just given him the most transcendent experience of his life. What he'd given her in return, he wasn't certain. He *thought* he'd satisfied her. But thinking wasn't the same as being sure and not being sure was threatening to eat him alive.

"Was it good for you, Mona Lisa?" he finally asked, opening his eyes.

He tried to keep the query casual. Judging by the abruptness with which his new lover levered herself up on an elbow so she could look at him, he failed to achieve this end.

"Don't you *know?*" she countered after a few moments, her brow furrowing.

"No," he said simply, gazing up into her wide, dark eyes. "I don't."

"But how—"

Adam lifted a hand, stopping the rush of words with the brief press of two fingers. "I think I know," he clarified. "But I've thought I knew things before. And I've been wrong. Disastrously wrong."

Mona Lisa blinked several times, a strange expression flickering over her gently rounded face. "Don't tell me," she said, a hint of outraged disbelief entering her voice. Exactly whom this emotion was directed at was impossible to say. "Felice's farewell present to you was some kind of slur on your sexual prowess."

The accuracy of her surmise stunned him. It also made him flush with humiliation. Disengaging as best he could, Adam sat up. He was trembling.

"I don't think this is a very good time to talk about my ex-wife," he declared when he found his voice.

"Oh, but I do," Mona Lisa disputed with remarkable calm, shifting to a sitting position, too. She linked her arms around him.

Adam groaned in protest and tried to turn away. What the *hell* had he gotten himself into? he wondered savagely.

"Listen to me, Adam," his friend-turned-lover insisted, tightening her embrace. "I understand that every couple is different. Even if one member of two different couples is the same person."

"Mona Lisa—"

"All I can say," she plunged on, "is that if you were *anything* with your ex-wife like you were tonight with me, she was a lucky woman." She inhaled on an unsteady breath then released it in an equally unsteady stream. "Although she may have been too stupid to realize it."

Adam stared at her for several seconds, conscious of the heavy *thud thud thud* of his heart. "Felice wasn't stupid," honesty compelled him to say. "But the way I am with you . . . God. Sweetheart. I never dreamed of being that way with her. I never dreamed of being that way with *anyone.*"

"Well, then." Mona Lisa smiled, the slow curving of her mouth ineffably lovely to watch. Her eyes were very bright. "I guess that makes me the lucky one."

"No," Adam responded huskily, shaking his head. He shifted his body and encircled her with his arms. "The luck's all mine."

She nestled against him, her body warm and yielding. He stroked her tenderly, breathing in her heady feminine scent. Her hair tickled beneath his chin.

"Felice hurt you a lot, didn't she?" Mona Lisa eventually asked.

Adam sighed heavily. "No more than I hurt her."

"But there was a time when you were good together. The perfect couple, and all that."

"Maybe." It seemed so long ago to him. Literally, another lifetime. "Right before she left, Felice accused me of being programmed like an android. She also said she was sick of playing Barbie to my Ken."

"She just walked out on you? No warning signs?"

Adam gave a humorless laugh. "Considering that Felice was in the throes of an affair at the time of the split, there probably were. But I didn't see them. Or if I did, I didn't know them for what they were. My first concrete clue that something was wrong was getting hit in the head with a bran muffin."

"*What?*"

He realized he'd said far too much to stop. And as unpleasant as the facts were to recount, he felt he owed Mona Lisa the truth. She deserved to know about the man he'd been before their lives had intersected in Central Park. He could only pray that she'd understand how hard he'd tried to change himself during the last three years . . . and what an integral part of that change she'd been.

Slowly at first, then with increasing fluency, he of-

fered her the story of his marriage. He said nothing to
justify himself, made no mitigating arguments for his
behavior. He finished with the words: ". . . and the
Saturday after my divorce became final, I met you."

Then he waited.

"If Felice was that unhappy, she should have said
something," Mona Lisa declared after a few moments.

"Maybe she did and I didn't hear her."

"She should have tried again." Brown eyes assessed
him candidly. "I can't say you weren't at fault for what
happened, Adam. Speaking as a pro at self-criticism, I
have to admit that you make a pretty good case against
yourself. But some of the blame belongs to Felice. And
just because she won't accept her share of the responsi-
bility doesn't mean you have to shoulder the whole
schmear." She waited a beat, then added, "Unless, of
course, you get off on feeling guilty."

"I'm finding it less appealing all the time," he admitted, his mouth twisting.

"Good. As for the issue of whether you made the
earth move for me . . ." Mona Lisa lifted her dimpled
chin as a flush of color entered her cheeks. "What happened between us was something for the Richter scale.
If I hadn't been satisfied—well, put it like this. *I don't
fake.* Not physical responses, anyway."

He regarded her steadily for a few seconds, seeing
the truth in her eyes. "What about emotional ones?"

The color in her face deepened, but she didn't glance
away. "Those, I have some trouble with. Like . . . fig-
uring out what mine really are and how to handle
them."

"We've both had some difficulty with that during the
last three years."

"At least you *knew* how you felt."

"Knew and did nothing for an awfully long time."

"Yes, well," she gave him an up-from-under-her-
lashes look that caused his entire body to tighten,
"you've definitely shifted out of the passive mode."

He gathered her close once again, claiming her lips
with a slow, sensuous kiss. She responded passionately,
her tongue flirting against his.

"No more holding back," Mona Lisa murmured as he eased her down against the mattress.

"Nothing but the naked truth from now on, sweetheart," he pledged.

Five

The next three weeks were among the happiest Mona Lisa had ever known. Her romance with Adam thrived, her business semi-boomed and her family basically left her alone. With a few exceptions—her inexplicable failure to win the New York state lottery and the discovery of a dead mouse inside one of her best black calfskin pumps, for example—everything seemed wonderful.

Which, naturally, prompted her to start contemplating the odds of being struck by an incoming asteroid.

"Let me get this straight," Adam said as he added a final portion of chicken broth to the risotto with fresh peas and porcini mushrooms he was preparing for their dinner. On top of all his other talents, the man could cook. Not merely microwave. *Cook.* Likewise bake, broil, blanch, barbecue, braise, stew, steam, stir-fry, fricassee, and poach. "You're worried that your life is going *too* well?"

"Not worried, exactly," Mona Lisa quibbled, studying his deft movements admiringly. Her stomach growled as she breathed in the scent of the risotto. The aroma exuded by the dish was sinfully rich, probably a couple of hundred calories per whiff. "I'm just not letting myself get . . . complacent."

" 'All good things must come to an end'?" the man who'd patiently handed her tissue after tissue two evenings ago as she'd snivelled her way through some black-and-white tearjerker quoted on a questioning in-flection, glancing over at her.

Mona Lisa's heart performed a quick hop-skip-jump as their gazes met. Casually dressed in a dark polo shirt and jeans, Adam looked as good to her as the risotto smelled. The clichés about propinquity breeding indifference definitely did not apply in this relationship. The more she saw of her friend and lover, the more she wanted him.

"I hope not," she said softly, remembering the promises they'd exchanged after the first time they'd gone to bed together.

Adam regarded her silently for several moments, the expression in his hazel eyes suffusing her with warmth. His voice, when he spoke, carried an unmistakable note of tenderness. "I hope not, too, sweetheart."

Mona Lisa took a sip of the excellent Napa Valley Sauvignon Blanc from the glass at her elbow. Adam went back to his culinary responsibilities, stirring with a smooth, steady rhythm as the rice absorbed the chicken broth.

Maybe she *was* being neurotic about the situation, she reflected with an inward grimace. On the other hand, there *were* times when what looked like the light at the end of a tunnel turned out to be an oncoming sixteen-wheel truck speeding along the wrong side of the road. She simply wanted to be careful. To enjoy what she had, but to keep in mind that there were no guarantees it would always be hers.

"Is this a regular routine with you?" Adam asked after a minute or so.

"What?"

"Worrying about your life going too well."

Mona Lisa nearly choked. She should be so lucky. "Hardly."

"I see." He sounded amused. "So what do you do when things aren't so great? Live in fear of a sudden flash of good fortune?"

"I stand around wondering what else is going to go wrong, actually." She took another drink of wine.

"A fatalist, hmm?"

"I suppose." Mona Lisa toyed with the stem of her glass and sighed. "I guess my philosophy of life is to prepare for the worst but hope to be pleasantly surprised."

Adam lifted his gaze to hers once again. "And have you been?"

"What? Prepared or pleasantly surprised?"

"The latter."

"Now and then." She felt herself start to smile.

One corner of her companion's well-shaped mouth quirked up. He stopped stirring the risotto. "Anything lately?"

Mona Lisa pretended to consider the question, her memory flashing back a scant ten hours. Not for the first time, she wondered how Adam's ex-wife could possibly have accused him of being boring in bed—or anywhere else. No, he wasn't into whips, chains, rubber suits, or spanking. Nor had he indicated a desire to have her dress up as a cheerleader, nurse or harem girl. Still, his sexual repertoire was in no way limited to doing it, wham-bam, underneath the covers with all the lights turned out.

"Are you by any chance referring to what happened in the shower this morning?" she countered dulcetly, conscious of a sweet, melting heat between her thighs.

The green in his changeable eyes intensified. "Could be."

"Well—" she paused, moistening her lips as she traced the rim of her wine glass "—it certainly was unexpected."

"But not altogether unpleasant, I trust?"

Considering that she'd practically swooned in his arms at the peak of her passion, Mona Lisa felt this was a safe assumption to make. She told her partner as much.

"Just checking." The comment carried a note of distinctly masculine satisfaction. Turning his attention back to the risotto Adam asked, "Would you mind making a salad?"

"That, I think I can manage." Although childhood lessons from her beloved Grandma Sylvie had given her a solid grounding in kitchen basics, Mona Lisa hadn't done much cooking in recent years. She'd found that there was something vaguely depressing about whipping up solitary meals for one.

Of course, there was something a tad unsettling about having her voice recognized when she called her favorite Chinese take-out and delivery place, too. But she'd learned to deal with that. One day she might even get the restaurant to spell her last name right on the top of her order form.

"There's lettuce in the crisper," Adam said as she opened the door to his refrigerator. "And I think you'll find a bottle of balsamic vinaigrette stashed someplace in the back."

The "lettuce"—a packaged assortment of organically grown baby field greens, to be specific—was very easy to locate. The vinaigrette, less so. Mona Lisa didn't mind having to root around, though. Had the contents of Adam's refrigerator been as organized as, say, the clothes in his closet or the books on his shelves, she would have been a bit nervous.

She'd once dated a man who kept all his provisions in alphabetical order. They'd gotten along all right until the fateful day when she'd made the terrible mistake of putting a bag of dried beans between a jar of applesauce and can of carrots. The guy had gone bonkers. Beans, it seemed, belonged between the *K* and *M* items in his larder, along with the other legumes.

Mona Lisa occasionally wondered what had happened to her ex-swain. Perhaps he'd found someone as compulsive as he. On the other hand . . .

"Got it," she announced, grabbing the dressing and straightening up. After shutting the refrigerator door, she moved to the wooden salad bowl Adam had set out on the counter to the right of where he was working.

"Great," he said, peering at the risotto. "A couple more minutes and this should be done."

"I'll try to control my drooling." Ripping open the plastic bag she'd retrieved from the crisper, Mona Lisa dumped its leafy contents into the bowl. Her thoughts drifted back to their discussion of a few minutes earlier.

After a moment she asked, "Do *you* ever worry about things going too well, Adam?"

He glanced at her, his brows contracting toward the bridge of his aquiline nose. There was a small bump on the left side of the feature, about halfway down. Mona Lisa knew it was the result of his having been hit in the face with a tennis ball when he was twelve.

"Once in a while," he allowed.

"Which makes you—what?" She cocked her head, her thick hair swaying against her neck and shoulders. "An optimist with occasional reservations?"

"Something like that."

"I bet you don't do it often." Mona Lisa began shaking the bottle of salad dressing.

"Worry about things going too well, you mean?"

"Mmm."

"I do it a lot more often than I used to."

She looked at him questioningly, startled by the intensity of his tone.

"I've come to realize how much I have," he explained simply. "Which means I've also recognized that I have a lot to lose."

She nodded, the comment he'd made three weeks ago about trying to break the habit of taking his life for granted echoing through her brain.

"Then again—" he grinned suddenly, obviously wanting to lighten the mood "—maybe I've just started to buy into that cockamamie cosmic theory of yours."

Mona Lisa blinked, confused. Then she figured out what he was talking about and started to laugh. "Oh, God. You mean my guy-in-the-purple-cape-and-plumed-hat theory?"

"Uh-huh."

"I can't believe you remember! It's been *ages* since I told you about that."

"Certain things transcend the passage of time, Mona Lisa."

"Yeah, right." She laughed again, unscrewing the top of the salad dressing. At some point in her life—she couldn't remember exactly when, but she thought it was around the time getting in touch with one's inner child had started to become really popular—she'd developed a nonsensical explanation of how the universe worked. She'd expounded it to Adam one rainy Sunday afternoon about two years ago over coffee at the Metropolitan Museum of Art.

The crux of her theory was that each human being was assigned a "guy" (sort of a guardian angel without any theological strings) to watch over him or her from birth. In addition to being garbed like characters out of some schlocky Hollywood costume drama, these guys came equipped with two boxes. One was filled with good stuff—the "cookies," in her parlance. The other was crammed with . . . well, crud.

Gazing down from their perches in the cosmos, each "guy" was expected to empty his boxes by doling out their contents over the duration of his assignee's life. Most did so in a fairly evenhanded manner. A few cookies. Some crud. A couple more cookies. Another fistful of crud. And so on.

Some guys, of course, dumped a whole *bunch* of crud on their assignees early on then compensated with a veritable deluge of cookies at a subsequent date. This, Mona Lisa averred, explained the phenomenon of "late bloomers." Likewise, so-called "overnight sensations" who'd actually slaved in obscurity for twenty years.

Other guys showered their assignees with a seemingly endless supply of sweet treats and successes. It was *these* folks who Mona Lisa Lefkowitz believed needed to be on the lookout for sudden disaster from the sky.

"I think my guy wears a toga," Adam announced, adding some freshly grated parmesan to the risotto.

"A *toga?*" She dribbled some dressing over the bowl of greens.

"Uh-huh. And a rhinestone tiara."

Mona Lisa rolled her eyes. "It sounds like your guy has a slight problem with historical accuracy, to say nothing of gender identity."

"Maybe so." Adam gave the risotto one last stir, then turned off the stove. "But he's still my guy."

She feigned a frown. "To tell the truth, I'm not so sure you can have a guy. I think you should come up with your own theory of how the universe really operates."

"Geez. You don't ask for much, do you?"

"You inspire high expectations, Mr. Hirsch."

"So I've been told. What if I start with something easier and work my way up to a cosmological construction?"

Mona Lisa tilted her chin challengingly, thoroughly enjoying herself. "For instance?"

"How about, rules to live by."

"Mmm . . . okay."

Adam picked up the pan containing their main course. "Rule one," he intoned. "When the risotto's ready, *eat it.*"

They did. Eat the risotto, that is. And it was delicious.

After they'd finished cleaning up, they went out for a walk. It was a lovely evening. Perfectly clear, with the temperature hovering in the pre-summer comfort zone of the mid 70s.

Ambling hand in hand, they window-shopped along Madison Avenue. Sylvie Seinfeld was departing for a long-planned visit to Israel in about ten days and Mona Lisa was keeping an eye out for a special going-away gift.

They were about to cross over to the west side of the avenue when Adam was hailed by a couple in their late thirties. Mona Lisa felt herself stiffen as the pair approached. Whether by accident or design, she'd met very few members of Adam's social circle during the nearly three years she'd known him. While those few she'd become acquainted with had been quite pleasant, she hadn't been able to shake the nagging feeling that each one of them had compared her with a mental image of the kind of woman they thought Adam should be with and wondered what the heck he was doing with her.

"Mona Lisa, this is my colleague, Elliott Greene, and his wife, Gabriella. She's a teacher," Adam said with his usual aplomb. "Elliott, Gabby, this is Mona Lisa Lefkowitz, a very special friend of mine. She runs an employment agency on the West Side."

There was an exchange of hellos and handshakes. Elliott was balding, bespectacled, and topped Mona Lisa's five-foot-five height by no more than four inches. Gabby was a statuesque beauty with dark, dancing eyes and a slight accent.

"Elliott's the source of the Carnegie Hall concert tickets we used a few weeks back," Adam remarked after everyone had done the polite thing.

If either of the Greenes wondered why such a bland statement of fact would cause their friend's "very special friend" to turn scarlet, they gave no sign of it.

"Oh, really?" Mona Lisa responded after a fractional pause, making a mental note to pay Adam back for his blush-inducing comment. She didn't doubt for an instant that he'd known what her reaction to it would be. "Well, they were much appreciated. Thank you."

"We were sorry to miss the concert," Elliott declared with a small sigh. "Especially after we read the review in the *Times*. But, you know how it is. The best laid plans and all that."

"Of course."

"Mona Lisa," Gabby said, rolling the syllables around on her tongue as though sampling their flavor. "You're part Italian?"

"Not that I know of."

"Then how—?" The other woman paused, brows arching. "Unless you think it is none of my business."

"You're not the first person to wonder, believe me," Mona Lisa assured her. She'd lost track of the number of people who'd asked about her odd combination of names. Even Adam had voiced his curiosity before they'd gone their separate ways the day they'd met. "My parents say they picked the name because I was conceived to the strains of the hit song by Nat King Cole."

"Hit song by Nat King Cole?" Gabby repeated. "I am not sure I know—"

Adam stepped into the breach, crooning the opening lines of the famous ballad. Elliott chimed in after the first few measures. While the two men sang with considerable feeling, they did so in entirely different keys, neither of them maintaining pitch for more than a couple of notes at a time. They also appeared to have trouble remembering the lyrics—except for the title phrase, of course. They substituted *la-dee-la-la's* for about half the words.

Their performance drew stares from several passersby and provoked a *yip yip yip* of protest from a miniature poodle.

"I *think* I may have heard this song on TV," Gabby declared when her husband and Adam finally gave up. Although her tone was solemn, her eyes fizzed with repressed laughter.

"Could be," Mona Lisa agreed, struggling to keep a straight face. "It's very popular. Although it's not usually performed as a duet."

"Am I picking up a subtle hint that you two don't think Elliott and I can sing very well?" Adam inquired in a pseudo-wounded voice.

"Of course not," Mona Lisa immediately denied. "I, personally, don't think either one of you can sing at *all*."

"*Less* than not at all!" the other woman concurred, finally giving vent to the humor she'd been holding back. Mona Lisa joined in a moment later.

The two men traded indignant looks then succumbed to laughter as well.

"And to think I was going to remember you in my Grammy award acceptance speech, Mona Lisa," Adam said, shaking his head.

"Remember me as what?" she demanded.

"Careful, Adam," Elliott warned, still chortling.

"One of the little people," Adam stated decisively. "Big stars *always* remember the little people."

The set-up for a putdown was almost irresistible. Mona Lisa was a split second away from inquiring whether she looked like a "little" person when something made her choke back the self-deprecating query. Suddenly her long-time strategy of laughing at herself before anyone else did began to seem pretty counter-productive.

Maybe instead of inoculating herself against others' jibes, she'd been inviting them, she thought with a pang. If she insisted on presenting herself as a target for mockery, who could blame people for taking potshots?

"It's a pretty name," Elliott commented. "Mona Lisa, I mean."

"Considering my parents' taste in music, I could have done a lot worse," she returned, still shaken by the flash of insight she'd just experienced. Adam seemed to sense her turmoil, because he slipped an arm around her waist.

"It's remarkable, really," Gabby observed. "That they believe they know exactly *when* . . ."

"I try not to think what that implies about their love life," Mona Lisa quipped quickly, soothed by the subtle stroke of her lover's fingers.

Everyone laughed.

"Uh-oh," Elliott said, consulting his watch after the merriment died down. "Gabby and I have to get a move on. Mona Lisa, I don't know why Adam's been keeping you a secret—"

"Because I don't want people like you ruining the good impression I've been trying to make on her," Adam inserted without missing a beat.

"Is *that* what you've been trying to do?" Mona Lisa asked with feigned innocence, recalling the small verbal score she had to settle.

"*Brava,*" Gabby applauded. "Keep him on his toes, Mona Lisa."

"I think you're in serious trouble, buddy," Elliott advised Adam, looking rather pleased by the prospect. Then he grinned at Mona Lisa. "In any case, it's been a pleasure meeting you. I hope we can all get together soon."

Mona Lisa inclined her head, feeling very happy. "I'd like that, Elliott. Thank you."

Not once during the rest of her walk with Adam did she check overhead for falling objects.

Six

$\mathcal{M}$ona Lisa Lefkowitz didn't think twice about answering the receptionist's phone at the Square Pegs Jobs Placement Agency the following Tuesday, either. But when she discovered who the caller was, she fervently wished she had.

She didn't usually do front-desk duty. Unfortunately, the agency's regular receptionist—an Alabama transplant named Evangeline who'd quit a better paying position at an X-rated phone service because she'd decided that working for Mona Lisa would be more educational—was on vacation. The rest of the staff, except for computer expert Herbert Zell, happened to be out to lunch when the call in question came in.

Mona Lisa was aware that some people believed Herbert was "out to lunch" as well—vernacularly speaking. She didn't agree. The man was a genius when it came to keeping Square Pegs' complicated personnel files and billing records organized and up-to-date. As for his almost pathological shyness . . . well, she had no doubt that he'd come out of his shell one day, given the right sort of encouragement.

"I'll get it," she announced brightly, behaving as though Herbert had been on the verge of leaping out of his seat and pouncing on the shrilling phone. She picked up the receiver and put it to her ear. "Square Pegs," she said. "No job's too odd for us. May I help you?"

"Mona Lisa?"

Her heart sank. "Oh. Hi, Ma."

"Why are you answering the phone? The owner of a business shouldn't answer the phone. It seems . . . menial."

So much for pleasant chitchat, Mona Lisa thought. "I don't usually pick up this extension," she replied, struggling to keep her voice level. "I made an exception this time because I had a premonition it was you on the line."

Out of the corner of her eye she saw Herbert lower the computer magazine he'd been hiding behind. He stared at her in unabashed amazement until he realized that she was watching him. Then he quickly jerked the publication back up in front of his face.

Mona Lisa felt a spurt of triumph. Herbert had never before manifested the slightest hint of curiosity about her personal life or anyone else's! His interest in this call had to be considered a good sign.

"Oh, fine," her mother huffed in her ear. "Go on. Make jokes. First impressions count, Mona Lisa."

Mona Lisa repressed a sigh. And the impulse to hang up. "You're right. I promise I'll never, ever answer the receptionist's phone again. Not even if it's ringing off the hook and I *know* it's the Publishers' Clearinghouse calling to tell me I've won their multi-million-dollar sweepstakes."

Herbert lowered his magazine again. She gave him a quick, conspiratorial smile. Although he retreated behind the pages as he had before, his withdrawal wasn't quite as hasty.

Her mother huffed a second time then changed topics. "Your father and I saw that thing about you on the news."

Mona Lisa stiffened in surprise, wondering if it was possible that she was about to be paid a compliment. "You mean the feature piece Channel Five did on the agency earlier this month?"

"I guess that was the station."

"And?" she prompted hopefully. The TV story had been a serendipitous bit of luck. Some assignment editor apparently had been thumbing through the telephone directory, come across the Square Pegs ad, and been intrigued by its motto. A perky blond reporter had subsequently been dispatched to get the scoop. The resulting piece—two minutes and fifteen seconds of cutesy video, pun-filled copy, and easily digestible soundbites—had netted the agency a number of new clients *and* provoked inquiries from several other members of the media. Square Pegs was now officially on the PR food chain!

"We didn't watch it live."

"Oh." Mona Lisa refused to succumb to disappointment. She and Adam had watched the broadcast together at her apartment. Afterward, he'd popped the cork on a bottle of French champagne and they'd toasted her television debut. "I see."

"We had to see a tape of it. We got it from Brenda."

"Brenda taped me?"

"Of course not. It was Mickey." Mickey was Brenda's son. "He was trying to record some other program and he hit the wrong button."

Mona Lisa almost laughed. That surprised her. Her usual reaction to conversations with her mother was to reach for a bottle of aspirin.

"You couldn't have called us before the show and said something?" The question was rife with accusation.

The impulse toward humor was swamped by a sense of remorse. "I'm sorry," Mona Lisa apologized. "I didn't get much advance notice myself. And . . . well, I wasn't really sure you'd be interested." She *had* taken the time to alert Grandma Sylvie about the report. The older woman had tuned in, then phoned Mona Lisa to offer lavish praise for what she'd seen. The call had come right around the time Adam had been opening the champagne.

"Do you have any idea how embarrassed your father and I were when people asked us what we thought of our daughter, the TV news star, and we didn't know what they meant?" her mother demanded.

Mona Lisa gritted her teeth. It was so typical. Her parents had only gotten to see her big moment on the tube because her eldest nephew had made a VCR mistake. What's more, they wouldn't have bothered with it at all if they hadn't cared about their image around the neighborhood.

"I *said* I was sorry," she apologized again.

"That pink wasn't so good on you," Renee Lefkowitz declared. "Donna, it would have been darling on. Especially with the new tint she's got in her hair. But at least you didn't wear black."

"The producer said I should try a bright color."

"Which is only what I've been telling you for years. Not that you listen." A martyred sigh came through the line. "That angle they shot you from was terrible, you know. Unless you're gaining weight again?"

"I haven't put on an ounce in five years." She'd actually been quite pleased by her appearance. Her full-figured look had apparently found favor with some male TV viewers, too. The agency had received several dozen phone calls soliciting her, ah, *personal services* since the story had aired.

"Oh, really?"

Mona Lisa shook her head at the skepticism in her mother's voice. In a few minutes, the woman would have her feeling as big as one of the balloon floats in the Macy's Thanksgiving Day parade! Drawing a steadying breath she asked, "Did you have some specific reason for calling, Ma?"

"Friday night."

"Friday . . . night?" A prickle of alarm skittered up her spine. She and Adam had been talking about going to the Hamptons for the weekend.

"You're coming to dinner, aren't you?"

"Uh—" Dinner? What dinner?

"The whole family is getting together."

Mona Lisa raised her eyes heavenward. Tough choice. Three glorious days at the beach with a man who cherished her for what she was versus an evening with a bunch of people who specialized in shredding her self-esteem.

"Actually," she said after a second or two, "I may have plans."

"Haven't we all."

"Ma—"

"Tell me, Miss I-May-Have-Plans. Who's going to explain to my mother why her favorite granddaughter can't be bothered to sit down to dinner with her before she goes to Israel?"

"Grandmere's going to be there?"

"I *said* the whole family."

"Well—" Mona Lisa was genuinely torn. She definitely wanted to see her Grandma Sylvie before the older woman left on her vacation.

"Who are these big plans of yours with?" her mother suddenly backtracked.

"H-huh?"

"Are you seeing someone? Your grandmother told me she was pretty sure you had a man with you when she called you at your apartment awhile back."

Mona Lisa choked down a groan of dismay. She'd noticed that Sylvie had seemed unusually eager to get off the line once she'd delivered her congratulatory comments about the TV story. But she'd never dreamed—

"Mona Lisa?"

"Yes, Ma," she affirmed flatly, knowing from experience that her mother would drag the information out of her sooner or later and make her life thoroughly unpleasant in the process. Spilling the beans sooner would save her some stress. "I'm seeing someone."

"Who?"

"No one you know."

"Excuse me, but I don't think you know everyone I know."

Mona Lisa silently acknowledged that she'd walked right into that one. "His name is Hirsch," she finally supplied. "Adam David Hirsch."

"Hirsch? Is he any relation to—"

"I have no idea."

"What? You haven't met his family?"

"No."

"Why not?"

"Because he hasn't asked me to!" Her feelings about

this situation were very mixed. She'd gotten the sense in recent days that Adam's were, too. But for all they'd promised to be open with each other, they'd yet to broach the matter head on.

"Oh." It was astounding how much disapproval could be jammed into a single syllable. "Well, maybe if you'd ask him to meet *your* family he'd get the idea."

Mona Lisa glanced toward Herbert. Although the computer expert still had his nose buried in his magazine, she had the feeling he was listening intently. She could only imagine his thoughts. "Uh—"

Having gained a tactical advantage by mentioning her mother, Renee Lefkowitz brought out the heavy artillery. "Unless you're ashamed of us, of course."

"I'm not ashamed of you."

"Then you must be ashamed of him. Which, considering some of the men you've brought home, means he has to be a real nightmare. Don't tell me. This one has a wife?"

"No, he doesn't have a wife!" Mona Lisa fought for control. "And I'm not ashamed of him! Adam Hirsch is a wonderful man!"

"There's no need to yell at me, young lady."

"I'm not yelling!"

"Well, it certainly sounds like—"

"Look," Mona Lisa interrupted fiercely. "I'll ask Adam whether he wants to come to dinner Friday night, all right? And even if he can't make it, I'll definitely be there. Tell Grandma Sylvie."

"Mona Lisa—"

"I've got to go, Ma. I'll see you at the end of the week. Bye."

And with that, Mona Lisa broke the connection.

"Uh . . . that was your mother, right?" Herbert Zell asked tentatively from behind the magazine.

She began to laugh. It was either that or cry. She shuddered to think how her computer whiz would deal with tears. To say nothing of how the other members of her staff might react if they found her blubbing when they trooped back from lunch.

"Oh, yes, Herbert," she replied feelingly. "That was *definitely* my mother."

Adam knew something was troubling Mona Lisa the moment she walked into his duplex that evening. But he was clueless about what the "something" was and wary of pressing too hard to find out. For all the intimacy they'd achieved, they each continued to maintain a few *no-trespassing* zones.

He found himself admitted to one of these deeply private areas as he and Mona Lisa lay in each other's arms in the sultry, satiated aftermath of lovemaking.

"Adam?" Gentle fingers drifted slowly over his hair-whorled chest.

"Mmm?"

"You wouldn't want to come to a family dinner at my parents' house this Friday night, would you?"

Easing her smoothly out of his embrace and levering himself up, he reached over and switched on the bed-side lamp nearest him. While the moonlight streaming through the sheer curtains on the bedroom's windows offered sufficient illumination for a lot of things, it wasn't enough to let him read the nuances of his lover's expression.

"I don't know, sweetheart," he answered carefully, gazing down at her face. "Would I?"

"It's sort of a bon voyage thing. For my Grandma Sylvie."

"Really?" He felt a spark of interest. "I'd welcome an opportunity to finally meet her, you know. All the things you've said over the past three years—she sounds like a remarkable woman."

"Oh, she is." Mona Lisa's wide brown eyes shimmered with emotion. "And I definitely want you to get to know her."

He stroked a finger down her cheek, savoring the softness of her creamy skin. "So?"

She glanced away, her features tightening. After a moment or two she muttered, "So . . . it wouldn't be just her, you, and me on Friday."

Adam paused, casting around for a scenario to explain her obvious reluctance to take him home. He came up with several. He put forward what seemed the most likely one by asking, "You think the rest of your relatives will disapprove of me?"

Her gaze slammed back into his. She looked flabbergasted by his suggestion. *"Disapprove?"* Her voice came close to shredding on the word. "For heaven's sake, Adam! They'll roll out the red carpet for you!"

"And that's bad?"

Mona Lisa sat up abruptly, clasping the sheet to her voluptuous, rose-tipped breasts. Adam sat up, too. Many seconds of silence ticked by.

"No holding back, sweetheart," he reminded her. "Whatever it is—please. Tell me."

She heaved a sigh, her lashes fluttering down to partially veil her eyes. "All my life, I've been the misfit Lefkowitz," she said slowly. "My family's biggest—and I do mean biggest—disappointment. I've always dreamed of changing everyone's opinion of me, you know? But I don't want to do it by going out with you!"

"I see," he replied, not entirely sure he did.

Mona Lisa lifted her lids and looked him squarely in the eye. "You think I'm nuts, don't you?"

"Well, maybe. A little," he admitted with a crooked smile. "On the other hand, I *know* your relatives are seriously crazy if they don't recognize how very special you are."

She blinked several times, her throat working. "Oh, Adam."

He gathered her into his arms, hugging her close. Pressing a kiss against her passion-mussed hair he said, "If you don't want me to have dinner with your family Friday night, I won't. If you do, I will. It's your call, sweetheart. Just tell me yes . . . or no."

In the end, she told him yes.

The dinner with her family was not the debacle she feared it might be. But it wasn't all that great, either. The tone for the gathering was pretty much set when her mother, exuding good will and Chanel No. 5, leaned forward and coyly said, "So, Adam. How long have you known our wonderful daughter?"

A few minutes of conversation with her maternal grandmother near the end of the evening lent some perspective to what had gone before. It also forced Mona Lisa to focus on what was truly important.

"I like your Adam," Sylvie Seinfeld declared forthrightly after she'd drawn her youngest granddaughter away from the other dinner guests.

"So do I," Mona Lisa replied, not repudiating the use of the possessive pronoun. While she had no formal claim on Adam, she felt he belonged to her . . . at least for the time being.

"Maybe *more* than 'like'?" The search of the older woman's chocolate brown eyes was shrewd.

Mona Lisa glanced toward Adam, who was standing on the opposite side of her parents' living room conversing with her older sisters and their husbands. He looked so handsome, so at ease. She could tell that he was making a terrific impression. She could also tell that her stock with her siblings was soaring. The latter realization galled her.

"Could be," she said after a moment, her throat tight.

"Is it him you doubt, *petite,* or yourself?"

Mona Lisa brought her gaze back to her silver-haired grandmother. She saw something very wise, yet ineffably sad, in the older woman's expression. She found herself thinking about the family lore surrounding the supposedly thwarted love affair of Sylvie's youth and wondering what the true story was. It was something she'd never dared probe into.

"Adam et moi sont très differents, grandmère," she said, slipping into French as she sometimes did with Sylvie.

"Which gives you a great deal to learn from each other." The older woman continued in her adopted tongue. "Too much of the same is boring."

"I'm not really his type."

Sylvie lifted a brow. "But he wants you still, *oui?* So

perhaps this 'type' of his which you really aren't isn't right for him after all."

Mona Lisa smiled a little at this charmingly convoluted piece of reasoning. A few moments later Adam came to join her and she found herself smiling a great deal more.

She smiled nine days later, too, when she was introduced to Adam's mother and father. But the expression was forced. Behind it she was nervous to the point of nausea.

"It's just a brunch," Adam had explained the previous Tuesday. "They give one every couple of months."

Whether his parents had discovered their affair and asked him to ask her—or whether bringing her along had been his own idea—hadn't been made clear prior to her acceptance of his invitation. Neither had the fact that the Hirschs' notion of "giving a brunch" involved hiring one of Manhattan's best-known caterers. Nor had Adam thought to mention that the guest list would include a number of the Big Apple's key movers and shakers.

Midway through the elegant festivities, it began to dawn on Mona Lisa that being the doted-upon only son of Barbara and Stephen Hirsch might be as tough— maybe even tougher—than being the unsatisfactory youngest daughter of Renee and Martin Lefkowitz. In a strange way, her family's attitude had freed her to find her own path. Adam, on the other hand, was restrained by the high expectations that apparently had been imposed on him from birth. His dutiful fulfillment of those expectations wasn't treated as anything special. It was simply a matter of him doing what he was supposed to do and doing it superlatively . . . and moving on.

No wonder he'd spoken to her of taking his life for granted!

Sometime after reaching at this disturbing conclusion —a few minutes into her fifth interrogation by one of Adam's many oh-so-gracious relatives, to be exact— Mona Lisa realized that there was a very good way to describe how she was being treated by most of the members of her lover's close-knit family.

It centered around the concept of killing a person with kindness.

"I'm sorry," Adam felt compelled to say as he and Mona Lisa began walking east from his parents' Fifth Avenue address.

"Sorry?" his companion echoed in an odd tone, allowing him to take her hand. Their fingers knit together.

"This is the first time I've been a guest at one of my parents' brunches in quite awhile," he explained with a grimace. In point of fact, he'd pretty much stopped attending them since his divorce. "I'd forgotten what they're like." He'd also forgotten what *he* was like in the context of such an event.

"It was nice to see Elliott and Gabby Greene again."

"They only showed up because I told Elliott you were coming."

"I doubt that," Mona Lisa said with a light laugh, brushing her hair back from her face with her free hand. "Anyway. I found the whole thing very . . . *interesting.*"

"You don't have to be so polite. I know you got the third degree from a bunch of my relatives. And as for my parents . . . well, they're pretty set in their opinions."

"Whereas my mother and father are paragons of flexibility."

"Well—"

"I think we should introduce them."

"I . . . beg your pardon?" He couldn't believe she meant what he thought she meant.

"Our parents," Mona Lisa clarified. "They definitely have something in common."

His muscles tightened at her tone. There was hurt beneath the flippancy. A very deep, very dark hurt. "Which is?"

"They all think you're too good for me."

Genuinely shocked, Adam came to a halt in the middle of the sidewalk. He forced Mona Lisa to stop as well. They turned to face each other.

"How can you say something like that?" he demanded harshly.

She lifted her chin in an achingly familiar movement, her gaze unflinching in its directness. "I can say something like that because it's true."

"You don't—" he swallowed, searching her face with something akin to fear. "God, Mona Lisa. You don't believe that, do you?"

Her chin edged up another fraction of an inch. Adam knew what her answer would be before she uttered it. "Sometimes." Her eyes flicked back and forth. "Yes."

"Why?"

"Why not?"

He dimly remembered their trading the same words the first time he'd asked her for a date. "You *can't,"* he insisted, shaking his head.

"Why not?" she repeated.

"Because if one of us is too good for the other it's *you!"* he practically exploded, the most powerful emotions he'd ever experienced geysering through his customary self-control. "Damnit, Mona Lisa! Don't you understand? *You're the best woman I've ever known.* If I could spend the rest of my life with you, I'd be the happiest man in the world!"

The blood drained from Mona Lisa's face. "The . . . the rest of your life?" she whispered.

He sucked in a deep breath, gazing into her eyes. He could see a future there. A future he wanted to be his— no, *theirs.* "Absolutely."

"Are we—" she trembled visibly "—talking m-marriage, Adam?"

"If you want to."

Mona Lisa's lips quirked suddenly then began to curl upward. The color returned to her cheeks, tinting them a delicate rose pink. "Let's."

Seven

*F*our days later, Mona Lisa Lefkowitz's past caught up with the man who wanted to marry her.

It was "crud" of the worst kind, or so Adam David Hirsch thought at first. But it wasn't dumped on him by some imaginary "guy" wearing a white toga and a rhinestone tiara. It was hand-delivered by a good friend in a navy blue Brooks Brothers suit.

Knock knock knock.

"Yes?" Adam glanced from his computer screen to the door of his office. "Elliott! I thought you were still in Chicago."

"I wrapped things up yesterday evening and caught the last flight back to New York," his friend said, walking forward.

"Congratulations."

"Maybe yes, maybe no." Elliott was holding a folded newspaper in his left hand. He made an equivocal gesture with his right. "The parties are going steady but they're not set to walk down the aisle."

"I know what *that's* like."

Elliott Greene was a great many things. Slow on the uptake was not one of them. "Are you saying you and Mona Lisa—?"

"I'm not saying anything—officially—at the moment," Adam answered with a quick laugh. "But yes. We're talking about it."

His "proposal" of four days ago had caught both him

and his prospective bride by surprise. While the desire to commit to Mona Lisa had been growing within him since the first time they'd made love, he hadn't thought he was ready to bring up the idea of marriage. Yet when he'd made his impassioned statement about wanting to spend the rest of his life with her and she'd called him on it . . .

It had felt right. A little ragged around the edges, maybe. But right.

He and Mona Lisa had a lot of things—a heck of a lot more serious things than, say, picking out china patterns—to work through before they got around to exchanging "I do's." They'd agreed on that. But they'd also agreed that what they had was strong enough and special enough to withstand their undeniable differences.

And their mutual uncertainties. There was no use pretending that the emotional baggage they were toting didn't include more than a few of those.

"That's great!" Elliott exclaimed, grinning. He dropped into the chair in front of Adam's desk. "Not that I'm particularly surprised. Gabby said she thought you and Mona Lisa were heading in that direction the evening we ran into you two."

"Actually, we were heading west on that occasion as I recall," Adam quipped, pleased by the other man's reaction. And by Gabriella's assessment.

Elliott chuckled. "Whatever. *Mazel tov.* She's a wonderful girl."

"Yeah. I think so."

"Not much like Felice."

"Definitely not." Adam paused, eyeing his friend narrowly for a few moments. "You were never a big fan of hers, were you?"

"Let's just say I didn't think your ex-wife brought out the best in you. Not that you didn't seem to have a lot going for you. I mean . . . well, a lot of people were stunned when you two broke up."

"Me among them."

Elliott grimaced. "I remember. I'm not going to claim I didn't feel a jolt when it happened but—oh, I

don't know, exactly. I always wondered whether there
was a *there* there for the two of you. If you take my
meaning."

Adam was pretty sure he did.

"You never said anything." He wondered fleetingly
how he would have reacted had his friend spoken up.
Not well, he suspected.

"What was to say?" Elliott countered rhetorically.
"Dumb enough to go criticizing somebody else's marriage. I'm not. Besides. You always acted as though everything was fine."

"It wasn't acting, Elliott. I thought everything was."

"Yes, well—Felice is in the past, right? Mona Lisa's
in the present. *And* the future. So, to repeat what I said
a minute ago—*mazel tov*. From Gabby, too. I know
she's going to be delighted when she hears the news."

"As long as a lot of other people don't hear it, too,"
Adam cautioned.

"Excuse me?"

"I told you. It's not official."

"Sure. No problem." Elliott paused, his expression
shrewd. "What do your parents think? *Un*officially."

"They don't know."

"I see. And hers?"

"They don't know, either."

Elliott gave a wry laugh. "Well, you can always do
what Gabby and I did. Elope first, announce later."

"A definite option." Adam was well aware that the
Greenes had married in the face of considerable famil-
ial opposition. Gabby's staunchly Roman Catholic parents had been appalled by the idea of their daughter
becoming the wife of an American Jew. And to say that
Elliott's mother and father had been less than thrilled
with the idea of their only son pledging himself to a
shiksa from Sicily was like calling the Great Depression
a period of minor economic adjustment.

At least he and Mona Lisa didn't have *that* problem
to contend with, he reflected.

They had, actually, talked about the idea of an elope-
ment. He had decidedly mixed feelings about going
through another big wedding and had said as much. But

he'd also stressed that if Mona Lisa craved white lace and orange blossoms, he wanted her to have them.

She, in turn, had revealed an ambivalence about the traditional wedding trappings. Part of her longed for the kind of nuptial extravaganza her parents had staged for each of her older sisters. Another part wondered whether the pressures associated with such an event were really worth it. He gathered that many of her misgivings stemmed from the fact that Renee Lefkowitz had taken to the role of mother-of-the-bride rather like George Patton had taken to the role of commanding general.

"You have to time it just right, of course," Elliott noted drolly. "Gabby and I were honeymooning in Hawaii when the notice appeared in the *Times*. And speaking of the *Times*—what did you think of the picture in this morning's Living Arts section?"

Adam frowned, thrown by the change of subjects. "What picture?"

"Of the painting."

"I—uh—" He'd skimmed the *Times,* the *Wall Street Journal* and several other publications when he'd gotten into the office, of course. Doing so was part of his daily business routine. But he couldn't remember seeing any photographs of paintings.

"I missed it, too," Elliott said. "I had my head buried in the financial pages. Gabby noticed the resemblance and pointed it out." He unfolded the newspaper he'd been holding. "I feel a little funny showing this to you now that you've told me you and Mona Lisa are talking marriage. I don't want you to think I'm having lascivious fantasies about your future wife. To tell the truth, I don't really see as much similarity as Gabby apparently does. Except, maybe, in the smile."

The word *lascivious* sent a weird jitter of alarm through Adam. He reached for the newspaper his friend was extending to him.

"There on page B3, below the fold," Elliott specified.

Adam David Hirsch looked.

Blinked in disbelief.

Looked again.

The photograph was of a nude portrait of a very lushly curved young woman with a wild tumble of dark hair. She was seated on some sort of fabric-draped bench, her voluptuous body partially turned toward the artist. Most of her left breast was visible, and so was her plump, birth-marked bottom.

She was smiling.

Shamelessly.

Seductively.

And oh . . . so . . . familiarly.

Adam's brain began to buzz, his vision to blur.

Mona Lisa, he thought, feeling his stomach clench. *It's Mona Lisa.*

There wasn't a doubt in his mind. No matter that the woman in the painting looked to be about a decade younger and a good thirty pounds heavier than the woman with whom he'd woken up that morning. They were one and the same person. He knew it with every cell of his body, every shred of his soul.

Mona Lisa Lefkowitz. The woman with whom he'd said he wanted to spend the rest of his life. Revealed . . . for all the world to see.

He suddenly remembered what they'd promised each other after the first time they'd made love—after he'd dropped his defenses and admitted to the humiliating doubts engendered by his ex-wife's accusations.

No more holding back, Mona Lisa had murmured.

Nothing but the naked truth from now on, sweetheart, he'd concurred.

Hah!

She'd never said one word to him about having posed nude! he thought furiously. She'd never so much as *hinted* . . .

"I guess maybe there's a kernel of truth to that old cliché about everyone having a twin somewhere in the world," he dimly heard Elliott comment. "But as I said, *I* don't think the painting looks that much like Mona Lisa. The article says it's going to go on display at—uh —Adam? Adam? Are you, uh, all right?"

Adam looked up from the photograph, temporarily beyond words.

"Oh, God," Elliott whispered, paling visibly. "It's not some look-alike?"

"No," Adam answered, finding his voice. Or, rather, some voice. "It's not a look-alike."

"You didn't know?"

"Just like Felice and her affair with Bruno Izbecki," Adam said, ignoring the tiny fragment of his brain that screamed this comparison was totally unfair. "I didn't have a clue."

Mona Lisa stared fixedly at the list of Square Pegs' newest "odd job" openings and told herself to ignore the seductive whispers that seemed to be coming out of the brown paper bag sitting on the corner of her desk.

Look at us, the bag's glossy-paged contents tempted. Look at us . . . right now.

Mona Lisa grimaced. Buying an armful of bridal magazines from the corner news stand had been foolish enough. To contemplate taking them out and perusing them in the office was insane! If any of her employees started to suspect she had marriage on her mind . . .

A shiver ran through her. Part anticipation, part apprehension.

She loved Adam David Hirsch and she wanted deeply to be part of his life. But committing herself with an "I do" required summoning up a terrifying degree of faith. Not so much in him. But in herself. And despite her prospective husband's passionate declaration that she was the best woman he'd ever known, she was still subject to flashes of dreadful self-doubt.

Fortunately, Adam seemed more than willing to be patient with her. He'd also been endearingly honest about his own nuptial hang-ups. As a result, they'd agreed to stroll toward the altar on their own terms, at their own pace. They didn't *need* to get married. When it was truly time for them to do the "ring thing," they'd know.

And while they waited for that time to arrive—

The door to her office swung open.

"Adam!" Mona Lisa started to stand up. Her instinctive reaction to his unexpected arrival was delight. Then she registered his expression and delight abruptly gave way to dismay. She sank back into her seat. "What's wrong?"

Adam shut the office door and walked—no, *stalked*—toward her. He had a folded newspaper in his hand. Reaching her desk, he tossed the paper amid the clutter on top of it and said coldly, "Would you care to tell me about this?"

Shaken and confused, Mona Lisa looked down. The paper was *The New York Times*. At first she couldn't figure out what Adam was asking her to explain to him. Then she focused on the photograph in the lower right hand corner of the page.

She felt the blood drain from her face.

"Ohmigod," she whispered, staring at the small, black-and-white reproduction of an oil painting of her naked, twenty-year-old self. Her head spun sickeningly. So did her stomach. "I can't believe this."

"You can't believe it?"

She raised her gaze to Adam's face, stunned by the anger in his voice. "I didn't know he'd actually finished it," she said stupidly. "To tell the truth, I'd just about forgotten—"

"To tell the *truth?*" The response was sharp as a scalpel blade and clearly intend to cut. "You want me to believe that you *forgot* you once stripped off your clothes for some boozed-up Parisian with a paintbrush?"

"Yes!" she flung at him, her temper flaring. "But now that I start to think back, I remember it was more than once. I stripped for Claude a whole bunch of times!"

"Too bad you never bothered to mention it to me."

Mona Lisa opened and closed her mouth several times. She hadn't been exaggerating when she'd said she'd all but forgotten the hours she'd spent posing for the sad-eyed, stoop-shouldered artist she'd known only as Claude. It had been several years since she'd spared a thought for that strange yet sweet episode during her junior year abroad. The memories were flooding back now, of course. But until a minute or two ago, she would have said that the chances of Claude's portrait of her (a portrait which had been far from finished the last time she'd seen it) ending up in *The New York Times* were about the same as . . . as . . .

As the chances of her being hit by an incoming asteroid.

"Adam—"

"Elliott Greene was the one who brought the picture to my attention. He didn't realize it was you at first. But he was sitting there when I did." Adam shook his head, his eyes bitter. "Do you have *any* idea how I felt?"

Mona Lisa's brain kicked into replay. Her mother's hyper-critical voice echoed in her ears.

Do you have any idea how embarrassed your father and I were when people asked us what we thought of our daughter, the TV news star, and we didn't know what they meant?

A lifetime of hurt reached critical mass in a single, searing second.

"No," she said rawly, clenching her hands to control the violent trembling of her fingers. "How did you feel?"

"I felt betrayed! I also felt like a fool! I'd barely gotten done telling Elliott that you and I have been talking about marriage—"

"You *told* him? I thought we'd agreed—"

"I didn't tell him we were *going* to get married! And don't try to turn this around and put me in the wrong—"

"Oh, of course not! Adam David Hirsch is *never* in the wrong!" Mona Lisa was on her feet now, lashing out verbally with every weapon she had. "He's perfect! He aces every test he takes. Succeeds at every task he's assigned. He doesn't slurp, snore or—or—*sweat!* He could probably pee one-hundred-dollar-an-ounce perfume if he really tried!"

"Damnit!" Adam roared, hammering his fist down on her desk. The brown paper bag containing the bridal magazines toppled off and hit the floor with a *thud.* "Don't you understand? One minute I was babbling about how close we are and the next minute I was looking at something that strongly suggests I may not know

you at all! You should have seen the expression on Elliot's face when he realized that I'd had no idea you ever posed nude. And I sat there like an idiot trying to think of something to say to him. Something that might explain—"

"You want an explanation?" Mona Lisa cut in. "That's easy. You had the misfortune to get mixed up with Mona Lisa, the big, fat misfit of the Lefkowitz family! But luckily, you found out the truth, the whole truth—the *naked* truth—about what a loser she really is before you did anything you'd need a lawyer to undo."

"You said it," he ground out. "I didn't."

"Oh, but you will," she informed him scathingly. "To your family. To friends. Maybe to a few of those women you claim would call off their engagements if you asked them for a date."

Adam flushed. "I don't need to listen to this."

"No problem," she retorted, glaring at him. "I'm done. You can leave."

"Fine."

"So, *go!*"

He did, slamming the door to her office as he went.

How long Mona Lisa wept, she never knew. Never cared. She simply swept the papers off her desk, put her head down and gave herself up to a torrent of angry, anguished tears.

She was almost cried out when she heard a tentative knock on her office door. She cringed, realizing what the sound signified.

Her staff, she thought miserably. They'd probably heard every word she and Adam had said—and screamed at—each other.

"Please, g-go away," she begged, wiping her streaming nose with the back of her right hand.

"It's Herbert," a quavery voice informed her. "Herbert Zell."

"H-Herbert?"

The door opened. Herbert stepped inside. He closed the door behind himself.

"I—" he swallowed nervously, knitting his skinny fingers together then unraveling them "—I'm here on behalf of everybody. They picked me."

"To do . . ." a hiccupy sob erupted from her throat ". . . what?"

"To say we're sorry. And to tell you that if there's *anything* any of us can do—"

Mona Lisa raised her hand in supplication. "No. Thank you. But no."

"Oh." The computer expert dipped his head. "Y-yeah. I . . . I figured."

"I appreciate the thought, Herbert." She tried to summon up a smile. She prayed the expression she produced didn't look as pathetic as it felt.

"Okay."

There was a long pause. Mona Lisa felt her eyes start to fill again. Herbert blanched visibly, but didn't budge.

"Hey," he said after a few desperate seconds. "How about a hug?"

Somehow, some way, Mona Lisa made it through the next few hours. In the wake of Herbert's amazing performance, her staff left her alone.

She considered leaving—going back to her apartment—more than a few times. Each time she told herself she had to stay put and gut it out. She had a business to run. Just because her personal life had crashed and burned in a hideously public way didn't mean she was required to flush her professional existence down the toilet, too.

The intercom on her phone buzzed about two-thirty, jolting her out of a bleary-eyed daze. She picked up with a shaky hand.

"Y-yes?"

"Hi, it's Evangeline," the Square Pegs' receptionist announced, her sexy drawl threaded with sympathy. "I am truly sorry to intrude on you, Mona Lisa, but you know that reporter from the TV station? The one who did the story on us? Well, she's on line two and she really, really, *really* wants to talk with you."

Mona Lisa really, really, *really* wanted to tell Evangeline to take a message but she knew she couldn't. She owed the reporter. The piece on the agency had been a boost.

"Thanks," she said, massaging her throbbing temples. "I'll pick up."

Click.

"This is Mona Lisa Lefkowitz."

"Oh, hi! It's Patsy from Channel Five. First of all, I have to tell you—everybody at the station *loved* the piece on Square Pegs. It was terrific TV. And it got terrific viewer response, too."

"Terrific."

"We're even kicking around the idea of a follow-up."

"Sounds . . . terrific."

There was a pause.

"Uh, look," Patsy resumed after a few seconds. "The reason I'm calling. Have you looked at the *Times* today?"

Mona Lisa went rigid. No, she thought. Please. No.

"Some of it," she said aloud.

"Well, there's this article and a picture on page B3 in the Living Arts section—"

"I've seen it."

"Terrific! It's an amazing story, huh? A young guy who's pegged as one of France's most promising painters in decades gets messed up in World War Two and goes totally off the deep end with drinking only to redeem his talent during the last few years of his life because of the inspiration of some unknown coed from America!"

Mona Lisa blinked several times in rapid succession. Is *that* what had happened? she wondered numbly. She hadn't been able to bring herself to read the story in the *Times.* Or look at the photograph of the painting again.

"The thing is, Mona Lisa," Patsy continued confidentially, "I was looking at the picture and—well, this may sound crazy—but I started to think the girl in the painting looked a lot like you. Heavier than you are, of course. And with more hair. *Then* I remembered you mentioning something about doing a junior year abroad in Paris—"

"It's me, Patsy."

"It *is?*" the reporter's voice soared excitedly. "This is terrific. Look. We want to do a piece. A huge piece. This is *such* a human interest—"

"No."

"What?"

"No," Mona Lisa repeated. "I won't cooperate with this 'huge' piece you say you want to do."

"But—"

"I think I've exposed myself enough for one lifetime, thank you."

Patsy called again. And again. And again.

Then, by some mysterious process, *other* reporters became aware that the naked woman on page B3 of *The New York Times* was Mona Lisa Lefkowitz, formerly of Brooklyn, now boss of the Square Pegs Jobs Placement Agency in Manhattan.

Mona Lisa refused to speak to anyone. She gave Evangeline a two word statement—"No comment."— to repeat to those who phoned.

When she watched the local news that night—checking out several different local stations—she discovered that telling a reporter *no comment* was a little like throwing gasoline on a fire.

She spent the next three days holed up in her apartment, listening to her answering machine.

"Hi. You've reached five-five-five-fifteen-oh-seven. Please don't hang up. You'll damage the machine's self-esteem. Leave a message after the beep."

Beep.

"Mona Lisa? This is your mother. I just heard. No. Worse. I just saw. I can't believe it! You. Naked. A size sixteen. This is going to kill your father. Don't call. I'm too upset with you."

Beep.

"Mona Lisa. This is . . . Adam. Look, I need—"

She hit the "Mute" button and deleted the message as soon as it finished recording.

* * *

Beep.

"It's Patsy from Channel Five again. We'll do you live. In the studio. Or a remote from your apartment. Anyplace! Call me. Please. I'm begging."

Beep.

"This is your sister, Donna. I just wanted you to know that your niece, Stacy, is upstairs crying her eyes out because one of the girls in her gymnastics class told her you're a porn queen. I hope you're very proud of yourself."

Beep.

"It's Adam. Please—"

Mona Lisa blocked her ears during the rest of the message.

Beep.

"Mademoiselle Lefkowitz, my name is Daniel Dorset. I represent the Baron Sevigny. He would very much like to speak with you about his half brother's portrait of you. Please. Telephone him in New York City at this number—five-five-five-three-oh-oh-seven—at your earliest convenience."

Beep.

"Mona Lisa. God. If you're listening—"
"No, Adam!"

Beep.

"This is Herbert Zell. Don't worry if you stay home Monday. We'll take care of things at Square Pegs. Evangeline says hello."

Beep.

"Mona Lisa! Sweetheart! Hey, this is Larry Bishop, editor of *Big, Busty Babes.* That's the magazine for the man who wants a lot to love. I've got an offer for you. Gimme a call ASAP. *Ciao!*"

* * *

Beep.

"Mona Lisa, this is Gabriella Greene. I don't understand exactly what's happened, but I know things have gone very wrong. I'm sorry. Your portrait is beautiful. If you would like to talk, my number is five-five-five-ninety-four-seventy-eight."

Beep.

"Your grandmother just called—long distance from Israel. I had to tell her. Reporters are pestering everyone in the neighborhood. I can't show my face. Why did you do this to us?"

Beep.

"I'm sorry. So sorry."

Mona Lisa awoke on Monday in a strange mood. Goaded by an impulse she couldn't put a name to, she stumbled into the bathroom and took a long, hard look at herself in the mirror over the sink. As she did, fragments of the telephone messages she'd listened to since Thursday night bounced through her brain. Two sentences in particular kept repeating themselves.

Your portrait is beautiful.
Why did you do this to us?
Your portrait is beautiful.
Why did you do this to us?

Do *what?* she suddenly demanded of her reflection. *What* had she done that was so terribly wrong? Shown off an excess of cellulite?

And then she heard her own voice, shouting at Adam.

You want an explanation? That's easy. You had the misfortune to get mixed up with Mona Lisa, the big, fat misfit of the Lefkowitz family! But luckily, you found out the truth, the whole truth—the naked truth—about what a loser she really is before you did anything you'd need a lawyer to undo.

"I'm not a loser," she said to the face in the mirror. It was an attractive face, even with the swollen eyes, she told herself. Not cookie-cutter pretty like her older sis-

ters', but did she really want to be a walking advertisement for Rhinoplasties 'R' Us?

"I am not . . . a loser," she repeated in a stronger
tone, trying out a smile.

She inhaled deeply, still studying herself.

Mona Lisa. The misfit Lefkowitz?

She shook her head. No.

Mona Lisa Lefkowitz, who made her own way in the
world.

Mona Lisa Lefkowitz, who'd been swimming up-
stream most of her life and had made too much progress to let herself drown in other people's disapproval
or her own self-pity.

Mona Lisa Lefkowitz, who was going to call Patsy
from Channel Five and give her one *hell* of a human
interest story!

Eight

*S*elf-righteous indignation had fueled Adam's stormy exit from Mona Lisa's office. Wounded pride had goaded him as he'd cabbed uptown. But by the time he sat down at the desk he'd departed from so precipitously after his conversation with Elliott Greene, he was beginning to realize that he'd committed a grievous wrong.

A variety of factors mitigated against his immediately trying to atone. Chief among them was a fear that what he'd done was truly unforgivable.

His sense of guilt became heavier with each passing moment. By the time his watch ticked off 4 P.M., he felt as though he was being crushed alive. That's when he reached for his phone and dialed the Square Pegs Jobs Placement Agency.

He was stonewalled by the staff, which he knew was no less than he deserved.

He called Mona Lisa's apartment but got no answer.

He called her workplace again and was informed she was unavailable.

He tried repeatedly to contact her during the three days that followed, failing over and over and over again. He was finally driven to telephoning her mother. He cut the conversation short when it became clear to him that all Renee Lefkowitz had to offer was complaints about her youngest daughter.

Sunday evening his own mother weighed in with a call to his apartment. He snatched up the telephone in the middle of the first ring, hoping against hope that he might hear Mona Lisa's voice on the other end.

"Hello?"

"Adam?"

He slumped. "Mother."

"How are you?"

Not bad for a man trying to endure a hell of his own making.

"Fine."

"I have to ask. *Did you know?*"

"Did I know what?"

"About this Lefkowitz girl's background when you brought her to our brunch."

"No."

A relieved sigh floated through the line. "I thought not."

"What the hell is that supposed to mean?"

"Don't swear, Adam."

"Answer the question, Mother."

"Very well. I simply couldn't believe you would have subjected our family and friends to her if you had."

"Subjected?"

"Oh, I'm not saying she wasn't amusing in an obvious way. And your father seems to think this business she runs has real possibilities. But really, Adam. She isn't the sort of girl I'd expect you to bring home."

"What *do* you expect? Another Felice?"

"There's no need to get into that!"

"Maybe there's every need. Come on, Mother. Tell me your vision of my ideal woman."

"Someone who's *worthy* of you."

Adam flinched. "And you don't think that's Mona Lisa?"

"Do you?"

"No," he said fiercely. "Right now, I think she's way too good for me."

"Adam!"

"I mean it."

"She's not our kind."

"Lucky her."

"What's wrong with you? You don't sound like your-self at all."

"Then maybe there's hope for me. Because the 'self' you're talking about, I don't want to be anymore."

There was a pause. Then:

"I wonder what the Baron Sevigny will think of her."

"The Baron *who?*"

"Sevigny. He apparently owns the portrait of your Ms. Lefkowitz. According to the *Times*, it was left to him by his half brother. The artist."

Adam frowned. The name Sevigny wasn't familiar to him. He'd only skimmed the *Times* article and didn't remember reading it. He hadn't heard it on the TV news, either. Although he *did* seem to recall one re-porter making reference to the painter of Mona Lisa's portrait having had a wealthy, titled half brother who'd come to New York—

Who'd come to New York.

Who was now *in* New York.

Adam expelled a breath he hadn't realized he'd been holding in a *woosh* of air. Maybe, he thought, just maybe, there was a way to reach Mona Lisa he hadn't tried.

"Adam?" his mother questioned.

"I'm sorry, Mother," he said abruptly. "I have to go."

"You are a very insistent man, Monsieur Hirsch," the Baron Sevigny declared quietly late the following after-noon as he extended his right hand. He was a tall, blade-thin man in his late sixties or early seventies. Im-peccably dressed; implacably mannered. He had cool gray eyes and a beautifully cultured voice.

Adam took the proffered hand in his own and shook it. "And you're a very inaccessible one, Monsieur le Baron."

"Yes. Perhaps." The older man sighed. "The last few days have been rather . . . difficult . . . for me."

"And others."

Sevigny's expression sharpened. "Yourself?"

"I was thinking more of Mona Smisa."

"Ah, yes. The elusive Miss Lefkowitz."

"You haven't reached her?"

"Not for lack of trying."

"I'm sure."

The baron studied Adam carefully. "When you requested this meeting you indicated you are acquainted with Miss Lefkowitz. How, exactly—"

"I've been her friend for three years, her lover for a month and a half, and for about four days last week, we were talking about my becoming her husband."

"Past tense?" The older man's tone was careful, like the hands of a physician probing a wound.

"For the time being, yes."

"Because of the portrait my half brother painted?"

"Because of things I did."

"And now . . . regret."

Adam gestured. "More than you can know."

The baron's gray eyes grew sad. "I know a great deal about regret, monsieur. It has been my companion for many years."

"Because of your half brother?"

"And other people."

There was a pause. The baron had received Adam in the sitting room of his hotel suite. After a few moments, he gestured to a sofa a few feet away.

"Shall we sit?" he suggested graciously.

They did.

"I'm trying to understand how your half brother came to paint Mona Lisa's portrait," Adam said when they were settled.

The older man's lips twisted. "As am I. One of the many reasons I hope Miss Lefkowitz will consent to speak with me is so I can hear her story of what happened. I have only fragments of the tale at this point."

"I don't understand."

"I'm not certain I can adequately explain. But—to begin, there was my family. Which was—you have a word for families which are not working?"

"Dysfunctional?"

"*Exactment.* My family was dysfunctional and . . . complicated."

"A lot of them are."

"D'accord," the baron agreed dryly. "In any case. My father had two legitimate sons. I was the younger."

"But you have the title."

"My older brother was killed in an accident."

"I'm sorry."

Sevigny nodded his thanks. "My father also had a number of children out of marriage. One of them was Claude. From an early age, he showed remarkable talent as an artist."

"You knew him?" Adam was surprised.

"One of the many complications of my family."

"Ah."

"Claude suffered deep distress during the war," the older man went on quietly. "Long before there was peace, he put his brushes aside for the bottle. At the time of his death, five years ago, I did not realize he'd taken them up again. I discovered this last March when an old acquaintance of his wrote asking what I wished done with the paintings my half brother had stored with him. I was *stunned.* Naturally, I rushed to see the man."

"And the pictures."

"And the pictures. The fulfillment, so unexpected, of Claude's early promise. Two dozen of them. Each signed and dated. The earliest of them, the portrait of your Mona Lisa."

A tremor of emotion went through Adam at the reference. Leaning forward, he asked, "Then what happened?"

"It seemed to me that the young woman in that first painting must be the key to my half brother's return to life. I wanted to find her. To thank her. So, I hired detectives. Made inquiries. All I could learn was that she was an American college student Claude met in Paris. I decided to bring the paintings to New York for a showing. I wanted to share their genius. I also hoped someone might identify the young woman for me. As it turned out—"

"Pardon, monsieur le Baron," a man who'd earlier identified himself to Adam as Daniel Dorset interrupted from the doorway of the sitting room. His manner was polite but urgent. "I just turned on one of the

local television stations. Miss Lefkowitz is going to be interviewed next on the news."

She looked like a woman who'd come fully into her own, Adam thought with a pang as he watched the screen of the large color TV in the baron's suite fill with a close-up of Mona Lisa's face. Although there seemed to be a hint of sadness in her wide, brown eyes, she radiated a new air of certainty.

His heart went out to her. This . . . *this* was the woman he loved.

The woman he prayed to God he hadn't lost forever.

"So, Mona Lisa," the vivacious blonde who was conducting the live interview said. Adam was pretty sure she was the same reporter who'd done the story on the Square Pegs agency. "You initially turned down our invitation to talk about this incredible portrait of you. What changed your mind?"

"Aside from your persistence, Patsy?" Mona Lisa quipped, drawing a self-conscious laugh from the blonde. "I suppose the simplest explanation is that I realized Claude Arnaud's painting is something to be proud of."

"You weren't at first?"

"No. I was embarrassed by it. And . . . by me."

"An esteem problem?"

"That's one way of putting it."

"You were shocked to see the picture, weren't you?" Mona Lisa cocked her head. "I had no idea it had ever been finished. I met Claude, the man who painted it, more than a decade ago when I was in Paris as part of my college's junior year abroad program. We used to frequent the same small cafe. I noticed him because he was always sitting by himself. He seemed very sad."

"You felt sorry for him?"

Adam glanced at the baron. The older man was staring at the TV screen with unblinking intensity.

"I thought he might enjoy a little company. And since I was trying to improve my French, I hoped he might be willing to let me practice on him."

"He was—?"

"In his fifties, I think. It was hard to tell."

"He had an alcohol problem, I gather."

"As I said, he was a sad man."

"She's very kind," Adam heard the baron murmur.

"So, what happened?"

"Claude wasn't very communicative at first. But I yakked away at him in French every time I saw him at the cafe. About two weeks after I started, he handed me a pencil sketch he'd done. It was of me and it was . . . it was *wonderful.*"

"How did the portrait come about?"

"He did more sketches of me. He said I inspired him. Eventually he asked me to pose for him in his studio. It was a garret, really. He lived there."

"Pose . . . in the nude?"

A tinge of color entered Mona Lisa's cheeks. Adam leaned forward.

"Yes," she said forthrightly. "My first answer was no. I tried to turn it into a joke, saying he'd need too big a canvas to fit me all in. He wouldn't have it. He talked a long time about being abundant of spirit and great of heart. Then he told me to go to the Louvre and look at some of the women painted by Renoir and Rubens and Degas."

"And?"

"I did." Mona Lisa's smile lit up the TV screen, piercing Adam through the heart. "One of the first things I decided was that my body had been born into the wrong century. I mean, there was a time when sixteen was the size to be. Anyway. I eventually decided to do it. I posed for Claude for an hour or two a couple of days a week for about a month. Then I went away for a week on a trip to Rouen. When I returned to Paris, he was gone. I tried to find out what had happened to him, but no one seemed to know."

"Are you aware that Baron Philippe Sevigny—the man who brought your portrait to the U.S.—credits you with allowing his half brother, Claude, to redeem his talent as an artist?"

Adam looked at the older man again. There were tears in his gray eyes.

"It was his talent, not mine," Mona Lisa said seriously, then flashed a mischievous look at the camera. "I just took off my clothes and sat around."

The reporter laughed for a second or two before becoming serious. "Several women's organizations are praising your portrait as a much-needed counterbalance to the national obsession with dieting. They say you represent an alternative beauty image. What do you think?"

"The only thing I represent is myself. Who I am. What I am. As weird as it may sound, I was comfortable with me—myself—when I posed with Claude. Then I lost it. The comfort, I mean. But I've got it back now and I intend to keep it."

And she will, too, Adam told himself.

"A special woman," the baron said as the reporter finished the interview.

"Very," Adam agreed.

"She reminds me of someone I knew many, many years ago."

"Really?"

"A woman I greatly wronged. I never found a way to put my mistake right. If I had it to do over again—"

"Yes?"

"There would be no limit. I would hand her my heart. Bare my soul before her."

The TV station arranged for Mona Lisa to be driven back to her building. The limousine they provided attracted the attention of several of the street's regular working girls and to her amazement, they started whistling and applauding when she got out of the car.

"Way to go, Mona Lisa!" one of the hookers called.

"Thanks," she called back.

She felt good about what she'd done, she thought as she climbed the stairs to her apartment. She felt good about herself, too. In fact, if she didn't have such an aching void where her heart should be, she would have felt perfect.

"Oh, Adam," Mona Lisa whispered tremulously, unlocking her front door.

She loved him. Still. In spite of. Because.

No, Adam wasn't flawless. But then, neither was she. While he'd precipitated the quarrel that had wrenched them apart, she'd done nothing to try to defuse it when she'd had the opportunity. Just the opposite.

He'd tried to reach out to her in the awful aftermath, too. But she'd turned him off. Shut herself away. She'd poured salt on both their wounds instead of working to salve them.

The counter on her answering machine indicated she'd had ten—ten!—calls since she'd left to go to the TV station. As she crossed to hit the playback button, she prayed that one of them would be from Adam. She also promised herself that even if none of them were—

Mona Lisa checked herself in mid-step. Someone was calling her name, she realized. Someone outside the building!

"Mona Leeeeeeeee-sa!"

She moved swiftly to one of the windows overlooking the street and peered out. She was trembling. Could it be? Was it possible—

Yes!

There, standing on the sidewalk, was Adam David Hirsch. Loitering not too far away were the same hookers who'd hailed her when she got out of the limo.

It took her a few, frenzied seconds to wrestle the window open.

"Mona Leeeeeeeee-sa!" he called again.

"Adam!" she yelled down, torn between laughter and tears. "What do you think you're doing?"

He flung open his arms. "Trying to talk to you!"

"About what?"

"About my being an idiot and a fool!" His voice was bold and brave. "About my being sorry from the bottom of my heart! About my being willing to do anything to make it up to you!"

"That—" she swallowed, her vision blurring for an instant "—that's *all*?"

"No! I also love you!"

Mona Lisa froze. He'd never uttered the words before, she realized. He'd shown her he loved her many times. He'd made her feel it to the marrow of her bones many others. But he'd never given her the gift of the words.

"What did you say?" she called.

"You heard him, girl!" one of the streetwalkers hollered exuberantly. "He loves you! And if that ain't enough—"

"Yeah!" Adam concurred. "I love you, sweetheart! And if that ain't enough—"

He started to undress. Standing on a public sidewalk, in full view of a bunch of hookers, Adam David Hirsch began shedding his clothes.

"What are you doing?" Mona Lisa practically shrieked.

"No holding back!" he shouted, shrugging out of his suit jacket and yanking off his tie. Then he went to work on his shirt. "It's the naked truth!"

The hookers applauded wildly. Several winos moved out of doorways to join in the fun.

Mona Lisa waited until Adam finished unbuttoning his shirt, then yelled for him to come upstairs because whatever else he was going to do was for her eyes only.

They fell into each other's arms, kissing and caressing, stammering out apologies and avowals of love. It was wild and wonderful and Mona Lisa wouldn't have changed a second of it.

"I was so proud of you," Adam said huskily, stroking his hands up and down her back and nuzzling hungrily at her lips. "That interview you gave this evening was wonderful. The baron was almost in tears—"

"The baron?" she repeated, dizzy with the joy she was experiencing. "You mean, Claude's half brother?"

"Yes." He eased back slightly, gazing down at her with his heart in his eyes. "I contacted him because I thought he might be able to help me reach you. He's a good man, sweetheart. And he gave me some wise counsel. He also told me I should bring you to meet him once we got reconciled."

"Very sure of himself, hmm?" She combed her fingers through his crisp, sandy brown hair.

"Very sure of us," Adam amended with a loving smile. "What do you think?"

"About us?"

"About meeting the baron."

"Well—"

At that point, there was a knock on the door to the apartment. It was Sylvie Seinfeld, back from Israel three days early to give aid and comfort to her favorite granddaughter.

All three of them ended up going to see the baron. What happened when Claude's half brother made his appearance caused Mona Lisa to abandon her philosophy of preparing for the worst forever. From that moment forward, she subscribed to the view that just when everything seemed just about perfect—life was bound to get even better.

The Baron Sevigny may have *said* he wanted to meet her, but within a second of his entrance into the main room of his hotel suite it was obvious to Mona Lisa that he had eyes for no one but her maternal grandmother.

"Sylvie?" he faltered, walking forward.

"Philippe?" the brown-eyed, silver-haired woman he was addressing responded.

"Mon amour, c'est bien toi?"

My darling, is it really you? Mona Lisa translated to herself.

"Je ne peut pas croire. C'est comme un reve."

I can't believe this. It's like a dream.

"Un rêve realisé . . ."

A dream come true . . .

"Sweetheart?" Adam whispered, slipping an arm around her waist. "What's going on?"

Mona Lisa snuggled close to the man she loved and who loved her in return. "Unless I'm very much mistaken," she whispered back, "Lefkowitz family lore about Grandma Sylvie's star-crossed romance is getting a happy ending."

Sylvie Seinfeld married the love of her life in a quiet ceremony two weeks later. Her favorite granddaughter did the same three months after that with considerably more hoopla.

The wedding of Mona Lisa Lefkowitz and Adam David Hirsch was the embodiment of what they believed a wedding should be. A happy time was had by all, including the two new mothers-in-law. Renee and Barbara were overheard comparing notes about what they would have done differently had anyone bothered to ask their advice.

The newlyweds' honeymoon destination was Paris. While waiting in the airline lounge for their flight to be called, they were approached by an overweight adolescent girl with kinky red hair and freckles.

" 'Scuse me," she said. "Are you . . . Mona Lisa Lefkowitz?"

"Mona Lisa Hirsch as of a few hours ago," the bride replied, glancing at her new husband.

"Oh, wow," the girl breathed. "You just got married? That's wonderful!"

"We think so," Adam agreed, raising his new wife's left hand to his lips and brushing a kiss against the back of it.

"Is there something I can do for you?" Mona Lisa asked gently.

The girl gulped and gazed at her with yearning eyes. "I've read all about you," she answered. "I really admire you. Could I get your autograph?"

Touched, Mona Lisa swiftly agreed. The roly-poly teen produced a piece of paper and a pen. "Write it to Beany, please."

"Beany?"

The girl blushed violently. "It's really Venus. But everybody makes fun of it 'cuz she was the goddess of beauty and love."

The former Mona Lisa Lefkowitz traded tender looks with her husband then did what any seemingly ordinary girl from Brooklyn whose portrait was currently hanging in the Louvre would do.

She wrote a message to the "real" Venus standing before her . . . and smiled.

Carole loves to hear from readers.

You can write to her at:

Carole Buck
P.O. Box 78845
Atlanta, GA 30357-2845

ANITA MILLS
ARNETTE LAMB
ROSANNE BITTNER

*Join three of your favorite storytellers
on a tender journey of the heart...*

Cherished Moments is an extraordinary collection of
breathtaking novellas woven around the theme of mother-
hood. Before you turn the last page you will have been swept
from the storm-tossed coast of a Scottish isle to the fury of
the American frontier, and you will have lived the lives and
loves of three indomitable women, as they experience their
most passionate moments.

THE NATIONAL BESTSELLER

CHERISHED MOMENTS
Anita Mills, Arnette Lamb, Rosanne Bittner
_____ 95473-5 $4.99 U.S./$5.99 Can.

Publishers Book and Audio Mailing Service
P.O. Box 120159, Staten Island, NY 10312-0004
Please send me the book(s) I have checked above. I am enclosing $_____ (please add
$1.50 for the first book, and $.50 for each additional book to cover postage and handling.
Send check or money order only—no CODs) or charge my VISA. MASTERCARD.
DISCOVER or AMERICAN EXPRESS card.
Card Number_____
Expiration date _____ Signature _____
Name_____
Address_____
City_____ State/Zip _____
Please allow six weeks for delivery. Prices subject to change without notice. Payment in
U.S. funds only. New York residents add applicable sales tax.   CM 5/95

Only in his dreams has Burke Grisham, the once-dissolute Earl of Thornwald, seen a lady as exquisite as Catherine Snow. Now, standing before him at last is the mysterious beauty whose life he has glimpsed in strange visions—whose voice called him back from death, and the shimmering radiance beyond, on the bloody field of Waterloo. But she is also the widow of the friend he destroyed: the one woman who scorns him; the one woman he must possess...

A Glimpse of Heaven

Barbara Dawson Smith

"An excellent reading experience from a master writer. A triumphant and extraordinary success!"
—*Affaire de Coeur*

A GLIMPSE OF HEAVEN
Barbara Dawson Smith
_____ 95714-9 $5.50 U.S./$6.50 CAN.

Publishers Book and Audio Mailing Service
P.O. Box 120159, Staten Island, NY 10312-0004
Please send me the book(s) I have checked above. I am enclosing $_____ (please add $1.50 for the first book, and $.50 for each additional book to cover postage and handling. Send check or money order only—no CODs) or charge my VISA, MASTERCARD, DISCOVER or AMERICAN EXPRESS card.

Card Number_____

Expiration date_____Signature_____

Name_____

Address_____

City_____State/Zip _____
Please allow six weeks for delivery. Prices subject to change without notice. Payment in U.S. funds only. New York residents add applicable sales tax.   GH 2/96

One of the most beloved storytellers of our time gives us her richest, most enthralling novel yet...

COMING HOME

by *New York Times* bestselling author
Rosamunde Pilcher

The author of the #1 bestsellers *The Shell Seekers* and *September* brings us her masterpiece, an unforgettable journey to a time when life and death, values and family, love, despair and joy changed lives forever.

COMING FROM ST. MARTIN'S PAPERBACKS IN AUGUST 1996—WATCH FOR IT!